She loosened the cord of her robe while he took hold of the collar, drawing it back off her bare shoulders and down her arms. The sweetness of her body's perfume reached his nostrils as she turned to him, smiling. Her heavy breasts rose and fell gently with her breath.

'This is the way it should be, dear. You must never let anyone tell you differently.'

Her hand caught his, squeezing the fingers for emphasis. He returned her smile, fighting the awkwardness he felt, and her smile softened. 'Come on, now,' she breathed and, still gripping his hand, led him barefoot across the kitchen, into the hallway and up the narrow staircase that climbed to the rear of the house.

LOVERS

G.M. Corrie

ARROW BOOKS

Arrow Books Limited
62-65 Chandos Place, London WC2N 4NW

An imprint of Century Hutchinson Ltd

London Melbourne Sydney Auckland
Johnnesburg and agencies throughout
the world

First published 1986
Reprinted 1986

Printed and bound in Great Britain by
Anchor Brendon Limited, Tiptree, Essex

ISBN 0 09 935340 7

To E.A.C.

PROLOGUE

A Letter to Rachel

I found *Lovers* again the other day.

'Found' might sound a little odd coming from the co-creator of the book that made his name. After all, Paul Hanna – 'the greatest photographer who never worked for *Life*' (I ought to pay a royalty to the reviewer who said that – it's brought me more commissions than I can shake a tripod at!) might be expected to have his walls lined with his own photographic works. And there *are* plenty there: my artistic ego is as big – and frail – as ever it was when you knew me. But *Lovers* has never been among them.

The reason is two-fold: those photographs were never intended for public view; they were made out of the love and joy and lovemaking of the two people in them; they were meant to refer to no one and to nothing beyond. Their public appearance was made without my knowledge or consent, and by the time I knew of it, it had already taken both of us down a path from which there was no return. I realize that now, after ten years of wrestling with guilt, of trying to expiate a sense of betrayal in a flood of work that would *prove* I would have made it anyway – without 'using' us, without exploiting our bodies and our emotions so much more ruthlessly than you or I had ever been exploited before.

But, more importantly, I am the *co*-creator, not the sole creator. *We* were responsible for that volume, as a man and a woman unite to create a child. *Lovers* is our child, the fruit of our love, and our loving. It should rest on *our* shelves, or nowhere, and since we are apart it must be nowhere.

O brave words . . .!

You always accused me of over-seriousness about my work. Humour in all things but that. My ultimate truth – or at least my own way of searching for it. Truth above all! Art above all! Only the truth is not always so easily found, or, if found, not so easily recognized for what it is.

I tell you this to let you know my thoughts before I chanced on that new-minted publisher's copy in a far corner of my attic, its discreet, black gloss, grey-lettered cover still wrapped in cellophane.

For a moment I was tempted to return it to its hiding place at the bottom of a forgotten chest. I regarded it as a man might regard the letters from a deeply felt and sadly ended affair. The sudden shock of recognition. A stomach-deep churning of ancient agonies that only masochism would wish to revive.

But, masochism or not, I tore open the dusty cellophane anyway. And then there was another, more selfish fear. Reputations are made as much by luck or fashion as talent. How gauche would that first effort appear now? How embarrassingly naive – like re-reading a prize essay from the twelfth grade?

I began to turn the pages and the attic, and all the complicated present, disappeared.

I was shocked.

Not shocked, as those first readers and reviewers were shocked, by the subject itself. 'Pornography masquerading as art', declared one newspaper, British I think. Do you remember that one? Or, 'Mr Hanna and his wisely anonymous companion undoubtedly enjoyed themselves taking these photographs but only Masters and Johnson or the dirty-mackintosh brigade are likely to share their enthusiasm.' (Definitely British, that!) Or, best of all, the commentator who almost beat the bleeper on networked television: 'Who wants to spend money to watch two young people fucking? Drill yourself a hole in your neighbour's bedroom wall and save yourself twenty-five dollars!'

Yes, those photographs showed fucking – not 'love-making' or 'erotic dalliance' or any of the other flowery euphemisms that pepper the introductory blurb. They were as explicit as anything you would pay twice the price for in Times Square or Soho or along the Reeperbahn – which explains, of course why they sold so well.

But where *those* photographs celebrate nothing but the possibilities of flesh, or the participants' disregard for it, ours were touched with an extraordinary rawness of emotion. They weren't – they aren't – porno or deliberate 'art', either; they are documentaries. Documentaries of love. They have a quality you see in Robert Capa or Donald McCullin, and that's not a boast – I mean a quality of present *truth* that's so nail-bitingly real you want to look away out of embarrassment but you don't because it has a crude, wonderful kind of beauty too.

Now that does sound like a boast or one of those arty-farty *Village Voice*-style critics I'm supposed to despise. The point I'm trying to make in my usual cack-handed way (see, I still haven't forgotten my British English!) is that the two young people in those pictures show a commitment, a self-respect, a wholeness I would never have believed either of us were capable of at the time.

The proof is in *Lovers*. Those photographs are a kind of prefigurement of the future, a turning point, a moment of healing for two young lives blighted by circumstance, by distorted views of what should happen between men and women. In some weird way – and the pun is fully intended – I *came right* in those pictures. And if I know you – and I still believe I am closer to you than any other person I've ever known – then you did too. I just wish I'd seen it at the time! When the obviousness of it first stared me in the face I went

9

through a good hour of anguish thinking of what might so easily have been . . . But this letter isn't meant to be a fruitless yearning after lost opportunities or any kind of glum remembrance of things past. I think the right term is an apology, or is it apologia?

I'm trying to say the publication of *Lovers* deserves an apology, even ten years too late. But *Lovers* itself does not, nor will it ever. It's private and beautiful and true in ways I've never managed to repeat because you created it just as much as I did. It cleansed us, it normalized us, it brought sex into a loving part of our lives where it had never been before — in a bizarre kind of way, it created *us*.

And that's why it will go back on my shelves tonight. That's why I've spent so long composing a letter I may never have the courage to send, even if I did know where you were or, perhaps just as important, who you were with. Old flames, I know, can be even newer embarrassments.

Perhaps, then, this is really just a letter to myself, a memo from my conscience to the fondest and most cherished of memories. If it is then it still has its purpose. Didn't we tell each other: you are more myself than I am?

Oh the embarrassments of youthful passion! Doubly embarrassing, of course, because it's still quite true.

With much love,

PAUL

Truro
Cape Cod
Massachusetts
USA

28 May 1986

10

1
PAUL
1969

He woke abruptly and with such immediate clarity of mind
it was as if he had never slept, as if the night's buzzing
thoughts had halted only for the shortest breathing-space.
But in that moment the sun had lifted over Nantucket
Sound, squeezing its rays through the half-drawn shutters,
filling his white-painted bedroom with fierce summer sunlight.

Instantly his heart was hammering. Flinging back the
covers, he reached for the watch lying next to his battered
Leica on the bedside table.

Six forty-six.

Six forty-six!

Breathing out, he flopped back onto the pillow. Nothing
and no one stirred in this house before nine. It was Aunt
Cora-Beth's invariable rule, even at Christmas or Thanks-
giving or when, as now, there were special guests staying.
She would hardly change that simply because it was his
birthday, even his sixteenth and the most important in his
short, sequestered life. The day when, by her own promise,
he would become a man.

Nevertheless, as he lay still, the sheet tangled about his
lean frame, he strained his ears for sounds of activity from
his aunt's room along the landing or Diana's next door.

He heard none, only the softest murmur of wind in the
pitch pine and the scrub oak in the dunes that kept the

11

house from the worst of the winter north-easterlies, the shrill echoes, too, of gull and plover and tern. Sounds as familiar, as unremarked, as the salt tang hanging on the faintest breeze.

Old admonitions of his aunt's echoed through his mind: 'Patience, Paul — that's the best lesson a young man can learn in his dealings with the female sex. I know you young fellows, it only takes a thought to get you ready and then you want to shoot off as quick as you can. Well, a woman isn't like that. She needs to be stroked and soothed and brought to readiness in her own good time. If every man was taught to do that, as I intend to teach you, there'd be a lot less unhappiness in the world . . .' Was that, he wondered, why she had let Diana see him naked earlier that week?

Alone in the house, when his tutors had gone and Joseph and Louisa had returned to their garage apartment, their domestic tasks done, he and his aunt often stripped and swam, costumeless, in the big, glass-roofed pool at the rear. It was a warm, intimate place, the echoing chill of the marbled surround cancelled by the carved wooden vaulting that looped low overhead, like the ribs of an upturned boat or the stomach of some vast whale — both appropriate similes since a rich whaling captain had built it as a conservatory a century and a half before.

But Paul's thoughts had been focused exclusively on the present when, finishing a light lunch at the poolside, his aunt suggested that Diana join them immediately in the water.

The girl gave him a quizzical glance across the small oak dining table, a look half wary, half amused.

'Will young Angel Face be safe?' she asked his aunt.

He recognized the remark as humorous, though the joke

12

eluded him, and Cora-Beth's face darkened. 'We don't,' she said briskly, 'have worries of that kind around here. As well you know, Diana.'

The girl laughed infectiously, but in a way that compounded the elusive joke so that Paul felt excluded, as Cora-Beth never excluded him, and self-conscious as a result. Or perhaps his consciousness was more of the girl.

She had been at the house almost a week by then, an encounter-group friend from Cora-Beth's excursions to the West Coast. For as long as he remembered he had seen his aunt naked almost every day, as she had seen him, and he accepted her beauty as a fact of life. But Cora-Beth was almost forty now; Diana was half that, tall, long-legged and blonde, with the sheen of youth in her scrubbed, Californian face. He had never seen a girl so close to his own age unclothed before and was frankly curious. And yet to have his curiosity acknowledged and mocked, as her laughter seemed to do, was strangely disconcerting.

As she bent, smiling, to draw her tee-shirt over her head, he turned away deliberately, busying himself unbuttoning his shirt and shrugging down his jeans until he heard the crisp splash of her dive. Then he watched her move swiftly away down the pool, cleaving the water as sleekly as the seals he photographed off the sand bars at the end of the estate shoreline. Cora-Beth's playful cuff caught him unawares.

'Come on, Paul. Don't dawdle now!'

She was stepping out of her own pants. Grinning, Paul kicked off his sneakers and beat her into the pool in a smooth double dive. Clear and body-hot, the water enfolded him like a liquid glove. Surfacing, he struck out towards Diana, overtaking her as he began to relish his own speed and power. Immediately, to his delight, they were racing, East Coast against West, Atlantic-trained against Pacific. For two lengths they were neck and neck. Then he drew ahead, stroke by stroke, until she was lost to view. He swirled to a halt in the shallow end, standing up, gasping, to look back.

There was no sign of her. Cora-Beth was ploughing a sedate width at the opposite end.

Puzzled, he hoisted himself out of the water, flopping down on the tiled side and dangling his feet. Instantly something brushed his toes underwater. A pale, sinuous shape rippled below him and Diana burst to the surface, tossing a swathe of damp-darkened hair from her face in the same movement and gasping with laughter.

'Hey, you're good!'

'Just practice.' His satisfied grin made nonsense of his modesty. The girl smiled and closed her eyes to shake more droplets from her hair. She was standing no more than an arm's length in front of him, hip-deep in the shimmering water. Rivulets trickled down her broad shoulders, funnelled into the steep valley between her breasts.

They were high, round breasts, smaller and firmer than Cora-Beth's. He had never seen such smooth, taut flesh. It had a lustre all its own, a glow of vitality that was more than the pale honey tan that covered her body, more than mere prettiness, too, for in features alone Cora-Beth was the more striking. It drew him in a way and with a strength he had never felt before.

'Have you seen enough?'

Her matter-of-fact tone sounded like a reproof, but when he switched his gaze to her eyes she regarded him with amusement.

'I didn't mean to stare.'

14

She continued to look at him, her expression growing thoughtful.

'How long have you lived here with Cora-Beth, Paul?'

'Since my folks died—when I was seven or eight, I guess.'

She nodded, as though digesting this, and he saw how her nipples were tiny pink buds hardly bigger than his own.

'You don't have many friends your own age, do you?' she said at last.

He shrugged. The thought had rarely occurred to him. He had his camera and the seashore, tutors to talk to in the day, Aunt Cora in the evenings, and Joseph and Louisa, when they were around. Once or twice a year Uncle Bernard brought his two boys from his new marriage in the South, but they struck him as a sullen pair, bored by the isolation of the estate, too intent upon their own business or private jokes they never shared.

'It doesn't bother me,' he said.

To his surprise, laughter bubbled into the girl's throat. 'Not a lot bothers you, does it?' she grinned.

He looked at her, then glanced down where her gaze had fallen. Though he had been only dimly aware of it, his penis had risen from his lap, thick and broad-capped, almost to its full stiffness.

'Oh,' he said, 'that happens all the time.'

'I'll *bet* it does!' Diana laughed so shrilly he stared at her. Her pale blue eyes shone with a brightness and a questioning he did not recognize.

'Cora-Beth never talked to you about things like that?' she queried.

He had no idea what she meant, but the fault, he sensed, was his rather than hers. Seeing the confusion in his face, she laughed again, dismissively, shaking her head so that

15

the damp curtain of her hair slapped against her cheeks.

'You know you're cute,' she said, and smiled such a broad, dazzling smile he felt the shock of it in the pit of his stomach. Then she turned and dived and, with a flashing glimpse of pale, smoothly rounded buttocks, struck out at speed down the pool. Paul watched her go, too uneasy for the moment to follow. He had never met anyone before who both attracted and provoked him so profoundly. It was the first time they had talked seriously, but there seemed to him no real seriousness in her at all. And yet she breathed the air of a wider, more complex, infinitely more exciting world than he had ever known, and his ignorance of it was very serious indeed.

So involved was he in his thoughts he was unaware of Cora-Beth approaching until her head bobbed out of the water at his side.

'I see you and Diana are getting acquainted,' she said. She was smiling. 'What do you think of her?'

He shrugged lightly. Nothing that he felt slipped easily into words. 'She seems . . . nice,' he said.

His careful tone didn't faze his aunt in the least. Her smile broadened. 'That's good.' Then, as she leaned back, swirling the water with her hands, something about him caught her eye. 'Mmmm. . . ' she added. She moved closer, reaching up and touching his knee, urging it gently but insistently open. 'I see you *do* think she's nice.'

Her eyes were on a level with his still visible erection.

'She didn't touch me,' he said quickly. But why should he feel guilty?

'That's all right, dear. Have I ever said you should worry about things like that?'

As she spoke, calmly and quietly, her hand slipped into his lap, her slender, red-nailed fingers curling about his

16

stiffened flesh, beginning the slow, steady stroking he knew so well. But, for once, he resisted, closing his knees over her hand. 'Diana,' he murmured, nodding awkwardly up the pool to where the girl was climbing out beside the lunch table.

Cora-Beth nudged his knee aside, neither turning nor slowing the movement of her hand. 'You mustn't be shy of Diana,' she said softly. 'She knows what young men are like. And *you* know I won't have you going about hard and uncomfortable. It's not the way I brought you up. Now relax – and let's get that stickiness out of you.'

But still he remained taut, keeping a close eye on the girl, waiting until she had padded nudely into the house in search of a towel, before he gave himself up to the sweet pressure in his loins . . .

It would be Diana.

There could be no other reason for her being there. No other reason for Cora-Beth's actions in the pool. The girl had been right about his lack of company. Normally he saw no one of his own age. The most frequent house guests were Cora-Beth's, women of around her age, who paid him only passing heed. And his aunt had never encouraged him to be naked before any of them. It would be Diana's tanned flesh he would penetrate. Diana who would give him the first coming of his manhood.

The thought brought a bubbling pressure to his loins and he watched his sheet tent from the force beneath. Abruptly a distant door clicked open; a board creaked on the landing. Tensing, he reached again for his watch. Only seven-thirty. The bathroom door along the landing gave its familiar squeak. Then, to his surprise, his own door rattled and opened.

Cora-Beth came in.

Later, when he gave his own version of his extraordinary childhood, most of his few confidants would express astonishment on seeing his aunt's photograph. Even in his most restrained accounts – and they became more restrained as he grew older – the impression given was of dissoluteness, or at least an overflowing sensuality allowed the freest hand. Instead they saw a woman of strength, of unmistakable, and unshakeable, determination.

There was enough to attract any man, of course, in her sharply sculpted features, her wide, bold eyes, the froth of rich, auburn hair that now hung, sleep-tousled, about her shoulders. But it was a beauty that almost dismissed itself, a convenient mask for the character, the force of will that dwelt within and never relaxed its hold. It was a mask that had beguiled and confused many men, including her former husband, and – though in a different way – Paul himself.

'Happy birthday, darling.'

Smiling, she crossed the room, bending to kiss his cheek. Then she pushed a small white envelope into his hand and sat down next to him on the bed as he tore open the flap.

Inside was a birthday card, cream-coloured and bearing an intricate and almost colourless drawing of a plain white flower. He opened it and saw in his aunt's handwriting 'To my own dear Paul' and a cheque for two hundred dollars.

As his mouth gaped in surprise, she touched his hand. 'Now you can send away for all those complicated lenses and zooms and whatever you're always complaining you can't afford.'

He laughed and kissed her cheek and thanked her. Then, with elaborate casualness, remarked: 'Was that Diana I heard moving about?'

18

Cora-Beth straightened, keeping her eyes on him. 'Diana has something for you, too, Paul. But you know that, don't you?'

His gaze slid awkwardly away from hers. 'I guessed.'

She tightened her grip on his hand, compelling him to look back at her. There was a strange hardness in her eyes.

'I've raised you differently from other boys, Paul. I've wanted you to have a respect and a love for your body, and the bodies of others, you may not find when you eventually leave here. There's so much joy to share, so much pleasure to give, but so often it's degraded and perverted by people who know no better. A woman knows that. Now that you have become a man you'll know it too and you won't be sucked in like the others.'

She spoke with a bitter note he had never heard before and which caught his attention far more than her words, which then meant little to him.

She seemed to realize this and paused, the narrow crease of annoyance in her brow abruptly fading. She nodded toward the spiked outline in his sheet. 'Do you need to go to the bathroom, Paul?'

He grinned, feeling the heat of embarrassment. 'I was just thinking about Diana.'

His aunt smiled. 'I'm glad. Now have your shower, slip on your robe and come down for a nice big breakfast.'

They ate alone in the kitchen, looking out over the straggling kettle pond at the back of the house, wrapped in a peculiar intimacy. To Paul it felt like Christmas, the Fourth of July and the day of his annual tutors' exams all rolled into one. Cora-Beth's quiet smiles as she moved about the old kitchen range, preparing sausage and eggs, pancakes and toast – food he was too nervous to enjoy – reminded

19

him of earlier, equally 'special' days: boat trips from Provincetown to watch the humpbacks pass, rare visits to Boston and beyond. Her pleasure nourished and fed on his. But today there was a new element. For the first time his thoughts and his emotions were directed beyond the circle of his aunt's warmth, threatening to break it and prompting the same nagging sensation of guilt he had first felt in the swimming pool.

Deliberately he made no mention of Diana's absence until they were drinking coffee, their plates empty.

'She had some toast and juice in her room earlier,' Cora-Beth told him. 'She wasn't hungry this morning.' She paused. 'When we've finished our coffee we'll go up and say hello.'

A sliver of ice trickled through his belly. As he put down his empty cup he felt a clamminess in his fingers and saw his aunt watching him.

'You mustn't be nervous, Paul. You're about to enjoy the most beautiful gift a man and a woman can give to each other. Just keep in mind all I've told you and it'll go just fine.' She set down her own cup. 'Now come here and let me look at you.'

Obediently he got to his feet and moved to her end of the table. She turned toward him on her chair, lifting a hand to brush a stray hank of hair from his forehead. 'Diana's right to call you Angel Face,' she murmured. 'Such a boyish, innocent look – you'll keep it, just like your father. You'll fill out, like him, in a year or so, too. Turn into a good, strong male animal who knows how to care for a woman properly –'

Her hand had dropped to his shoulder blade, fanning and tracing her fingers down and across his chest so that his bathrobe slipped open. Now she unknotted its cord,

20

smoothing the fabric back from his nakedness. He looked down at his manhood. It had sufficient stiffness to have lifted perhaps half an inch from its nest of hair, but the foreskin still covered its helmet and the ball sac beneath was slack.

Cora-Beth's fingers scooped it, buoying the loose flesh in the warmth of her palm. Her look grew wistful.

'All the women who will love this and know joy from it,' she said softly, 'and not one of them will have what I've had . . .'

And she leaned forward and pressed her lips quickly to his shaft, causing him to start and look at her in surprise. Never before had she touched him there with her mouth.

But she gave him no time to think further, rising abruptly to her feet, and tugging at his sleeve. 'Off with that now, Paul!' She spoke briskly. 'We have nothing to hide in this house. This is a day for us all to be proud of our bodies.'

He shrugged off the robe, laying it carefully over a chair as Cora-Beth turned her back.

'Help me, Paul,' she said.

She loosened the cord of her own robe while he took hold of the collar, drawing it back off her bare shoulders and down her arms. He placed the garment next to his. The sweetness of her body's perfume reached his nostrils as she turned to him, smiling. Her heavy breasts rose and fell gently with her breath.

'This is the way it should be, dear. You must never let anyone tell you differently.'

Her hand caught his, squeezing the fingers for emphasis. He returned her smile, fighting the awkwardness he felt, and her smile softened. 'Come on, now,' she breathed and, still gripping his hand, led him barefoot across the kitchen, into the hallway and up the narrow staircase that climbed

21

to the rear of the house.

It was a time when he only cried at night, quietly but bitterly into his lonely pillow. Tears of self-pity and growing resentment. Why had they gone? Why had they left him? What had he done to make them do that?

And all the careful explanations by over-earnest adults of how his parents' plane had struck a freak storm on a ski trip to the Grand Tetons, side-slipping into a sheer rock-face, meant nothing. That was a fairy tale for grown-ups. All he knew was that his mother and his father had left him in summer camp — for ever.

And when the other youngsters had packed up and been collected he stayed, alone with a flustered counsellor and an embarrassed policeman, until two neighbours appeared — an elderly couple he called 'aunt' and 'uncle' but who were not related to him at all.

'There are no close relatives, we're sure of that,' they said.

'No grandparents? Uncles, aunts?' the policeman persisted.

'Only us.' The old man shook his head. 'Oh this is so terrible, so terrible . . . '

'There was a younger sister,' the old lady recalled suddenly. 'Vicki told me last Christmas. Married some kind of a banker, but I think they divorced. She and Victoria had quarrelled, apparently; they didn't speak. But I'm sure now . . .'

'Where is this person?' The policeman seized his chance. 'Do you have a name? An address?'

The old lady blinked. She looked at her husband. 'Didn't they live out East somewhere? Wasn't it Connecticut, Massachusetts . . .?'

'On the Cape,' the old man said with sudden emphasis. 'A big old house on Cape Cod. But she's there on her own. Quite a young woman, too. You remember telling me —

The old lady nodded so slowly and thoughtfully it was impossible to say whether she remembered or not. 'Well,' she said at last, with a trace of sigh, 'if she's got so much space she can hardly refuse one little boy . . . '

Which was how he left behind his home, his quiet, mid-western neighbourhood, his school, his friends, and found himself in a rambling, old-smelling, cedar-tiled house between a blue, silent lake and a green, crashing ocean. How, too, he came to live with the prettiest and strangest lady he had ever met. A lady who ignored his childish embarrassment as she watched him undress for bed, who seemed as forgetful of her own clothes as she was of his, who took him one day without explanation to the large, grey-roofed double garage over which Joseph and Louisa lived, close by the lichened wall that ringed the estate.

In silence they had climbed the wooden stairs to the gabled entrance door, passing unannounced into the narrow kitchen beyond. 'They're all out,' — he had murmured, conscious of trespass in a place he had never been before, glancing at his aunt's face for confirmation or denial. But she had simply smiled and led him forward into a large, cluttered lounge where an ancient television flickered noiselessly in a corner.

The set's hum had masked the sounds at first and, when he did become aware of them, it seemed that they might still be emanating faintly from the speaker. But then came a high, shrill gasp, issuing unmistakably from an open door across the room. And, as his aunt drew him closer, other sounds shaped themselves: soft grunts and moans, the creak of springs, the faintest liquid sucking sound — all counterpointed by a woman's low, steady, panting breath.

A short corridor led into the bedroom; the view from its windowless gloom was unimpeded. The couple on the bed could have been posed. Only much later did it occur to him that they almost certainly had been.

Both were naked. Louisa rested on all fours, alternately sinking onto her forearms or lifting her head high over her arched back as she

23

kept time with Joseph's thrusting rhythm between the upthrust cheeks of her rear. She was a plump, bosomy young woman of Latin extraction, the abundance of her olive flesh only serving to exaggerate the fullness and roundness of her hips and breasts. Thick dark hair, normally worn tucked into a convenient bun, danced halfway down her back, trailing in a thin film of perspiration.

Joseph, who knelt behind her, his deep-set eyes squeezed shut in concentration, his broad hands gripping and kneading the flesh of the dark girl's thighs, was older — a hairy, big-boned, crudely handsome man who still spoke with the Greek accent of his parents.

Paul absorbed this tableau in an instant, feeling within himself the growing stillness of unease, of non-comprehension. He was abruptly aware of a far graver trespass than merely wandering uninvited into a strange home. This was a glimpse of an alien, an adult world — a world of fierce and unfamiliar emotion, frightening in its intensity, its inexplicable violence. Instinctively he wanted to retreat.

But, as he went to turn, Cora-Beth bent her head to his and murmured in his ear: 'Aren't they beautiful? Don't you see how beautiful they are together? Come and look, Paul . . . They want you to. They want to show you how beautiful they are.'

And she was urging him forward, pushing him through the doorway, into the small bedroom which Louisa's frantic panting seemed to fill, close up to the bedside so that he saw the thick, scarlet, glistening organ of Joseph's love, like the pizzle of some unfamiliar beast, spearing over and over the dark profusion of hair that sprouted and spilled between Louisa's buttocks. Smelled, too, the sharp, musky, pleasant-unpleasant odours of their coupling. And caught the look on Louisa's plump, flushed face as she turned her head and saw him.

A look of sudden sly exultation, conspiratorial yet demanding, making its secret, unsettling appeal to an adult, a masculine aspect of himself he scarcely knew existed . . .

24

His heart had reached a slow and steady thunder by the time they paused outside Diana's room at the far end of the landing. His aunt knocked. Diana answered more brightly than Paul felt appropriate for such an occasion, but today was a day of revelations — his own expectations seemed a poor basis for any judgement.

He followed his aunt into a room full of sunshine. Smaller than his, it was tucked into a corner of the house, with windows on two sides following the circle of the sun. Both were open. Below one was a small double bed, hardly larger than a twin, its top cover pulled back to reveal a rumpled white sheet. Below the other was a simple Victorian dressing table painted a pale green. Diana sat at it, one long, bare leg tucked under herself, peering into the small square mirror. She turned quickly, immediately smiling that dazzling smile that had so disturbed Paul in the pool.

'My, we are doing this in style, Cora-Beth!'

If his aunt replied, Paul heard nothing. His eyes were fixed on the girl in a gaze too wary to be bold, too hypnotized to be merely curious. She was wearing a man's faded, collarless striped shirt, the old-fashioned kind with rounded flaps to front and rear; it was unbuttoned to her midriff.

Paul blinked at it; he had mentally prepared himself for Diana's nudity. Even such a skimpy garment as this was a further blow to his fragile peace of mind, doubly so since the shirt's selective concealment only served to increase her body's attractiveness.

She saw where he was looking and her smile grew more subtle. 'Guess I'm not playing the game,' she said, with a look of sly mockery that included both Paul and his aunt. She uncurled herself and stood, crossing her arms to grip

25

the bottom of the shirt, but at the last minute paused.

'No – Paul. Best you learn how to do things properly. Why don't help me get this off?'

He glanced at his aunt, but she said nothing. So, uncertainly, he stepped forward. Diana stood before him, smiling directly into his face. He smelled a muskier perfume than his aunt's, fresher but richer too, pricked with a curious citrus tang that reminded him obscurely of oranges. It was an odour that would haunt his mind for many years afterwards.

There was another surprise too. He realized that, shoeless, Diana was almost half a head shorter than him.

He reached down and gripped the bottom of the shirt. Then, with a confirmatory glance at her face, began to draw it up her body. She remained perfectly still until the rucked fabric reached the soft jut of her breasts. Abruptly she lifted her hands and brought them down over Paul's, pressing his palms onto her flesh. Through the shirt it was the warmth and firmness of her bosom he felt more than its shape, but it was more than enough to send a sharp stab of excitement through his loins.

Instantly the girl snatched the shirt from his fingers and drew it over her own head, shaking her hair free of it. Startled, Paul looked down, glimpsing the curve of her belly, a curious wave of dusky blonde at her crotch.

Then Cora-Beth was at his shoulder. 'Isn't he beautiful?' she said quietly. And he jumped as her fingers glanced his thigh and lightly brushed the underside of his shaft, now fully erect. At once irritation replaced his former guilt. Surely it should be Diana, and Diana alone, touching him now?

The girl seemed to share his thought. The teasing look returned to her face. 'If I didn't know better, Cora-Beth, I'd

26

say you were planning to enjoy this almost as much as Paul. Are you going to stay with us?'

Paul made no effort to hide his dismay. He had assumed Diana and he would be alone. This would be a moment to prove himself on his own terms. Having Cora-Beth hold his hand, or his manhood, was hardly the way to achieve it.

To his relief it was clear that Diana, for all her mockery, had made the same assumption. 'I'll be in my room,' said Cora-Beth quietly. 'I'll look in in half an hour.' She kissed Paul's cheek. 'Good luck, dear.'

Then, padding softly from the room, she was gone.

Paul looked back at Diana, his relief returning quickly to uncertainty. Nude, her honeyed flesh glowed in the morning sunlight, highlights glinting in the sweep of light blonde hair – freshly washed, Paul realized, despite her casual air – which played about the tips of her breasts. He had never seen anyone more strangely, more excitingly beautiful.

Her eyes sparkled with that wry, questioning look he had seen before. 'Are you sure you've never done this, Paul?'

He shook his head, puzzled. Surely his aunt had talked to her?

'Do *you* do it often?' he asked.

She laughed out loud. 'Oh, I fill my time! I think you count as my first younger man, though.' She grasped his hand. 'Let's sit down, shall we?'

She led him to the bed and they sat together at the pillow end, the flesh of her thigh warm against his.

'Your aunt has some wild ideas, Paul. You'll find that out soon, but the main thing that I have to teach you is that sex is fun. So just relax, enjoy those nice warm feelings and have a ball. OK?' She paused and suddenly made an ugly face. 'So serious!' He grinned as she squeezed his hand,

27

drawing it further across her thigh.

'That's better,' she said. 'Now – did you like it when I made you touch my breasts a minute ago?'

He nodded, swallowing as his gaze fell to them. They seemed perfect smooth-fleshed globes. 'Touch them again, Paul,' Diana said. 'No kidding now. Hold them, stroke them gently.'

He breathed in, swallowing again as his fingers closed over their taut warmth, feeling the perfection of their shape, their soft weight.

'They're beautiful – 'he whispered.

'Circle the nipples with your thumbs.' Diana spoke equally quietly, watching him. 'See if you can make them stand up for you. That's it. Gently now.'

Her face was inches from his as he stroked her, and the only sound in the room was the faintest whisper of their breath. Diana's tone changed subtly as, miraculously, first one small pink bud, then the other blossomed into tiny red-tipped stalks.

They smiled at each other, sharing the triumph, and Paul felt a surge of pride, just as a more physical surge seized his over-strained erection.

As his face registered the crisis, Diana pinched his arm sharply making him gasp. 'Paul,' she said quickly, 'if you feel yourself coming, tell me. Can you hold back?'

He took a deep breath, nodding once, then twice as her eyes stayed on him.

'Sometimes it's easier just to let it happen. I don't mind getting messed up a little. I'll help you if you like – '

'No!' He shook his head so violently her eyes widened in surprise. That was what Cora-Beth did. Instinctively he knew this must be different. This must be something new and right.

28

The girl's look softened. 'Now I'd have said you had quite a taste for that . . . .'

Her lip curled teasingly as Paul frowned at her. Then, as realization dawned, a deep flush rose from his toes. 'You saw – at the pool. . .?'

'I'm not dumb – or blind, Paul. Don't get me wrong – if that's what turns you both on, fine. I've got a kid brother who'd wash cars for a year to get jerked off by a pretty lady . . . ' She paused, seeing his flush, and his confusion, deepen.

She was treading, she realized, on dangerous ground. It still astonished her that Paul actually existed, that Cora-Beth's bizarre accounts of her nephew's 'wholly Reichian' upbringing really were factual and not the fantasies Diana heard all too often in such encounter groups.

But now that she had made the trip East – if only for a free vacation and the possibility of an unusual sexual experience (both equally valid reasons, as far as she was concerned) – the presence of the phantom nephew himself posed problems she had never faced before. He reminded her of a wealthy Arab student at UCLA she had once known – a young man with values that seemed quite familiar on the surface but underneath were wholly and unpredictably different. She could respond only with the directness she had learned to use in all situations.

'Hey, why are we talking? You came up here to learn how to fuck. Well, let's fuck. You do want to, don't you?'

He nodded quickly.

'Well, I hope it's me you want to fuck. By the look of that nice-looking hard-on you've got there I'd say it was. But let's hear it from you, OK?'

He nodded again. She was suddenly like one of the brash ra-ra-skirted cheerleaders he saw on TV – bright, depersonalized and demanding. He found himself smiling lop-sidedly.

'I want to – fuck you – Diana – '

'Great! That's what I like to hear – enthusiasm!' She grinned and patted the bed. 'Come on, let's lie down.'

She lifted her long legs and rolled sideways beside him, pushing herself up the bed until her shoulders were propped against the pillow. Less easily, Paul settled at her side, their flesh touching on the narrow mattress.

'Give me your hand,' she ordered. Taking it, she drew it slowly down her body, watching his face as she made his fingers trace the slope and summit of her breast, the valley of her navel, her stomach's gentle swell and the beard of dark blonde beneath.

He raised his head to look as he felt the wiry tightness of her hair. Where Cora-Beth was dark and sparse, neat bands of thickness angling downward like a pubic arrowhead, Diana was bushy and undisciplined; the lightest dusting of golden-tipped fuzz thickened abruptly into two swirling and opposed crests, framing her sex like dense cowlicks of salt-marsh hay.

She made the softest grunt as his longest finger sank into her hair, pressing the folded flesh beneath, feeling its slickness and heat.

'Gently,' she reminded him. Abruptly she swivelled, crooking one knee, to make it easier for him, but dislodging his hand and causing him to glance at her. She touched his shoulder. 'Go on, you can get closer than that. You have seen a woman up close, haven't you?'

'Sure.' He frowned at her. 'I don't miss things either – '

She screwed up her face and punched his rib cage lightly as he bent towards her splayed thighs. 'We're not *all* like Cora-Beth, Mr Experience – '

30

He was walking through the darkened house to his room, open-pored and damp from a late shower, pleasantly weary from a day spent trekking to a distant brook to photograph the alewives churning the water in their spring spawning.

He had not seen his aunt and barely registered the thin line of light beneath her door. In a house where privacy had little meaning, Cora-Beth's bedroom was the single, qualified exception — a status conferred on it as much by Paul as his aunt, who liked to read late and undisturbed. But as he passed quietly by, expecting not to see her until the morning, she had called him in.

She was in bed, reading by the soft light of a bedside lamp. Putting down her book, she had patted the mattress at her side, inviting him to sit. As he did, the towel, which was all he wore, slipped from his waist. He started and quickly bent to replace it, but she stretched out an arm to stop him, letting her hand fall into his lap, her fingers sifting his fine, damp, curls.

'So much hair for a fair boy,' she said at last, smiling up at him. 'That's from your mother. She was like a bird's nest down there.'

He blinked at her, his smile crooked and embarrassed. Hers had faded, though her hand remained where it was.

'You're starting to have warm, exciting thoughts these days, aren't you, Paul?' she said. 'Thoughts that make you big and hard and tingly . . . . Who do you think about? Is it Louisa — ?' Her dark eyes studied his face for confirmation and saw surprise and a deep, spreading blush.

Her perception astonished him. He did think of Louisa — and of all women. Flesh — soft, rounded, sweet-scented, female — haunted his mind, feelings compounded of vague sentimentality, gross prurience and the most basic curiosity. They unnerved him, embarrassed him by their urgency and — worse — their total unpredictability: even the hint of a sexual thought brought him stiffly and instantly erect. He would walk for long hours along the foreshore or through the pitch pine, alternately lost in burgeoning fantasies or vainly trying to think away

31

the unrelieved pressure in his loins. Suddenly – in weeks and months too short to remember – baffling and unbridled emotion had rearranged his consciousness, leaving him uncertain and confused and secretive as a result. Yet Cora-Beth knew.

'You mustn't hide those feelings, Paul. They're lovely feelings. They are meant to be shared. You'll feel bad if you keep them bottled up . . . '

And to his horror he was rising, his flesh thickening and stretching between her fingers.

'There, Paul – doesn't that feel nice? Isn't that a good feeling? Oh you're splendid – don't turn away like that! Be proud of yourself.'

So he had brought his gaze down from the bedhead, where it had climbed in embarrassment, to his aunt's bright smile and the broad-capped column of flesh between his legs.

'You're not alone, you know. Women have those good feelings too. In different places, of course. Come here, Paul – it's time you found out.'

She was moving across the bed, patting the vacated portion of mattress. Wondering, dry-mouthed, he hesitated – would they do what he had seen Joseph and Louisa doing? Images of that groaning, sweating frenzy – whose violence now made so much sense –filled his mind. But he couldn't impose Louisa's loose-lipped, half-abandoned look on Cora-Beth's unruffled self-assurance. And he was right.

For a fraught hour he knelt below her outstretched thighs, naked pupil before nude mistress, torn between great embarrassment and greater curiosity, watching as she traced the soft convolutions of her sex, seeing its avenue of whorled flesh thicken and unfold under her touch into glistening receptivity.

'Give me your hand, Paul. Come on – just watching won't do you any good.' Grasping his hand in hers, she directed his finger to the edges of her tenderest flesh, probing its sticky warmth, its softness so extraordinary against his rigidity.

'Relax, Paul – let your hand relax . . . . There – '

32

And he touched hardness, a curious, truncated echo of his own, peeping from a hooded fold of flesh. She winced as he pressed it. 'Softly, Paul! That's very sensitive. Never touch it directly. Move up to it, move around it. Take your time. Here . . . '

He glimpsed her face, flushed, he realized, not from the glow of the lamp but from her own warmth — her eyes, too, aswim with a brightness she seemed to fight, blinking, not meeting his as she brought his finger in slow, easy, spiralling strokes toward the nub of her pleasure . . .

'Hey!' Diana looked at him with a kind of amused disbelief. 'I thought *I* was teaching *you*.'

'Don't you like it?' said Paul.

Her lips were narrow and thin, skimpy even when engorged. Her nub was tiny; he had to search for it, using the soft, exploratory stokes he remembered.

'Of course I *like* it —'

She winced as he found her, jerking her hips upward in an involuntary spasm, wiping the amusement from her face.

'Whooh, Angel Face.' She moved away from him, squirming onto her back, her knees still outspread. '*I'm* supposed to be in charge here. Remember?'

'No one's in charge. Our feelings are in charge.'

The girl grinned at him. 'Now if that isn't pure Cora-Beth I don't know what is!'

But Paul's face remained serious. 'Aren't we going to do it, then?' he said.

'Are we going to do it?'

There was a real anxiety in his voice, a deep confusion as his aunt bucked and panted beneath him, grinding his knuckles into the damp flesh between her legs while her mouth stretched and her eyelids

33

*flickered in fierce concentration. She seemed lost in a world as frantic
and private as Joseph and Louisa's. A world where he intruded.*

Then her eyes flashed open, blinking rapidly as if hardly focused.

*'I'll show you — Paul — this way — climb up — climb up on me — '
She had released her numbing grip on his hand; she was clutching at
his thighs, pulling him forward awkwardly, down onto the mounding
expanse of her breasts. Their flesh stuck; her breath warmed his
throat; his aching stiffness compressed the rasping curls of her mons.*

*And her hand was pushing down, between them, clasping his
swollen length, squeezing its veined edge against the hard bone
beneath her sex, rubbing herself with it . . .*

*He had no breath. The ache in his abused cock was a pent-up
agony. He should be inside — if that was what they were doing — why
this play-acting? Why this mad teasing . . . ?*

He was in her.

There was the slightest awkwardness as she guided him
to her opening, a subtle shifting of her pelvis to allow him to
negotiate the double gates of flesh. And suddenly she
enclosed him. A warm, silken smoothness gripping the
heart of him. It was a comfort, a homecoming, an intimacy
as total as it was daring, as strange as it was wholly natural
and right.

He swallowed, matching her careful breathing, lifting his
gaze from her stiff-nippled breasts to her smiling, high-
coloured face.

'Nice?'

He nodded, three, four times, breaking into a broad grin.
'Oh yes.'

'Good.' She lifted her head from the mattress, reaching
down and touching his buttock gently with her fingertips.
'Come all the way in,' she said softly. 'You don't want to
catch cold out there.'

He nodded again, smiling, looking down between their bodies to watch his bloated cock slide impossibly between her parted lips. A shudder overtook him as their hair meshed. He gasped, jerking up his head to meet her eyes, suddenly wide and tremulous.

'Are you all right?'

He bowed his head. 'I think – '

'Don't worry if you can't stop yourself. I won't mind.'

'No!' He blinked fiercely. 'No. I want to make you come.'

'You want to make *me* come?' Her chuckle transmitted itself to his enclosed penis, squeezing it as her diaphragm rose and fell, and making him wince. 'That's nice,' she smiled, stopping and pecking the skin of his chest. 'Well,' She sighed pleasantly, 'you better start moving then. Nice and slow to begin with.'

The door latch clicked behind them.

A sick certainty that a moment of triumph was sliding from his grasp suddenly invaded Paul. He forced himself to withdraw carefully, fighting an instinctive urge to thrust and thrust again. Sweet perfume assailed his nostrils.

'How's my boy doing?'

Diana stirred under him as he eased forward again. 'Oh he's doing fine, Cora-Beth. He's promised to make me come, too.'

'Well, of course. I brought him up to be totally considerate. Does it feel good, Paul? Doesn't Diana feel marvellous?'

Sweat broke on his brow as he turned to his aunt, inches from his face. Go away! his mind screamed. Go away and leave us, leave me alone this once!

'Come, Paul – it's easy – just let it happen – we'll come together – we'll do it together – '

35

His aunt's words hissed semi-coherently in his ear. He was wrapped in the maelstrom of her emotions, simultaneously repelled and excited by them. He saw the sheen of perspiration on her forehead, he saw a dark flush speckle the vee of her breasts, he saw — shockingly — her habitual coolness crumble and dissolve.

Then his thoughts were scattered by a surge from his loins, a surge so powerful he no longer had the power to control it. For an instant he teetered unsupported on the edge of an abyss. And then, miraculously, release came. The pressure went; his agony burst outwards in sharp, pumping thrusts, as though his organ had taken on a life of its own, and each thrust a peak of the most intense, the most delirious, the sweetest pleasure he had ever known.

'Yes!' he heard his aunt whisper. 'Yes — oh yes — do it on me — do it — do it!'

'Oh *yes*, Paul!'

It was Cora-Beth who caught the change in his face a second before the spasm took him, before Diana, bright-eyed beneath him, instantly jerked her pelvis downward to meet his stabbing thrust, closing her eyes, her lips curving in a Cheshire-cat smile of triumph and consummation as he spent himself again and again and again. And then, grunting, slumped heavily across her, feeling his aunt's hand brush his buttock, hearing her purr: 'That was wonderful, *wonderful*, Paul.'

And it was. It *was*.

But still it could not stifle the slow canker of disappointment that wormed and burned within him. He *was* a man, but Cora-Beth's man, and he would not be free of her — free to be himself — until he had left this place.

2

RACHEL

1974

She would be a woman tonight.

The thought came with the force of revelation, a whispered secret that shocks as much by its absolute truth as its total unexpectedness.

Yes, she thought. *Yes, of course*. And it was as if her body had spoken, as if the power that so recently had swelled her hips, shaped her legs, rounded her bosom so fully she still slipped into a self-conscious round-shoulderedness, had also created its own urgency, its own inexorable timetable.

The moment stilled her. It drowned out the street games of the children beyond her bedroom window, the whine of May's transistor radio from the kitchen below. She sat, almost without noticing, at her small, cluttered dressing table.

A woman. Tonight.

The maleness which had stroked her and held her, grasped her hand in the darkness of cinema or disco, probed her mouth with its warm, darting tongue would *take* her . . . breach the final barrier of her selfhood. She would open to it like a flower, like the soft, sensitive flesh between her thighs . . . . A sweet thrill of fear made her shiver.

She dropped her hand into her lap, pressing her fingers lightly against the warm bulge in her white cotton pants, her eyes widening in wonderment.

If her body reached decisions like this, undermining her

mind, her conscience, it could be anyone, any time . . . simply an instant, unthinking surrender to maleness.

Then she smiled. It wouldn't just be maleness. It would be Donny. Lean, dark-haired, soccer-mad Donny with the deep, dark eyes and the long, long lashes. Donny from the same northern town, the same unruly school – three years on . . . . *Her* Donny, who waited while others grew impatient and annoyed and moved on . . .

'But why not, Rache? You know I won't hurt you.'

'You know why.'

A male sigh in the intimacy of the old Ford. Yellow lamps flickering in the night-cooled streets. Venus high in the dimming sky.

'I don't see why you've got this thing about being sixteen. There are girls down at St Mark's been on the pill since they were fourteen.'

'Well I'm not like them!'

'I never meant – I just said – '

'Well, don't.'

A heavy silence. A car swished past the shaded lay-by. She found his hand in the dimness, sought the glimmer of his eyes.

'I love you, Donny.'

A soft squeeze. He didn't turn.

'I feel the same way, Rachel, but it's difficult – '

'What is?'

The sigh again. 'You won't even let me see you undressed.'

'I don't want to be stared at!'

'Bloody hell, Rache! You've seen me. You've even touched it.'

'You showed it to me.' She felt the spasm of his hurt pride and pulled him closer, her tone softening. 'I was glad you did, Donny. It proved you trusted me.'

His breath caught and she stopped. He squirmed in the driver's seat. She waited.

'It's just' – a vague gesture with his free hand – 'when people see

your stepmum and you they — assume — you do, that you and I do.'

She froze, her grip slackening on his fingers. 'What people? Assume what?'

His glance was swift, embarrassed. 'You both just look — sexy — as if you'd enjoy doing it. I'm not saying I — '

She flared. 'You mean spotty kids with dirty minds! Well, she may be a rotten tart, but I'm not. I'm not like that. I'll never be like that!'

Old hurts, old resentments raked through her afresh, shaming him into silence, leaving her hot and shaken. If only her father had waited. Things were getting better, she was growing up more every day, knowing him more, understanding him more; they would have been fine together, alone. But he had not waited. In his weak, impatient way he had married her.

Just because she looked like the girls in the magazines, because she did the things they did . . .

And, as the anger seeped from her large, brilliant eyes, Donny waited, both attracted and alarmed as ever by the flashes of passion from so bird-like and petite a frame — but not surprised. For it was there in the soft triangle of her face, the frankness of her gaze, the pouting fullness of her lower lip. A look of sullen intensity, of bruised sensuality that sparked its answer in the eyes of every passing male. Did she really not see it? Did she truly not realize that unspoken invitation? 'Yes — can you satisfy *me*? Do *you* have what it takes?'

And later, in the fevered daring of his imagination, alone at night in bed as his fingers teased his stiffness, would come the impossible surrender — her unholy lushness unfolding naked beside him: 'Yes — yes, it's *you* I want — I want *you* to take me — I want *you* to fill me to overflowing. Please — *please*, fuck me. Oh fuck me — now!'

That was what he would wait for, that was what would keep him content with jocular hints to his friends that all was well, that they sucked and fucked and cavorted every night, because they had only to

39

look at her to see the promise in her face.

He started, feeling her fingers on his knee, aware that his thoughts had made him rigid. She was quiet again, regarding him warily as if her outburst might have turned him against her.

'Donny?' A whisper. 'Donny, I don't care what anyone else thinks. I only care about us.' Her fingers tightened. 'We will, I promise you. As soon as I'm ready. Don't push me _ please. You know there's only you, don't you . . .?'

And they were kissing, their breath accelerating as his hand cupped the soft roundness beneath her sweater and her fingers brushed the warm ridge down his thigh, clasped it, rubbed it . . .

She shuddered, feeling the prickle of stiffening nipple beneath her bra cup. It had been so close that night, she could so easily have let herself drift into that mindless swoon where responsibility and self-respect faded to nothing. And when Donny had cursed and the thickness beneath her fingers had jumped and the warm dampness risen through the fabric of his jeans, her guilt and her disappointment had vied with a sensation of the most intense relief.

She breathed in and her eyes focused on her reflection in the dressing-table mirror.

Did her face really show what Donny had said? It seemed to her only ordinary – pretty, yes, but she knew three or four girls at school who were much, much prettier. A woman teacher had once told her she had 'good cheekbones' rather gruffly, as though in envy, and she had hoarded up the phrase, only appreciating it with a flush of pride when she heard a top model described in the same terms.

An early boyfriend had called her lips 'kissable' in a way that suggested he had just read the word somewhere but which pleased her enormously for the whole of one summer.

40

Yet she felt certainty about none of these things. Only her hair, shoulder-length and thick, a rich dark thatch shot through with chestnut, seemed worthy of admiration. Hadn't her father called her 'my little gipsy'? Once.

'Rachel! Rachel – you up there?'

May's voice echoed up the stairwell. A shrill London voice. The woman didn't even come from round here. Rachel frowned in the mirror, knowing her prejudice was unfair, irritated that she knew.

'Rachel!'

'*Yes!*'

'Do you want a snack now, love, or will you wait till we get there?'

Get there? Get where?

Rachel stood up, reaching for the lemon yellow ribbed sweater Donny liked, the pleated beige skirt she'd brought to go with it. 'Be right down!' she called, dressing. She wasn't going anywhere with May tonight. Donny was calling. It was pre-arranged.

The stairwell smelled of frying fat. Sizzling sounds and the thump of pop music issued from the open kitchen door. May stood just inside, wincing as she straightened the lid on a chip pan.

She had a striking face, not a pretty one, Rachel decided, full-lipped and dark-eyed but with a kind of lushness that forever toppled over into obviousness: the constant mascara, the overlong lashes, the bleached honey-blonde hair almost as pale as her well-rounded flesh.

Obvious, Rachel thought, with all the puritanism of youth. As obvious as the way she was dressed now, a skimpy, kimono-style robe wrapped loosely over her full bust, barely covering her thighs, where the lace edging of a slip showed. Just to show off her legs, even if they were good

41

legs. She was thirty-four, not some eighteen-year-old sexpot.

May turned and saw her, making her blush suddenly for her disapproving thoughts.

'I was just getting your dad some egg and chips,' her stepmother said. 'You know he hates to drink on an empty stomach. Do you fancy some?'

Rachel shook her head. 'I'm seeing Donny tonight.'

'That's right.' May nodded brightly. 'You can come along with your dad and I, make up a foursome.' Her expression altered as Rachel's face dropped. 'Didn't your father talk to you?' She glanced back into the kitchen. 'You're a right so-and-so, aren't you, Jack? Rachel doesn't know a thing about it.'

Rachel stepped through the kitchen doorway. Her father sat at the small table under the window, his dour, handsome face sunk into an evening paper. He looked up vaguely. 'What's that, love?'

Switching off the radio at her side, May told him.

'Oh yes, Rachel. May thought it'd be a good idea if you came along to a camera session tonight. You're a big girl now – you'll enjoy yourself.'

'We *both* thought it'd be a good idea,' May corrected snappily, and tripped across the room to snatch the paper from his hands. 'Watch these chips – I've got to pay a call.'

She went upstairs as Jack rose wearily to his feet. Rachel stared at her father, aghast.

'Daddy – '

'I know what you're going to say, Rachel, and I don't want to hear it. We ask you to do precious little in this house. You can please May just for one evening.'

He paused over the cooker, his face set in that stiff obstinacy she hated, with nagging overtones of betrayal

42

and blame. *It's not* me *who betrayed you!* she wanted to scream. *I didn't invite that woman in.*

Her father's eyes flickered toward the stairs and his voice dropped. 'I'm disappointed, Rachel. I've got to say it. It's nearly two years now since May's been with us and she's made every effort to be nice to you. And all you've done is moon about and be obstructive. I expected better. A lot better.'

The flagrant injustice set Rachel's heart thumping and colour racing to her cheeks. Her voice shook. 'I don't want to watch her prancing about, making a fool of herself –'

'Shut it! Just shut it!'

It was the darkness in his eyes more than the sharpness of his tone that silenced her. She felt an iciness down her spine. For a brief moment she had seen real hatred there.

He breathed in. 'There's a nasty touch of your mother's temper about you, Rachel, and I've already had too many years of that. I won't have any more. Now run and get yourself ready. We're going in half an hour.'

Shaken and still inwardly fuming, she turned. There was a clatter on the stairs and May bustled in.

'All settled? Jack – you've let these burn!' Fussily she nudged her husband back from the cooker, turned off the gas and reached for a plate. The others watched her in silence.

'Well?' she said, glancing up.

'I won't take my clothes off,' Rachel snapped.

'Oh, for God's sake!' May cried. 'What have you been telling her, Jack? What do you think we get up to, love? It's not a Roman orgy!'

'Don't ask me,' said Jack, moving back to the table. He picked up his paper. 'I don't know where she gets her ideas from. Certainly not from me.'

43

May looked at her stepdaughter. 'It's only a bit of fun, love. You'll enjoy yourself. Anyway, it's time you saw a bit of life.'

'I'm seeing Donny!' Rachel's eyes stung.

'That's no problem. Donny's coming too. He wants to.'

Rachel blinked, shocked into silence, her gaze wavering on her stepmother's bright, flushed face. There was a blankness in her mind.

'What do you mean?' she said at last.

'What I say.' May turned to the cooker, igniting the gas beneath a crusted frying-pan. She picked up two eggs. 'He popped by yesterday afternoon – just on the off chance. I told him you were staying late at school. We had a nice chat. He's very keen on coming.'

She gave a half-glance backward, a look that seemed sharp with challenge. But her stepdaughter was incapable of responding.

'What did you tell him?' Rachel's voice was toneless.

'That we were having a little get-together at Ted's place – something to drink, something to eat – and taking a few snaps. Donny's very interested in photography. He thought my album was fantastic –'

'You showed him *that*?'

Her mind's emptiness was giving way to shivers of rage and humiliation. She thought of May's treasured 'album' – a tattered ring folder between garish covers with plastic sleeves of glossy eight-by-tens: May in a swimsuit, May in an over-tight bikini, May in a baby-doll nightie with her pink-nippled breasts moulding the all-but-transparent fabric, the dark triangle between her legs a shadowy outline in her briefs. Pouting at the unseen photographer, wet-lipped and heavy-lidded . . .

Had Donny sat beside her as she leafed through it,

44

inflated with her own ego, watching him for his reaction the way she watched every man . . . ?

Her thoughts were confused. Donny wouldn't have let her . . . he'd walk out, disgusted . . . . But he thought she was sexy, he'd said so . . .

'He was *very* complimentary.' May swivelled, scooping the fried eggs and sliding them onto a plate, unaware of the sudden paleness in Rachel's face. Jack grunted as May put the meal in front of him.

'Who's that?' he asked, dropping his paper.

'Young Donny – being very appreciative of my modelling work.' She did a mock pirouette, her robe lifting over bright pink pants as Jack's features broke into a grin.

'You cheeky bitch!' He slapped a broad arm round her hips, snatching her to him while she shrieked. 'You love it, don't you, showing it all off? I don't know what to eat first – you or the meal.'

She shrieked again as he plunged his nose into her lightly covered cleavage. 'No, Jack, no! Not in front of – ' Shiny-eyed, she twisted her head as Rachel shot from the room and thundered upstairs. 'Now look what you've done – '

Jack's face darkened. 'Leave her – she's such a moody cow these days. If I didn't know any better I'd say she was rotten with jealousy – '

'Of me, Jack?' May's voice rose in exaggerated disbelief. 'No! What on earth for . . . ?'

Their words faded along the landing, lost in fresh giggles. Rachel closed her ears to them, shutting them out as she slammed the bedroom door. It was horrible, *horrible*. They made her feel excluded, a pettish child, an intruder in her own home.

But it was her, not him. She saw that clearly. Her father was right – she *was* jealous, but her jealousy paled beside

45

May's. Rachel was his flesh, May only had her own flesh —
her face, her figure, her 'modelling' work . . .

Scoffing, Rachel sat on her bed.

*The letter had been tucked in the back of a bottom drawer in the
living-room dresser, under an old folder containing the few household
accounts her father kept. Normally Rachel never went there — it was
part of the unspoken household segregation between his and hers that
had grown up since her mother's departure. But her father was out
and she needed writing paper.*

*She saw the edge of a lined sheet and pulled it out into the open. It
had been torn from a child's exercise book and the handwriting it
contained was childish and ill-formed.*

> *Hi! [it read] I was so pleased you answered my ad. I hope you
> didn't mind the small charge. Film and postage are so expensive
> these days, but I'm sure you know that!*
>
> *My measurements are 36(C-cup)-24-35 and I have posed
> regularly for several photographic clubs, so I am not short of
> experience. I am, however, happy to pose for individuals, though I
> am obliged to ask for help with my expenses.*
>
> *I have many exciting costumes of my own and some very sexy
> lingerie, but I will gladly pose without them! Nothing kinky,
> though.*
>
> *I hope you enjoy the enclosed sample of my work. You can get in
> touch with me by writing back with your phone number and I will
> ring you immediately. As you can see I really enjoy modelling and I
> know we can have a really exciting photo session together.*
>
> *Looking forward to hearing from you, Marilyn.*

*A grubby Polaroid was paper-clipped to the back. Rachel turned it
over and saw May.*

She was wearing a dark, ill-fitting wig and her make-up was different, but the face as unmistakable. She was sprawled against a purple counterpane, grinning up at the camera. Her knees were bent back and spread wide; one hand cupped a full breast, the other pushed into the light, gingery fuzz between her legs. Apart from black fishnet stockings and a thin gold chain around her midriff, she was naked.

To Rachel the photograph was gross and foolish. It astonished her that men could take such a thing seriously. But her father had, because a week earlier she had come in to find him and 'Marilyn' sipping drinks together on the living-room sofa.

'This is May,' he had said. 'She's been helping us out at the camera club.'

'Helping yourselves, more like,' May had grinned at him, rising to take Rachel's hand. And by that grin Rachel had known instantly that this strange woman regarded her father as her conquest, her trophy. The photograph and the letter only showed how.

A two-tone horn bleeped below and Rachel leapt up from her bed and hurried to the window, in time to see Donny's mauve-painted Capri bump over the kerb and park on the grass verge opposite. He got out and waved up at her.

Frowning, she rushed downstairs and met him on the front step.

'What the *hell* do you think you're doing?'

His welcoming smile froze. 'What's the matter, Rache?'

'We were supposed to be seeing each other tonight!' Her eyes blazed.

He shrugged, uncertainly. 'May asked me especially. She said you were going anyway – '

'I'd *never* go. You know that.' Her voice dropped to a hiss as high heels clicked behind her.

'Hello, Donny! We ready to go then?' May bustled forward, smiling, in a cloud of heady perfume. She was wearing a peasant-style skirt of dark, fluted gauze, decorated with a lacy floral pattern; through a sleeveless bodice of the same material a red, satiny bodice was just visible. Even to Rachel's eyes the outfit looked stunning.

'Hello, Mrs Turner.' Donny smiled hesitantly and Rachel caught a brightness in his eyes that stilled her simmering anger. She was abruptly unsure of herself, unsure of him. May's attractiveness *was* obvious, but men liked that; even Donny liked that . . .

'Come on, Rachel, stop dreaming!' May thrust a bulging plastic bag into her arms. 'That's for the sandwiches. *Jack!*'

Donny drove at speed, showing off a little, borne along on a tide of ebullience from May in the back seat. Rachel sat quietly at his side, watching the sure movements of his left arm in his white short-sleeved shirt as he changed gear, the flexing of leg muscles in his newly pressed narrow-leg jeans. Once, he caught her glance and smiled warily, then with greater confidence, realizing he had been forgiven.

He's beautiful, she thought. But there was only a look of soft trust in her face. She felt small and vulnerable, needing to be cherished. She did not trust May, nor even her father in these circumstances. Donny, for all his strange maleness, would have to look after her. Knowing that, she felt close to him again.

The house where the camera club was to meet was on the far side of the town, halfway down a dusty cul-de-sac already jammed with parked cars. Expertly Donny manoeuvred the Capri into the last remaining space.

While Rachel stayed at Donny's side as he helped her father unload boxes of camera equipment, lager packs, groceries and holdalls belonging to May, May herself skipped excitedly up the path to the house.

48

The front door opened as she reached it and Rachel heard a loud whoop of joy. She looked up as May was lifted and hugged by a small, balding man no taller than her shoulder.

'Put my wife down, Ted!' Rachel's father shouted, grinning. 'You don't know where she's been!'

'I know where she's going, you lucky sod!'

Laughing, his arms full, Jack led Rachel and Donny to the front porch, where Ted lolled against May's shoulder, gripping her tightly about the waist.

'You're a cheeky bastard,' Jack said.

Ted pulled a face. He was in his late thirties, a lean, bony man with a leprechaun's face and darting eyes. 'The best-looking pair in the North!' he cried. his head diving toward May's cleavage. 'Yourself and your good wife, I mean!' he added, rising.

Pouting, May slapped his chest. He made a mock groan and his gaze fastened on Rachel, his eyes widening with interest.

'And who's this, then, Jack? You're not planning something a little different tonight, are you?'

Rachel blushed, uncertain how to react.

'Don't you remember my Rachel?' Jack said. 'It can't be that long.'

Ted's face dropped. 'Not *little* Rachel. My God –'

His hot stare left Rachel nowhere to look. She felt foolish, the crimson deepening in her cheeks.

'Rachel's helping out with the food,' said May quickly. 'With her boyfriend, young Donny here.'

Ted's eyes flickered past Rachel, noted Donny for the first time and flickered back.

'Pick your tongue up, Ted,' May chided with a sharp smile. 'Someone'll trip over it.'

Ted's grin snapped back into place. He gave May a loud smacking kiss on the cheek. 'Isn't she gorgeous, Jack? Best model we've ever had. Well, don't hang about here. We've been set up for half an hour. Everyone's here . . .'

He ushered them into a narrow, ill-lit hallway. Muted rock music and a murmur of male voices came from an open doorway to the left. As May stepped through it there was a sudden roar of welcome.

Rachel followed hesitantly, keeping close to Donny. Inside was a large through lounge, the windows tightly curtained. The ceiling lights were on but reduced to a dull orange by a brilliant glare from the further end. There four photo-floods on stands were directed at a length of wide, light blue material pinned against the curtains.

Half a dozen men were crowing around the delighted May, greeting Jack loudly as he squeezed in behind her. Rachel hung back. As the hubbub wore on the men would glance toward her, eyeing her speculatively in a way that made her increasingly uncomfortable. All were about her father's age, fortyish, perhaps a year or two younger, married men on a spree. She recognized two of her father's pub friends, but they did not acknowledge her, either uncertain who she was or waiting for an introduction from Jack. None came.

Then May was breaking away, urging her back into the hallway. 'Let's get this stuff into the kitchen, shall we, love?'

They moved toward a doorway at the far end. Behind them, Jack, Donny and Ted jostled with grocery bags and cans of drink.

'Well, why not?' Rachel heard Ted's voice, low and insinuating.

'Give it a rest, Ted,' her father murmured. 'It's only her first time for God's sake —'

'Nothing too strong. Couple of underwear shots. Doesn't even have to do topless if she doesn't want. You know how the lads go for the mother-and-daughter bit. You wouldn't mind a bit of that, would you, Donny . . . ?'

She was about to turn round, but May spoke loudly, drowning out the voices as she entered a tiny, overcrowded kitchen. Quickly her stepmother began unloading groceries onto a central table. 'I've got to run and get ready, love. Can you make a start on those sandwiches? Whatever you like – they're not fussy. Where'd you put my bags, Jack?'

'Top of the stairs.' Jack and Donny began piling lager cans into a fridge. There was no sign of Ted. 'You can change up there.'

'I hope to God Ted's missus left her little mirror this time,' May muttered, hurrying out.

'Where is Ted's wife?' Rachel asked.

Her father turned quickly, as though surprised she had spoken. 'Ted's missus?' He went back to his loading. 'Oh, she's not too keen on photography. Out, I suppose. Donny, you going to give me a hand in the lounge? I'll show you how the gear works.'

Donny gave a bright nod as Jack slammed the fridge door, pushing a spare can into the boy's hands and rushing out. Donny grinned and snapped the can open. 'Not bad, eh? They don't stint themselves, do they?'

'I want to go, Donny,' Rachel said quietly.

His smile slipped. 'Now? We haven't even started.'

'That's why.'

Donny sighed. 'I can't do that, Rache. Run out on your dad and May. It's so bloody rude –'

'Please.'

Her need to be gone, to step out into the gathering dusk was suddenly so overwhelming she could barely articulate

51

it. Something wrong would happen here, something bad.

Her strength of feeling trapped Donny for a moment. She saw his indecision, his yearning to see what happened in that long, over-bright lounge. Then her father called him from the hallway.

'Let's give it an hour or so – just to be polite. Then we'll see. All right?'

Donny ran from the disappointment in her face, not waiting for an answer. The door swung shut behind him.

She felt abandoned. Nobody listened. Nobody cared. A fluttering panic grew in her, scattering her courage. If there had been a back exit she would simply have slipped away. But leaving meant passing the lounge door. Being seen, having to explain . . .

The panic reached its peak. Chewing her lip, she held on tight, letting the force of her feelings dissipate. She was being silly, she told herself. Donny would come back, he always came back. She breathed in, thinking more clearly. It was her sudden insistence that had alarmed him. She had seen it before. Sometimes he seemed almost frightened by the depth of her emotion – foolishly. She didn't understand why; she was still herself, still the Rachel who cared for him.

A little happier, she looked down at the groceries on the table. Then she turned and began searching for a knife and plates.

Down the hallway the rock music rose in volume. May's high heels bumped on the stairs, there was a burst of catcalls and excited shouts, and the lounge door slammed shut.

Rachel worked quickly, glad to lose herself in the steady production of sandwiches. Occasionally laughter or loud cries would rise above the regular thump of the music. Once, the lounge door opened and a fat, sandy-haired man

52

she did not know stumbled into the kitchen and made straight for the fridge. He was red-faced and sweating, his shirt open to his navel.

'On your own, love? Come and have a drink. It's a great session,' he said.

'Just finishing these,' Rachel replied uneasily, indicating two sandwich-filled plates.

'Great! Do with a bite soon.' The man grinned, hoisted two lager packs from the fridge and went out.

Time passed. Rachel sat at the table before half a dozen plates, staring out at the darkness of a small yard. Resentment alternated with a sense of relief. Perhaps this was all there would be. Soon Donny and May and her father would reappear and they would simply go home. She did not want to think what Donny might be doing next door.

But it was May who reappeared first.

A sudden babble of voices came from the hallway, then female shrieks and a clatter of footsteps. Abruptly the kitchen door burst open and May flew in, giggling wildly, twisting to beat away the hands of a pursuer.

'Get *away*, Ted!' she squealed, pressing the door to. 'Go and keep my husband quiet. Go and play with your focal length. I need a break!'

There was a grumbling moan from beyond the door. Laughing, she turned to meet Rachel's startled gaze, and sucked in a deep draught of air.

Rachel blinked. May's skirt was gone. In its place her long, well-shaped legs rose inside dark fishnet stockings, cut off just below the fullness of each pale-fleshed thigh. Black suspenders, slightly askew, disappeared under frilly-edged nylon pants drawn up tight into her crotch. The suspenders were clipped to the lower half of her bodice, which hardly covered her waist. The top half was equally skimped, leaving only the suggestion of a half-cup, over which her breasts spilled, heavy and round and flushed. Her face was flushed too, her eyes wide and shining, as if she were drunk.

'God,' she murmured, 'it's hot under those lights!'

She tottered to the fridge past a silent Rachel, opened the door and bent to fan cooled air into her cleavage, where sweat had beaded and run. 'Whoo-eee! That's more like it. You've done enough to feed the five thousand here, love.'

'You're not wandering about like that, are you, May?' Rachel asked.

'You what?' May straightened with a frown. She glanced down. 'This is my best outfit. Cost your father a small fortune, the lovely man.' Then she saw where Rachel was looking. 'You mean these?' She giggled, wriggling her shoulders so that her breasts bobbed together. 'Not bad for thirty-four, eh? Old Ted can't keep his hands off them, the randy little bugger!' Her face changed as she saw Rachel's expression. 'I'm not embarrassing you, am I, love?'

'Of course not!' Rachel reddened. 'Why should you do that?'

May's eyes narrowed, a spark of venom rising in them that made Rachel flinch. She did not want to fight their unspoken battle here; she was not sure if she could fight it openly anywhere yet.

'I'm proud of what I've got, darling,' May hissed. 'If I want to have a laugh – and Jack does too – I have it. What I don't need –'

A chorus of yells from the hallway saved Rachel. May lifted her head, her expression clearing. Swiftly she bent to the fridge again and pulled out two six-packs.

'I said I'd only be a minute,' she murmured. 'They'll go off the boil. Bring a couple of those plates, Rachel. Come on! You can't hide away in here all night.'

Reluctantly Rachel rose and picked up the plates as May kicked the fridge door shut and clip-clopped to the kitchen door, elbowing it open.

'She's back!' came Ted's voice.

May laughed, exaggerating the sway of her hips as she tripped down the hallway.

'And little Rachel!' Ted boomed.

'Keep your hair on,' May cautioned, skipping through the lounge doorway as Ted aimed a pat at her rear. He glanced at Rachel, whose eyes darted away instantly, and a remark faded on his lips. Instead he hurried in behind May as the men inside crowded round her.

Steeling herself, Rachel followed.

The room was darker now, hot and fuggy with the slow swirl of cigarette smoke in the glare of the photo-floods. They were the only illumination, transforming the men into lumbering silhouettes, catching the odd sheen of forehead perspiration, the gleam of excited eyes. But it was the atmosphere that whipped at Rachel's senses: a tension-filled mixture of male sweat and alcohol fumes, souring perfume and unfulfilled yearning. It settled on her skin like a slickness, raw and sensual, as repellent as it was subtly, disturbingly exciting.

She heard her father call from the circle around May. 'This is my idea of heaven, lads! An ice-cool lager served by the best pair of tits in Britain! Aren't they lovely?'

She saw him reach around May's shoulders, scooping her bared breasts in his palms, tweaking the pink stubs of her nipples while she shrieked through the men's laughter. 'Get off, Jack! I'll drop the lot!'

'Here,' Ted chimed in, 'why should Jack have all the fun? He can have a fondle any time!'

55

'Poor diddums!' May blew him a kiss, twisting from her husband's grasp and pushing the lager cans into his hands. 'We mustn't let poor Teddy feel left out.'

She turned towards her host, rising on tiptoe and pulling his startled face down into her deep cleavage, wriggling her soft flesh against him. 'Christ!' he bellowed, surfacing. 'I've come!'

The others roared with laughter. 'Cheeky devil,' May grinned.

'*Me*, cheeky?' Ted reeled back in mock outrage. '*Me*? You want to see what *you've* done to young Donny there.'

His name broke the spell for Rachel. She turned in the dimness, feeling a sudden dread. The men quietened as they looked too. Then she saw him. He was slumped on a sofa below the front window, gazing drunkenly down his own outstretched body, his knees spread wide. A thick and obvious ridge bulged down the inside of his right thigh.

'He can't get the bloody thing down!' Ted bellowed as the laughter soared again.

'Tell you what else we can't get down!' another voice cried. 'Knickers! May's knickers!'

The others joined in at once, chanting together.

Rachel slipped behind them, setting the plates down on the carpet, easing onto the sofa beside Donny. He was breathing heavily, his gaze unwavering. He reeked of spilled lager.

'Donny!' She squeezed his arm. 'We've got to go. You can't stay here like this.'

For a moment he didn't respond. Then, slowly, he turned his head and blinked at her. 'Touch it, Rachel,' he said thickly. 'Touch it for me and make it better. I only want you to. You know that.' His hand found hers, clutching her fingers, drawing them down onto the warm bulge in his lap.

'Please, Donny,' she whispered. 'Not here – ' She looked round, unable to free her hand, certain they were over-looked. But the others were busy snatching up cameras, fanning round the further end where May stood grinning in the scalding light, running her fingers lightly up and down the seam of her pants. As shutters clicked, Ted called, 'Don't tease, May. Just get them off.'

She laughed. 'They all look the same, you know, love.'

'Only in the dark,' Ted replied. 'You've got a lovely pussy, May. Let's see it.'

Donny's hand squeezed tighter and Rachel looked down. He was opening his zip, crushing her fingers in his own as he drew the catch down.

'Take it out for me, Rache,' he murmured. 'Take it out and suck it. Nobody'll see. They don't care here anyway.'

She watched, numbed, as the white of his underpants tented through his open fly. The evening was turning into a nightmare from which she couldn't awake, every hoped-for wonder changing into something raucous and strange, every finer feeling mangled or distorted.

She heard a soft giggle from the other end of the room. The noise had faded in the steady clicking of cameras. May faced away from her audience, bending from the waist, her back arched to round the naked cheeks of her buttocks. Between them fierce light detailed the swollen fig of her sex, its carroty halo of hair, the puckering of glistening, pink-ridged flesh.

There was a rush of harsh breath. The air was electric. Rachel felt a pulsing warmth against her hand. Donny stared at her. His stiffness, pale and blunt and alien, rose from his lap. She did not know how to react. This was not a Donny she recognized, or who recognized her.

His hand reached to her shoulder, to her neck. Before she

realized what was happening, he was pulling her head forward, downward onto his exposed penis.

'Fantastic, May,' Ted cried. 'Now let's try it on your back. That's it. Get comfortable. Knees bent – nice and wide apart. No, keep your fingers on your pussy. Good. Now I want you to imagine Jack's giving you the grinding of your life. That's it . . . . Incredible!'

Panic flashed through Rachel. She had not done this thing before. She would not do it now. Donny grunted as she squirmed aside, tearing herself from his grip.

'Donny –'

'Bitch!' The word hissed out, shocking her. She was staring at a stranger, hard-faced, blank-eyed in the shadows.

'Bitch!' he repeated, and turned away, blinking slowly, as though to wipe out sight and memory of her.

May giggled. 'This is making me feel bloody fruity. Do I have to be having it off with Jack? I fancy a change of Cock Robin now and then –'

Abruptly Donny was lurching to his feet. A flailing arm struck Rachel across the cheek, knocking her head back, though she felt nothing. He staggered forward, drunken and exposed, tearing at the belt of his jeans.

'How about this for size, May?' he bellowed.

The shutter-clicking stopped. Heads turned. There was a ripple of laughter.

'Got room for this inside?' Donny boomed again. He stumbled as his jeans dropped over his thighs, his hand clutching his bloated organ, holding it forward like an obscene offering.

Laughter soared into whoops of incredulous delight. As he elbowed his way between two crouching men, May sat up, gaping at him. 'Donny –' she began , and shrieked as he tumbled forward, crashing to his knees between her out-spread legs and slumping across her body.

'Careful! You're crushing me!' Her protests turned to involuntary laughter as he raised himself, his head lolling. Instantly he dived, licking and kissing her stiffened nipples, making her squeal again.

There were cheers. The fat, sandy-haired man knelt and tugged at Donny's shoes. Two more grabbed his jeans, jerking them down and off. Bare-bottomed, he sprawled between May's thighs, spreadeagling her on the carpet.

'Keep still, keep still . . . !' she cried, pushing him back, peering down between their bodies. '*My God!*' she hissed suddenly. 'I *thought* that felt thick . . . '

The cheering turned abruptly to baited silence. The air hummed afresh. The onlookers strained forward, closer to the semi-naked couple. Voices murmured, a low, grumbling chorus, sharpened with urgency: 'Give it to him, May . . . . Let him have it, girl . . . . Go on, May . . . . Do him . . . . Fuck him . . . . *Fuck* him . . . '

May breathed in with a shudder. With an effort she lifted Donny's bloated, beer-reddened face, holding it between her hands. 'Well,' she gasped. 'I don't think Rachel can begrudge me an inch or two of you.'

With a frown of concentration she squeezed her hand below Donny' waist, forcing a grunt as she took hold of him. She straightened, closing her knees to grip his thighs, urging him onto, into her body, and gave a sudden gasp. 'Oh yes – oh, *yes*!'

At once Donny's thighs began to pump, hard and sure, mechanically fast, as though a switch had been pulled, a source of hidden power abruptly engaged. May's eyes widened above his shoulder. Her hand clutched at his dimpling buttocks, gripping his thrusting flesh.

'Oh come *on*, lover,' she breathed. 'Don't you dare stop —
don't you *dare*!'

Her head lifted a last time. In the glare of the lights, the
press of bodies, she would have found it difficult to see
beyond the circle of eager-eyed cameramen. But, at the
door, Rachel knew without any shadow of doubt that she
did. That final look mirrored the first she had ever seen
from her stepmother. A look of triumph, of conquest, of
possession. A look only rivals could exchange in a moment
of long-sought-for victory.

It lasted barely seconds, then a spasm wiped it from
May's face. But in that brief instant Rachel had gone.

Until she reached the bus station in the centre of town she
had no idea that coaches ran so late. Two waiting students
— a couple clinging together in duffel coats — told her
differently. The overnight service went to London via
Birmingham and Coventry.

From the rent money she had taken from the living-room
dresser she paid the driver for the full journey. Inside she
sat in the first unoccupied seat, stuffing beneath it her
holdall, which contained a single change of clothes, a toilet
bag, a towel.

As the coach pulled out of the station and climbed the
steep rise past the Gothic shadow of the town hall, she
glimpsed the dimly illuminated face of the clock tower
above. Ten minutes past midnight. She had just reached
sixteen years of age.

She grunted softly, ironically. It was hardly the
birthday she had planned.

Then she slumped, closing her eyes instantly. She was
asleep before the coach had reached the motorway
entrance.

Sleep was easy. She was leaving nothing; she was going nowhere. There was very little else to do.

3
PAUL
1970

'Come in, Mr Hanna,' said the Dean of Freshmen. 'Good of you to drop by.'

The man rising behind the carved oak desk was sprightly, middle-aged, clean-shaven and smiling. He wore a grey rumpled suit, a pink striped shirt and horn-rimmed glasses whose colour toned precisely with the dark wood panelling that surrounded him.

Paul closed the door behind him and advanced with some trepidation across the faded oriental carpet. He distrusted such effortless and apparently non-sarcastic urbanity, particularly when it was prefaced by a written invitation stating the exact time and place of his appointment. Did the man really imply he had a choice about being here?

The slight, ironic twist to the Dean's smile showed Paul his proffered hand was a mistake. But the Dean took it anyway, then indicated the tall leather-backed chair in front of the desk.

'Hope I haven't interrupted your orientation too much,' he said when they were both seated. 'But we like to take these things in a fairly leisurely way at Curwen. A full week before the academic year proper begins gives us all time to settle in – lets us both see if we've made the right decisions.'

Paul felt alarm bells ring in the back of his mind. Until this moment, only halfway through his second day on campus, he had been fully occupied by a dazzling series of adjustments to a wholly new way of life. The fact that he might not make those adjustments – or that others might think so – had never occurred to him.

'If there's a problem with my major –'

'Oh no. I'm sure you'll be an asset to the Fine Arts faculty. Academically, I see no difficulties at all. Your SAT scores were exemplary. Exemplary. Those photographs of Cape Cod you submitted for your CLEP tests were remarkable. I know it's a spectacular part of the country but you made it look quite dreamlike.'

The fulsomeness of the praise only served to increase Paul's unease – something which dawned on the Dean, who paused, his pale blue eyes dropping to his steepled fingers.

'You are, of course, a legacy,' he went on. 'Your late father did very well, here, I believe – though on the scientific rather than the artistic side. And your guardian, Mrs Van Ost, has been very generous to the college.'

Paul's face darkened. He was unaware of the extent of Cora-Beth's 'generosity' but its existence had annoyed and embarrassed him since he had first heard of it – significantly from a tutor who had links with Curwen and not from his aunt herself. But why was this man referring to it? Was he suggesting that Paul had bought his place?

The Dean's eyes lifted again, his expression almost quizzical. 'A remarkable woman, your aunt. I understand she had you educated privately. No mean feat to keep the education authorities at bay these days – especially in Massachusetts!' A smile formed and faded instantly. 'There was no special reason for that – medical, for instance – you weren't able to cover in your application, was there?'

Paul shook his head. 'My aunt had very strong views about education. And she likes to get her own way.'

'Quite clearly!' The Dean's smile was back. 'And no harm in that to judge by the academic results.' But his eyes were sliding away again, giving a disquieting impression of shiftiness, of an issue still untouched.

'Of course,' he resumed, 'good SATs and grade averages – and special talents – are a very important, but not the only part of qualifying for Curwen. We have never claimed to be in the forefront of what, for want of a better term, we call the "Ivy League" colleges. Nor have we intended to be. We aim to produce the fully rounded student, someone in whom academic excellence sits happily with social and community awareness. That's why we pay more attention, perhaps, than many other colleges to an applicant's extra-curricular activities, his sports, his hobbies, even his friends – ways in which he's relating to his community.'

Paul's struggle to draw meaning from all this was giving him a glazed look, which the Dean misinterpreted as boredom. His eyes narrowed.

'My point, Mr Hanna' – he spoke more briskly than before – 'is that you appear to have pursued a somewhat lonely path. Whether by choice or not –'

'It wasn't.' Paul cut in, and faltered in his own abruptness. 'My own choice, I mean. I would have preferred it – otherwise – if that had been possible . . .'

As the words petered out, the Dean's look gradually lost its sharpness. Eventually his eyes softened. 'Please believe I had no intention of prying. My only concern was that you felt yourself able to make what for most of our freshmen is a pretty drastic transition.'

Paul was nodding. 'I think I can cope OK. I really want to make up for lost time as soon as I can.'

The Dean nodded in return, faintly once, then more definitely, as if making up up his mind, fixing Paul with a sudden and brilliant smile.

'Good. Good!' He rose abruptly. 'I'm glad we had this little talk, Mr Hanna.'

This time it was the Dean's hand which caught Paul unawares. He rose to shake it uncertainly across the desk, tightening his grip as he felt its firmness.

'Now, any problems you have, anything your student advisor can't handle, come straight to me. And do give my regards to your aunt.'

The Dean was not, Paul realized, about to leave his desk. As he started to turn away he heard the door open behind him.

'Oh, I'm sorry. I thought you were alone.'

A girl not much older than Paul leaned in the doorway, her long face flushed, smiling vivaciously. The smile remained vivacious as she focused on Paul.

'No, it's all right, Barbara. We're just finished.'

With a hesitant smile, Paul skipped back towards the door. The girl stepped inside to let him pass, her bright, clear blue eyes flickering over his face. She wore faded jeans and a tight yellow turtleneck which, Paul noticed, showed the outline of well-shaped breasts.

'Barbara,' he heard as the door closed, 'I thought you were helping your mother with dinner –'

Then the door thumped shut.

Give my regards to your aunt. Was that the point of this little exercise?

Frowning, Paul moved down the dark tiled corridor that led to the entrance hall of the administration building, the slap of his rubbered soles echoing against the high corniced ceiling.

Did Cora-Beth's tentacles extend this far?

It was barely forty-eight hours since he had driven

through the gates of the Cape Cod estate, watching his aunt, Joseph and Louisa retreat, waving, in the taxi's rear mirror, feeling a sudden draught of lightness and freedom and sheer exhilaration surge through him.

Gone! Gone for ever as far as he was concerned. This was a new beginning, a new life. From now on he need never look back.

Until this moment.

A scattering of freshmen, who looked lost, and early returned sophomores, juniors and seniors, who did not, hung about the notice-boards in the entrance hall. Paul eased through them and out of the swing doors, onto the broad stone steps overlooking Curwen Big Yard.

Warm late summer sun splashed on the tops of the plane trees that filled it, casting deep shadows on the clipped grass and the asphalt paths beneath, drawing darkness or scalding brightness by turns from the high mock-Victorian brownstone pressing in on every side. The solidity of the buildings – the nearest rimmed and softened by the ivy – distracted and impressed Paul. It reminded him of the timeless calm of ancient forests, though he knew the oldest building had been built less than forty years before: a grandeur both warm and austere, but, unlike the forest, so securely rooted in itself he could not clearly see his own relation to it.

Or, for that matter, to the rest of this place.

He had arrived here with a mixture of excitement and dread, twin poles of emotion between which he had ricocheted ever since. Both were feelings with which he had become well acquainted during the past eighteen months.

Paul's adulthood – at least, as Cora-Beth defined it – had

wrought considerable change in his life at the Cape. The gift of a small Honda had enormously widened his experience of his immediate surroundings – not only in terms of fresh subjects for his camera, but in terms of other people too. Hesitantly he had begun to make acquaintances of his own age, forming tentative links with a world of high school and 'proms', illicit liquor purchase and 'hot' dates. A world he looked on with a mixture of envy and incredulity, a fierce urge to belong and an ever growing awareness of his own isolation.

His aunt's desire to involve him more thoroughly in her own very different world, for which his stage-managed 'initiation' had, in her eyes, qualified him only exaggerated his sense of separation. The advent of Diana, it seemed, had ended a long period of self-imposed exile for Cora-Beth. Overnight the house had filled with names and faces she had referred to only obliquely before – friends, acquaintances, conquests from excursions to California and New York, from her life before Paul.

They were smart, self-consciously bright people, the men in their thirties and forties, the women generally younger, all affluent, attractive – for the most part – and united by an abiding interest in matters sexual. Their sophistication – a kind of deliberate insouciance barely an inch off rudeness or hostility – had unnerved Paul.

Despite Cora-Beth's reiterated assurances that her regular gatherings were 'free, loving, orgasmic experiences' for the dozen or so couples who generally attended, he detected little beyond the orgasmic. Even in sex the participants had struck him as purely demanding, their deeds as self-conscious as their words. More than once he had found himself missing Diana's brash directness. But she had

67

flown back to Los Angeles within days of Paul's 'initiation', reappearing at the Cape only fitfully and not at all during the past winter.

'I think it's for the best, Paul,' his aunt had told him. 'It's so easy, with a first lover, to become overly attached. Think of Diana as the first of very many happy experiences.'

But his first, and less than kind, thought was that his aunt was interfering again, as she had done at his most intimate moment with the blonde Californian girl, maintaining a hold he was unable to throw off even at a hundred miles' distance.

A party of co-eds clattered up the steps beside him and collided with a second group emerging from the swing doors. Loud shrieks of recognition and exaggerated delight split the air, scattering Paul's thoughts. He blinked at a mass of bobbing hair, lithe figures, flushed, excited faces, abruptly aware that more than one pair of eyes was flickering in his direction as if to judge the effect of so much uninhibited enthusiasm.

Caught off balance, he moved on down the steps, but not quickly enough to miss a sudden flurry of whispered comments.

'You *don't*!'

'Why not?'

'He looks about *twelve* _ '

'He reminds *me* of Jon Voight –'

'*Everyone* reminds you of Jon Voight –!'

'I bet he's a virgin – '

'I *adore* virgins!'

Springing off the bottom step, he glanced back at that, causing an explosion of stifled giggles and one blossoming red face.

He strode off into the shadows of the trees, a warm glow

68

enfolding him. His feeling when he left the Cape had been right. This *was* a new life, a source of experience much richer and more varied than anything Cora-Beth could devise. He began to feel confident for the first time since he had arrived. 'Orientation' – that process by which newly enrolled students were for a short time encouraged to act as tourists on the campus – was as loosely structured as the Dean of Freshmen had implied. Paul had nowhere special to be before registering for classes late that afternoon.

He left the Big Yard by a small gated archway at the far side, emerging a short distance beyond into a larger airier square named, by a peculiarly academic logic Paul had yet to appreciate, Curwen Little Yard. Here the buildings were more modern, at least in appearance. Broad, five-storeyed and greyly unprepossessing, they housed the freshman dormitories. Paul's was on the immediate right, marked by a brass plaque that read 'Jackson House'.

He arrived on the front step in time to hold the door open for a middle-aged man and a small, worried-looking student manoeuvring a huge cabin trunk inside. The entrance hall was long and narrow, its floor space diminished still further by a long train of similar trunks, suitcases and bags.

Not all freshmen, Paul had discovered, arrived on the day requested, and he had spent the night alone in his shared room, finding an envelope addressed to 'Kyle Stevenson Jr.' in their pigeonhole that morning. The letter, he noticed now, had gone. He stepped over a large wicker hamper and gained access to the stairs.

He climbed past three echoing floors, all equally utilitarian and distinguished only by the traces of different-sized posters now removed from their landing walls. At the top he pushed through a fire-door into a corridor buzzing with voices. The source of only one was visible, a tall, bespectacled youth propped against a door jamb, hands in corduroy pockets, guffawing into the room beyond.

Paul was about to pass him by when he realized this was his room. He halted, causing the tall youth to falter in mid-guffaw with a curious hiccuping sound as he did a swift double-take in Paul's direction. Then he moved back as Paul glanced inside.

Three young men occupied the room, one perched on a desk, another sprawled across Paul's bed, a third rummaging in a gigantic pile of suitcases, bags and boxes which occupied the middle of the floor. The two seated noticed him first and responded with blank looks. Eventually the rummager caught their expressions and turned.

'I think this is my room – ' Paul began.

The rummager's square, ageless face – almost saturnine in its blankness – suddenly sprang to life in a broad, white-toothed smile. He dropped a large rolled-up rug and stepped over the debris towards the door, his hand extended.

'You must be Paul Hanna. Kyle Stevenson.' Paul moved inside and shook hands. 'This is George Manton.' The rummager indicated the youth at the door, who nodded, lifting his hand slightly and prompting Paul to offer his; they shook hands self-consciously. 'That's Lawrence Hoffman on the desk and the sophomore slob you see on your bed is George's brother Schuyler.'

The other two nodded, the latter rolling into a sitting position on the rumpled sheets.

'The guys are just helping me move in – George and I were at prep school together,' Kyle went on. 'George, of course, being obsessionally well-organized, had his room straight hours ago.' As George grinned, Kyle paused,

70

taking a deep breath. '*So* – I'm told room-mates are supposed to have something vaguely in common, Paul. You weren't at Deerfield by any chance, were you?'

Paul blinked; the name meant nothing. 'I've just come from the Cape.'

'The Cape?' Kyle's face brightened instantly. 'Oh, whereabouts? We have a place at Osterville.'

'Mashpee,' said Paul. 'On the Sound.'

'Uh-huh!' George and his brother spoke together, exchanging knowing smiles. Paul and Kyle glanced at them questioningly.

'I *told* you,' Schuyler grinned. 'Jackson is Privilege Palace. Can't you just smell the affluence?' He leaned forward. 'Paul, I'd lay odds you're a legacy.'

Paul nodded hesitantly. 'My father was here –'

Schuyler beamed. 'I rest my case.'

'Oh *come on* –' Kyle broke in. 'Lots of people summer on the Cape –'

Paul looked at him. 'We live there all the time.'

'Even in the winter?' Kyle gaped with such a look of incredulity – feigned or not – that Paul smiled.

'Sure – I like the winters.'

'The point Schuyler's making,' George interrupted, 'is that Cape Cod residences on the ocean are not exactly inexpensive. *Ergo* –'

'Ergo,' Schuyler spoke over him, 'Jackson House is Nob Hill around here. Hey, don't knock it. This is where all the local talent heads for – this is where they grab their little banker-lawyer-investment-broker-to-be before he realizes there are other women in the world. The opportunities for parallel parking within these walls are unbelievable –'

'What happens if you happen to be poor,' said Lawrence Hoffman glumly.

Schuyler shrugged. 'Who talks about money? Let people assume what they want to. In any case, if you got in here without being rich you're obviously a genius and you'll get rich anyway.'

He looked down at his watch and winced. '*Jesus*, I should be seeing my advisor. I've got to bolt. I'll see you fellows around.'

And, pausing only to brush George's arm non-committally, he had gone. There was a pause. George glanced down the corridor after him, then came in, pulling the door to.

'He hasn't even got an advisor for this semester,' he told Kyle in a confidential tone. 'He's seeing some co-ed at McAllister House. She came up early too.'

Paul, who in the intervening moments had only just begun to appreciate the sheer volume of his room-mate's belongings, looked up and asked, 'What's this about parallel parking? I thought cars weren't allowed in the Yards?'

To his astonishment his three companions burst into loud laughter.

'Oh, classic,' said Kyle eventually. 'I'll remember that.'

'It's probably what my dumb brother is going to be doing in about ten minutes,' explained George, sobering. As Paul, feeling conspicuous, went to reclaim his bed, Kyle's eyes widened.

'You're not serious?'

'He'll need a forklift for all the rubbers he's got hidden in his trunk.' Sighing, George sat heavily on Kyle's bed. '*And* he's seeing this other woman back home. I don't know how he does it. He's not even good-looking, for God's sake.'

'It's the extra year,' Lawrence Hoffman contributed. 'I think experience makes a big difference.'

72

Kyle nodded thoughtfully, lifting and hefting a pair of skis. He glanced round at his new room-mate. 'Anyone pining after your tender young body back home, Paul?'

Paul was abruptly aware that the question, pitched so casually, had aroused a peculiar tension in the room, as if the three youths, who all now looked at him, were teetering on the edge of the most appalling abyss.

At once he thought of Diana and then of his aunt's 'free, loving, orgasmic experiences'. He felt the colour rise up his neck, not, he realized obscurely, because of his embarrassment at his memories, but because of his companions' obvious sensitivity.

'Hey,' Kyle said quickly, 'we're all biding our time too. I mean, everyone knows college is where the real talent is. Who wants to waste their energy on teeny-boppers . . .?'

The nods were tacit, the embarrassment universal, and in that brief moment Paul understood with a shock that of the four people in the room he was the only one who was not a virgin.

He had waited for the shot half the afternoon, planting the tripod in three or four dozen spots among the beach grass and the soft sand, guessing the position of the sun as it would set behind the wind-blown hulk of the fishing shack.

He had found the place the way he usually did — en route to somewhere else which was now forgotten. A summer colony near the very tip of Sandy Neck where the low, dune-piled spit of land curved back toward the mainland like the claw of some gigantic and decaying lobster. A dozen or so grey cedar-tiled cottages clung to the water's edge, extending frail single-plank jetties into the turquoise calm of Cape Cod Bay.

Paul saw no one and the place had an air of abandonment. But it was only the second Friday after Memorial Day, the summer hardly

73

begun, and the season's visitors might still be trekking eastward from Boston and New York.

The shack clearly was abandoned. It bordered a shallow inlet, its doors and windows gaping, its roof and walls threadbare. Silhouetted against the sunlight, the ragged geometry of its exposed beams, the stumps of an adjoining jetty had for Paul the stark complexity of a Chinese or Japanese ideogram. With a background of blue sky and white dunes, or the image mirrored in the placid waters of the inlet, the picture would already have been an intriguing composition. But Paul was curious to see the effect of sunset.

When it came, a warm glow stealing over the ocean, turning the pale dunes golden, he worked at speed, changing positions rapidly, bracketing exposures, stopping down and down and down as the light faded, until his elderly Leica could no longer cope on its own and he was guessing time-exposures in semi-darkness.

He sat eventually in the cooling sand, his heart thudding, his mind exhausted. Doubts about his final exposures racked him but underneath he felt a suspicion that he had done all he could — a prickling excitement that among these photographs were some of the best he had ever taken.

So much tension, so much energy, so much sheer agony to get a picture even half right! It was like banging his head against a brick wall he had laboriously constructed himself: back-breaking work of dubious necessity, fraught with uncertainty, and bliss when it was over. But it was still the most deeply involving, the most purely exciting thing he had ever done.

The stars were beginning to show when he packed his equipment, loaded his trailbike and set off down the winding track that led to the nearest road. It was eight o'clock before he drew up in front of the estate's double garage, surprised to find the doors blocked by half a dozen expensive-looking cars, most of them European.

Then he remembered Cora-Beth had mentioned guests might be calling that evening. He had assumed they were her usual women

74

friends, an arty, waspish crowd from Sandwich and Brewster, mostly divorced and wealthy, but unlikely to stretch their alimony to the BMW's and Porsches parked here.

Laughter from the direction of the house distracted him. Propping the bike, he noticed the glow of porch lights from the rearward side facing the kettle pond. Puzzled because his aunt rarely ventured onto the estate grounds after dark, he followed the driveway round the edge of the house.

A broad lawn sloped gently from the porch towards the pond. As Paul came in sight of it from the cover of some bushes he heard a loud splash, a shrill cry, then distant giggling against the rippling of water. Something bobbed in the pond, scattering the dim reflected light from the porch, where storm lanterns hissed and voices murmured.

'Clive?' a woman called nearby. 'Clive, are you there?'

Abruptly someone stepped from the bushes directly in front of Paul, bumping into him with a soft impact and recoiling with a piercing shriek.

'Jesus Christ! Who the hell are you?'

'I'm sorry — I didn't see you — ' Paul gabbled, as startled as the woman. 'Is Cora-Beth here?'

'Cora-Beth?' The woman's tone lightened as she repeated the name. She moved her head to one side, allowing the porch light to fall on Paul's face. The same light caught the edge of her own features. Paul was aware of bright eyes, sharp cheekbones, hair to her shoulders or beyond and — with a jolt — the gently rounded outline of a breast, a shadowed thigh. The woman was naked.

'It's Paul, isn't it?' she hissed suddenly. Paul nodded, then realized she might not see in the gloom and began to say, 'Yes, I — ' when the woman turned toward the porch and yelled excitedly, 'It's him! He's here! It's the boy!'

Instantly she clutched at his hand, pulling him forward across the lawn, her bare feet slapping on the grass, her teardrop rear joggling in

75

front of him. 'Cora-Beth! Everyone!' *she called.* 'He's back!'

As Paul opened his mouth in protest he saw three or four strangers on the long porch turning towards him, drinks in hand. At once they parted hurriedly, laughing, as a man slipped between them and skipped down the porch steps. Flushed and bright-eyed, naked like the woman, he hopped in tight circles about the grass, his gaze darting from side to side.

'Paula! Paula!' *he bellowed.* Then he spotted the woman and dashed across to her, tearing her hand from Paul's. 'Come on! I'm not doing this on my own.' *And he whisked her away, breathlessly, towards the pond.*

'Go and see Cora-Beth,' *the woman flung in her wake.* 'She's waiting for you —' *A shriek and a loud splash cut her off in the darkness.*

No more enlightened, Paul mounted the porch, nodding vaguely at the drinking guests. Nods were returned. An attractive brunette in a long gown smiled at him sweetly. 'I think Cora-Beth's upstairs,' *she said.*

Paul thanked her and moved through the screen doors into the rear parlour. Half a dozen more people, men and women, sat about in a straggling group, chatting quietly by the glow of sidelights. Music played unobtrusively. One or two glanced up as Paul entered. He recognized no one.

The transition from the normal quietness and solitude was so abrupt and total he almost suspected he had wandered into the wrong house. Then in the soft light a face suddenly mirrored his own uncertainty.

It belonged to a girl sitting in an armchair next to the far door. Her features were darkly Italianate, moodily attractive; she looked much younger than the others, perhaps only a year or two older than Paul and, though she was surrounded by the group, her tense expression set her apart from it. Her gaze caught Paul's and her frown softened momentarily before she looked away.

He eased through into the hall, just as a burly, balding man, his large barrel-like chest thickly matted with hair, rolled past him from the direction of the kitchen.

'Darling,' he declared languidly and apparently to thin air, 'I've got to eat no matter how wonderful it is for you.' He bit deeply into a hunk of Italian bread and turned suddenly through the door of the main living room. Paul blinked after him. The man had only been wearing a towel wrapped loosely round his prodigious waist.

Skinny-dipping was one thing but near nudity for guests inside the house was something else. Beginning to wonder if Diana was about to reappear, Paul went to the living-room door.

The door was ajar but the light inside so dim and ruddy he thought at first the room was in darkness. He ducked his head in further and heard a soft masculine grunt, a giggling exhalation of breath. A couple sprawled on a low mattress only a few feet from the doorway; they were both nude, their limbs intertwined, their flesh almost indistinguishable in the roseate glow of a distant brass lamp.

For a moment Paul was back in the apartment over the garage, watching Joseph and Louisa, thinking Cora-Beth had arranged a fresh performance for her friends. Then a slow, caressing movement brought a woman's head into view: a thin, skull-like face, heavy eyelids smoothly closed, a wide mouth curving in pleasure. A broad thigh hooked a slimmer one, and a second face moved from shadow. It was older, fleshier, but indisputably female.

Paul gaped in surprise; he'd read about such things but the sight of it was something for which even Cora-Beth hadn't prepared him. The masculine grunt came again, and Paul realized in the same instant that other couples occupied the room, curled together or stretched out on armchairs and sofas in the gloom. Opposite him the burly man sat watching the two women, chewing dispassionately on his snack as a naked blonde knelt between his splayed legs, her hand pumping slowly at his lap.

The scene lashed at Paul's senses, disturbing and exciting him at

77

once. Suddenly all Cora-Beth's rules of discretion, even of secrecy before all but a few house guests — rules that had seemed unshakeable, unbreakable for eternity — were crumbling about him. It was this, more than anything else, that shocked him.

Though no one had even acknowledged his presence, he backed out quickly, colliding with a newcomer.

'Oh, Paul — are you joining us?'

With an effort he recognized the begowned woman from the porch, smiling at him warmly. A tall man hovered behind her.

'No — not — in a minute — ' He broke away to the stairs, missing the woman's sad shrug.

A male voice filtered down from the landing: 'I'm so pleased about this little gathering, Cora-Beth. There's been nothing in this neck of the woods since the Marion crowd broke up. Did you hear about the big div — '

The voice paused as Paul rose into view. Cora-Beth stood by her bedroom door, listening to a tall, distinguished-looking man in his forties. Her face lifted as she saw Paul approach.

'Darling! I've been waiting all evening for you!' She was dressed in a bright red kimono, her hair piled high. 'Paul,' she said, turning to her guest, 'this is Martin Hornsiger, a very dear friend of mine from Connecticut. Paul — Martin has a very special favour to ask of you.'

Paul found himself shifting his camera gear to shake hands with the man, who smiled with a kind of nervous warmth. His palm felt moist.

'Glad to meet you, Paul. I've heard a lot about you.'

'I'd really like to get washed up and a bite to eat,' Paul said, turning towards his room.

'Of course, darling,' said Cora-Beth quickly as the man nodded. 'When you've showered Louisa has a spread organized in the kitchen. But I think you ought to listen to Martin first.'

Unease flickered across the man's face as he gave Cora-Beth a *swift glance. 'I really think you ought to, Cora,' he said, but she cut across him.*

'Paul isn't a child, Martin. He'll be more than happy to help, won't you, darling?'

The man puzzled Paul. He had every sign of affluence, of professional sangfroid, and his nervousness seemed as uncharacteristic as it was obvious. Yet whatever its cause it was not enough to deter him.

He glanced awkwardly up and down the landing. 'Is your room close by, Paul?' he asked. 'Perhaps we could pop in there for a little chat. Man to man.'

Shrugging, Paul moved to his own door. As he pushed it open and switched on the light he saw Cora-Beth smiling at him encouragingly, her eyes bright. He went inside and Martin slipped in behind him, closing the door softly and advancing with his hands pressed together.

'You see, Paul,' he began, 'it's about my daughter —'

Sweat gleamed on his upper lip.

'Hi, I'm Paul.'

'Anna — ' The girl paused within a yard or two of the door, apparently content merely to look round the large, deeply shadowed bedroom.

'It's my aunt's room,' said Paul, stepping away from the bed and the small lamp, which was the only source of illumination. 'It's the most comfortable room up here. I thought it would be more private than — downstairs —'

The girl nodded faintly, her gaze moving over a row of samplers on a far wall, seemingly unimpressed.

Paul felt a flutter of uncertainty. Perhaps he should never have agreed to this. But when he had seen the girl in the parlour she had smiled at him, and he had liked her. Her face intrigued him. It was balanced between prettiness and real beauty, a smooth oval with full,

79

down-curving lips, almond-shaped eyes with a bruised Latin look that bespoke a very different ancestry from her father. It was a mobile face, with a fleshy softness that added years in these heavy shadows, but the flesh itself was smooth and youthful. And now it bore an expression of melancholy that seemed irremovable.

'Look,' said Paul suddenly, 'this is your father and my aunt's idea. If you feel bad about it we can call the whole thing off —'

She shook her head, the dark curls of her short-cut hair bouncing against her slim neck. 'It's OK.'

She stepped further into the room, still glancing about as she came, but focusing her dark, suspicious gaze finally on Paul. She was, he saw, a good inch or two shorter than Diana. The top of her head was level with his chin; she was tiny.

Paul drew in breath. 'So — you've never done this before?'

Her eyes darted away from his. 'I've played around — you know — petted — with guys.'

Paul copied her slight nodding as her gaze slid over him again.

'But never all the way?'

'Somehow it never came up.' This time her faint grin mirrored Paul's smiling enjoyment of her unconscious pun.

Emboldened, he said: 'I think you've really very attractive.'

'Thank you.' She nodded again, not meeting his eyes, her smile fading.

A silence grew between them. Paul could think of nothing to add. The girl was shy or indifferent or both, a far cry from the kind of uninhibited enthusiasm he was used to from Diana. But whatever her true feelings she showed no inclination to go. That had to be in his favour.

He shrugged. 'Well, I suppose we ought to get undressed. The light's OK for you, is it?' he added quickly.

'Could you put it on the floor?'

'Sure.'

He darted across the room, setting the bedside lamp down on the

80

carpet. 'I'm not so keen on bright lights myself. Those people down-stairs — they must get a special kick out of an audience — ' Turning, he halted, his breath catching.

The girl's back was to him, the party dress she wore bunched about her slim hips, just below the white edge of pants. Only the thin line of a bra strap marked her slender back, its olive-toned flesh warm and golden in the lamplight. His heart thumped. He watched as she slid the dress down her thighs and stepped out of it, reaching out to drape it over a chair. Her hips were narrow but her waist was pinched, her legs slim and shapely: she was exquisite.

'Have you — done this before?' she asked suddenly. Abruptly Paul turned his own back, plucking open his shirt, aware that his cock was responding to the girl's undress.

'Quite a few times, yes.' He spoke more airily than he intended, coughing as he scuffed off his moccasins and smoothed down his corduroys.

'With a lot of girls?'

'No — not really — '

'Good.'

The memory of a smile crossed her face as he turned to her again, replaced immediately by a look of vulnerability and real fear as every expression dropped from Paul's features.

She stood facing him in the dimness of the room's centre, nude but for a pair of tight white briefs, her hands by her sides. Strictly speaking, her breasts were out of proportion to her size, pendulous and very large but beautifully full and rounded, the areolae perfect soft brown saucers topped by thimble-sized stubs of nipples.

As she saw where he was looking she brought her arms up protectively, cushioning herself, avoiding Paul's stare. 'They're really an embarrassment. I just can't get blouses that fit, and people are always staring — '

'They're beautiful!' Paul interrupted, stepping forward in front of her, heedless of the erection that tented his pants. He shook his head in

81

wonderment. 'They're the most beautiful I've ever seen – really.'

Even in the semi-darkness the girl's flush was discernible. Then her gaze, slipping self-consciously under his, caught sight of his pants. She gasped softly, framing a shocked grin. Paul glanced down. His erection poked through the fly, rising stiffly against his waistband.

'Jesus.' He looked up at the girl and grinned. Then he lifted his eyebrows half-apologetically. 'Well, I guess there's no point in keeping them on –'

As he bent to disentangle himself, the girl half turned, tugging hesitantly at her own briefs before sliding them off in a rush. No more than a foot away she stared up into his face, blinking rapidly as they straightened, facing each other.

Paul swallowed thickly. He took in only vaguely the shadowed mat of fur between her legs. His heart drummed in his chest, pumping a slow fire of excitement through every vein. She was beautiful, utterly heart-squeezingly beautiful.

Breathing in, he lifted his arms, hesitating as the girl visibly tensed. Then, when she did nothing more, he moved again, folding his fingers round each slender arm. Her flesh felt satiny warm but the tension in her body was unmistakable: a fine, barely controlled trembling which broke into a sudden bout of racking, panting shivers as Paul clasped her, bent and kissed her.

Her head turned up to him, her mouth fastened on his, her tongue probing the barrier of his teeth, darting and flickering inside while she rose on tiptoe, squirming against him, pressing the full weight of her remarkable breasts into the flesh of his chest.

Astonished, Paul felt his senses explode. It was hardly the time to point out that he had never kissed a girl before, that his encounters with Diana had proceeded directly from fondling to fucking, and sometimes even without that preliminary.

When they broke apart he was wide-eyed and gasping, his nostrils swimming with the heady smell and taste of her. And she stood back

*from him, watching him as quietly and warily as before, as if nothing
had taken place.*

'My God,' he whispered.

*'That's the one thing I do well.' The ghost of a first unrestrained
smile curved her lips, transforming her face. It spread as Paul nodded
enthusiastically.*

He turned and glanced at the bed. 'Let's lie down, shall we?'

*The girl's smile froze. 'I think we're supposed to be down here.'
She looked floorwards at the outline of a large circular carpet.*

*Paul followed her gaze. 'Oh — right —' He took her arm, aware
that their awkwardness had reasserted itself. Clumsily they knelt,
twisting sideways to stretch out side by side.*

*'Not as dusty as it looks,' Paul murmured, brushing a hand over
the carpet, attempting a grin.*

*She interrupted him. 'Don't go too crazy — you know —' She was
below him, her eyes round and bright in the dimness.*

*'Oh, sure.' His eyes moved over her body, her legs pressed together,
her breasts rounded and proud. 'No problem,' he breathed.*

*His blood was moving again, prompting a soft ache not just in his
heart but in his penis too. He held his breath as he brought his fingers
up the girl's ribcage, letting it ease out slowly as he cupped the firm,
surprisingly heavy fullness of her breast. Licking his lips, he bent and
kissed the soft tip of her nipple. He felt her chest sink, her breath
whisper through her nostrils. Pleased, he rubbed his lips against the
taut breast flesh, teasing the nipple with flicks of his tongue. She
breathed in again, deeply, but when he raised his head to see her
reaction she was gazing at him coldly and clearly.*

*'You're doing this because you like me — just a bit — aren't you?' she
said, her voice level.*

*He blinked uncertainly. 'Yes — course — I like you a lot. I mean, I
couldn't do anything if I didn't.' His gaze darted towards his cock,
which now pressed hard and swollen against her pale thigh. What on
earth was the girl talking about? Wasn't it obvious she drove him*

83

wild? 'Why are you *doing it?'* he asked.

The girl's lip curled cynically. She glanced away. *'Oh, that's easy. Because my father wants to fuck me and he's too scared to do it. That's why.'*

He fucked her, he thought, quite well — certainly in a way that Diana would have approved, probing her with slow, lengthening, explorative thrusts until she opened for him, withholding his first climax for much longer than ever before, though mainly out of a fear of encountering some obstacle of which he had only read.

He was puzzled, and then excited to find her curiously passive under him (the contrast being so great with Diana's frantic writhings); he felt his maleness challenged, and so reinforced in a new way. But, as he approached his climax, watching her breasts bounce with the motion of his thrusts, he had suddenly imagined he was fucking not a girl but a warm and perfect doll, a sexual facsimile made for masturbation and not the sticky, sweaty actuality of sex.

Then the girl's brooding, all but silent stare had begun to annoy him and he had pushed all the harder, desperate to get some response. And it was only as he burst in her, lifting his head in the instant of ejaculation, that he realized her gaze had not been directed at him at all, but past his shoulder to the two figures who had slipped into the room quietly and unnoticed at his back.

Or rather the one figure, standing in the heavy shadows beside the door; Martin Hornsiger, his eyes fixed on the couple on the floor, while a woman knelt in front of him, her figure pale and shapely in the dimness, her dark head bobbing back and forth from his loins. A woman who might have been the begowned guest who had spoken to Paul downstairs. From where he was it was impossible to say because she, like the girl's father, was nude. But the greatest mystery of all was the girl herself. As he curled exhausted across her, his head sinking against her narrow shoulder, he felt her cheek and throat awash with silent tears.

'My God!' said Kyle Stevenson. 'To actually deflower a genuine, apple-cheeked, rosy-arsed *virgin*! To arouse that sweet, pubescent body to full, sensual, pulsating woman-hood! Can you *imagine* that? Can you *just* imagine that!'

'Sure,' said George Manton, his head buried in Rousseau. 'All the time.'

Kyle made a high-pitched strangled sound halfway between a whimper and a death-rattle. He was hunched on the back of a battered chesterfield in the corner of the Jackson House student lounge, gazing intently out of the window across Curwen Little Yard. Snow winnowed from a leaden sky.

With a sigh, he slumped down onto the seat. 'O Julia,' he pleaded. 'Julia – Julia – Julia!' George lifted an eye from his book. 'You don't mean Julia Niles? Is she out there?' He stood up from his armchair and began squinting through the window.

'She's gone. Ages ago,' Kyle pointed out sourly; he took a consolatory swig from the afternoon's third can of Carlsberg.

'Miles and miles of Niles, eh?' said George, sitting again and grinning. 'You don't think *she's* a virgin?'

Kyle scowled at him. 'Of *course* she's a virgin. Any woman I love – any woman with legs that long – has to be a virgin. That's self-evident. Anyway' – he sniffed – 'if she refuses me what else can she be?'

'Oh-whoah-ho!' George guffawed with rich enjoyment.

'Oh and how many nights of bliss have you experienced with Nancy Burger Queen or whatever she's called?' Kyle interrupted loudly.

'The name's Hamburger,' said George, sobering and spelling it out. 'We're making good progress.'

'Like swapping spit? Like sucking face?' Kyle's features

twisted with heavy sarcasm. 'That's no way to reel in the biscuit, George!'

George's gaze returned to Rousseau. 'You're a real pain when you're loaded, Kyle. It's not even four o'clock yet, for Godsakes. And I do happen to have an exam tomorrow morning.'

Kyle swallowed a burp with a look of sudden guilt. 'I'm *not* loaded yet – that's the problem,' he said dully. 'I'm trying to be because I'm so damn horny it hurts.'

Ignored by his friend, he sighed again, his gaze wandering across the broad, untidy, all but deserted room. It lighted on a figure, just beyond George, lying on a heavy sofa with a ring folder, which he appeared to be studying intently, propped against his knees.

'Hey, Paul – my old buddy, my esteemed room-mate – how come you appear to remain aloof from all this surging pulchritude? How do you restrain yourself? Let us share your special secret.'

Paul, who had been listening to every word, replied without raising his head: 'Vitamins.'

George made a soft snorting noise.

'No, come on, Paul,' Kyle persisted. 'Don't tell me there isn't someone in this mass of talent you haven't got the hots for. How about that cute little blonde from Bryn Mawr in your fine arts class?'

'*Bryn Mawr?*' George grimaced. '*Now* you're talking virginity.'

'Or that redhead with the big – you know – ' Kyle prompted, straightening on the chesterfield as he warmed to his theme. '*You* know – sat by us in the dining hall Monday lunchtime. Got a funny mouth too. Sally something.'

'Howell?' Paul offered.

'*Powell*,' said George. 'You're thinking of the Dean's daughter.'

Kyle's eyes glowed. 'Barbara Howell! Now there's a cookie to conjure with!'

George frowned. 'She's not even a student.'

'So what? She's around, isn't she?' said Kyle. He leaned forward, his brow knitting in concentration. 'I have a very astute theory about this woman, which I hope to put to the test in the not too distant future. You know there are two basic types of the genus female?' He paused while George finally abandoned Rousseau with a look of resignation. Kyle already had Paul's attention.

'There are,' Kyle continued, 'foxes – and family. Foxes promise the earth – and deliver it. Family are the nice girls you end up marrying. They don't deliver anything until you're practically engaged.'

'And Barbara Howell?' George asked tolerantly.

Kyle pursed his lips. 'A very interesting case. Obviously an attractive girl – pretty face, nice bod – does wonderful things to a tight sweater. Friendly too – obviously curious to know what it's all about – but just a teeny bit uptight about the whole idea. Clearly something to do with the close proximity of daddy. In other words,' he added quickly, catching boredom cloud his friend's face, 'she is teetering on a fine edge between fox and family. Left to herself she'll probably do what daddy wants. But with a careful nudge from the right person – bingo!'

George smacked his glasses higher onto his nose in a gesture of annoyance. 'You really talk a load of horse manure sometimes, Kyle,' he snapped. 'The reason Barbara Howell is uptight about anything is that no student is going to screw around with a faculty member's daughter – unless he's made the Dean's List, at least! You are just not in that league. And anyway I thought you were obsessed with Julia Niles?'

Kyle sniffed and retreated to his Carlsberg. 'No one said I had to be faithful.'

'*Je-sus.*' George flipped over a page of his book and patted it flat.

There was a pause. Paul resumed his reading. A far door opened and laughter echoed from the entrance hall. Kyle brooded, his face growing heavier as he began to drum his fingers steadily against his lager can. The drumming increased in volume.

'For Chrissake, Kyle!' George shouted in genuine anger.

'Damn!' Kyle shot to his feet and began stamping up and down the scuffed carpet. 'Damn, damn, *damn*! I have so much untapped sexual energy! *Why* doesn't Julia Niles let me? All she's got to do is lie there while I stick it in and jiggle it around – is that so much to ask? She can read a book while I'm doing it if she likes!'

George sighed, impressed in spite of himself by his friend's vehemence. 'Why don't you have a word with Lawrence Hoffman? He's got every single *Playboy* from June 1966 to December 1970 inclusive.'

'I don't want – ' Kyle snapped, and then stopped. He spun round, his eyes widening. '*That's* it! That is it!'

'There's a logical connection here I seem to have missed,' said George.

'*Playboys*!' cried Kyle. 'We don't have the right image. Here we are reeking of wealth and what do we do? We lie around in this hole all day, studying and jerking off! All those women out there are looking to us Jacksonites to show them the way – to give them the time of their lives!'

'What do we do then?' said George sourly. 'Monogram our underwear?'

'We have a party,' said Kyle.

Paul looked over his folder. 'The rooms here are pretty small.'

'Not *our* rooms.' Kyle frowned. He swung his arm. 'This room – or all of them. A Jackson House party. Well, why not? Since Christmas this place has been like a tomb.'

'We *have* had two weeks of exams,' George pointed out.

'All the more reason to break out – to make the *big* gesture.' Kyle laughed. 'No wonder the women around here think we're the dullest freshers since the Depression! It's about time we woke up! And besides' – he nodded towards his room-mate – 'if we don't introduce Paul to someone nice soon he's going to die a virgin . . .'

Talk of sex worried Paul, or rather talk of obtaining it. He had no qualms about the act itself – contrary, he became aware, to many of his contemporaries. But finding himself in a position to prove that was an increasingly complicated problem.

At the Cape his opportunities had been almost as un-limited as they were constant, though the number of partners his own age had been small. Here, the number of potential partners was huge – and the opportunities apparently non-existent.

He saw couples showing every sign of friendship and affection, but public displays of any other kind were rare – drunken petting at parties, a languorous embrace on the lawns of Little Yard during a brief sunbathing spell early in the fall term.

Once, he had returned overnight from a photographic trip to the coast, arriving unexpectedly in the small hours to find his room reeking of alcohol and a tousle-haired, bleary-eyed co-ed in a rumpled party dress tucked into his bed;

and Kyle, in a similarly rumpled DJ, snoring on the other side of the room. Paul's arrival had prompted a whispered explosion of embarrassment, accusation and counter-accusation, resulting in Kyle escorting the girl back to her dormitory and exhorting Paul to preserve an eternal silence on the incident.

Paul had been astonished – not by the fact that Kyle had done such a thing, but because clearly nothing had happened. The couple had been fully clothed; they had not even shared the same bed. And yet equally clearly Kyle suffered from the most intense sexual frustration.

Such abysses of non-comprehension seemed to open at Paul's feet whenever he began to feel at ease in his new surroundings, adding to a natural reticence and throwing a pall of deep uncertainty over his social activities. For the first time Cora-Beth's gospel of total freedom started to make a kind of sense; bottled-up frustration *was* uncomfortable; it did create the most appalling tensions, which, more and more, came to colour every aspect of his life.

Once, he would have lived quite happily with full female nudity, being hardly aware of his own bodily reactions. Now the sight of a well-filled sweatshirt, a pert rear, the slightest hint of cleavage, would set his heart pounding, the blood racing to his face and to the swelling tissues of his cock. Suddenly it was as if the clock had reversed three or four years, back to the dawn of his sexual awareness with all the confusion and embarrassment he had since blotted from his memory.

And in odd despairing moments he even suspected that his aunt's keenness to launch him into this wider world was simply an attempt to produce just such a self-justifying reaction.

How *did* you invite a girl to bed? he wondered. Did you

simply move from everyday conversation to 'Let's fuck'? If you did, Paul's fellow students were remarkably discreet about it. Talk was plentiful – action only to be judged by innuendo, chance remarks, personal accounts that seemed more lurid than factual. Often Paul found himself suspecting some gigantic copulatory conspiracy from which he alone was excluded – clandestine coupling behind every other dormitory door. At other times he wondered if sex ever took place here at all.

But in his misunderstanding way Kyle was quite right. Paul *was* a virgin on Curwen campus, and a party could well make a difference.

'But this is a San Juan night,' said the girl in the sheet. 'Kyle Stevenson told me it was a toga party.'

'Well, it is and it isn't,' said Lawrence Hoffman, losing audibility as he retreated behind the entrance-hall door to allow a Hawaiian-shirted couple to pass. 'It's a kind of a mixture,' he added, reappearing.

'You mean fancy dress? Well, Kyle might have said.' The girl turned in annoyance to her sheeted male companion. 'I've got this marvellous harlequin outfit left over from Sugarloaf last Christmas.'

'I'm sure you'll have a great time,' said Lawrence.

Paul, who had heard this exchange while staggering across frozen grass under the weight of a beer crate, arrived in time to catch Lawrence's sickly grin.

'Jesus,' Lawrence murmured, holding the door open. 'That Kyle is such a dork. You know he's told every woman he fancies this is a toga party. Everyone else thinks it's an ordinary bash.'

'Why?' Paul frowned, depositing his crate among a pile of coats as he shrugged off his anorak. 'Does it make them easier to spot in the crowd?'

'He figures they'll be wearing less, I guess.' Lawrence's expression was so glum Paul burst out laughing. 'That's great,' Lawrence went on. 'I'm supposed to be watching the door and I have to explain it's all a big mistake. Two women have already gone to look for a real toga party.'

Grinning, Paul nodded at his crate. 'Let me deliver this and I'll come back and relieve you.'

'You're the third person to promise that, Paul,' Lawrence pointed out flatly. 'Hey!' he added as Paul turned to the student-lounge door. 'I nearly forgot. There was a phone message for you.'

'For me? Who from?'

'I don't know. Some woman. There's a note on the lounge board.'

Woman? He only knew one woman who was likely to ring him up. Frowning, he went down the hall to a wall telephone in the shadow of the stairs. Personal ads, notices and scraps of messages dotted a pinboard to one side. He found a piece of paper with his name on it and turned it over. 'Lady rang,' was written in a spidery scrawl. 'Mrs V? Arriving tonight. Shitty line. Sorry.'

Paul's heart plummeted. He had cut the Christmas break to a minimum, stayed over for Washington's Birthday; Cora-Beth's curiosity would have been piqued. It was her style to act without warning. And on this of all evenings –

Shit, shit *shit*!

Lawrence was arguing with another group of neo-Romans when he went to collect his crate. He had to nudge a group of impassioned conversationalists before he could enter the student lounge.

It was crowded, noisy and very dim. Doors music

92

thumped over a hubbub of loud voices, laughter, clinking and occasionally breaking glasses. It took him several minutes to elbow his way to the drinks table at the far side, ignoring a sudden outbreak of cheering as his burden was recognized. He set it down beside a flushed and bright-eyed Kyle, who was arguing vociferously with a tall blonde girl in a toga.

' . . . A joke,' he heard his room-mate explain, a considerable infusion of lethal punch slurring his words. 'Tha's all. I mean – you look great – you really do – '

'But I don't see the point. Why did you tell Mary-Lou Ratner and Lisa Halprin to wear the same? Were you trying to make us look silly?'

'Why should I do that?' Drunkenness turned Kyle's look of outraged incredulity into a bizarre parody of human facial expression. 'Julia – I wou'nt lie to you – never in the whole world. I've got – too much – respect for you – ' He burped suddenly and violently just as a chorus of male voices bellowed for him from the crowd.

'Oh go on, Kyle,' the blonde girl snapped. 'Go and play with your drunken friends. Perhaps *they'll* see the joke.' She turned abruptly to Paul as Kyle lurched away with a stricken look. 'Will you fill my glass, please?'

Paul, who had been unloading beer bottles from his crate, glanced round in surprise. 'Oh, yes, sure.' He took the proffered wine glass and scanned the table for wine bottles. 'Oh, punch'll do,' the girl said.

She looked at Paul as he handed back a full glass. 'You're Kyle's room-mate, aren't you?'

'But I don't know anything about toga parties,' Paul said hurriedly. 'I only just found out about it myself.'

The girl's face broke into a smile. It was a distinctive face, sharp-chinned and strong, with a small, full mouth and rosy, well-rounded cheeks that rounded still further when she smiled.

'Oh, I'm not blaming you.' She glanced up at him from under her eyebrows with a peculiarly sly look. 'After all, you're a man of discretion.'

Paul blinked at her. 'I think we met before. In your room. Fairly late one night . . . ?'

Something clicked in Paul's memory. The girl's face had been flushed then, puffy with sleep, half hidden by tangled hair.

'Julia Niles,' she said, offering a hand. Grasping the small, blunt fingers, Paul introduced himself.

'I really wouldn't have recognized you – '

'I'm still grateful I didn't hear it all over Econ 102 next morning. This place is so indiscreet.' Paul nodded warily. 'You're majoring in Fine Arts, aren't you?'

'Yes I am. What's your major?'

It was the first 'normal' conversation Paul had had with a member of the opposite sex at Curwen – and perhaps anywhere else. And it happened so naturally and easily he could have been talking to a male friend or an older acquaintance of Cora-Beth's with whom the question of sex would never arise.

But it did arise here – almost literally – as he studied the girl's face, finding a slight crookedness in a front tooth, a curiously timeless quality in her high cheekbones, her russet colouring: features that could be preserved forty or fifty years hence. He glimpsed too the outline of a shapely leg between the loose folds of the sheet which she wore knotted over one shoulder, leaving the other bare.

And as they talked he was aware – or as aware as his new uncertainty allowed him – that she was studying him in turn, finding his face pleasant, his trousers questionable, his hair appealing. *Yes*, was the verdict of her unvoiced deliberations. *Yes, I find you interesting too. Yes, I would be open to your advances.* Or did he imagine that?

Every instinct told him that he did not. Every new-found inhibition warned him that this was not the Cape, this was new and dangerous territory.

The conflict created a strange tension, a kind of mutual electricity of which Paul had previously been only dimly aware. In his efforts to control it – and his fear that only he truly felt it – he took generous draughts of the punch which had so devestated his room-mate. As he did, he was surprised to notice that the girl – who had shown little tolerance of intoxication in Kyle – appeared as keen to keep up with him. To Paul this was another unconscious sign of her acquiescence, her favour, and just as gratifying and confusing.

Fortunately for Paul, the girl's head was turned away at the time and she did not see the importunate way he flung out a gesturing arm, only to connect with a passing tray of drinks, which upended over both of them.

'Oh Jesus! Jesus! You *moron!*' Julia shrieked, her hair dripping beer and red wine, while the owner of the tray, who was too drunk himself to realize he was innocent, bumblingly apologized. Paul dabbed at Julia's sheet and his own shirt and trousers in guilty silence.

'Look – I've got plenty of clean sheets upstairs,' he found himself saying. 'You're welcome to come up, get cleaned up.'

'Jesus! *Jesus!*' Julia repeated, but with Paul's hand clutching the point of her elbow she was turning, easing damply through the crush, heading for the entrance hall . . .

Guile. That was what he lacked. That provided the key

to the mysteries of seduction. The art of manipulating chance events, twisting them to his own advantage. It was more than the only practical way of dealing with hideous social complications, it was actually expected – it was allowed for.

The thought came to him in a moment of alcoholic clarity on the stairs – along with a profound suspicion that things were happening interestingly and excitingly but, on the whole, just a little too rapidly for him to register them properly. At that moment Julia, who was negotiating a twist in the staircase a step ahead of him, halted abruptly and he nearly fell over her. He had started to apologize before he realized she was shaking with laughter.

'Look at us!' she cried. 'Just *look* at us!'

Paul began to laugh, too, feeling his balance go and gripping her arms more for that reason than any other. But she lurched into his embrace – by accident or design, he couldn't tell – and he was suddenly kissing her as deeply and enthusiastically as Anna Hornsiger had kissed him a hundred miles and a whole world away.

Even allowing for the inconvenience of their position, she felt angular and awkward to him. She crushed her lips against his with considerable force but allowed his tongue to pass her teeth only hesitantly, as if uncertain what he intended or that she should permit it. Finally her chest began to heave, her breath exploded in a panting rush and she broke away abruptly, pressing her hands against his sopping shirt with a look of blinking confusion.

'Hey – ' She breathed in deeply then broke into a broad grin. 'We *thought* you couldn't be that quiet.'

'Quiet?' He frowned. 'Who's we?'

'Oh, you know, girlfriends.' She dismissed the thought. 'I really like shyness in a man. Mostly it's the complete nerds who aren't shy. Any guy with straight teeth thinks you're just dying to throw yourself at his feet. You're not like that. I think that's nice.'

Her grin was suddenly a brilliant smile. She tucked an arm round his waist, pulling him proprietorially against herself. They moved on up the stairs.

Confidence spread through Paul for the first time that evening. He knew desire in a woman, if he knew nothing else. She wanted him as much he wanted her. Everything would be all right.

And when they halted again on Paul's landing she told him with sudden seriousness, 'I'm really *not* this forward as a rule. It's just that dreadful punch – I think I'm the teeniest bit blasted.' He found her reticence appealing, even touching; his certainty allowed him to be generous.

Other couples moved along the corridor, exuding an air of anticipatory excitement, of giggling secrecy – or so it seemed to Paul. He felt he had at last cracked the great Curwen sex conspiracy, and qualified mysteriously but unmistakably for the hidden, orgiastic life of the place.

His room was a mess, thanks largely to Kyle's ever expanding possessions. But Julia, hovering in the middle while Paul rummaged for clean sheets, seemed unaware or uncaring. She stood quietly, looking round with bright eyes as though more impressed by her daring at being here than anything else.

'Here –' Paul gave her the only clean sheet he could find. She thanked him as he moved back to the door in search of a half-empty wine bottle he had vague memories of Kyle concealing behind his skis.

'Oh it's OK,' Julia added suddenly. 'You don't have to wait outside. I can trust you, can't I?'

He was too nonplussed for a second to respond to her

teasing smile. It had never occurred to him to leave. Then he grinned back.

'But no peeking, mind,' she warned. 'Turn around.'

Still grinning, he faced the closed door. If she wanted to play games then that was fine by him – now that consummation was literally within touching distance.

He heard the soft rustle of descending fabric and felt his cock stir. A sweet, skin-tingling delirium surged through him. He had been so long without the immediate prospect of sex his sudden need for it shocked him with its power.

'Can't get these damn – safety pins – out – ' the girl murmured.

Paul turned his head. She was facing away from him, bent forward over the gathered material of her sheet. She wore a sensible white bra, full white cotton briefs. Her back was long and narrow and bony, her shoulder blades like broad paddles, her spine visibly stippling her pale flesh. Not a back as smooth or as sculpted as Anna Hornsiger's or Diana's or even Cora-Beth's. But its angularity, its vulnerability caught at Paul's throat.

'I've probably got some pins somewhere,' he said thickly.

'O don't worry. I've got it sorted.' There was a smile in her voice as though she suspected him of making an excuse to turn round, which she liked.

Paul reached up and began to unbutton his shirt. As he bent to slide off his trousers he almost lost his balance, realizing with surprise how much the punch had affected him.

The girl had discarded her soiled sheet and was shaking the fresh one into a usable shape. 'I don't know why Kyle is so keen on togawear,' she was saying. 'I get the feeling he'd prefer me not to wear anything underneath. Don't you find

98

he's a little over-eager? He got me up here that time with the feeblest ex – '

Her voice shut off in a fierce gasp as Paul's lips brushed her neck. Simultaneously his fingers slipped the catch on her bra, sliding beneath the sagging straps, under her arms, lifting the loosened cups and scooping her small, pointed breasts.

He wanted to overwhelm her, devour her, touch every inch of her flesh in the same searing instant.

She froze, her limbs locked into a kind of spastic immobility, so that as he turned her around, bringing his head and tongue down onto the blunt tips of her nipples, she leaned backwards, pulling him with her. Only when it seemed they would both crash full length on the carpet did her knees bend. They tumbled sideways onto the edge of Paul's bed, Julia falling back across the mattress and Paul sprawling between her thighs.

The impact released a violent sob from the girl as Paul plucked at her briefs, peeling back the top and plunging his face into the first musky curls of her pubic hair.

'No – no – no – !'

He felt the shock of her scream through her body, a second before a flailing fist struck the side of his head. Stunned, he fell away from her, jolted still further by the wild kicking of her long legs. Finally a bare foot caught the base of his exposed erection, doubling him in a sudden flare of agony.

'What's the *matter* with you? Why did you *do* that? Just what do you think I *am* . . . ?'

Her breathless, sobbing gabble reached him through waves of pain. He was aware of her stepping over him, snatching up clothing from the floor.

99

'You were so *nice* — why did you have to be like that? — why?'

The door opened, then slammed thunderously. Outside, dimly, he heard a girl's voice ask: 'Julia, are you all right?' Then a sob and running feet. A male voice murmuring: '*I don't know. Probably just a row with Kyle —*'

Then silence.

Paul stayed where he was for what seemed a long time, curled foetally on the carpet, his eyes tight shut until the urge to retch had passed. He felt violated in mind and body, confused and abused, swamped by a flood of emotion so violent and conflicting he could barely contain it.

When the soft knock came at the door he shut his eyes again and pushed his head harder into his knees. Then the catch clicked open and a familiar voice said, 'My, Paul, don't they let you use the beds around here?'

His eyes snapped open in disbelief. He twisted round.

She stood in the doorway, shapeless inside a bulging, thigh-length down coat, her straight blonde hair tucked into its collar, cupping her grinning, cold-flushed face.

'Diana!'

Her soft grey eyes crinkled impishly. 'Hello, Angel Face. Fancy a swift fuck?'

She came inside, closing the door and easing a large well-packed flight bag off her shoulder as Paul sat up, blinking.

'I don't understand. Where's Cora-Beth?'

'Having a wild time on the Cape, I imagine,' said Diana, unzipping her coat. She shrugged it off to reveal a tight, pale pink tee-shirt, and glanced round the room. 'I must admit I expected something a little more stylish —'

'But I had a telephone message. A Mrs V something,' said Paul.

'Well, I called. I gave someone my name. Diana Vaughan — he probably misheard it, he sounded half asleep. Oh, Paul!' She stamped her booted feet and frowned at him. 'I haven't seen you in six months and all you do is interrogate me! I'm the lady who took your cherry, remember? Doesn't that mean anything, or are you too busy screwing all these teeny-boppers? You're certainly dressed for it — '

Breaking into a grin, Paul rose to his feet, clasping her to him. 'It's great — it's fantastic to see you.'

'Good,' she said, pulling away, 'because I was hoping to use your hospitality for the night. I've got to meet this guy I've been going with in Hartford tomorrow. He's a complete shit but he's got a schlong that ought to be in movies — ' She paused as she saw Paul's hesitant expression.

'I've got a room-mate,' he said.

'Well, I don't mind an audience if you don't,' she beamed, making him laugh. Then her face straightened. 'You haven't gone all po-faced and serious on me, have you? The Ivy League bit hasn't got to you, has it?'

Paul shook his head and shrugged. 'I don't think so.'

'Great!' She relaxed. 'You have no idea how uptight you were when we first went together. You made me feel like a schoolma'm! Now it's your turn. Any of those co-eds downstairs shown you some nice ways of doing it?'

Paul was grinning again, overwhelmed by her enthusiasm, her energy, her glamour. Instantly, matter-of-factly, she caught the bottom of her tee-shirt and pulled it swiftly over her head, shaking her hair free. Her bra-less breasts, fuller and rounder than he remembered, seemed the fulfilment of a promise Julia Niles could never have met.

'Come on, Paul, there must be *something* we haven't done before,' she prompted, sitting on the bed and pulling off her

101

boots. She glanced up at him as she unzipped her jeans, then frowned. 'Look at you! I know I've put on some winter fat, but I don't even get a flicker of interest. I bet you've been at it all night. Come here.'

Shaking his head, Paul moved closer. 'I wish to God I had,' he grinned. He halted just in front of her, his loins on a level with her face. Without a word she lifted her hand, easing her long fingers through his dark blonde hair, gently bearing the weight of his limp flesh in her warm palm.

He breathed in deeply and swallowed. Diana's lips curved in a quiet, gratified smile. She looked up at him.

'I've missed this little baby,' she murmured, her smile broadening as Paul echoed it, until a surge of feeling wiped his face of expression. Diana's head dropped, her straight, clean-smelling hair brushing his thighs with a feather touch.

'Let's see how much he's grown,' she whispered.

The warmth of her breath against the very tip of his cock sent a violent shudder through him. The first liquid touch of her tongue was as subtle and as delicate, so that the spasm which pushed his swelling knob through its cloak of foreskin seemed a response to some inner stimulus. But then, as he stretched, the soft lapping back and forth from tip to base, urging him on to greater length, greater rigidity was unmistakable, inescapable . . .

'Jesus, Diana,' Paul gasped through the acceleration of his heart. 'Oh Jesus God!' And he was back in the world of the Cape, where the richest fantasy was reality, where the sweetest, most undeniable joy of all was never denied him—

He did not hear the clatter of feet in the corridor, the rumble of angry voices, the whispers beyond the door. Until it opened.

'Paul! What the hell have you been trying to pull with

102

Ju – ' Kyle's raucous, alcohol-bleared tones cut off as though a switch had been thrown. In an echoing silence another male voice said quietly but very distinctly: 'Jesus fuck.'

With the slowness of dream, his mind and his emotions still engaged by the shaft of pleasure sliding between Diana's lips, Paul turned his head. He glimpsed the circles of blank faces – male and female – clustered in the doorway. Then someone's arm moved across and the door itself shut off the view.

It left the blankness of those faces in his mind – the blankness of separation, of isolation, of a yawning gulf between worlds which made his hammering heart ache.

But all he could think to say, on a dying gasp, was: *'Shit.'*

4

RACHEL
1974

It was the morning of her tenth birthday, only weeks after her mother had gone and the shouting and the shrieking and the crying, long into the night, had finally stopped. That was good because the arguments had frightened and alarmed her and given her bad dreams, and now the dreams had stopped too.

But it was not so good because her mother was no longer there to tell her if it was a mac day or a coat day before she went to school in the morning or to check her buttons (even though that annoyed her) or assure that everything, deep down, was really all right. If she was on holiday as her father said, even an especially long one, people ought to send a postcard at least. She was glad, then, when the first post brought a birthday card from her mother. It said very little, wished her well, sent her love. But her excitement was such she ran straight to tell her father, forgetting it was so early, that he was gruff and short-tempered in the mornings because he hated his job, and never liked to be disturbed until he came down to breakfast.

He was a strange man with a cold, serious face who rarely smiled at her or her mother, but she loved him.

She thought she would wake him as she pushed open his bedroom door but he was already awake. He was kneeling on the bed, facing the pillow so that his back was to her. She was puzzled because he was not wearing his pyjama trousers and he was trembling. Thinking he might be sick, she moved closer.

There was a picture lying on the pillow in front of him, a picture in three folded sections like the maps at school But this wasn't a map. It was a picture of a lady, a pretty, smiling lady, and it was rude because she hadn't any clothes on.

Then, just as she was about to ask what he was doing, her father spoke, but not to her. He spoke to the lady in the picture, in a halting, gasping voice. 'Jesus,' he said. 'Oh Jesus – I love you.'

And that was when she saw what he was doing.

He was holding his winkle, the thing that boys peed with, or something that was there in its place, because it had become long and fat and stiff, so massively big it didn't seem a part of him at all. In fact it couldn't be a part of him because he was squeezing it and pulling at it so hard it would have hurt him terribly.

'I love you,' he murmured, over and over again. 'I love you. I love you . . .'

Then, to her utter astonishment, he had peed. A strange, thick, milky pee that splashed right up the pillow in little spurts. And he had groaned, as if he had been hurting himself after all.

Then he turned and saw her and his face went scarlet with anger. 'Get out!' he had roared. 'Get out! Get out! Get out!'

But she had known by his expression, before he had shouted a word, that she had witnessed something awful and grown-up and secret which she had no right to see. And it was only later, in the quietness of her room, that she wondered what was so special about the lady in the picture that her father could say so easily that he loved her when he never said that to Rachel.

The coach jerked to a halt with the explosive hiss of air brakes. Rachel opened her eyes slowly, aware of an uncomfortable grittiness behind them, a film of grease on her skin. Beyond the coach window, grey early morning light filled a large and apparently deserted bus station, though the strip lighting against the steel and glass roof was still on. As she looked it flickered out.

The place seemed larger but no different from a dozen

105

other stops throughout the night – stops that had roused her from numbed sleep to a permanent half-wakefulness, as passengers clambered on board and off or the coach simply waited, once for almost an hour. Thoughts and dreams had interweaved inextricably. Teeming images full of resentment and longing, self-pity and a bitter anger that had brought her so vividly awake she had sat bolt upright, her heart racing, gazing into the darkness beyond the window until the feeling ebbed.

Now those thoughts still worried her, but dimly, inside a bubble of fatigue as grey as the morning. She had no idea how divorced she was from the outside world until she realized abruptly that the usual bustle of departure around her was universal. The whole coach was emptying. She was in London.

With a shock she straightened, shrugging on her dark woollen coat, fumbling under the seat for her holdall. As she got up the two duffel-coated students she had got on with squeezed past, smiling at her briefly. They looked as tired as she felt but there was an aura of happiness about them that caught in her throat. She waited until half a dozen more passengers, as silent and self-absorbed as herself, passed before joining the file.

The tarmac outside smelled of petrol and rubber. The air, crisp with an autumn chill, clouded her breath. As she stepped down her fatigue vanished. The other passengers were scattering purposefully.

She had no idea where to go.

The enormity of what she had done came over her in a rush. Last night all she had wanted was to get as far and as fast away as possible. To spite them all by her absence, to rid herself of them for ever. Any thought of life beyond that had simply not occurred to her. But here it was – here she was – in a city she had only visited once before, briefly, as a child, where she knew not a soul. Her realization of the stupidity of her action vied with her panic and almost won. Couldn't she have gone to friends or relatives? There was an aunt in Preston, a best friend she'd lost touch with since Donny. And her mother . . .

The coach-driver climbed down behind her, forcing her to step aside and making her aware she was now alone. As he glanced at her, she moved away quickly, suddenly self-conscious.

Her mother was a dream – a scattering of cards at Christmas and birthdays, with postmarks so various she had long ago realized they were part of a deliberate policy of concealing her whereabouts. The aunt and the girlfriend meant nothing – not compared to what had happened. Nobody she knew could mitigate that. It cut off the past as cleanly, as irrevocably, as a death.

She glimpsed an exit to the street and walked faster. She had been alone, she realized, since her mother left. Donny might have changed things, but in the end Donny had been no different from her father. That was a simple fact, independent of her feelings for him, of her present sense of betrayal. So nothing really had changed.

It was hardly a comforting thought, but it was the nearest she could manage to a feeling of resolve. For the moment it would just have to do.

She breakfasted in a half-empty Wimpy bar, and, refreshed, then walked all day, almost forgetting her discomfort and new situation in unabashed curiosity at new streets, new shops, new faces and fashions. She found Oxford Street and window-shopped up one side and down the other, crossing to Hyde Park to lunch on a sandwich and a canned drink, whose price shocked her.

She found an empty bench overlooking a green slope and risked shedding her woollen coat in a sun that had grown unexpectedly warm. When she had eaten she leafed through a copy of the *Standard* – purchased, she thought, with commendable initiative – and received an even larger shock at the rents asked for flats and bedsits.

What she needed was digs, somewhere small and friendly and cheap, perhaps with a family, a refuge until she decided what she wanted to do. But the newspaper ads didn't mention anywhere like that, and there seemed no small family houses among the shops and the hotels and the office blocks soaring around her.

She was so absorbed that she was only dimly aware of the little old man sitting down at the opposite end of the bench, until he spoke to her. She looked up in surprise, and then gratitude at her first conversation of the day.

The man was bowed and sixtyish, with the wizened face of a Mr Punch and a shapeless, grey postal worker's jacket. His voice was so soft she had to beg his pardon and lean closer. Then her ears caught the low, rasping tones, still indistinct but with the key words thickly emphasized: ' . . . love . . . fuck . . . your . . . juicy . . . cunt . . . '

The words lashed her with the force of a hard slap, freezing the smile of her face. In the same icy instant she saw the shocking urgency in his small, narrowed eyes, the slow rubbing movement in his dark baggy trousers.

Without thinking she snatched up her coat and holdall and ran. Twenty minutes later, safe in the bustle of the Oxford Street crowds, she was still trembling.

It was the least prepossessing of the small, inexpensive-looking hotels that littered the side-streets between the coach and railway stations at Victoria, in a white-painted, flat-fronted terrace opposite a row of small, bright shops balanced between dinginess and a kind of faded trendiness.

Rachel hovered in front of a travel agent's window, gazing at the posters inside without seeing them. It was late – how late, she wasn't sure, because her watch had stopped, but the shops had closed and the traffic had the same bustling urgency she had seen this morning. More relevantly, she was tired.

Her feet ached and she felt sticky and soiled. The urge to find somewhere warm and comfortable with hot water and a bed – regardless of cost – was almost irresistible. But she had seen only one hotel with any indication of prices outside and the smallest figure was pence more than she had in her purse. The dowdy hotel behind her could surely not charge as much as that.

Torn between frugality and fatigue, annoyed at her own indecisiveness, she wandered to the next shopfront. It was a secretarial agency, job upon job scrawled in blue felt pen on three window-high displays: PA and telephonist, copy typist and receptionist. The salaries offered made her blink. She had no idea jobs like that could pay so much. She had done some shorthand and typing at school, though some time ago. Could that be enough to get her started?

The possibility was the boost her confidence needed. The lights inside were still on. She looked between the displays and saw a man and a girl talking beside a desk. She wondered if she dared go in now, but the thought reminded her of her travel-worn state. She would need to be refreshed, to look presentable to enter such a place. The hotel was more than justified.

A pair of glass swing-doors opened onto a dim, musty-smelling hallway, incongruously narrow after such a broad entrance. Wallpaper with a thin, dull red stripe completed the alleyway effect. The carpet was patterned and anonymous.

Rachel came to a small reception desk tucked into a corner at the end. Television ads blared from a room to one side. She saw a row of armchairs through an open doorway. One was occupied, a man's head turned away toward the invisible set. No one else was in sight.

She was about to call to him when she noticed the sign over the door: *lounge*. The man was obviously a guest. Perhaps she should wait for someone in charge. The sudden indecision pricked her confidence; but at that moment the man swivelled his head and glanced at her quickly. Immediately he looked again, his eyes widening with interest; he leapt up and skipped athletically through the door.

'Can I help you, love?'

The speed and enthusiasm of his approach startled Rachel, not least because it seemed designed to impress. He was tall, too, leaning over her from a good six feet, so that her gaze dropped defensively from his urgent, scruffily handsome face as his eyes swept speculatively down and up her body. Thick hairs curled through his open shirt front. He was in his late twenties, his features rounded, his hair dark and close-cropped like Donny's.

'I'd like a room,' she said, blinking, discomfited by his blatant interest.

'Why not?' he beamed, reached behind a yellowing credit card display on the counter and punched a small bell. Rachel felt herself redden, embarrassed by missing something so obvious.

'Malik'll be right up. He'll look after you.' His gaze flickered the length of her figure again; she wished he would not stand so close; she was caught between the desk and the wall.

'Come down to see the bright lights, have you?' he said at last. His eyes held the slightest hint of mockery, but underneath she saw the hardness and hunger of the old man in the park.

'Just visiting,' she murmured, forced into the faintest deprecatory smile and cursing herself for it instantly as she glimpsed a spark of encouragement flare in his face.

'Oh *well!*' he beamed. 'You're going to be lost without a guide and it just so happens, being a native, as it were, I have the rest of the week *entirely* free. Now, what I suggest is, we have a little drink in the pub round the corner and discuss this – '

'I don't know,' Rachel cut in, stammering. She was out of her depth and sinking fast. To her immense relief a small, brown, bespectacled face appeared through a doorway behind the desk.

'Malik, old son!' the young man cried. 'I have a lovely young lady here who wants your very best room – '

'No!' Rachel snapped quickly. 'Just somewhere small, please. Nothing fancy.'

'I have a single at the back,' said the newcomer. 'It's very comfortable, but a little bit cramped.'

'I don't mind. Sounds fine,' said Rachel hurriedly. The small brown man opened a registration book. 'How many nights?'

'Just one – for now.'

'Oh, she can do all that later,' the young man cut in. 'I'll give you a hand with this.' He grasped Rachel's holdall so swiftly it slipped from her fingers. She scowled at him, feeling a scream of frustration rise inside her. Why did

111

people want to organize her all the time? She wasn't an invalid or an idiot.

'Can you tell me how much the room is?' she asked the man behind the desk. Mildly he told her.

And a pit opened in her stomach. It was over a pound dearer than the other tariff she had seen.

She became aware that the two men were staring at her curiously. Embarrassment and panic erupted in her simultaneously.

'Are you all right, love?' the young man began. But abruptly Rachel was turning, snatching the holdall from his grasp, tripping down the hallway, casting a muffled, 'Thank you very much. Changed my mind – ' over her shoulder.

Then she was outside, in bright daylight, her face burning and her heart thudding. *Fool! Stupid fool!* She wanted to shriek uncontrollably, to sink into the pavement, to explode in a ball of flame – anything to wipe out her own appalling idiocy.

Opposite her a fair-haired man and a young girl were locking up the secretarial agency. As they glanced across the road, Rachel looked away, aware of her scarlet face and her frantic mugging. And to her horror the hotel's swing-doors opened behind her.

'No – wait, love!'

She started off at speed, sliding between two parked cars and across the road.

'Don't be silly. I'm sorry about all that inside.'

She didn't turn. On the opposite pavement the fair-haired man was unlocking the door of a pale blue Jaguar, staring in open curiosity as she swerved past him.

'Please, love, no more bullshit. Please!'

The young man from the hotel had drawn level, outpacing her, spreading his arms in supplication, but not attempting to restrain her physically. For that reason, and her mounting embarrassment, she paused.

'I don't want to have a drink with you!' she snapped.

'Oh forget about all that.' He screwed up his face dismissively. 'Look, I was out of order back there – all right? I was trying it on. I don't often see a girl with looks like yours – even in London. I just got a bit overheated, acted like a burke and I'm sorry. OK?'

Rachel blinked at him, still too confused from the events of a few minutes ago to make any judgement. The hardness, the urgency had gone from the young man's eyes but his frowning sincerity could have meant anything. He saw the confusion in her face and his brow cleared.

'You're a lot younger than you look, aren't you?'

She turned away abruptly with a flash of annoyance: she did not need to be patronized.

'Hey, give it a rest!' Now he was laughing, touching her elbow lightly. He snapped back his hand as she threw him a fierce look of warning. 'I just want to help.' He spoke through his laughter. 'If you're not interested – fine. Forget everything I say. But half a minute isn't going to cost you anything, is it?'

He took a breath as she sighed, watching him carefully.

'Now I may be completely wrong but I get the feeling you're not exactly flush,' he went on. 'If you've got nowhere to go tonight, for instance, don't just wander the streets with your little bag. There are some nasty people about – much nastier than me.' He reached into his pocket. 'Here's somewhere where you can clean up, put your head down and it won't make a hole in your purse. It's pretty basic, but it's a lot better than a park bench.' He sniffed and pushed a leaf from a notepad into Rachel's hand. 'Girl I knew once

113

stayed there, gave her the chance to find her bearings . . . OK?'

He was grinning at her again. 'And if you fancy that drink sometime, when you're settled, come and look me up. Ask for Derek. I'm always somewhere around the hotel.'

He was backing away from her, his grin broadening. 'See,' he called, 'I'm quite a nice fellow really!'

He turned and broke into a run, vanishing between the parked cars.

Nonplussed, Rachel stared after him, until she noticed the fair-haired man, still standing at the door of his Jaguar, gazing at her with an amused smile.

Annoyed, she turned her back and began walking. But after a few steps she stopped and glanced at the note in her hand. Scrawled on it was the name of a hostel with an address and a rough map. To her surprise the address was close to Oxford Street – she had passed within yards of it only this morning.

A wave of guilt overtook her. Even if Derek's motives weren't exactly pure he had been extraordinarily kind to a complete stranger, when she had been frosty throughout. But still the image of the old man in the park – mirrored, she was certain in the young man's eyes – haunted her, undermining her contrition.

Pushing the note into her pocket, she began her long walk northward.

She woke to the smell.

At first she thought it was the pillow under her cheek, its granulated foam interior knobbly against her skin. Then came sourer, muskier odours, unmistakably feminine, and she opened her eyes, shocked it might be herself.

114

A girl, short and grossly fat inside a shapeless, hand-knitted cardigan, her hair tangled in rats-tails, sat on the bunk opposite; she was drawing on a cigarette, watching Rachel with small, dull eyes.

Rachel blinked at her, lost for a moment. Then she remembered where she was. What on earth was the girl staring at?

Rachel stretched her facial muscles, frowning and lifting her head. The rest of the room seemed unoccupied. Daylight seeped through a row of high, dusty-looking windows opposite. It showed brown-painted walls, thick with graffiti, a dark lino floor, scuffed and frayed, chipped paint and drooping springs on metal bunk beds packed tightly together. In the corridor outside someone was at work with a mop and bucket.

Now she knew the source of the smell. An amalgam of unwashed female bodies and ancient decay, shot through with traces of cheap perfume and cheaper disinfectant. She swallowed thickly, fighting a rising horror. The place was a slum.

'You got nice clothes.'

'I beg your pardon?'

The plump girl breathed out smoke, her face as expressionless as her voice, as dowdy as her surroundings. 'You buy them yourself?'

Rachel sat up quickly. Her coat and jumper were crumpled at the end of the bed but her skirt lay on the floor beside her. She bent and snatched it up, brushing off dust and hairs.

'Couldn't you have picked it up? she snapped without thinking. 'This floor's absolutely filthy.'

To her surprise the plump girl shot to her feet. 'I don't

115

touch other people's things!' she snarled, dropping her cigarette and stamping it into the floor. '*I* don't nick nothing!'

'I didn't mean – ' Rachel protested, but the girl was halfway to the door, slapping her feet resentfully on the lino.

Rachel watched her disappear then took a deep breath. What had prompted that? Were her clothes that much better than the girl's? Was the girl just simple? She felt her unease grow. This was a world she didn't understand, where she didn't fit.

The hiss of water came from the farthest end of the room. Turning, she saw a doorway and strip lighting beyond it gleaming on white tiles. Thank God there was somewhere to wash. She hadn't even bothered to ask the night before.

She swung herself out of bed, pausing to find her shoes and slip them on before stepping on the floor. Then, on an impulse, she pulled on her skirt, put her sweater into her holdall and carried it with her.

The washroom smelled damp and fetid. Tidemarks lined the ancient sinks that formed a double row down the centre. More graffiti grooved the wooden doors of toilet cubicles to the left. To the right, half a dozen elderly shower fittings hung over a sunken area awash with soap-slimed water. A girl stood under one, soaping herself in a sputtering stream, her face to the wall.

Rachel felt a surge of distaste close to nausea. She couldn't wash here; she'd put on more dirt than she washed off.

Then the girl in the shower turned, shaking bright red, tightly curled hair, and saw her. Rachel was aware of a swift, raking stare.

'Come on in. The water's almost warm.'

116

The accent was broadest Glaswegian, grating and thick. Rachel smiled uncertainly. 'I must have overslept,' she said.

The Scottish girl grunted. 'You did yourself a favour. You wouldn't have got a look-in at these showers half an hour ago. That's why I hang about. This place is a fucking cattle market.'

Rachel nodded non-committally. The thought of fighting off a couple of dozen strangers to get into showers like these was even more appalling than actually using them. Frowning, she put her holdall across a sink top. Then her frown deepened. The entry qualification here seemed to be a rough tongue and a habit of staring. The Scottish girl was doing it now, quite blatantly as she faced Rachel, water chasing the suds down her short, thick body.

She was quite blatant about that, too, though Rachel could hardly see why. Her legs were short and squat, her breasts boyish and flat. Only the mass of hair, drawn into a dripping beard between her legs, made Rachel in the least appreciative of her immodesty. Her own dark profusion had worried and embarrassed her since it had first appeared. Even May – the only other woman she had seen completely naked – seemed quite skimpy down there. But this girl more than made up for that.

Increasingly self-conscious, Rachel turned her back as she eased off her skirt. 'Does everyone have to leave early?' she asked over her shoulder.

The Scottish girl laughed. 'You don't think anyone'd hang around this dump if they could avoid it? Anyway, if you do, they have you cleaning the place. That's why they let Fatso outside stay on. Catch me doing that!'

'I think I upset her – the fat girl,' said Rachel, unclipping her bra and draping it over the holdall next to her tights. A new pair would be today's first dent in her purse. She had no spares.

'Everyone upsets her – the silly cow. She's daft in the head.' The girl watched while Rachel bent and quickly smoothed off her knickers, reaching a towel out of the holdall and wrapping it round herself in the same swift movement. 'You got a fellow?'

Rachel turned in surprise. Somehow boyfriends and a place like this seemed an unlikely combination. Then she thought of Donny and her brow knitted. 'No. Not so's you'd notice.'

The other girl gave a grunting laugh. 'Yeah, I've had a couple like that. I've got this right pig at the moment. He's a fat sweaty little shit. It's like a ton of potatoes when he gets on top of you. I won't let him lay a finger on me until he makes it worth my while. Here – come under this one.'

Rachel hesitated, halfway to the furthest shower. The Scottish girl waved her hand. 'Come *on*! It's the only one that works properly. It's OK. I've finished.'

Nodding gratefully, Rachel put her toilet bag and towel on the floor and let the other girl move past her before stepping into the vacated space.

The water was as lukewarm as predicted. She gasped then sighed, closing her eyes in sheer physical enjoyment of its liquid grasp, momentarily forgetful of the slurry of scum about her ankles, the spidery cracks in the tiling, yellow with age, next to her face. Even the Scottish girl's grating comment.

'I'm sorry?'

'They're wankers! All men are wankers. You've got to find yourself one with cash, and plenty of it. Make him pay for everything. Every fucking thing.'

The girl was towelling herself briskly only a few feet away,

118

her eyes narrowed in her square, bony face, her gaze fixed on Rachel. Rachel had known consciously 'hard' girls at school and disliked them, both for the hardness itself and the posing it involved. Here, this girl made her doubly uneasy.

'You won't have any trouble – not with a body like that.'

'You what?' Rachel gave her a crooked glance as she bent to lift shampoo from her toilet bag. The other girl was drawing her thin towel up and down her abdomen, fluffing the gingery-gold hair at her crotch into an extraordinary bush, curling inches from her pronounced mons.

'Screwing some fellow with money. Making him pay for putting it up.'

Rachel turned away quickly, massaging shampoo into her scalp. She didn't like the girl's desire to shock, to show herself off, or the way she stared. There was something insidious, unpleasant about her, beyond all posing. She wished the girl would go.

'I can't see the point of them myself. I can have a good time on my own. Or with a friend . . .'

Rachel glimpsed her again as soap drained from her hair. The girl was still towelling her abdomen, but slowly now with a steady, purposeful rhythm, her narrow hips thrust forward; her eyes, still fastened on Rachel, were half-hooded, her thin mouth fractionally open.

The realization of what was happening struck Rachel like a draught of arctic air. And, seeing it in her face, the Scottish girl grinned. 'Am I embarrassing you?' she said softly. 'Don't you like a wee feel now and then? You could help me if you liked.'

'*Out!*'

The word burst out of nowhere, startling Rachel as much as it did the girl. Suddenly a tall, rangy young woman was there, her narrow features working in rage. Smacking the handle of a mop across the Scottish girl's thick waist, she sent her staggering back toward the sinks.

'Get your fucking hands off me!'

'*Out!* Get dressed and *get out!* I don't want to see you in this hostel again!'

The woman's screech drowned out the girl's shouted protest. Swearing, she slapped the towel and charged out of the washroom, swerving to avoid another sweep of the mop handle.

'*Bloody* little whore!' the woman hissed, her thin chest heaving. '*Christ!* As if we don't have enough trouble . . .' Then her gaze focused on Rachel, hunched against the tiling, arms crossed protectively over her breasts, eyes bright and round and staring.

'And *you* should have the sense not to encourage her!' the woman snapped.

'Let's see what you've done.'

The notebook was snatched from Rachel before she could even open her mouth in protest.

'Hmm.' The agency manageress scanned the gappy transcription, her full lips tightening. Then, unsympathetically, she sighed. 'This doesn't really seem much better than your typing.'

Rachel swallowed her annoyance. She had intended to talk to one of the younger interviewers, but the woman had seized on her the moment she had stepped through the door, peremptorily, as though she doubted whether Rachel should enter at all.

She reminded Rachel of May – a smarter, more business-like May, but with the same fondness for strong perfume, the same exaggerated cleavage, the same predatory air. A woman with little interest in other women, especially if they were prettier, and younger, than herself.

'I think it's just a bit of practice I need – '

'Well, you can hardly expect our clients to pay you while you get that.' The woman sighed again, shortly. 'No, with some "O" Levels filing clerk *might* have been possible, but companies are much choosier these days, even for temps. They'll only pay good rates for experience.'

Sensing the woman was about to turn away, Rachel blurted: 'What about telephonists, receptionists?'

'Can you work a PABX?'

Rachel looked blank. The woman smiled icily. 'And, of course,' she said, 'personal appearance is *very* important on a reception desk. Sorry.'

And turning her back she immediately began talking to another interviewer.

Cow! Rotten, savage cow! In the busy street outside tears of anger and frustration pricked Rachel's eyes. She stamped fiercely on her feelings, refusing to allow the woman her victory. But the tears came anyway, forcing her to turn her face to a chemist's bright-lit window and pretend dust had caught in her eye.

It was the sixth in a day of rebuffs and only different from the others in its callousness. The message of each was painfully similar: she had no secretarial skills to speak of and no evidence of any academic ability. A girl in the very first agency had suggested waitressing and Rachel had laughed; only now did she realize it had not been a joke.

But the manageress had aroused a more corrosive fear. Was it the way she looked that was wrong too? She knew her coat was too thick and heavy for weather as mild as this, and did not really match her beige skirt; she knew the white cotton blouse she had unearthed from her holdall needed an iron, which was why she kept her coat closed. But there were girls passing who looked much more dowdy and still oozed self-confidence.

Was it her make-up? Her hair, which she had had to towel dry this morning? Then her mind touched on the worst suspicion. Had her clothes absorbed the sour odours of the hostel? Her heart plummeted at the appalling thought. No wonder no one would send her for an interview. Quickly she unbuttoned her coat, flapping it wildly to let the petrol fumes of Oxford Street permeate the fabric. Then, realizing where she was, dashed into the chemist and squandered a quarter of her remaining money on an inexpensive perfume spray, which she applied liberally – until she noticed the curious looks of passersby – to the lining of her coat.

The effort restored some of her confidence, but the traumas of the morning and the day still cast oppressive shadows. Her watch, re-started now, told her it was nearly four.

The prospect of further rebuffs, and the grim possibility of a second night in the hostel, made her spirit quake. Suddenly more than anything else in this wide, bustling, heedless city, she needed to see just one friendly face.

Only pausing to remove a smear of damp mascara she glimpsed reflected in the chemist's window, she started briskly toward Victoria.

The reception-desk bell sounded angry and off-key, its clattering trill absorbed into the dusty fittings of the hotel lobby. At least that was what appeared to be happening, because no one came to answer it.

Sighing, Rachel stuck her head through the lounge door again. It was still empty, a scattering of ill-assorted armchairs facing a blank television set. Until she arrived it had simply not occurred to her that Derek might not be here, slouched in an armchair, whiling away his free week.

Unless, of course, that was just another part of his chat-up technique . . . . There could have been half a dozen lonely females passing through since then – girls who could afford to stay and to accept drink invitations on the spot.

Smarting, Rachel controlled herself. She was leaping to all sorts of conclusions. He had said 'around the hotel', which could mean anything. And he had been kind to her when she had promised him nothing in return.

She was debating whether she dared sit and wait in the lounge when the front doors opened and the small, bespectacled Asian she had seen the day before came in, smiling at her briefly in a way that suggested he did not recognize her.

'Mr – Malik, is it? Is Derek here?'

'Derek?' The Asian frowned thoughtfully, bending to place the carrier-bag he was holding under the reception desk. 'Oh no,' he said, rising, 'not today. Tomorrow perhaps.'

Rachel looked at him in surprise. 'Doesn't he work here?'

'Work for me?' The man seemed to find the idea amusing. 'Oh no, he's just a friend. He drinks here. He's a good customer. Shall I give him a message?'

Chewing her lip, Rachel glanced away. 'No – thanks. You don't know where he lives?' she asked suddenly.

The man shrugged, smiling softly. 'I'm sorry.'

Rachel nodded, feeling a last lifeline slip away. She turned to go. 'I still have a room free,' the Asian said. 'It's very nice, very inexpensive.'

'No, it's all right.' Rachel smiled stiffly. 'I'm fixed up, thanks.'

*

She stepped on to the pavement. The day had been almost spring-like but now the chill of dusk was in the air. Opposite, the shops were still open. Rachel crossed to them.

She was, she realized, close to her lowest ebb. The only certainty the future offered was just two more nights in the hostel, with all its attendant horrors. For the first time, and only for the briefest second, she allowed the consideration of a return home. Her emotions recoiled with a violence that made her blink.

'Hello. Looking for refuge from your boyfriend again?'

Rachel looked round, momentarily lost. She had been standing in front of the secretarial agency, gazing sightlessly at the window displays. Now the door was open. A man in shirtsleeves and a waistcoat was leaning out, grinning at her.

'Yesterday?' he prompted. 'Out here? You went past me like a bat out of hell. I thought you were going to jump in my car, order me to put my foot down –'

Rachel's face lightened in recognition, then she flushed. 'Oh that wasn't my boyfriend.'

The man's eyebrows shot up in mock horror. 'All the more reason to do my Galahad bit.'

Rachel broke into a hesitant smile and then blushed a deeper red. She couldn't have conversations like this with total strangers. Not on the street. The man, who had been only an impression of smartness and affluence the day before, was obviously young, younger than Derek. His hair was wavy, his face long and cleft-chinned, his eyes crinkly with laughter lines under gold-rimmed spectacles. It was a bright, brash, confident face. Awkwardly, Rachel turned away.

'Aren't you coming in?'

She looked back at him. 'Why?'

'Well, you don't look at job ads unless you want one, do you? You do want one?'

Rachel stared. The possibility of hope from so unexpected a quarter was too sudden to register. 'Yes, yes I do,' she said at last.

'I'm Barry Drew,' the man said, ushering her inside and asking her name. When she had answered, he said: 'That's Wendy.'

A pretty blonde girl of about nineteen glanced up from behind a desk and smiled.

'It's nearly half-five. You might as well call it a day, love,' Barry told her airily. 'I'll look after Rachel, here.'

With a look that Rachel could only describe as old-fashioned, the girl rose and picked up her handbag. Bidding a crisp goodnight she left.

Barry indicated an empty desk. 'Let's get a few details, eh, Rachel?'

It did not go well. He leaned over her as she copy-typed, nervousness making her fumble even more than usual. Halfway through the shorthand test she put down her pencil in despair. 'Look, I really think I'm wasting your time – '

But as she went to get up, he touched her shoulder, pushing her down again. 'Don't be so hasty! It's probably my fault. I usually get my girls to do these tests. And anyway, personality counts for a great deal in a job. Anyone can pick this stuff up as they go along. Believe me.'

She wanted to, more than she could say. And seeing that in her face he smiled.

'I think we really ought to talk about this a bit longer, but it's well past our closing time and I went without my lunch today.' He leaned forward as the disappointment showed in her eyes. 'So I'm going to grab an early dinner. Why don't you come along and we can carry on? You haven't got to be anywhere for an hour or so, have you?'

Rachel shook her head. 'Great! You can leave your bag upstairs. I've got a little flat there I use in the week. It'll be safer than in here. Let's get going, then.'

Rachel rose hesitantly, her instincts telling her he had just got away with something Derek had bungled hopelessly. But Derek's interest had been undisguised and honest, and a rebuff had instantly turned him into a friend. This man hadn't even looked at her legs.

She was immediately seized by an even more worrying thought. Would she have to pay for her own meal? After the day's purchases she had barely enough for two more nights at the hostel and perhaps two coffees and buns.

Barry was holding open the door, looking back at her expectantly, keys jingling in his hands. A rumbling stomach made up her mind.

The dinner was a nightmare.

She had started by being uncritically impressed – by her first ride in the cushioned comfort of a Jaguar, though their destination was only two streets away; by the flowery intimacy of a restaurant she would never have dreamed of entering otherwise; by Barry's unruffled familiarity with exotic-sounding food, with wine, with the restaurant's rotund Spanish manager, whom he called by his first name.

Rachel's discomfort began when the same man had insisted on taking her coat, revealing her crumpled and by now less than wholly white blouse. It had increased as other couples had gradually filled the tables – girls who looked cool and elegant and utterly self-confident, men who made loud remarks in posh London voices. Barry's conversation – about the two agencies he owned with a partner, about his house 'Marlow way' (she had no idea where that was and didn't ask), about his plans for expansion – covered her first, fumbling experience of asparagus. But when she had started to speak, made unexpectedly voluble by wine she was unused to, she found herself talking of home and school friends, odd relatives, days and outings she'd enjoyed, even, guardedly, of Donny and suddenly she saw the boredom in Barry's face and heard herself as he must. Gauche and provincial and utterly trivial.

She immediately lapsed into a sullen silence, only worsened by Barry's attempts to bring her out of it. She couldn't understand why he was bothering. Someone as self-assured, as affluent, could be spending his time with any of the other girls in this restaurant – girls with perfect make-up and expensive clothes, girls who were bright and witty and sophisticated. He could only be patronizing her, even making fun; she began to grow increasingly resentful.

She let him drive her back to the agency only because she had to collect her holdall. Her urge to be gone, to disappear into the darkening streets was so powerful by now it seemed impossible he couldn't see it. She was astonished when he insisted she come up to the flat and fetch her bag herself.

Lacking the courage to object, she hung back as he unlocked a front door next to the agency entrance, plodding reluctantly after him up a narrow staircase beyond. Another door at the top opened directly into a living room.

There was a thick cream shag-piled carpet on the floor, abstract prints on the walls; a tulip lamp overhung a wide, dark blue leather couch; a large gold cigarette lighter rested on a chrome and smoked glass coffee table in front of it.

Rachel's eyes widened in surprise.

'Like it?' Barry grinned at her in undisguised delight.

'It's fantastic.'

'So it should be. Cost me a bloody fortune.' He peeled off his jacket in a single swift movement. 'But what's the point of making money if you don't spend it?' He patted the couch. 'Sit down a minute. Enjoy it while I find your bag.'

Wonderingly Rachel stepped forward, feeling her street-dusty shoes sink into the deep pile. She'd no idea places like this existed outside magazines. Her depression evaporated, lost in her sense of entering a world so different in quality from her home, from the squalor of the hostel, that it seemed almost dream-like. She was overwhelmed.

The leather of the couch felt as soft as kid under her fingers. As she sat, Barry reappeared, setting down on the table in front of her a heavy, rounded glass with amber liquid swimming in the bottom. 'Brandy OK? I'd have ordered it in the restaurant but I've got better stuff here.'

Rachel looked up at him uncertainly.

'Well, taste it. If it's no good, tell me.'

She lifted the glass and sniffed, suddenly too ill at ease to admit that she had only ever drunk brandy with lemon and honey. It smelled thick and oily. She took a swift sip, grateful that she could swallow it smoothly without sputtering.

'It's fine.'

'Five-star. Best there is.' He sat on the arm of the couch, looming over her. 'Let me take your coat. You can't enjoy your drink all wrapped up.'

She was unbuttoning the coat before a natural wariness overtook her. She knew that she was not in control here, that he had her at every disadvantage. The fact that he had made no untoward moves only disconcerted her even more. Nobody was this generous without a reason. She didn't even know if she liked him.

'I really think I ought to be going,' she said quickly,

128

pulling her coat together again.

Barry simply nodded sensibly, so that Rachel was unable to judge whether he was disappointed, or relieved.

'Fine,' he said, 'but if you're not in a hurry you don't have to worry about tubes or buses. I can run you back in the Jag in five minutes. What sort of place have you got, by the way? Is it a flat or a bedsit?'

Rachel hesitated, her confusion growing. She had fudged the issue of an address simply by giving the hostel's without saying what it was – just as she had fudged her previous work record, hinting at numerous unspecified temporary jobs.

Awkwardly she began to explain, putting as good a gloss on it as she could, fighting her nervousness as she saw his face darken, until finally he burst out, interrupting her; 'But that's only for dossers! You get the dregs in a place like that! God, you'd need disinfecting after putting your head through the door!'

Rachel blushed furiously, caught between an angry desire to defend her own actions, however ill-advised, and the obvious truth of his words. But he gave her no chance to react.

'I'm not running you back to a dump like that. You can stay here tonight. And I'm not taking "no" for an answer. Jesus! I wouldn't leave my worst enemy in a hole like that.' He tapped her arm. 'Now come on, give me that coat. You're going to enjoy a bit of luxury for a change.'

The shower water splashed over Rachel's shoulders, needle-sharp and warm, so vivid a contrast to the luke-warm trickle of the morning that that now seemed like a bad dream. But this was no less dream-like, and not because the small, clean, sweet-smelling bathroom that

129

surrounded her lacked reality. If anything it was too real. Too many impressions were crowding in on her, scattering her thoughts, making resolution of any kind almost impossibly hard.

She knew she had been manipulated, outpaced, outclassed in ways she would have objected to loudly under normal circumstances. ('You can sleep on that if you like,' Barry had said when she asked if there were blankets for the couch, 'but there's a perfectly good bed next door. You don't mind doubling up for one night, do you?') But these weren't normal circumstances. She was tired, she was penniless, she was in desperate, aching need for the slightest scrap of certainty, of security, even if it lasted only a single night.

But underneath, just as insistently, another need continued to assert itself. A need for someone, anyone, to say, 'Wait. Is this right? Surely you should give this more thought.' A need her father had once fulfilled – if infrequently and imperfectly – but well enough to deter Donny at times. Now there was no one.

Turning off the shower, she dried herself, stretching the time as long as she dared.

There was no dressing gown in the bathroom and her coat was elsewhere. Rachel wrapped herself in a large, damp bath-towel, drawing it tightly around her shoulders. Then she turned out the light and opened the door.

The bedroom was next door, dimly illuminated by a single shaded lamp next to the curlicued wicker headboard. The bed itself was smaller than she had anticipated. Barry sat up against the lefthand pillow, bare-chested, his spectacles gone, his head bowed over a magazine.

She saw that his face looked younger and more raw without glasses, that his chest was as hairless as Donny's,

130

that he wore a thin gold chain, that he had nice shoulders. Then he glanced up and saw her and grinned.

'Do you mind?' she said quietly. 'Could you put the light out?'

A frown creased his brow, then his grin broadened. 'Yeah. Sure. If that's what you want.'

He rolled sideways, stretching almost full length across the mattress to do it. Rachel blinked as the duvet slipped from his waist, revealing the top of a lightly haired thigh, the absence of shorts or pyjama trousers.

In darkness she felt her way to the side of the bed and lifted the duvet. She wanted to keep the towel on, but it was too damp. Letting it fall, she squeezed herself onto the mattress, keeping as close to the edge as she dared.

She lay on her back, perfectly still, sensing rather than feeling Barry's dull, alien weight on the opposite side of the bed. She didn't know whether to feel exhilarated or resentful, grateful or resigned. So she did nothing.

The sudden touch of his hand against her side sent the breath exploding from her nostrils in a high-pitched grunt.

'Here, you're wet! Couldn't you find a dry towel?' His voice was astonishingly close, warm and intimate, as if his mouth were pressed against her ear.

'I used them all up,' she said, swallowing. In this enforced proximity she wanted to whisper, but a whisper implied affection and she didn't feel that.

His hand was still flat against her left thigh. She tensed as it began to slide upwards, following the contour of her hip.

'You're damp all over,' he said, an odd wonderment in his voice. 'You'll catch your death.'

Rachel's eyes were tight shut, her body frozen, her heart thudding within it like the heart of a small, trapped animal. Barry's hand moved onto her stomach, onto the flesh of her

131

ribs; it touched the swelling undercurve of her left breast, fingers spreading to cup the soft weight, to measure its rounded width, closing on the puckering stub of her nipple.

Then, strangely, he stopped, as if reminding himself that she might choose to object, allowing her the opportunity of some small token gesture. But Rachel, even if she had felt herself able to protest, would not have done so. An odd lassitude had invaded her – a detached awareness that confined her physical apprehensions to her rapidly beating heart, leaving her mind free to observe, almost neutrally but with an intense curiosity, the things Barry was doing to her, the reactions of her own body.

A sharp intake of breath marked the end of the hiatus. 'Oh, Rachel,' he gasped. 'Oh, Rachel, oh, darling – ' And he was twisting, squirming against her, grasping her and lifting her as his mouth came down onto her breasts, rubbing his lips against the firm flesh, licking and sucking each nipple into tender erection.

Rachel grunted, snatching air in quick gasps as she knew alarm at the suddenness and urgency of his movements. She felt his weight and his strength, both considerably more than her own. She felt too the pressure of a solid, fleshy rod butting her upper thigh. He was kissing her now, her face, her throat, the tips of her breasts, while his hands roved downward, stroking, caressing, exploring. His touch was rougher than she would have preferred, but not unpleasantly so; she was annoyed most by his repeated 'darling's; she wasn't his darling, and making such a point of it seemed a fake, a sop to her emotional conscience. She was letting him, wasn't she? Wasn't that enough?

At the same time she was surprised, and even guilty, at how little she had to do. His own excitement seemed sufficient to fuel the entire enterprise, while she hardly moved, clutching uncertainly at the sharp peaks of his shoulder blades, letting go the occasional involuntary gasp, waiting to be swept up by the same tide of emotion. She was pleased, then, despite a sudden wild fear of violation, when his hand slid between her legs, rubbing against the folds of her sex so that she could feel her own slickness. She held her breath as he parted the outermost ridges of flesh, lightly probing the mucus-thick warmth within with the tip of a single finger.

'Oh, Rachel,' he murmured. 'Oh, I must – I can't hold back I've got to – got to –'

It seemed odd to her that he should apologize; she had made no objection. Did he have a conscience of his own about this? But then all speculation ceased as he moved across her and she felt his full weight on her body.

He loomed above her, a curiously dense shadow now that her eyes had adjusted to the gloom, and though his harsh breath and the trembling of his flesh was real and immediate she was grateful for his anonymity. His hand fumbled between her legs, he leaned forward and he penetrated her.

She felt a sudden, breathless dread that blotted out all thought. But only for the briefest fraction of a second. Abruptly her detachment had gone, her thoughts snared and churned by the wild hammering of her heart. Guilt, regret, a sense of loss for something precious squandered recklessly, was swallowed in a single, ringing thought: 'He's in me. A man is in me. I'm doing it – I'm doing it –'

And in that burst of heightened emotion it was impossible to say whether her excitement came from her own guilty awareness or the queer, sliding pressure inside her.

Barry's weight bore down on her, his heaving chest crushing her breasts, and she became aware that he was

133

moving again, rocking himself backward and forward on her pubic bone. She felt the edges of a warm, tingling response where he entered her and in a sudden urge to increase the contact squirmed on her back.

Instantly Barry let out a groan, whispered, 'Rachel – oh take it, love – take it – take it!' And went suddenly rigid but for a series of short, sharp jerking movements of his thighs. Then, with a loud sigh, he slumped forward across Rachel's body, gradually sliding down her side.

She lay quietly, blinking and confused for several minutes before she realized it was all over. Had he really done it inside her? She hadn't *felt* him come.

The sense of anticlimax grew slowly, then engulfed her in a rush of resentment, just as something small and slippery slithered from her sex. She reached down between her legs. She realized the limp, sticky thing she had between her fingers was Barry's cock, no bigger now than a little boy's. It felt so small and pathetic she was torn between a sense of wonder that it had actually been inside her and a temptation to giggle.

She was almost glad now that it had not been Donny. To have done it with someone she loved and to have felt like this afterwards would have been unbearable.

She sighed, gazing upward into the darkness, wondering if Barry's silence signified sleep and whether she dared ease her arm from under him before it went entirely numb. Then she thought of the appalling Scottish girl from so long ago this morning. *All men are wankers. You've got to find yourself one with cash, and plenty of it. Make him pay for everything. Every fucking thing.*

She sniffed. Every *fucking* thing was right.

And with frightening suddenness a feeling of the most profound loneliness burst over her and she wanted nothing

134

more than the strange body at her side to hug her and squeeze her and hold her tight for as long as she needed. But in the silence she heard only the soft breathing of sleep and she was too afraid to touch him in case he woke.

5

PAUL

1971

'Hey Paul! Paul Hanna!'

Halfway across Big Yard, Paul turned, stepping back out of the early morning flow of scurrying, chatting, steam-breathing fellow students onto the frost-crisp lawn. He could see no familiar faces.

Puzzled, but in no mood for mysteries, he moved back onto the path – just as a stocky figure in an elderly flying-jacket, the fur collar pulled high, jostled his elbow.

'Paul – Schuyler – Schuyler Manton.'

The broad, grinning face suddenly registered. 'Oh, hi.'

'How you doing, Paul? You settling in OK?'

The grin, warm and self-indulgent, remained as they began walking. Paul shrugged non-committally. Since their first meeting in Paul's room, Schuyler had acknow-ledged his presence with no more than the odd, perfunctory nod. Such unexpected interest made him wary.

'I hear you had quite a celebration last night.' The grin was a sidelong leer now. Understanding dawned on Paul.

'Now wait – that was just a stupid misunderstanding.'

Schuyler laughed. 'That's not the way Julia Niles is telling it. According to everyone in McAllister you're a cross between Little Boy Blue and the Masked Rapist.'

Scowling, Paul swore under his breath.

'What are you complaining about?' Schuyler cried. 'It'll take me *years* to get a reputation like that! I mean, two different women within minutes of each other – that's the stuff of which legends are made!' He glanced round, ignoring Paul's stony expression. 'Hey, is your great-looking blonde friend around? Where did you find her? She's not at McAllister, is she?'

'She's a visitor,' said Paul flatly.

Schuyler looked back at him and frowned. 'Don't be so down in the mouth, Paul. Look, I'm seeing this girl from Grant House Thursday night. Why don't you bring your blonde friend along, make it a double date?'

Paul shook his head and paused; they had reached the steps to the Fine Arts building. 'Sorry. She left early this morning. I don't think she'll be back for a while.'

'That's too bad.' Schuyler screwed up his eyes and stared across the busy square. A buzzer sounded distantly from inside the building.

'I've got a lecture starting,' said Paul, turning to the steps.

'No, wait!' Schuyler spun to him suddenly. 'This girl I'm seeing has a friend. She's engaged or something but if I say it's you there shouldn't be any problem. We'll make up a foursome anyway. OK?'

His grin returned as Paul shrugged and nodded. 'Great! See you in Jackson lounge, eight o'clock Thursday. We'll have a sweet time. I guarantee it.' Hands deep in his pockets, Schuyler turned happily to go. 'Oh,' he added, spinning back, still retreating, 'I'd keep away from Kyle for a day or two if I were you. You really pissed him off jumping on his girl and spending the night on George's floor just about finished him! What a dork, heh!'

Laughing, he broke away into a sprint.

Perched high in a seat at the very back of the lecture hall,

Paul let the lecturer's droning tone waft over him, losing himself in the welcome gloom of a slide show.

The effects of last night's party punch, not to mention his exertions with Diana, had left him feeling light-headed and frail. Certainly in no mood to appreciate a rambling discourse on Masterworks of the Early Florentine School (with special reference to Giotto).

He had not wanted Diana to leave this morning. Waking with her in the pre-dawn darkness, her naked body tucked spoon-fashion into his in his narrow bed, had been an odd, an illuminating experience. In all the times they had shared a bed together at the Cape – and that, now he came to consider it, could not have been more than half a dozen times – he had never actually *slept* with her. Never seen her with her hair not shining and well-combed, her eyes slitted and sleep-fugged, her breath less than sweet.

Becoming aware of that, as he first stirred, his morning erection hard against her buttock, he had felt a twinge of unease, even of anticipatory distaste. But then she had stirred too, murmuring awake, twisting abruptly to give him a swift, tight hug before rolling out of bed.

And watching her pick her way, barefoot, through the discarded clothing on the floor, reassembling her belongings with a kind of brisk incompetence, he had been seized with a feeling that was half pity, half tenderness. Pity that her body looked pale and vulnerable and almost ordinary in the cold glare of the room's ceiling bulb, her shapeliness somehow subsumed in the mere fact of flesh. Tenderness from an unreasoning urge to shield that vulnerability – with clothes, with his arms, with himself.

It was a moment of sudden and almost overwhelming sentimentality, to which he did not give way only because he sensed that Diana would reject it. So he remained, chatting sleepily, companionably from the bed as she dressed, extracting a pleasure almost as secret and thrilling as sex from these moments of curious domesticity.

She had insisted he stay where he was, pecking him briefly, almost primly on the forehead – to his disappointment – before slipping out into the corridor. 'Maybe see you in the spring,' she whispered, flicked his light-switch and with a grin was gone. He had lain in the darkness for a long time before dozing off again, filled with a kind of heady, wondering glow he did not recognize.

All he knew was that Diana formed the centre of it. Diana offered a warmth, an excitement, an intimacy which mysteriously seemed to begin and not end with the release of orgasm. It would have been good to have explored such a feeling further.

A sudden flickering of light set him blinking. The slide projector clicked off; there was a groundswell of shuffling feet and murmuring voices as the audience rose. The lecture was over and Paul hadn't taken a single note.

Sighing, he slapped his ring folder shut and joined the crowd moving slowly toward the exit.

Now, it seemed, he did not have Diana but he did have a spurious notoriety. *According to everyone in McAllister* . . . . How did Schuyler Manton know what *everyone* in a co-ed dormitory thought at eight-thirty on a Monday morning?

Paul could guess.

His attitude to Schuyler had been neutral to begin with, shading into mild dislike when the sophomore seemed disinclined to encourage friendship. Instinctively Paul disapproved of his raucousness, his predatory approach to sex, which turned it into a contest rather than an equal sharing of pleasure.

But he couldn't deny that Schuyler's methods seemed to

work in this confused and frustrating atmosphere. Nor that he was flattered by the attentions of a local 'expert' in sexual matters.

The thought enlivened him as he came out onto the steps of the Fine Arts building. As he started down, a face caught his eye in the swirl of students at the bottom. It belonged to a girl in a bright red ski jacket; it was lean and full-lipped and pretty, framed by two swathes of dark, curling hair. Wide eyes returned his gaze in the same instant so that he found it impossible to say whether she recognized him or that he should recognize her; the face had a nagging familiarity.

She seemed to hesitate as he approached and his lips were just forming a tentative smile when he felt a sudden sharp jab in his side. A female voice hissed in his ear: 'Hanna – you're such a *shit!*'

Astonished, he glimpsed a small, red-headed figure darting away up the steps, vanishing in the crowd. Curious looks, even faint smiles flashed on either side. One expression was a deep, questioning frown. It came from the dark girl who had now drawn level with him.

He opened his mouth to speak but the incident had been so unexpected, so bizarre his mind was a blank. He shrugged vaguely and moved on down the steps.

At the bottom the dark girl's identity suddenly came to him. Her name was Barbara Howell; she was the Dean of Freshmen's daughter. But when he turned and looked at the steps again she had gone.

The black VW squeaked to a halt at the kerbside. Through the chill night air a pink and green neon sign winked garishly: PARADISE AL EY.

'Oh *no!*' shrieked the girl in the front passenger seat. 'A real motel! He really *meant* it!'

'Of course I meant it,' Schuyler said, turning from the wheel. 'I always say what I mean.'

'But I thought we were going back to Cheryl's room at Grant,' chimed in the girl in the back seat; she leaned across Paul's knees to do it.

'Well, if you want to have an intimate party with about four hundred co-eds passing the door, it's up to you.' Schuyler shrugged.

'Oh yes?' Cheryl nudged his shoulder, a look of knowing and gleeful suspicion spreading across her snub-nosed features. 'And what kind of *intimate* party did you have in mind?'

Schuyler remained straight-faced. 'Oh, a few drinks, some music, pleasant conversation – isn't that right, Paul?'

'Absolutely,' Paul nodded encouragingly from the back seat.

The girl at his side looked at him uncertainly. She was small and plump, with rounded features almost babyishly soft, straight dark brown hair, even softer eyes that reminded Paul of does. Her softness attracted him, but a hint of something harder underneath, a kind of wilfulness, even obduracy, had made him keep a polite distance.

'Well of course *he's* going to say that!' Cheryl twisted round to grin brilliantly at Paul. Her eyes, still shining, narrowed. 'I think we're being railroaded, Bernice . . .'

'Nonsense!' Schuyler let in the clutch so sharply the car leapt forward, squeezing a shriek from Cheryl. 'Want to be sure of a room.' He shot under the neon sign, swerved across the motel forecourt past a bright-lit office and bumped to a halt in an empty parking slot.

Instantly he turned and gave Cheryl a loud, smacking

kiss on the lips, pulling back a second later from her startled face and nodding to Paul. 'Time to do the business, buddy.'

Both of them piled out of the car. As they hurried across the forecourt, Paul said, 'I'm beginning to think she's right about being railroaded.'

Schuyler glanced at him and grinned. 'Well, naturally – and doesn't she love it!'

Paul frowned. 'You mean you've been with Cheryl before?'

'Twice – after parties. Get her wrecked and it's open sesame! She blames it all on the demon booze.' Schuyler laughed through his frosting breath. 'Jesus, I hope they've got the heating turned up in this place.'

'I can't see Bernice doing that,' Paul said. 'Isn't she supposed to be engaged to someone?'

Schuyler shook his head dismissively. 'Oh, just some crew jock. He's in the tank all winter – she never sees him. Anyway those guys are all slam-bam types. She's obviously in need of some subtlety, some finesse – or she wouldn't be out with you.' Chuckling, he nudged Paul's elbow. 'She *knows* your reputation. If she doesn't, Cheryl's told her. I've given you quite a build-up, young Paul. I'll be calling in a favour like that, too.'

They were at the office door. Schuyler pushed it open and went inside.

'What did you have in mind?' Paul asked, following him.

'Oh, we'll think of something.' Schuyler thumbed a buzzer on the counter, then turned, his voice dropping. 'I tell you, Bernice has a pretty nice body – not exactly skinny, but very cleverly stacked. I've seen her in the pool. You're a lucky – oh, we'd like two rooms, please.'

His tone changed as an old, blank-faced man in a base-ball cap shuffled into view. 'Might as well have them next to each other,' Schuyler added and glanced at Paul with a crisp smile.

'It's not,' said Bernice quietly, 'that I don't find you attractive.'

She glanced at Paul warily, trying to judge his reaction, her face a pale oval in the bedroom's gloom. He was gazing at the dim ceiling.

'It's just that I feel bad about John. Cheryl told me we were only going to have a drink.'

A low, throaty laugh filtered through the half-open door beside the bed. There were soft murmurs then Cheryl's voice whispering distinctly: 'No – I don't *want* the door open.'

A moment's silence was followed by a scuffling of feet. A hinge creaked. Turning and glancing across the bed, Paul saw the door between the two rooms close silently, cutting off the faint glow from next door.

Dropping his gaze, he realized Bernice, stretched out beside him in a frilly white blouse and jeans, her body barely touching his, was watching too. She sighed as the door clicked shut.

'Would you like another drink?' Paul asked. He reached for the half-empty gin bottle under the bedside lamp.

'No – it's OK. I don't really like it that much.'

Paul emptied the dregs in his own glass and set it down next to the bottle. He felt assailed by a curious lethargy – partly absorbed from the girl and her doubting uncertainty but arising just as much from himself. He could want her easily – her over-elaborate blouse, he guessed, was intended to diminish an intriguingly large bust, though in fact the garment's fussiness only drew attention to it. But, it seemed to him, its secrets held only a marginal, almost an

143

academic interest. He had the capacity for sex but something had sapped his will for it.

It wasn't a fear of repeating the Julia Niles fiasco – he
must be on surer ground here, if only because the girl had
made no attempt to leave. It wasn't even a resentment that
she could lie with him on a bed in semi-darkness and
discuss the impossibility of intimacy for well over an hour.
It was, instead, a kind of laziness, a knowledge that he
could do this so much more easily, so much more satis-
factorily with somebody else. He would not have wasted
even a minute – if Diana had been here.

The girl was talking again about her fiancé, her soft voice
reaching him through a fug caused, he now realized, by
alcohol; he couldn't remember whether he had just
finished his third or his fourth drink.

' . . . I think trust is so important. I mean, if you're going
to marry someone – eventually – it would be awful never
knowing who they were with, what they were doing. You'd
never feel right together otherwise.'

Something snared Paul's attention. 'That's true,' he interrupted her. 'It's got to *feel* right.'

The girl nodded, blinking at him. 'I'm really glad you
understand.'

'So it's really good with you and John?' Paul turned his
head to face her directly for the first time in minutes.

No more than a few inches from his in the dimness, her
eyes were suddenly wide and hesitant. 'We're very – close –
yes. John's very gentle. And good-looking, of course. He's
obviously got a fantastic future. And I realize, with all the
training he has to do – he's got a really hectic spring coming
up – he can't spend as much time as he wants with me –'

'But the time you are together,' Paul cut in, 'you can
make up for that?'

144

'Oh, certainly. Certainly.' She nodded twice, wrinkling her chin for emphasis. 'We have some really wild times. Next weekend we're going up to Vermont to ski – John's family have got a cabin we can borrow. There'll be about eight of us.'

'I was thinking more about bed,' Paul persisted.

The girl paused, her eyes darting away and back again instantly, as though nervous of meeting his gaze but even more nervous of not keeping a watch on him.

'That's OK.' She made an exaggerated shrugging motion, moving her whole upper body. 'It's fine. It's neat. John and I have a really nice time – really nice.'

For a moment she paused. Then she sniffed and looked away. 'Anyway, I think an awful lot of garbage, to be frank, is talked about sex. I mean, it's only part of a total relationship, after all. If two people have trust and respect for each other it doesn't really matter what you do or you don't do together. That's what John feels and I –'

Paul's attention wandered. He found himself concentrating not on the girl's words but her face, the way her lips moved, the fleshy curve between nostril and upper lip. For this reason he heard the noises first.

Initially they barely punctuated the girl's hushed tones; they were muffled and vague, only just penetrating the thin partition wall behind their heads – a grunt, a cough, a giggle that could only be Cheryl's. But as their volume grew, and the thinness of the wall became apparent, Paul saw in Bernice's face her growing awareness of their involuntary eavesdropping. Her blink rate increased, her voice faltered. Clearly the bedhead next door directly abutted theirs.

'*Schuyler!*' Cheryl hissed. And then the movements began – a steady, rhythmic pounding, composed of abused bedsprings, snatched breath, explosive gasps.

Bernice's eyes seemed to be swimming in her head, her cheeks turning darker by the second. Yet she seemed unable or unwilling to acknowledge the cause of her unease, gabbling on instead in an increasingly rushed and disconnected way.

Paul was fascinated by the cocoon of highly charged emotion that had so suddenly enclosed them. The girl appeared almost fearful, but her fear did not blunt her sexual sensitivity – on the contrary, it seemed to fuel it. Paul was aware of a sexual energy arising from them both, an energy he knew only too well, but for once it seemed to pivot on him, on his reactions. At the Cape he had been a receiver of others' desires, hardly ever an instigator. He had only glimpsed this kind of personal power with Anna Hornsiger, a power that seemed able to undermine, to override female reticence and uncertainty, paradoxically to take its strength from those doubts.

His eyes widened with this new realization, drawing an instant response from the girl, who took his change of expression for the sudden onset of passion.

'Hey – I think we should – just say something.'

Paul rose on one elbow, turning his body to her. Her hand rose awkwardly, lightly touching his chest. Her eyelids flickered. It was as if she were fending him off but only in the feeblest, most token way.

'Please,' she said.

Her duplicity intrigued and amazed him. She wanted him, but she needed to be subdued – by his overwhelming desire, by his power – whether *he* actually felt it that strongly himself or not. It was an excuse, like Cheryl's need to be drunk, or to appear to be.

The thought suddenly struck Paul as absurd. He

grinned, wanting to share the joke with her, but as he reached for the buttons of her blouse, she simply swallowed, fixing her eyes more firmly on his face, as though by not seeing what he did she somehow absolved herself of responsibility for it.

The illusion grew harder to maintain as Paul's desire began to stir, scattering his detachment. As he undressed her – and she had to help him with the elaborate catch of a support bra – her nervousness turned to a kind of resignation, a blinking withdrawal as though to forestall pain or disappointment.

Then Paul lost himself in her breasts' soft spillage, seeing her no more. They were broad, deep breasts, not sculpted like Anna Hornsiger's, but shaped by their own size and weight into loose, mounding pillows of flesh. Their warmth, their pliancy, their generosity entranced him.

Stripped, her body was the same, as softly padded as it was shapely, so deep in flesh that Paul felt he could wallow in it, finding its only tautness in the silken socket of her cunt. As he moved between her broad thighs, she winced and groaned under him, but when he glanced down, half breathlessly, her eyes were hard and open, staring into his chest.

'What's the matter?' she hissed. 'What's the matter? Why haven't you done it!'

There was an urgency, almost a desperation in her voice. She *expected* him to have finished after no more than two or three strokes.

Guilt pricked him. He was not giving her good sex – he was simply assuaging his own sexual curiosity, simply fucking her flesh, when originally he had had no real desire to fuck her at all. But he could hardly make that point now.

Deliberately he slowed, lengthening and deepening the

angle of his strokes, massaging her slick inner surfaces with the sides of his shaft. Under him he heard her breath catch. 'What are you doing?'

Concentrating, he matched his breathing to each thrust, squashing the urge to spurt swiftly, self-indulgently, building a rhythm that would include her too.

'What are you . . . ?' She started. He glimpsed her face, fearful, wide-eyed, wondering, her self-restraint, her unease forgotten.

And then the response began. A sudden panting spasm. An upward jerk of thighs that until a moment before had received him passively. A shaking rush of breath.

'Oh – oh – *oh*!' Abruptly she was frantic, clutching at him wildly, flailing her limbs, thrashing under him so violently he had to press himself to her to avoid being thrown off.

'What are you doing to me! What are you *doing* to me!'

Then, just as suddenly, she froze, her back arched; her body was whip-taut as her breasts lolled over her rib cage. And with a long, shuddering sigh she sank back into the mattress, inhaled softly and was still.

Paul stayed where he was for some moments, snatching back his breath in case she continued, then, as the sound of her breathing deepened, afraid that he might wake her. Eventually he raised himself, letting their flesh unstick slowly, and withdrew with as much care. Bernice made a faint murmuring sound, slipping onto her side, but that was all.

Paul sat up on the bed, astonished and rather pleased that he had managed not to ejaculate, even though his erection now ached abominably. The thought of spending himself, unacknowledged, in inert flesh did not appeal.

It had just occurred to him that silence now reigned in the adjoining room when the door eased open. Schuyler's tousled head moved cautiously into view. He beamed as he saw Paul. Nodding toward Bernice, he put two hands to his cheek and mimed sleep.

When Paul nodded, Schuyler beckoned him. Paul picked up his shirt and, knotting it loosely around his waist, went over.

'Ooh – eee!' Schuyler chuckled, rising on his toes in the shadow of the door. He wore only underpants, his thick chest dark with coiled hair. 'Quite a noisy lady, little Benny.'

Paul shrugged faintly, unwilling to respond to Schuyler's air of gleeful conspiracy. 'I don't think she'd come before.'

'Of course she hadn't! Not with a dumbo like John the jock sticking it in – I *told* you she needed finesse. You have a very grateful young lady over there.'

He ducked his head past Paul's shoulder. Paul turned. Bernice lay with her back to them, her buttocks round and pale in the shadow of the bedside lamp. When Paul turned back, Schuyler's eyes were gleaming.

'Look, is Cheryl awake? We ought to get back. I've got a seminar at nine tomorrow.'

'Hey, slow down.' Schuyler frowned. 'We haven't even begun yet.' His grin reasserted itself. 'Cheryl's just dozing for a while – but she's in a very accommodating mood . . .' He paused, meaningfully. Paul stared at him.

'Paul, do I have to spell it out? I've broken her in – she's raring to go. And she thinks you're cute – she told me.'

'You want to do a swap?'

'Fantastic!' Schuyler's eyes shone with mock surprise. 'I'm getting through! Come on – you owe me one. You haven't got anything special going with Bernice, have you?' he added suddenly.

Paul shook his head. 'She seemed pretty uptight to me.'

'Not when the Master gets going – Mr Super-erotico!' Schuyler punched Paul's smooth chest lightly. 'Cheryl is a peach – she's so sweet and tight. And she loves it from behind. That's a hot tip.' He nudged Paul aside to peer at the bed; sweat glistened on his upper lip. 'Look at that arse – *Jesus.*'

With a reassuring pat on Paul's arm, he eased past him and moved swiftly across the room with a kind of bulky stealth. Paul watched him go, then, as Schuyler knelt tentatively on the edge of the mattress, he turned through the open doorway.

The room beyond was in darkness, but the drapes were only partially closed. A neon glow picked out a patch of anonymous carpeting. At its far edge was the dark outline of the bed. Paul held his breath and listened. Cheryl made no sound.

He had liked the girl for her friendliness and vivacity, and admired her fresh, blonde looks. But he had been unsure of her slim, angular figure, which reminded him of Julia Niles. Any serious thought of actually having her, though, had only come with Schuyler's suggestion – and the sophomore's judgement still failed to impress him.

The undifferentiating ache in his crotch made up his mind. He approached the bed, items of discarded clothing snagging his bare feet. He was beside it before he realized the narrow bank of greyness he saw was a back. It was half turned away from him, sinously, a sheet wrapping the lower part, pillows hiding the head. Bending, he saw the steep inclines of shoulder blades, the rippled line of vertebrae.

He reached out and touched the skin. It was warm and taut, much tauter than Bernice's. He smelled a musky warmth. A soft sigh, half a purr, came from the pillows. The

150

spine stretched and the shoulder blades closed and opened beneath the flesh.

Paul felt his crotch stir, driving his hand. He fanned his fingers, spreading them into a caress.

The girl's purr broke into a low chuckle. 'That's nice . . . ' She breathed in as his hand moved downward.

Paul watched it move, absorbed by its progress and its daring, allowing it the illusion of a will of its own. He could believe that it didn't matter whether she knew who he was or not, that the anonymous intimacy, the extraordinary possibilities of this darkness were the only things of importance.

Cheryl lifted her shoulders from the pillows, keeping her head dipped so that a dark curtain of hair hid her face. She chuckled again, but her body was tense to the touch and, as Paul's hand reached the flat of her buttocks, she arched her back, letting the covering sheet slip away.

He came on her then, in a rush, catching the same note of sharpened breath as he felt her soft dampness. Yet still, when he climbed on the bed behind her and drew her cheeks back onto him in the darkness, she halted suddenly and twisted, fumbling backward to find and grasp his stiffened cock.

'Now *that's* better,' she purred. Then she straightened, just as abruptly, tossing her head and readying herself with almost businesslike efficiency.

This time there was no attempt at holding back. He plunged hard and deep, with a fierce, bucking energy that made her cry out. And immediately a sharper cry came through the wall. 'Who are *you*? Who are *you*? Go away! Get out! *Get out!*'

Panting, spent, Paul felt the girl under him go tense. 'Oh *no*,' she hissed angrily. Then she was gone altogether, squirming away, pulling herself free of him.

Instantly the door crashed open. The main light flared with blinding brilliance.

'She's *crazy*!' Schuyler's voice bellowed. 'The woman's goddam *crazy*! What did *I* do! What did I *do*!'

'Oh, Schuyler – you're such an *idiot*!'

The mattress heaved, rolling Paul onto his side as Cheryl flung herself off it. Blinking and utterly confused, Paul glimpsed her over-bright figure storm toward the doorway, elbowing Schuyler aside and disappearing into the adjoining room. A slamming door cut off a burst of sobbing.

'I don't get it.' Schuyler, taking shape now as Paul's eyes adjusted, gestured dramatically. He looked wide-eyed and flustered and very naked. 'I mean, you don't come to a place like this to play pat-a-cake, for Chrissake! Well, do you?' His gaze danced wildly, questioningly in Paul's direction. 'Well, *say* something!' he snapped. 'You're supposed to be the guy who handles situations like this!'

Paul weathered the other's stare for a full five seconds before the combined effects of alcohol, fatigue and coitus interruptus struck him in a wave of nausea.

'Oh for Chrissake,' he murmured, and buried his head in the pillows.

The image surfaced slowly like a reluctant apparition. A stretch of Long Island dune, two intersecting folds of wind-smoothed sand, anchored by bristling clumps of beach grass. In the ruddy half-light of the dark room it looked more than ever like the contours of a woman's body, barely abstracted.

Paul grunted and shifted the print in the developing tray. He had been thinking of Diana when he had taken the shot and, of course, nothing of her showed now. But the photograph still had a charge, a sensual impact that appealed to him. It would make a 'possible' for his portfolio.

Its monochrome tones reached their full darkness in the developing fluid. Lifting the print out, he rinsed it then moved it across the bench to a tray of fixative and dropped it into the clear solution. Knuckles rapped on the door at his back.

'Two minutes, I promise!' Paul cried automatically. Curwen's photographic department was still new, and darkroom facilities were in short supply. But a familiar voice responded hesitantly. 'Paul – is that you in there?'

Frowning, Paul threw a cloth over the fixative tray, then turned and unlocked the door.

Kyle Stevenson hovered immediately outside. He was wearing a dark green down vest over a faded blue shirt, a heavy sweater knotted incongruously round his shoulders. He looked glumly wary.

'I'm not disturbing you, am I? You haven't got a woman in there by any chance?'

Paul smiled thinly. 'Not today.' He glanced across the busy studio space beyond. 'You better come in or they'll think I've finished.'

He stepped back to let Kyle enter the narrow, cramped room, then locked the door again.

Since the Julia Niles incident Paul's relations with his room-mate had moved from strained silence to a discreet mutual avoidance. Only in the last few days had anything like normality been restored, mainly due to Kyle's sudden acquisition of a new girlfriend. But it was still a surprise to see him here.

'I didn't think historians ventured this far afield,' said Paul, returning to his trays.

'Oh, you never know – I thought I might stumble on the

153

odd nude life-study class. God, this place'd turn you into a vampire.' Kyle turned from squinting at the rows of drying prints and dragged a small envelope from his vest pocket. 'I was coming up here anyway to get my sweater back from Lisa and I saw this in your pigeonhole.'

Paul glimpsed the college crest on the back of the envelope and felt his heart sink. He had been wondering if anything official would follow Schuyler's motel disaster. On the ride back to Grant a tearful Bernice had threatened everything from legal action to castration. It had been just as well Schuyler hadn't heard it; Bernice had refused to get in the VW with him, and Paul had had to drive the girls home.

He pulled the print out of the fixative, rinsed it under the tap of a nearby basin and added it to the row of drying prints. Then he switched on the white light and took the letter from Kyle.

'Bad news?' Kyle asked.

Paul shrugged. 'Dean Howell wants to see me.' He glanced at his watch and straightened immediately. '*Shit* – in about twenty minutes! Thanks, Kyle. I was sleep-walking this morning – I didn't even bother to look.' He grimaced as another thought struck him. '*Dammit*, I'll never get back in here today.'

He began stacking prints frantically as Kyle resumed his wary expression. 'So it's true, then?'

'What's true?'

'That idiot Schuyler tried to jump on some woman from Grant in a motel the other night. And you were with him.'

Paul paused in his stacking. His room-mate's unexpected appearance now made sense. But he was still grateful for the interest. ' "Idiot" is right. It was my woman he jumped on, but I didn't see it happen.' Paul grunted. 'And *I*

154

was an idiot to go with him in the first place.'

The note of contrition was only half calculated, but it had its effect. It was easier to forgive the Niles episode if Paul appeared to have suffered in the same way. Kyle grew expansively reasonable.

'Well, I've known Schuyler quite a while through George, of course, but he always struck me as a little over-enthusiastic, if you know what I mean. I mean, we all spend enough time *talking* about sex. But Schuyler seems to need to *do* it whether the mood's right or not.'

Paul's faint smile was wry. This was the Kyle whose untapped sexual energy had threatened to pin a heedless Julia Niles to the carpet. A sexual outlet tamed the passions wonderfully.

'I wouldn't worry, Paul, seriously. If Schuyler wants to dig his own grave that's his concern. I'm sure you'll be able to square it.'

Paul nodded without conviction. He slipped his prints into a folder, tucked it under his arm and cast a quick glance round the darkroom. 'I've got to go. You coming down?'

Kyle shook his head. 'I said I'd see Lisa for coffee.'

Paul's eyes narrowed. 'Lisa? You mean, Lisa Halprin – that blonde from Bryn Mawr?'

For the first time since they had met, Paul saw his room-mate flush, if only mildly.

'Uh-huh. The one in your fine arts class.' Kyle's lips contorted in an effort to avoid mirroring Paul's sudden spreading grin. 'She's a great girl,' he persisted. 'And she's got this thing about togas.'

'It's about my daughter,' said Dean Howell.

For a dizzying moment Paul felt the floor and all the dark

panelling of the Dean's office recede at breath-taking speed. Could Bernice's – or Cheryl's – surname really be Howell?

Then he realized the Dean was smiling over his bunched fingers, using them to hide an uncharacteristic embarrassment. He even laughed, sliding back in his desk chair and glancing up at the ceiling.

'I'm sure you're not aware – and there's no reason why you should be – that Barbara recently had her eighteenth birthday. I know twenty-one is traditionally regarded as a more significant age for special celebration, but these days eighteen seems to me equally noteworthy.'

Paul nodded encouragingly, not at all sure where any of this was leading. It struck him that the Dean appeared to be wearing the same crumpled suit he had worn at their first meeting, only his shirt was now a yellow rather than a pink stripe.

'Mrs Howell and I have never been particularly adept with cameras, and we do seem to lack any suitable photographic memento of our daughter.' The Dean lowered his ceilingward gaze with a sudden darting glance at Paul. 'I'm sure you get my meaning – '

Paul's look was blank. This time the Dean's laugh was more strained.

'I'd be deeply grateful if you'd consider taking Barbara's picture – as a belated birthday present to her. I don't mean from you – naturally I'll reimburse you with whatever you consider appropriate.' He paused at Paul's expression of astonishment, which was in fact relief.

'I – er – ' Then Paul's mind caught up. 'I've concentrated mainly on landscape. Are you sure I'm the right person?'

'You are, according to Mr Wolcowitz – he's still your tutor this semester, isn't he?' Paul nodded. 'Apparently he's very pleased with odd portraits you've done – he likes

their spontaneity, and I'm happy to follow his judgement.'
The Dean shrugged expressively and smiled.

Paul raised his eyebrows, still surprised. The only portraits he had taken had been chance snaps to finish off rolls of film. He had shown them to his tutor no more than a couple of times, and with no apparent reaction.

'Well.' He smiled, realizing he was pleased and very flattered. 'Thank you, sir.'

'Don't thank me. Just make them as fine as those Cape photos of yours.' He was rising, rounding the desk and drawing Paul toward the door. Paul got up from his chair and followed. At the door the Dean lifted suddenly onto his toes as if to overshadow him, though their heights were similar.

'Your first commission, Mr Hanna,' he beamed, and, swooping for the door handle, pulled the door open. 'I'll talk to Barbara and we'll sort out the details. Oh here's the lady herself.'

Paul turned, to glimpse a bright red ski jacket emerging from the dimness of the corridor. Barbara Howell looked up, seemingly startled by the two figures in the doorway. Then she smiled, her long face springing to life.

'You'll be glad to hear I've been successful, Barbara,' the Dean announced. 'I've persuaded Mr Hanna here to immortalize you on film.'

The girl slowed as she drew close, looking from her father to Paul in a bright-eyed, wondering fashion, tugging awkwardly at a neck strap on her jacket until it popped open.

'Well – that's fantastic.' She appeared embarrassed, either by what her father had said, or Paul's presence or the entire situation – he couldn't tell. Whatever the cause it seemed right for him to go.

157

'I'll see if I can borrow a studio in Fine Arts.'

'No need for that!' the Dean boomed; generosity clearly made him effusive. 'My wife has a room at home she uses for her painting. Plenty of light, superb views. It's ideal. I'll organize it. Would the weekend suit you, Mr. Hanna?'

'Yes sir, yes. Fine,' Paul replied, without even thinking about the extraordinary offer. He found himself returning Barbara's uncertain but far from unhappy gaze.

'This is really good of you,' she said.

'We'll be in touch,' the Dean cut in brightly, with a brisk, dismissive smile, and ushered his daughter into his office and shut the door.

The house was a leftover from grander times, a warty accretion of ill-assorted gables and turrets and porches, marooned at the end of a wide and very modern suburban avenue which might have been only a farm track when the house was built. Flanking trees masked it from full view until Paul halted his trailbike directly in front. The steely light of spring was not kind to the flaking clapboard façade.

At least the house's size matched the pretensions of a college head of faculty; its age and its incongruity in these surroundings seemed to Paul peculiarly appropriate to Curwen.

He felt a ripple of unease as he propped the bike and unstrapped his metal camera case from the carrying-rack. *He* knew what he was doing here – he had travelled a lot further than this to explore new photographic possibilities. What worried him was everyone else's motives.

It didn't bother him at all that Dean Howell was plainly exploiting a student's enthusiasm to save himself money. He was more concerned to know why the student should be him. There were at least two other members of Paul's course who had taken a particular interest in portraiture. Why should he be so favoured?

He couldn't quell a suspicion that Cora-Beth was somehow involved, though in what way or for what reason he couldn't fathom.

He walked past a dusty station-wagon and climbed the steps into the gloom of a vast porch. A stout, strong-featured woman with silver-grey hair tied back in a bun answered the doorbell. She was dressed comfortably in baggy Levis and a paint-spattered checked shirt. Her fierce, pale eyes scrutinized Paul minutely before she broke into a swift polite smile, as if she were donning a mask.

'You must be Paul Hanna. I'm Judith Howell. Do come in.' She sounded as brittly effusive as the Dean. Paul stepped inside, wondering which of them had been like that first.

Inside, the house was smaller and lighter than he had expected. Untidier too, after the faded austerity of the Dean's office. There were books and magazines everywhere: literary for the Dean, artistic for his wife, Paul presumed. She led him through to a long, low-ceilinged living room with french windows overlooking an unkempt lawn.

'Of course,' Mrs Howell was saying, 'we've always tended toward traditional forms of representation. They always seem to me more personal somehow. But I suppose a photograph is so much more immediate.'

Paul nodded politely, only noticing as Barbara entered, interrupting her mother, that the wall nearest him was covered with small paintings and sketches of the Howells, all clearly by the same hand.

'Hi. I was just changing.' Barbara smiled with a kind of gawky grace Paul hadn't noticed before. Then she shrugged, dropping her eyes half-apologetically to the long, puffy-sleeved gown she wore. 'I hope this isn't too formal. I wore it at my last prom, but it's the only decent thing I've got.'

'I think it looks lovely, darling,' Mrs Howell said with a sudden warmth that surprised Paul. 'It shows off your colouring marvellously.'

Paul looked at it again and saw that she was right; its pale blue matched the colour of the girl's eyes, and threw into vivid contrast the darkness of her hair. She looked very attractive.

He became aware that the two women were looking at him as if for comment. 'It looks great.' He glanced round quickly to cover his inability to think of anything more startling. 'Is there any place in particular where you thought . . .?'

'I'll show you,' said Mrs Howell.

They trooped upstairs behind her, passing two landings, to a broad, sun-filled attic which seemed to span the house. There was a desk and a massive chintz-covered sofa at one end, an empty easel and the paraphernalia of oil-painting at the other.

'My little hideaway,' said Mrs Howell, as if she were not at all keen on sharing it. She immediately began to bustle about the room, pointing out odd items that could make props – a polished wooden seat in a dormer for 'the ideal setting', the blue swirl of the Connecticut River over the rooftops beyond for 'a superb background'.

Paul endured it with a sinking heart and rising irritation. He was here because Mrs Howell couldn't operate a camera. They didn't want a portrait photographer, they wanted a cut-price camera technician. Until with a wry exasperation – more exasperated than wry – Barbara broke in: 'Mo-ther . . . '

The older woman paused and looked at her daughter with a surprise that was clearly feigned.

'Mr Hanna knows what to do – he's extremely competent. And Father wanted spontaneous pictures. They can't really be that if you're telling us exactly what to do all the time.'

Paul, who had been watching and making motions of polite assent from the middle of the room, saw the mother's face change subtly but instantaneously, as though one mask had suddenly and miraculously evolved into another. A battle, it seemed, had already been fought and this was no more than a final, face-saving skirmish.

'I'm sure you're right, dear. I'll be downstairs if you need anything at all.'

She left in silence.

'Look,' said Paul, as soon as she had gone, 'I don't want to tread on anyone's toes here – '

The girl shook her head abruptly, her expression shadowed. 'It's not your fault. My mother and I argue – we always have. I'm going to college in the fall, anyway.' She glanced at him and her face cleared. 'Oh I'm really sorry,' she said. 'The photo was Dad's idea but I thought it would be more fun to use a person from college. I never meant to embarrass you.'

It was Paul's turn to shake his head. 'I'm not embarrassed. This is your mother's home – she can do what she likes. If you want to leave things for now I'll understand.'

'No! No – don't do that. You've brought all your things – and I spent *hours* getting ready!' She laughed then, infecting Paul with her sudden vivacity. Some of his unease lifted.

161

For someone he had seen no more than four or five times, and spoken to hardly at all, their rapport surprised him. And she was pretty too.

'Well.' Paul grinned back, lowering his camera case to the floor. 'I suppose we better start.'

She watched with interest as he knelt to unload a telescopic tripod, a flash unit, a roll of film, his Leica. 'God, that looks so gnarled and professional! It looks as if it's been through a war!'

'It has,' Paul told her, pleased at the remark. 'My father brought it back from Europe. He used it for years. The lens is incredible. It's even been through a plane crash.'

Barbara's eyes widened appreciatively. 'And your father passed it on to you?'

'Only in a way.' Paul opened the camera and reached for the film. 'The crash killed him. It was the only thing left.' He glanced up at her quickly, instantly conscious of being stupidly flippant, even brutal. Seeing her start, he felt a spark of perverse pleasure in the effect and an upswelling of shame that he did.

'I'm really sorry,' she said.

'No.' He shook his head; he was playing games again – the games he'd learned to play away from the Cape – and there was no need for them here. 'Thanks, but it was a long time ago.' Hurriedly he finished loading the film. 'You know, I think your mother had a point about that window seat –'

But she still watched him, with a wariness midway between sympathy and solicitude. Embarrassed, Paul grinned. 'Do you want to sit over there?'

She went thoughtfully, settling herself inside the dormer, her body half turned towards Paul, her face lit by sunlight from a window opposite.

'That's nice,' Paul said, rising and framing her within the viewfinder. The shutter release clicked softly.

'My mother actually isn't my mother at all,' Barbara said suddenly. 'My father was divorced. It's really why my stepmother and I don't get on too well. I know most of it's my fault, but sometimes it's so hard to control your emotions.' She paused, and a stiffness overtook her features as if she was revealing too much too quickly. 'I know what it's like to lose a parent, especially one you're very fond of.'

Paul paused too, lowering the camera. He was aware that Barbara was making an effort to be open with him and, presumably, to demand the same in return. His immediate reaction was to resent the invasion of his privacy; the situation was fraught enough as it was. But he found himself saying, 'You never really forget, even if the details get fuzzy.'

Her eyes sparked immediately. 'I *knew* it! I knew we had something in common when I first saw you. I have a real instinct for that kind of thing.'

Her enthusiasm made Paul smile.

'No, seriously!' she insisted. 'It's happened to me several times before. I only need to look at a person, before we've said a word, and I know if I'm going to be able to talk to them or not. Do you remember your father really well?'

The question caught Paul unprepared. 'I suppose – I mean, I was pretty small at the time – ' Then, in spite of himself, he did remember, and, remembering, began to talk, self-conscious at first then less so as Barbara nodded encouragement, her clear blue eyes concentrating on him, until he was surprising himself with recollections he had not thought about for years. The past had never been taboo at the Cape, but Cora-Beth had not encouraged him to dwell on it either – '*This is your new life, Paul . . .*'

163

And when he paused she began to talk, just as freely, of her real mother, of herself, of the stepmother downstairs. As she did, Paul picked up his camera again, excusing himself at first as he took a picture. Then another, and another, moving about the seated girl for fresh angles, letting her expressions dictate the rhythm of the shots.

The lustre, the plasticity of her face fascinated him. By seconds it changed – with the movement of muscles, the changing sunlight, the shadows of darkly rippling hair. It was a landscape sprung to life, but a landscape more subtle, more exciting, more beautiful than any he had photographed before. And it was only when she burst out, laughing, 'Hey! How much nearer do you want to get? Aren't you going to leave me any clothes on!' that he realized how physically close he had come.

Grinning, he sank back on his haunches. 'I think some of those shots are going to be great,' he said.

Barbara beamed down at him, her eyes round and shining. 'I think so too. I really felt it – a nice kind of electricity.'

Paul nodded and glanced down at the camera. He was at the end of a roll. He rose, and was immediately aware that the excitement of the shooting had had a more physical effect. He drew in his stomach, hoping that the folds of his jeans would hide any obvious tumescence – as a hand touched tentatively against his thigh.

She stared up at him, her gaze brimming and intent. She rose in front of him. 'I'm sorry – I didn't mean to – ' Then her mouth turned up to his and they were kissing.

Her lips were soft and sweet-tasting, folding back on his with the pliancy of Anna Hornsiger's. Paul felt sucked closer and closer as the mounds of firm breasts pressed into his chest and the girl's thighs locked with his. Then the reactions of his body outpaced all thought; his cock surged to stiffness and he was grasping the girl's slim back, lowering her to the floor when a sudden awareness of where he was, who he was with came to him in a flash.

'What is it? What's the matter?' Barbara hissed as he pulled back, snatching breath. 'Don't you want to?'

He smiled wanly. 'It's not a question of wanting or not.' He took a deeper breath. 'We're not exactly alone, are we . . . ?'

Barbara shook her head. 'She won't come up here.'

Paul's eyes widened. 'Well, I'm not so sure.'

Then he froze as footsteps thumped just beyond the door. With a start Barbara moved back from him.

'Barbara!' Mrs Howell called. 'Your father's having trouble with the car again. I'm going to fetch him in the station-wagon. Will you be all right?'

'Oh sure!' Barbara coughed as her voice squeaked. 'We'll be just fine. It's all going really well!'

'See Mr Hanna out for me, will you?'

'No problem!' She turned to face Paul as the footsteps retreated, a smile spreading, then turning into a full grin as the front door slammed distantly. 'No problem at all,' she murmured.

Dusk was falling as Paul sped from the Howells' street, passing the Dean's dusty station-wagon as it turned from a side avenue. If the occupants recognized him, or even saw him, they gave no sign.

The cool air ruffling his hair added to his sense of buoyancy. It had been so easy, as easy as falling off a log, as easy as a Cape seduction. Suddenly all the months of subterfuge, of guile, of endless persuasion and sheer effort were swept away. Cora-Beth, in her own bizarre way, had a kind of wisdom: when all guilt, all hypocrisy vanished only enjoyment remained. And spending himself between Barbara Howell's thighs – thighs as slim and as sweetly tender as Diana's – had been very enjoyable indeed.

'You know it was me,' she had murmured, nuzzling the curve of his chin as they had lain semi-naked on the huge chintz sofa. 'You know I got my father to pick you for my pictures. He'll do anything I say.' Then she had giggled at a sudden thought. 'I dreamed you'd get me to strip – and then *do* things to me. With my parents right downstairs. Isn't that wicked?'

'Oh, that's *really* depraved,' he had encouraged her, feeling her small, round breasts squash into his chest as she burst into soft chuckles.

The incident was a turning-point for Paul. There were rules in the world beyond the Cape, rules that changed subtly and unpredictably with each new circumstance, but rules which could be learnt, which differed not in essence from those he had grown up with. The discovery boosted his confidence enormously. All he felt he had ever needed was a key, an edge, and now it seemed that he had it.

The photographs underlined his new confidence. Seeing them appear in the developer Paul felt that stab of surprise which signalled something fresh and exciting. Later the doubts crept in – technically large numbers of the shots were poor, the focus variable, the framing odd. But in more than a few there was a vitality that pleased him immensely, a vitality that seemed the best part of the subject.

In the end, unable to select the most representative, he assembled a simple montage, a series of six, featuring as many changes of expression. Each, in itself, was mobile, incomplete; viewed together they made a whole, a continuous portrait. Or so it seemed to Paul.

And so, apparently, to Dean Howell. After delivering the photographs to the Dean's office Paul received a brief but glowing note of thanks, promising a settlement of accounts following an imminent conference at Wheaton. 'I think our little experiment more than justified itself,' the note finished.

Two days later, crossing Small Yard by the light of a spectacular sunset, Paul heard footsteps accelerate along the pathway behind him and felt a sudden nudge in the middle of his back. Startled, he spun round. A slight figure in a hooded windcheater stood behind him. Backed by the lurid sky, the face was shadowed and indistinguishable. Then the hood was yanked back.

'Cheryl!'

Her snub nose came up, her teeth gleaming and even in the dusklight. 'If you hadn't recognized me, Paul Hanna, I'd have hit you again – harder!'

Her tone was impish. Paul grinned, flattered that she remembered him at all. 'Well, I wouldn't have if it hadn't been so dark.'

'You!' She aimed a sharp elbow at his ribs, causing him to leap aside onto the grass. Laughing, he regained the path, warmed by Cheryl's look of mock wrath. So there was no hypocrisy, no guilt here, either.

They continued toward the ochre-washed façade of Jackson House.

'I meant to tell you,' Cheryl said. 'I had a pretty nice time on our big night out – especially towards the end.' She brushed against Paul as they walked, glancing up at him.

'So did I. I'm really sorry about the trouble with Schuyler.'

167

'Oh, Schuyler!' The girl hissed exasperatedly. 'I haven't even *talked* to him since. Some people are just so unsubtle it's unbelievable.'

'How's Bernice?'

Cheryl drew in her breath. 'She and John are having a few problems. He doesn't know about – that night,' she added quickly, then shrugged. 'I've never gone for muscles, myself. I prefer something more subtle.' She was grinning at him again, sidling closer. 'You did some pretty nice things to me, you know. I was kind of surprised you didn't give me a call.'

They had paused at a junction in the path, one way leading straight on toward Jackson and Big Yard, the other branching leftward toward the female dormitories. Paul dug his hands into his jacket pockets.

'Well,' he said, 'I don't need to call if you're here already.'

Cheryl's expression was speculative. 'That's true.'

They regarded each other, slow grins forming.

'So,' said Paul, 'why don't we get together sometime this evening?'

Immediately the girl launched herself forward. 'My room – 301 – Grant – eight o'clock,' she hissed. Her lips pecked his cheek in a swift, dry kiss, and she was gone, haring off down the branching path. 'Don't be late!' she called.

Paul watched her go, a smile replacing his look of shocked surprise. He felt mildly stunned and highly de-lighted. Every day should be like this. Perhaps every day *could* be a day when he behaved as he had at the Cape – more circumspectly, certainly, but with much more control of his own destiny.

When he turned back toward Jackson, students were

streaming from the passageway leading from Big Yard, blinking and raising their arms against the glare, suddenly aswim in horizontal sunlight. A splash of red caught Paul's eye. He frowned, uncertain at this distance, then lifted his arm.

'Barbara!' he called. The figure in red immediately turned and darted back through the crowd, disappearing.

Puzzled, Paul moved closer as a voice called: 'Oh hard cheese, Hanna, only *two* women to screw tonight! Looks like a quiet night after all!'

Sniggers rose from the passing crowd and spectacles flashed in the dying light. Paul recognized George Manton. He was walking with Kyle Stevenson and Lawrence Hoffman. They slowed as he went to join them.

'What's up with you, George?' he asked.

George's expression was dour. He sighed. 'Cheryl Thingamajig is actually supposed to be Schuyler's girl. I suppose you realize that?'

'I thought *everybody* was Schuyler's girl,' Lawrence pointed out.

'George is pissed off because Nancy Hamburger is playing the field,' Kyle explained boredly. Then his tone brightened. 'But what I want to know is why does the sight of my room-mate send the Dean's lovely daughter into a panic?' He grinned. 'You haven't been a *really* naughty boy, have you, Paul?'

'Nancy and I have just agreed to enlarge our relationship – that's all,' George resumed tartly. 'And I don't see what the hell difference it makes to anyone else!' He bounded up the front step of Jackson House and crashed through the door, leaving it to slam behind him.

'Well, of course, that is an interesting point of view, George,' Kyle said amiably. He turned to Paul. 'We're

169

going for a beer. You coming?'

Nodding, Paul followed the other two into the entrance hall. Lawrence made for the stairs, then paused when he saw that Kyle was moving in the opposite direction. 'Aren't you coming up? I've got half a crate of Budweiser just sitting there.'

Kyle frowned. 'I'm not going into your room again without thick sunglasses, Lawrence. You live inside a centrefold. You have naked female flesh on every inch of your walls. I don't know how you can stand it. Your nerve ends must be raw.'

Paul was grinning as he finished. Lawrence merely blinked. 'Well, over-stimulation doesn't seem to be a problem for me, Kyle. In fact I find masturbation has quite considerable advantages over conventional sexual outlets. It's easy, it's inexpensive, you meet a really available kind of female . . .'

He dashed up the stairs as Kyle lunged at him. Paul stepped back, laughing. 'Ugh!' Kyle grimaced, just missing Lawrence's retreating back. 'I won't touch you! You're unclean!' He halted, gasping on the stairs, as the noise of running feet continued above. 'Aren't you coming?' he called upward.

'Too much work!' Lawrence's voice echoed down the stairwell. 'Anyway, my women need me!'

'Jesus,' Kyle whistled, grinning as he rejoined Paul. 'I just hope he's as intelligent as everyone seems to think. Sometimes I think I'm the only normal human being I know.'

'Thanks,' said Paul. 'Is it my webbed feet that bother you, or the fact that I keep pushing your stuff back onto your side of the room?'

They moved down the hall to a small lobby which contained coffee and Coke machines. For a short time in the early evening canned beer was sold here, too. Buying two cans each they took them back into the lounge and found an unoccupied corner.

'Seriously, Paul,' Kyle said, cracking his can, 'there's more to life than fucking and taking photos. I mean, for a basically normal kind of guy you don't need to carry on like Schuyler Manton.'

Paul lowered his beer, grinning. 'A minute ago I was some kind of Martian.'

Kyle looked peeved. 'Listen to me. I *live* with you, I *know* you. You're not trying to prove you're Superdong –'

Paul shook his head, surprised and amused by such seriousness from his room-mate, at least in a state of sobriety. 'You listen, Kyle. You're having a great time with Lisa – she makes you feel marvellous and that's great. So why not lie back and enjoy it? And when you meet somebody else who's just as nice, enjoy that too. It's that simple. It really is.'

Kyle glanced away and back again, grunting. 'It's not that simple, Paul. It really isn't.'

Someone called Paul's name from the lounge entrance. When he waved his arm a face in the doorway said, 'Call for you' and vanished.

Paul gave his beer to Kyle for safekeeping and went out into the hall. It was empty, but the receiver of the wall telephone under the stairs was hanging down. He picked it up and gave his name.

A small, taut voice said very distinctly: 'You didn't call me.' For a blank moment Paul had no idea who was speaking. The statement tangled with his conversation with Cheryl, confusing him. Then he thought the caller might have misheard his name. Then he realized who it was.

'Barbara! How are you? You sound strange.'

'Who was she?'

Paul frowned, lost again. This sounded nothing like the bright Barbara he knew, yet too odd to be a joke. 'I don't know what you mean.'

'The girl outside. The blonde with the hood. The one who kissed you.' Her voice sawed, gratingly. Paul blinked.

'I *thought* I saw you. That was a friend. Her name's Cheryl. She's at Grant. Why didn't you come over?'

'Have you been to bed with her?' The question shot out, in a single rush of breath, jostling the words.

'Once, yes.'

The silence was so long Paul thought she had left the phone. Then, close but muffled, he heard a single strangled sob.

'Barbara, are you sick? Can I do anything?'

'You could have phoned me!' Her voice sawed again, strained through invisible tears that instinctively made Paul wince. 'It's been *three* weeks. You didn't even show me my pictures. You didn't even do that.'

Paul sighed. None of this seemed to be making the slightest sense. 'I gave them to your father. He commissioned them. I only did what he asked.'

'Did he ask you to *screw* me?' This was a sharp hiss in his ear. 'Oh I'm sorry, I'm sorry, I didn't mean that.' There was another sob.

Paul gazed impotently up and down the hall. Beyond the entrance hall glass, dark now from the falling night, a male face was looking in at him. He leaned out from the angle of the stairs to see it more clearly but it vanished.

'Barbara,' he murmured.

She seemed to reply from a great distance. 'Didn't what

we did *mean* anything to you? I thought we were so close – we talked so easily – and we did such wonderful things – ' Her voice broke momentarily. 'You don't think I do things like that all the time, do you? Is that it? I've *never* done anything like that before – with anyone!'

'It was fantastic, Barbara,' Paul said quickly. 'One of the best times ever. I'll always remember it.' His voice fell as several students passed from the lounge and went upstairs.

'I *knew* it! I *knew* you felt it too!' The earpiece was suddenly buzzing with her excitement. 'I don't care about the pictures – I mean, seeing them – they're lovely, I really love them. I just want to see you. Can I come round tonight?'

Paul hesitated. He liked the girl, he desired her, he had enjoyed making love to her, though no more than to many others, and their one time together had been against his better judgement. Now her sudden and bizarre intensity worried him. But he had no wish to be hurtful.

'Let's talk tomorrow.'

'You're seeing that blonde girl tonight.' The tension was back immediately.

'Yes I am – '

'And you'll sleep with her – I *know* you will! Oh, you shit, Paul! You little shit! You're just like everyone said. And I was so sorry for you when that girl was so rude to you outside the Fine Arts building – I thought *I'd* never be like that to anyone, no matter how shitty they were to me. But I expect *you* don't even remember her name – '

Paul tried to interrupt but she swept straight on.

'Oh, I've been so stupid – I feel so *stupid*! Well, you just wait. One day someone you really care for'll treat you like nothing. *Then* you'll know!'

The receiver crashed down.

Blank-faced, Paul replaced his own receiver and found his hand trembling. The fury, the hatred in the girl's voice, and all they had ever done together was enjoy themselves . . . . Familiar uncertainties began to curl about his heart. Surely it wasn't all going wrong again?

A muted ripple of laughter from inside the lounge distracted him and he remembered Kyle and his beer. He straightened up. No. People were different. Barbara Howell's oddness didn't make all girls the same. He was still right. He was still on course.

The outside door opened. Paul stepped away from the stairs and saw the face which had peered through the glass during his call. It belonged to a tall, fair, heavy-built youth in a sweatshirt and what looked like tracksuit bottoms.

He came in hesitantly, nodding toward Paul. 'You're not Paul Hanna, are you?'

The youth's face was square and fleshy and pink, his eyes shadowed and red-tinged, as though he had been drinking or jogging in a sharp wind. Paul did not recognize him.

'What's the problem?'

'You're a friend of Bernice Stettinger – over at Grant?'

Paul nodded, frowning. 'I know Bernice, yes.' Why didn't the other youth look at him? He seemed almost diffident or distracted by something, his gaze darting about the deserted hallway.

'She wants to see you right away.' He immediately turned back toward the door.

Paul laughed. First Cheryl, now this, in a single day. 'Hey, wait. Jackson isn't exactly out of bounds, there's the phone – why does she need messengers?'

The youth sighed. 'Look – I was asked, I happened to be passing here, I volunteered. OK? Ask her yourself. Are you coming or not? I've got to be at Grant in two minutes.'

Paul shook his head, grinning. He had been convinced Bernice had had everything out of him she needed. But the day seemed destined to prove the unpredictability of women.

He shrugged. 'OK. But this is crazy – I'm due at Grant at eight anyway.'

The youth skipped through the door ahead of him and set off to the right at a cracking pace.

Curwen Little Yard was in moonless gloom, its pathways pegged by circles of dim light beneath infrequent lamp standards. Once they had passed the spreading glow of the Jackson lounge they were in semi-darkness.

'Don't you have any idea what this is about?' Paul called to the figure in front of him.

Abruptly the youth spun round, reaching out his hand and slapping it hard against Paul's chest, stopping him dead. If Paul hadn't been rendered breathless out of sheer astonishment he would have been winded.

'Yeah. Sure I know what this is about. It's about trust, it's about decency, it's about taking advantage of women who are officially engaged to be married. But mainly it's about this – '

Paul didn't see the fist. He simply felt the stinging crack to the side of his face. Then his head snapped back and he was sprawling somewhere leafy and damp-smelling. There was movement all around him, but the numbers of feet seemed wrong.

Broad hands clutched at his arms, yanking him upright again, propping him. Faces bobbed to left and right, but only the one in front of him, grey in the darkness, seemed familiar.

The youth who had hit him was breathing heavily. 'There's always a patch of rottenness in every year, Hanna

175

— some little dickhead who thinks he can stick his cock wherever he fancies. Well, some people won't stand for that. Some people have principles. Some people think you ought to learn some too!'

This time the blow came from below, swinging upwards into his stomach. Paul doubled up, belching air at first in a rasp of agony, then a spattering of half-digested food.

'Jesus! Mucky bastard!'

He swung, groaning, between his captors as each tried to avoid the dribble from his lips. 'Hit him again, John.'

A second blow struck the side of his face, making his head ring. He didn't know where the third arrived because it knocked him unconscious .

6
RACHEL
1974

'Barry, I feel silly – '

'No you don't. You look absolutely fabulous. Lean forward a bit more. Now don't move!'

'Barry – these things are too small!'

Bent from the waist, her hands outstretched to touch the edge of the bathroom vanity unit, Rachel broke into uncertain laughter. She lifted her head and looked at her small, flushed features in the oval wall-mirror, then down where her breasts bulged absurdly from the cups of a tiny white filigree-edged bra, then further still to the similarly patterned suspender belt and the white stockings beneath.

'I feel like a tart, Barry.' Her brow knitted as she realized he was no longer behind her. 'Barry!' she cried suddenly. 'You're not getting that camera again!'

The flash lit up the bathroom, doubling in the mirror and blinding her as she turned. 'Oh you rotten swine,' she said, blinking. 'Why are you always doing that? You know I hate it. Oh *God*, I didn't even have my knickers on! Give me the picture!'

'No, I can't – it's not ready yet.' Chuckling, Barry pushed out an arm to hold her at bay as he knelt, depositing the Polaroid camera round the corner of the door-frame. Then he rose, pulling Rachel against his bare chest, wriggling his pectorals against the taut cups of her bra, and

177

watching the constricted flesh above them wobble and pout.

'What are you *doing*?' His renewed chuckling brought a reluctant smile from her. 'I said these were too small – they're really uncomfortable.'

'They look all right to me.' He glanced up into her face as her frown deepened. 'I told you, I get them off a mate in the trade. Freebies. I can't quibble about the odd inch here or there. Here, go back where you were.' With a broadening grin, he began to turn her round.

'I'm supposed to be in the office at nine today.'

Barry shook his head quickly. 'Holford's won't miss you for ten minutes. Dozy old wankers. You're only there to make up numbers, anyway. Go on, bend over – look what you've done to me! I can't go out like this, can I?'

Rachel twisted her head to glance back. The thick towel which Barry had tucked about his waist – his only garment – bulged massively at the front.

She looked away, glimpsing in her mirrored face the nervousness that leapt inside her, allowing herself to be guided by Barry's hands, one at her waist, the other between her shoulder blades, bending her forward and down.

'I thought you just wanted to see me try these things on.'

'Come on, love. I'm only human, aren't I?' As she stretched out her arms to balance herself against the vanity unit once more, he reached down her back, breaking the clip of the bra. 'That's better, isn't it?'

His eyes found hers in the mirror and he grinned, lifting his hands beneath the released cups, cupping them to receive the pronounced curves of her breasts.

'You've got fantastic boobs, Rachel,' Barry breathed, watching his hands gently knead the firm flesh. She felt him

178

shudder against her. 'Jesus, I've never seen such incredible boobs.'

His face had that look Rachel knew of old – an anonymous rapacity. The frantic activities of the last two weeks had shown her quite clearly what it involved. But now there was something else there, too: a kind of awe. It pricked her vanity, redeemed some particle of self-esteem from a maelstrom of conflicting emotions she hardly dare examine.

'Christ, Rachel.' Barry swallowed, his eyes glazing momentarily. 'Sometimes it's just not enough to fuck you.' But as he spoke something rigid and warm prodded her inner thigh. She dipped her head. The red, bell-shaped tip of his erection protruded from the gap between her half closed thighs, parting the thick hair of her mons.

A rasping chuckle came from Barry's throat. He was clutching her tightly now from behind, moulding his body to hers so that she felt every movement. 'Looks like young Percy's going to insist on his oats.' He began to heave his thighs backwards and forwards in a sawing motion, rubbing the soft tissues of her sex with the veined edge of his shaft.

She tensed, feeling her body respond in spite of herself. 'Don't you want to lie down?'

'Why? It'll be all right.' He was moving more urgently now, each stroke drawing the tip of his cock further back along her crease, closer and closer to the point of penetration. Rachel twisted uneasily, suddenly terrified of being hurt.

Abruptly Barry reached downward, palming her mound, squeezing his length hard against her moistened lips so that it sank between them.

'Get your bum higher!'

His other hand rose between ner legs, urging them apart.

Rachel moved her feet awkwardly, feeling him slide further down her back, bending at the knee as he sought the right angle to enter her. She shuddered, seeing her face in the mirror, pale and blank-eyed, someone she couldn't recognize.

'Barry – '

Then she gasped as his tip slipped suddenly between her inner lips, rolling into and out of the ring of muscle that marked her vaginal opening.

'*Shit* – I can't – ' He gave a breathless laugh. 'You'll have to get longer legs, Rachel!' She tried to look at him as he straightened again, but immediately he was drawing her backward and down.

'Come on, love – we'll do it on the floor.'

They had had sex in this fashion only once before, early one morning when he had seized her from behind as she climbed from bed. She both hated and welcomed its impersonality.

When he lay on top of her she could see his face and gain some sense of intimacy from the proximity; she could judge her own reactions by his expression; she could feel confident that what she did was right. She could also enjoy that single special moment just after he was spent when his urgency changed abruptly into a childlike softness: the one moment between them that promised to match her expectations of tenderness.

None of that could happen in the rearward position. Then, she simply received him blindly, unable to gauge his excitement except in the most obvious ways. Yet his face-lessness absolved her of responsibility, turning his stabbing thrusts into a kind of masturbation, so that it could be anyone making love to her, phantom lovers from her fantasies, even Donny.

180

She tried to imagine that now as his cock probed her moist opening, sliding between the upraised cheeks of her rear. But the trick would not work. She was too annoyed with herself for agreeing to put on his tarty underwear – the sort of thing May wore.

Barry came quickly, in short, deep, jerking movements, grinding his pubic bone hard against hers to leave her hot and gasping. And then he was gone, withdrawing abruptly and still partially erect as he did whenever he did not fall immediately asleep.

'You'll be the death of me, Rachel,' he murmured, patting her rump as he stumbled past her to the shower.

She dressed in the bedroom while he washed. The clothes were new – a skirt and one of three blouses she had bought on her first weekend in London when Barry had gone to Marlow for 'urgent consultations' with his partner. He had lent her the money to buy them as an advance out of her first week's wages, temping in a dusty barn of a typing pool high over a warehouse at the back of Liverpool Street.

Alone in the flat for two days and two nights, she had begun by exulting. She had money, she lived in plush surroundings, she had a lover who was young and rich and generous and who desired her utterly. For long moments a roseate glow would enfold her – all that her life required to make it perfect was for Barry to declare his passionate love, perhaps even set a wedding date . . . . The thought shocked and thrilled her with its daring.

But then, as the long evenings had worn on, the glow shaded with doubts. Barry did not telephone – he had not said he would, but that was hardly the point. For almost a week she had made love with him, tidying the flat by day and preparing his evening meal for his return, and yet within a day all that was forgotten – or so it seemed to her.

181

When she saw the Jaguar pull up outside late on the Sunday night her relief had almost choked her. She had flung herself at Barry as he opened the door to the flat, clinging to him fiercely and feeling tears sting her eyes. But he had pushed her back with a look of blank surprise and annoyance, and with a rush of blood to her face she was suddenly convinced that he had not expected her to be here at all.

Then he had smiled. 'Christ, Rachel, let me get through the door first.'

Kissing, she had felt his desire stir and responded as fervently as she knew how, forcing him never even to dream of forgetting her again. In his urgency he had taken her on the edge of the leather sofa, only yanking down her pants in his eagerness to enter her. Then, as he did, he paused, gazing down at her so wonderingly she thought that this of all moments would be the one to declare himself.

'Bloody hell, girl,' he had murmured, 'you just can't get enough, can you?'

As she left the bedroom, Barry brushed past her, shrugging on a shirt.

'I'm just off,' she told him.

'No, hang on.' Drawers rattled behind the bedroom door. 'I've got to go up west this morning. I'll give you a lift.'

Barry's head popped round the door jamb, bobbing as he stepped into trousers. 'By the way, I'm off to Marlow tonight, so I'll see you Sunday – all right?' His expression darkened as Rachel's face fell. 'Now come on, Rachel, don't throw a moody. This is business – the last thing I want to do is go barging about the countryside at the weekend.'

'I don't see why your partner can't come here for once,'

Rachel snapped, not hiding her sourness. 'It's been every weekend I've known you –'

'Moneymen, love.' Barry had disappeared again. 'Fellows who hold the purse-strings. You have to keep them sweet. It's sad but it's a fact of life. He insists on going over the books – in person – every week.'

'But I thought you were rich.'

There was a high, bright laugh. Barry reappeared, shoe-less, pulling on his suit jacket. 'Not that rich, love. Not yet.' He yanked something from his jacket pocket. 'I've got one quick call to make. Go and sit in the car, eh? I'll be two minutes.'

Rachel hesitated; Barry's sense of time was extremely flexible. 'Shall I make you a coffee?'

'No!' Annoyance flashed across Barry's face. He slapped the car keys into Rachel's palm. 'It's a confidential call – all right? I just need a bit of peace and quiet.'

Stung, Rachel half turned away. 'Wendy'll be in the office by now. I'll go down and say hello.'

'*No!*' This time real anger seized him, shocking her. 'For Chrissake, girl, how many times have I told you I don't want you in the office! It's not that hard to understand, is it? Now go and get in the bloody car and don't give me bother!'

His arm shot out suddenly, snatching at her elbow, spinning her round and shoving her forward. She stumbled, almost crushing the Polaroid, which still lay on the carpet outside the bathroom door. She glimpsed the developed print sticking from the back: a huge, bleached close-up of her rear and upper thighs, her puckered sex picked out in its ring of dark hair.

She plunged blindly across the living room, bumping against the furniture, seething with humiliation and rage and a horrible fear. He had never struck her before, never shown such a total dislike, almost *hatred*. And a moment before he had been inside her . . .

A stiff lock slowed her at the front door. As she tore it open the purr of dialling sounded from the bedroom. 'Sorry, Rache. Two minutes, eh?'

She halted in surprise. Then turned back, just as Barry's voice – so matter-of-fact before – became animated. 'Hello, Roger? Where've you been, you old bastard? I've been trying to get hold of you all month – '

Calmer, Rachel walked slowly down the stairs to the street door. It had not been hatred – it had been the frustration of a single moment. Relief flooded her, but it did not conquer her fear. Fear that she had done something to provoke him, that she had upset him by not enjoying that stupid underwear or objecting to his silly photographs. . . . And then her spirit rebelled.

Why did it bother her so much what he thought? He was good to her, yes – he shared his flat with her, he found her work through his agency. But she cleaned the flat, she cooked meals, she washed for him. She never went out with him, she never saw him at weekends, she was forbidden to have any contact with him at work – even during the first week when she had been at home upstairs and he had been working in the office directly beneath.

It was as if he were ashamed of her, but not too ashamed to make her wear ludicrous underwear, to take pictures of her almost naked, to screw her every night he was there.

That was the nub. *That* was what bound her to him. The fact that he *had* her – and she let him – over and over again. And that splendid, terrible deed dominated every thought of him, confusing every emotion so that most of the time she had no idea whether she loved him, liked him or, sometimes, even fancied him.

A white envelope lay on the mat. Picking it up she saw it was addressed to Barry. It was the first letter she had ever seen delivered to the flat. Another sign that they lived in a kind of limbo.

She told herself she was being silly and slipped the letter into her bag.

The Jaguar was parked outside, but it was a bright, crisp morning and she felt like clearing her lungs; Barry's penchant for keeping the central heating at full blast left her throat prickly and dry.

As she waved at Wendy through the glass door of the office, a voice said: 'Hello, stranger! Come back for that drink, have you?'

Startled, Rachel spun round. Derek stood grinning at her, his hands plunged into the pockets of an open reefer jacket; underneath, typically, he wore only an open-necked shirt.

'You don't even remember me, do you?'

'Course I do!' Rachel cried, seized by the fiercest urge to hug him. As his grin broadened she gave into it, rising on tiptoe to plant a swift, affectionate kiss against his cheek.

'I believe you!'

She moved back, reddening. She had glimpsed him twice in the street from the flat's window. She had been tempted to seek him out at the hotel during her lonely weekends, but a sense of loyalty, and perhaps shame, had stopped her.

She felt that now as he nodded up at the flat. 'I see you've gone up in the world.'

Rachel's blush deepened. 'It's just somewhere I'm staying –'

'Hey – ' Derek reached out to touch her arm. 'I'm not chucking stones. You're doing very well. Seriously! I didn't expect a girl like you to be on her own for long. As long as

185

you're all right –'

'Yes, I'm – fine –' She hesitated, embarrassed to talk about Barry. A woman slipped past her toward the office with a brisk, 'Excuse me.'

'I've got a job too.'

'Fantastic!'

'I only started on Monday. It's in the City –'

She paused, her sudden flush of pride cut short. The woman who passed her had not gone into the agency. She was opening the street door of the flat. Frowning, Rachel watched her disappear inside.

'Look, I'm sorry, Derek. I've got to go.'

Derek caught her arm again as she started back toward the flat. 'I'll be in the hotel bar tonight. Half-six. Pop in for five minutes. Bring your boyfriend, if you like.'

'Yes, I'd like that. I'm sorry, Derek –'

Who on earth . . . ? Rachel's heart gave a single thud as she eased open the street door and began to move up the stairs. Something was very wrong. The woman, whoever she was, could not have mistaken the address; she had her own key. She couldn't be a thief, either, because she had clearly gone straight up, quite undeterred by Barry's voice, which still filtered down the stairwell.

The front door was ajar. Rachel opened it fully. The living room was empty. Then she saw a handbag – burgundy leather, polished and expensive – lying open on the sofa. A rich, fruity perfume – equally expensive – hung in the air. Barry's laughter came from the bedroom.

'I'm *not* joking, Rog. A genuine bloody virgin! Really bloody, too – you should have seen the sheet the morning after. Yes! I thought I'd never have one. And she is a little doll – tits that'd make you weep, and her arse – Christ! My

186

cock's going to need splints if she stays much longer – '

The woman Rachel had seen stepped out of the kitchen. She was slim and sharp-featured, striking rather than pretty. The fur coat she wore was open and pearls showed against a dark jersey beneath. Her eyes, a cold and livid green, focused on Rachel without surprise.

'And I suppose you're the little doll,' she said, her accent London and crisp. Her hand came up, a long cigarette between slim, red-painted fingers; she drew on it quickly, hardly inhaling at all. 'Barry's tastes seem to be getting younger. How old are you? Eighteen, seventeen? I suppose you *have* left school?'

Contempt showed through the woman's tone, intimidating Rachel as much as her self-possession, her obvious familiarity with the flat and Barry.

'Who are you?' Rachel's voice sounded ridiculously frail.

The woman inhaled again, even quicker than before, moving to stab the cigarette into a glass ashtray on the coffee table.

'Just the person who pays for this little love-nest.' She spoke through neat streams of smoke. 'Signs the cheques for Barry's little toys. His car, his suits, his tarts – '

Rachel felt the colour sweep up her neck. 'But he's got a partner who gives him money. In Marlow.'

'That's right.' The woman straightened and the look in her eyes made Rachel flinch. 'A marriage partner. Or did he neglect to mention that little detail?'

From an accelerating beat, Rachel's heart slowed. She felt herself retreating, from her surroundings, from the present, from a revelation that suddenly made perfect sense.

'I didn't know.'

'You surprise me.' The woman's gaze narrowed and

Rachel saw that her nerves were as taut as piano wires and that she was younger than her clothes and her manner had suggested.

There was a click from the bedroom as the telephone went down and Barry bustled down the short hallway.

'Rachel, I thought I told you to wait in the – '

His mouth dropped open as he saw the two women. 'Oh, fucking hell.'

'More like fucking *heaven* from what I hear,' his wife snapped. 'Shall I throw her out, Barry, or will you?'

Barry hesitated a moment as if struck dumb. Then he lifted his arms in a gesture of helpless innocence. He gave a brief, hollow laugh.

'Sonya, you surprised me, love – I expected to see you tonight.' He assembled a smile. 'This is Rachel, she just started downstairs. I was just running her to a booking.'

The smile wavered under his wife's unblinking stare.

'You or me, Barry. We don't want an ugly scene, do we?'

Without a word or a backward glance, Rachel turned quickly and left. As she went down the stairs high heels thumped across the carpet and the door above her slammed shut.

She passed her working day in a curiously anaesthetized state, punctuated by sudden bouts of relief and, increasingly, a dread that was only partially rational. When she finished and asked the snuffly, cardigan-wearing middle-aged man for whom she had made tea and sorted files all week to sign her time-sheet, he told her that the girl she had replaced would be back the following Monday; Rachel was no longer needed. The news added a further notch to her unease, but did not surprise her.

It was dark when she returned to the agency. The

windows of the flat were unlit and there was no sign of the Jaguar in the street. Rachel passed the office twice before she was sure that Barry was not inside.

She opened the door as Wendy was shrugging on her coat.

'Hello there. You don't have to bring your time-sheet in, you know. Posting's all right .'

'I thought I might get the money tonight.'

'Oh, that isn't how it works.' Wendy was brisk but not unfriendly. 'We pay on Thursday. By post, or you can pop in if you like. But I don't suppose you want to do that.' Her eyes caught Rachel's, holding them for a moment until Rachel dropped her gaze in hot embarrassment.

'We heard the battle all morning,' said Wendy. 'I thought for a while the ceiling wouldn't take it.'

'I just had no idea,' said Rachel quietly.

'No.' Wendy picked up her bag with a smile and began switching off desk lamps. 'Doesn't exactly advertise his marital status, does our Barry.'

'Why does she put up with him?'

Wendy shrugged, raising her eyebrows. 'Don't ask me. I just interview the girls, make the coffee and tell him to keep his hands off my knees.'

She echoed Rachel's faint smile. 'He asked me to get the key off you if you popped in. But I'd nip up now and pick up your things, if I were you. Sonya'll have the locks changed by Monday.'

She turned away to switch off the main light. When she turned back her expression had softened. 'I honestly wouldn't take it too much to heart. You're not the first and you certainly won't be the last. And if you're going to take a pair of scissors to his wardrobe, or a flame-thrower or whatever, have a couple of blasts for me while you're at it!'

*

189

'Chin up,' said Derek.

Smiling, Rachel lifted her glass and drank. 'That's nice. What is it?'

'Campari and orange. Don't you watch the telly?' He frowned at Rachel's blank look. 'Your education has been sadly neglected, my love. Stick with your uncle Derek and enlightenment will be yours.'

They sat on stools in the bar of Malik's hotel: a small basement room as faded and over-decorated as the rest of the establishment. A ventilator hummed above glistening ranks of spirits and exotic liqueurs. They were alone.

'That was a genuine offer, by the way,' Derek went on, more seriously, as Rachel's smile subsided. 'Free access to my sofa until you find somewhere better. Share expenses. Give me some rent when you can afford it. And I promise no funny business unless you feel like it – in which case I demand first refusal.'

This time Rachel did not smile. She looked down at her glass, then sighed. 'I can't give you any money until next week. I don't know after that. I think I only got work this week as a favour to Barry.'

Derek drained his beer glass in a single draft. Breathing in, he shook his head. 'Live one day at a time. Next week is next week. OK?'

Rachel turned to him. 'You're really kind,' she said.

He laughed. 'Hey, slow down. This is pure self-interest. A couple of days being seen around with a girl like you and my reputation's going to rocket. I'll have more offers than I can cope with.' He put down his glass and rose from his stool. 'Now sit tight. I've got to have a slash.'

When he had gone Rachel sat quietly, fingering the stem of her glass. She felt wrapped in a peculiar vulnerability, balanced on the finest line between exultation and despair,

190

confidence and complete uncertainty, but still balanced – just.

Live one day at a time. She hated the uncertainty of that, and had no choice but to accept it. And if Derek wanted what Barry had had – and she was learning to trust no man on that score – then she would give it, as Derek deserved it more. But she hoped he would not ask, because she needed a friend now much more than a lover.

Her nose prickled. She lifted her handbag and looked inside for a tissue. Frowning because she could see none, she rummaged deeper, turned over an Underground map and saw an unfamiliar white envelope tucked between the folds. Puzzled, she pulled it out and recognized Barry's mail from the morning. Her first impulse was to tear it up. But intruding on even this small part of the life Barry had kept so secret seemed a better revenge. She opened it.

It contained a single sheet of pale cream paper. At the top in dark blue hollow capitals was the word 'Prince' with a London address beneath. She read:

Dear Mr Drew,

Thank you for letting us see your photographs of your girlfriend, Rachel. We agree that she is extremely photogenic and could well model for *Prince* magazine.

Could you ask her to telephone me at the above number and arrange an interview?

I am afraid I am unable to give you a definite figure for a modelling fee. This will depend on the results of any photo session we might arrange. But our minimum payment to models would be in the region of £100 a day.

Your finder's fee will be payable when Miss Turner's pictures are accepted for publication.

Thanks again for your interest and I look forward to hearing from Miss Turner in the near future.

Rachel read it again twice, blank incomprehension changing to a scalding embarrassment that began at her crotch and finished at her scalp. Barry had shown *those* pictures to complete strangers, to the staff of a magazine –

A cover, bright, colourful, a girl pouting over a scrap of a bikini, flashed before her mind's eye; something Donny had bought, snatched away with teasing laughter as she reached for it. But she had glimpsed the warm expanses of flesh, the pouting lips, the sly smiles . . . poses from May's 'album'.

In a fit of anger she crumpled the letter and flung it away.

'Malik'll be down in a minute. Here, you dropped something – '

'Leave it!'

Derek was bending as Rachel twisted on her stool. '*Prince* magazine!' He rose, frowning as he smoothed the sheet; his brow cleared as he read on. 'Bloody hell – '

'*Derek!*'

He turned away as Rachel made a grab for the letter. 'But this is fantastic!'

Rachel paused, staring at him. 'What do you mean?'

'Well, it's not some tatty tit-and-bum rag, is it?' Derek looked up, his eyes gleaming. 'It's a classy mag. I mean, you get top models in a thing like this.' He gave a grunting laugh. 'A hundred quid a day! Aren't you flattered?'

Rachel's expression wavered. She had not anticipated this kind of reaction – not from someone she regarded as a friend. It undermined the certainty of her anger, confusing her.

'I just don't want to do anything like that.' Even to

herself the reason sounded limp. She blinked at Derek's repeated laugh.

'Have you ever looked at *Prince*? I mean, looked through it properly?'

Rachel did not reply.

Derek reached towards a coat-rack and lifted off his reefer jacket. 'Come on, ' he said quickly. 'I must have a copy lying around at home. If you're going to throw away a hundred quid you might as well find out why!'

Derek's flat was five minutes away, on the second floor of a large, terraced Edwardian building whose tall porticoes peeled grey-white paint so evenly as to resemble some form of fungal growth. In the broad, tiled hallway a side-table shed avalanches of unclaimed mail. The air smelled musty and old.

There were faint cooking odours on the linoed landing. As they reached Derek's flat a door slammed higher in the building and footsteps clattered, but no one appeared.

Derek's living room was long and narrow; a high ceiling and truncated cornices showed it had once been part of a much larger room. The furniture was sparse, ill-assorted and cheap. It looked like a place to spend the night in, not to live. The contrast with Barry's luxury lifestyle could not have been greater, and a part of Rachel groaned at its loss.

She sat on a tall, plain brown sofa, feeling springs twitch under her, while Derek rummaged in a chaotic bedroom to the right of a tiny kitchenette. He returned, triumphantly, with two magazines, one missing a cover, and dropped them beside Rachel.

As he made coffee, she looked through them – gingerly at first, as though wary of what she might find, then with increasing interest.

'Well?' Derek asked, plumping down at her side and handing her a warm mug. He bent forward to switch on a small fan heater.

The pages opened across Rachel's knees showed a centre spread: a girl in her late teens, tall, blonde, clean-looking and nude; she stood facing a wall, glancing back over her shoulder with a look of wary invitation.

'There's some very attractive girls in it,' Rachel said.

Derek nodded. 'Didn't I tell you? They don't have rubbish. They get actresses, girls off telly ads. All sorts.'

Rachel turned the pages, cautious of acknowledging his enthusiasm. To be sitting next to an attractive man, poring over pictures designed to titillate him, made her nervous – both pleasantly and unpleasantly. She was glad his jacket was still on and buttoned. Deep down, a sudden thought – instantly expunged – wondered whether it was to hide his erection.

'I think that's a good picture.' She prodded a view of a girl sitting against a tree, her head tilted back, eyes closed against bright sunlight, her white blouse open, exposing pale golden breasts.

As Derek grunted, she turned the page. Now the same girl sprawled on her stomach sacross a fur-covered divan, bare buttocks uplifted to the camera, black lace knickers stretched into a thin line between her widespread thighs where the darkness of the material mingled with the shadowed tangle of her pubic hair.

'And that's ridiculous!'

'Why do you say that?' Derek frowned. 'That's a horny picture.'

Rachel's lip curled scornfully. '*No one* looks like that. It's not how people behave. You just wouldn't lie around like that.' To her consternation, she found herself blushing.

'You'd feel silly. *I'd* feel silly, anyway. Do *you* know anyone who lies around like that?'

To her relief Derek seemed oblivious of her burning face. 'I wouldn't mind getting to know them,' he muttered. He picked up the magazine and flicked through it. 'It's fantasy, though, isn't it? It's just meant to be a turn-on. It's not meant to be real.'

'But the girls *are* real people.' Rachel stabbed a finger at a passing page. A dark girl, naked from the waist down, squatted on a sofa, her knees splayed. '*She's* real! You're not *imagining* you can see – between her legs. That's *her*. And it doesn't even look sexy. It's like saying, "This is what mine looks like. What do you think?" It's just crude.'

She was trembling as she finished, but Derek simply shrugged.

'Blokes are curious about things like that – and you can't tell me women aren't. Anyway, what's it matter what blokes think? The girls are only putting on an act for the camera. They're not doing it front of anyone, are they?'

'What about the photographers?'

'They're top professionals for a thing like this. They've got to be. They're guys with reputations. I'm sure they have their fun, but they're not going to make much of a living if they have non-stop orgies all day!'

Rachel grunted, her expression dark. 'You don't know that.'

Derek sighed. He slapped the magazine shut, threw it aside, and grinned at her. 'I'm only trying to help, love – I'm not even going to get the finder's fee . . . . ' He shook his head, wonderingly.

'You tell me you're not qualified, you can't get work, you've got no money. But you're a beautiful girl – you could knock half the women in that mag into a cocked hat.

They're even *offering* to give you a chance!' He paused, suddenly more serious. 'You've got to grab your chances in this life, Rachel. You've got to learn to capitalize on what you've got. I wish I'd done that years ago.'

He was quiet while she put the second magazine on the floor. Then she sat gripping her coffee mug. 'What would you think if you had a girlfriend – who appeared in that?'

Derek's laughter was sharp and sudden. 'Fantastic! Bloody fantastic!' His jollity disconcerted her. 'It's a laugh, Rachel – that's all. Treat it as a big laugh – on all the silly wankers who'll buy the mag, if you like. For a hundred quid a day you should worry – seriously! Seriously!'

Rachel stared into the pale brown swirl of her coffee. The fan heater hiccuped and began to make a grating sound. She felt very serious indeed.

He had come home late and they had gone straight to bed, making love swiftly and fiercely but with an energy that seemed to burn itself out a moment before consummation. Ejaculation followed penetration within the same heartbeat, and as his dead weight pressed her into the mattress Rachel felt puzzlement and disappointment.

It deepened when he roused himself only to ask for cigarettes – he had forgotten to buy any on the way home. There was an off-licence on the corner which would still be open.

'Barry, it'll be freezing.'

'It's mild out. Oh come on, Rachel, I've had a knackering day.' She went, stifling feelings of grievance with gratitude, her desire to show willingness, to impress him. Wearing only her coat, her skirt and shoes, she took longer than she'd thought – someone was stocking up for a party.

She undressed again in the lounge and tiptoed into the bedroom. Barry was propped on one elbow peering at something spread across her pillow. As she pressed the side of the mattress he swivelled in surprise, his face flushed, as though he had been unaware of her till then.

She saw the magazine first: the photograph of a young woman, blonde, deep-bosomed, nude, spreadeagled across a quilted bedspread, her hand between her open thighs in a posture Rachel knew from May.

As a chill touched her breast, her eyes caught Barry's hand. It rested in his lap, the purple tip of his erection squeezing between his curled fingers.

The chill turned to ice. His gaze faltered as it met hers.

'What are you doing?'

She saw his face change, from embarrassment to boldness to a kind of deliberate recklessness. 'I'm enjoying my magazine.'

'But I'm here.'

'I know. This is different.' He twisted towards her, pushing back the sheet, reaching out to take her arm. 'Here, kneel down.'

Hesitantly, she complied, not knowing what he wanted, nervous of him.

He moved closer to the edge of the bed, reaching up to draw her head down, turning his erection towards her.

'No.'

'What's the matter?'

'I won't. Not that.' Her eyes were dark and frantic, startling him. He shrugged.

'Don't move.'

He rose onto his knees, looming over her. As she looked up at him he edged closer, balancing himself with a hand on her shoulder. The curving shaft of his penis butted the tip of her breast, slipped sideways into her cleavage. He reached down, scooping each breast, urging the rounded flesh inward until it covered all but the bulb of his erection.

He began to pump slowly from his thighs, rubbing himself against her. 'We really need some powder, or oil.'

She blinked at him, steadying herself as a more vigorous thrust rocked her. He was glancing back at the girl in the photograph.

197

'Why do you like her? Is it because she's blonde?'

'I just like the picture, that's all.' He grunted and breathed in sharply.

'Is it because she's got a bigger bust than mine?'

He shuddered violently, gripping her shoulder again. Rachel looked down. The bulb of his penis, already thickly engorged, swelled faintly: there was a bubble of moisture in its eye. Then he gasped, his whole body stiffening; his thumb rubbed across her nipple.

'Christ _'

She flinched as the first spurt of seminal fluid splashed against the underside of her chin. A second spattered the flat of her chest. As the thick liquid began to dribble between her breasts he let go of her, gulping air as he slid back onto the mattress.

'Jesus, Rachel. That was incredible. . . . '

She looked down where his head rested on the magazine, the girl's expression of calculated ecstasy crumpled next to his closed eyes. Already his semen was cooling on her flesh.

She got up, went into the bathroom and turned on the shower. When the water was almost scalding she stepped beneath it and soaped herself, over and over and over again until long after she was sure he was asleep.

Typewriters clattered in the high attic room. Entering, the stocky, moustachioed young man frowned momentarily at the huge colour proofs that seemed to cover the entire floor, but his annoyance hardly dented his grin.

Across the room one of the typists looked up from his machine. 'Don't tread on those, I'm just about to do a cut-up!' He paused as he noticed his colleague's expression. 'You saw her?'

The stocky man nodded enthusiastically. He picked his way to his desk, snatching up a packet of cigarettes.

The third occupant of the room, who was pale and

bespectacled and even younger, stopped typing too. 'The little yummy with the dark hair?' he asked.

The stocky man nodded again, even more enthusiastically.

'Did you get her to strip?' The guardian of the proofs rose from his chair.

The stocky man sniffed. 'Wouldn't take her bra and pants off. Great little bod, though. *Very* sexy face.' He made loud lip-smacking noises of approval.

The proof-guardian frowned. 'If Alastair finds out you've been seeing models behind his back he'll go bananas.'

'He's not here and she wanted to see someone today. What could I do? The editor *is* supposed to delegate occasionally.'

The bespectacled typist grinned slyly. 'And the fact that you get a nice kickback from the photographer if you pass her on privately has nothing to do with it.'

Lighting a cigarette, the stocky man shrugged. 'Perks of the job.'

As the other groaned, the proof-guardian asked, 'How old is she?' When the stocky man told him he hooted in delight. 'Gaolbait! Alastair'll cream his pants. Who did you give her to?'

The stocky man breathed out smoke. 'Max Wallace.'

'A sixteen-year-old to that old wanker!'

'He pays better than anyone else.'

'Only because he has to!'

The stocky man looked peeved; by his own lights he had made a good deal. 'She'll be all right. She's a little toughie. You've only got to look at her to see that.' His grin re-formed itself. 'What a cutie, though! I reckon she'll make a centre. I might give her to the Swedes as well.'

'Mercenary sod,' said the proof-guardian. He knelt to sort his proofs, losing interest.

The stocky man chuckled and rubbed his hands together gleefully. He beamed. 'I feel lucky today. Anyone fancy a quick thrashing at backgammon?'

The middle-aged man who had been staring fixedly at Rachel from Regent's Park left the train at West Hampstead. Deliberately she turned away as he passed the carriage window opposite, still eyeing her as he went down the platform.

She breathed in as the train gathered speed again, only mildly relieved by his departure. It still astonished her that some men could be so blatant, or so unself-conscious, in the way they looked at girls. Once she would simply have been irritated and embarrassed. Now she was aware that a subtle and heady game was underway, a game in which she could find herself a player without warning and usually without choice.

But it was a game she was determined to master, just as she had mastered her own fears and misgivings when she had unzipped her skirt and lifted her jumper in the offices of *Prince*. Just as she would do again this afternoon.

It had not been easy contacting the photographer called Max Wallace. The two numbers given by the man who had seen her at *Prince* – for home and studio – seemed either constantly engaged or unattended. Eventually, late at night a dry, rasping voice, gruff and off-hand, had answered from the home number.

'Yeah, sure. Come on up tomorrow. I've got a shoot after lunch. We'll do some test shots.'

She had to draw his studio address and directions from him. By the end of the call he had still not asked her name.

She had only reached her first name when he interrupted, 'Yeah, fine. Fine.' And the line went dead.

In a way his rudeness made everything easier. If she had to do this thing, she wanted to do it angrily, defiantly, showing how much she despised herself for it and everyone involved in it. Anger, too, was a more reliable emotion than self-possession.

She came out of the Tube station into a busy North London thoroughfare, clogged with heavy traffic and wind-blown refuse. In dusty side-streets lunch-hour street markets were packing up. The ugliness of the area reminded her of home; its unheeding bustle seemed peculiarly London.

Following Wallace's directions, she found a turning of Victorian terraces, jostling and ornate. Halfway down, a row of garages interrupted the pattern. Above them was a single storey of what appeared to be offices, the windows metal-framed and blinded. Stairs led up the side. The door at the top was open.

Inside, Rachel found herself in a short corridor with two doors opening off it. The one at the far end looked like the entrance to a storeroom; the second, which faced her, had frosted glass. A large beach umbrella and some folding chairs were propped against the wall to one side.

Uncertain, she knocked at the glass. When there was no answer she turned the handle.

The room beyond was tiny and chaotic. If it had once been a reception area, or simply an office, only a desk and two padded office chairs bore witness to the fact. All three were piled high with rolls of coloured paper, strips of plastic film, boxes, magazines, and odd lengths of plywood and polystyrene, which spilled onto the intervening floor space.

As Rachel hesitated a door on the opposite side of the

201

room burst open and a girl entered, wafting bars of low rock music with her. She was short and dark, with Italianate, almost over-lush features that instantly struck Rachel as both extremely attractive and faintly sluttish. The heavy breasts that lolled, apparently bra-less, beneath her loose, vee-necked sweater added to the effect.

Her face set in a look of childish rage, she ignored Rachel, clattering behind the desk, where there was a small cleared space, ringed with used paper coffee-cups. She sat, sweeping her long, thick hair back from her forehead in a gesture that was as practised as it seemed careless.

With a shock Rachel realized who the girl reminded her of; it was herself – the girl could even be her age. Did *she* look as obvious, as available, as this?

The thought kept her silent as the girl flicked rapidly through a desk diary, then stood up, slapping it shut with an impatient gesture.

'Is Mr Wallace in?' Rachel asked at last.

The girl's dark eyes barely flickered at her. 'He's got a shoot on.'

'Is he going to be long? He did ask me to call.'

The girl gave a swift, mirthless smile as she rounded the desk. 'All bloody night at the present rate.'

She snatched up a jacket from a pile of cardboard boxes and made for the door, pausing just as she reached it to give Rachel a single, searching look. Her smile returned, wry now and curiously bitter. 'Why don't you pop in, anyway – see the master at work? I'm sure he won't mind.'

Rachel turned her head toward the door through which the girl had entered.

'Yeah – the studio's through there. Go on in and say hello.' The girl's expression was almost mocking, its

202

mystery annoying Rachel as much as it disconcerted her.

'Have fun!' The girl laughed and went out, banging the door.

Rachel nearly turned and left too. But she told herself this was a new world, probably quite different from the view May and her father had given her. What had Derek said? *These are top professionals . . . guys with reputations.*

No more reassured by the thought than before, she sighed softly and went to the studio door.

She opened it a crack. The music still thumped, louder if anything; as she listened a man's voice grunted, a woman's replied, followed by laughter, a sharp clicking sound like high heels on a hard surface.

Rachel opened the door further. Behind it was a narrow, windowless passage; the only light issued from the open doorway of a cupboard-sized room to the left. She glimpsed the edge of a mirror ringed with light bulbs, a shelf piled with make-up, female clothes heaped on the end of a small table.

The opposite end of the corridor, only a short distance beyond, opened into a dim, shadowed area.

As Rachel stepped through the office door, closing it quietly behind her, the man's voice called out, 'Come *on*, Josey. Don't piss me about. I got Steph and Teri to shoot today. You're costing me money as well as time – '

It was the voice Rachel had spoken to on the telephone. There was a sigh, the scraping of a heel.

A large wooden frame filled with sheets of hardboard, which towered over Rachel's head, marked the end of the passageway. She looked through the end struts into a room of almost Stygian darkness; walls, floor, ceiling were painted a uniformly matt black, momentarily confusing her sense of perspective, making it impossible to judge whether the further side was a hand's breadth or some vast distance away.

Then her eyes adjusted. She saw the faint shadows cast by black-painted window recesses in a wall to her immediate left and in another wall a good twenty feet in front of her. She saw the room stretching away to her right. In the same instant a girl moved into view from that direction.

Blonde and tall, her height emphasized by white high heels, she was wearing a pale halter-neck top, which barely reached her waist, dark sheer stockings, and nothing else.

Her face, which was round and pretty with delicate, rather doll-like features, was contorted with annoyance. She drew on a cigarette, staring into the dark wall to Rachel's left. 'Max, I told you I wasnt't going to put up with this kind of rubbish any more,' she snapped.

'Come on, Josey. Don't be a bloody pain. Just get back on the couch, Come on! I haven't got all day.'

Drawing again on the cigarette, the blonde girl tossed it to the floor and crushed its spark under the point of her shoe. She turned, folding her arms, blinking. 'I'm hired to be a model, Max. Not an outlet for your sick little fantasies. I wouldn't even let my boyfriend do that in front of me —'

'I'm not your boyfriend, Josey,' Max interrupted her, tiredly.

'Thank God for that.' The blonde girl took a deep breath and stepped back out of view.

Rachel moved to watch her.

The far end of the room was ablaze with light, revealing it to be at least twice as distant as the wall opposite. Two large photofloods were directed at an L-shaped screen covered in a plain cream material. In front of it was a low, dark red divan; in front of that a camera on a tripod.

A man stood beside it, silhouetted by the fierce light at his back. Rachel could see only that he was short and thick set, his legs bare below the knees, his feet in sneakers.

He turned as the blonde girl passed him, and Rachel glimpsed the square, careless face of a man of about forty, a forceful face which the years had rendered dissolute rather than weary. He was wearing a loose, kimono-style wrap, which ended just below his thighs, and his hands were deep in the pockets.

Two more young women, one tall and dark, the other small and bosomy, leaned against a trestle table to one side. Both were dressed in similar wraps and apparently little else. They watched with glasses in their hands, the dark girl with sly tolerance, the redhead with a look of giggling incredulity.

'Have a drink, Josey,' Max advised as the blonde girl settled on the edge of the divan, stretching out long, shapely legs towards him. Suspender straps stretched tight against the pale smoothness of her thighs; the pubic hair that sprouted between them was reddy gold and luxurious, a rich inverted beard that made Rachel think of her own.

'I don't need to get pissed to do my job,' the blonde girl snapped.

Hunched over the camera, the photographer chuckled throatily. He began to take pictures. 'Lean back, Josey. Further than that. Open your legs a bit more. Wider! Get your twat up in the air. Come on, love – put a bit of life into it. *That's* it! A nice bit of contempt. Let's see what you think of all the wankers out there – '

'The only wanker's in here,' the blonde girl muttered. Her expression was coolly bland, only her large clear eyes flaring at the camera.

205

'Great! Great! That's the way to do it. Shit!' Max darted from behind the camera. 'I can't see enough pink. Spread that lovely big bush of yours. Here, I'll show you what I want –'

'No you bloody well won't!'

The blonde girl leaned forward, looking down between her legs, while Max stood over her, chuckling again. Between wary upward glances, the girl licked the fingers of both hands, then carefully divided her soft, pubic waves. Under the bright light, even from where Rachel stood, the wrinkled fissure of her sex was plainly visible.

The photographer's shoulders shuddered. 'Jesus, I love to see a woman do that. That is so horny.' The shoulders jerked again and became a rhythmic movement.

Seeing it, the blonde girl's face flushed angrily. 'Max, I'm warning you!'

'What's the matter?' The photographer gestured airily. 'We're taking horny pictures, aren't we? If it doesn't turn me on it's not going to do much for the punters. I'm not bothering Steph, am I? Or Teri?' He spun toward the other women, the edge of his wrap flapping.

Only then did Rachel realize it was hanging open. With a twisting sensation that began below her stomach, she saw between his coiled fingers a dark red bulb of swollen flesh.

'You're like a kid with a new toy, Max,' the dark woman replied, her eyes glistening slyly as she raised them from his crotch to his face. 'I'd have thought you'd seen enough bare pussy in your time.'

The photographer was grinning, his face bright. 'You can't have enough pussy, Stephie. I'd have thought you'd know that.'

The little redhead exploded into giggles; her eyes were round, transfixed by the man's slow-moving fingers. 'Is he always like this?' she breathed.

'Often enough,' said her companion. She sipped at her glass, her smile mirroring Max's over its rim.

'Well?' He laughed as the redhead gaped at him. 'Which of you ladies is going to put me out of my pleasure, then? Josey's obviously not in a party mood – '

'Jesus Christ, Max!' The blonde girl shot to her feet, flushed with anger and close to tears. 'You really piss me off – if I don't get a good set out of these I don't get paid, and all you do is fuck about!'

'You want to learn patience, Josey.' The photographer spoke affably, advancing on the trestle table. With an excited squeak the redhead retreated behind it. The dark girl stayed where she was until Max butted against her, his pelvis nudging her stomach. Swearing, the blonde snatched up a thin dressing gown, throwing it around herself.

The dark girl's face was inches from the photographer's and slightly higher, regarding him with quizzical amusement. Her tongue flickered over her thin lower lip. 'You're a dirty old sod, Max,' she said softly. 'Why don't you finish Josey's pictures for her?'

He bumped his crotch companionably against hers, making his low throaty chuckle. 'Because I want to f—' he murmured, so indistinctly Rachel could not catch it. Simultaneously his hands moved upward, smoothing open the girl's wrap.

She glanced down with a frown as two tautly globular breasts, projecting with incongruous size and perfection from a reed-like frame, rose into view.

Max breathed in deeply, his fingers cupping each well-defined mound. 'I tell you, Stephie, you still got the best pair in the business.'

The girl nodded, watching him. 'Oh yes? A moment ago

207

it was Josey giving you a hard-on.'

'Come on, Stephie . . . .' Max was grinning, a hand sliding down the girl's slim back to mould a pale buttock; beneath her wrap she was plainly nude.

'Careful.' Her smile returned, then vanished abruptly in a shocked gasp as his hand darted sideways between her legs. '*Max!* You rotten – ' She broke into involuntary laughter as he bent forward to murmur in her ear, gripping her round the waist, preventing her from twisting away.

' . . . Lie down . . . burning . . . ' Rachel heard.

The girl lifted her head, grinning and shuddering as Max rolled a nipple against the flat of his palm. 'I promised Frank there'd be no funny business this time.'

She laughed again as the photographer whispered in her ear. Then Max was turning, drawing her back toward the divan. 'Just rest your legs. You'll love it. Make a happy man very old,' his voice rasped, cajoling.

'Stephie?' the redhead called from the shadows. 'You're not going to do it with him!'

Still murmuring in her ear, Max brought the dark girl to the divan. She sat, stretching out her legs, her wrap falling back from her shoulders. Naked, her body seemed to Rachel over-slim, almost stringy, all her roundness and softness concentrated in her bust.

'Frank'll kill you if he finds out!' the redhead called.

'Oh shut it, Teri!' the dark girl snapped. 'Frank's not here, is he?'

'Lift your knees,' said Max. He was in front of her, reaching down toward her thighs.

'Like this?' The girl squirmed further onto the velvet padding, dropping her hands to balance herself as her legs bent and rose, tilting her backward. She gave a wary laugh as Max opened her thighs, leaning between them with his hands on her knees. 'Not wasting any time, are we?'

'Not polite to keep a lady waiting —'

Her giggle was cut short with a dry gasp as the photographer fumbled where their crotches touched. Then with a grunt he rose onto the balls of his feet, slipping forward suddenly and down.

'Jesus Christ!'

The dark girl's wincing cry stabbed at Rachel's heart. At once she felt light-headed and strange, aware of shame and embarrassment for having lurked here so long, of a bodily excitement that roused disturbing memories of Barry.

Heels smacked on the hard floor. With a shock Rachel saw the blonde girl aiming straight for her, her shadowed face set in a mask of cold anger.

'Christ — go careful — that's so *deep* —'

Confused, Rachel stepped back awkwardly against the hardboard rack, just as daylight flared behind her.

The young girl from the front office, coatless again, entered the small corridor in a rush, her head lifting speculatively as she saw Rachel's startled face. Trapped, Rachel blinked at her, her mind blank. But the girl simply brushed past her, rounding the hardboard rack and halting as the blonde drew level.

'Max! *Prince* on the line again about Josey's pictures —'

The blonde slowed, casting a scornful glance back at the couple on the divan. The dark girl's legs now stretched high over the photographer's shoulders as he moved almost horizontally between them.

'Bugger off, Tracey,' Max grunted, momentarily breathless as the dark girl moaned. 'I said — no — calls —'

Rachel saw his assistant's lush features twist into a sly smirk. 'Then you won't mind seeing this new girl, will you?

After all, you've kept her standing here a good half hour – '

'New g—?'

His reaction was convulsive, letting one of the dark girl's legs drop, trying vainly to twist round while his companion gasped in protest.

'Fucking *Christ*, Trace – what the bloody hell are you . . . ?'

There was a ripple of amusement from the girls at Rachel's side. As she glanced at them, colouring fiercely in the semi-darkness, Josey turned to her, lifting needle-fine eyebrows sarcastically high.

'Welcome to the world of glamour!' she announced.

And, shaking her blonde head, swept out.

7
PAUL
1971

Paul came back to the house on Cape Cod prepared to despise it, only to be shocked by its size. Something which had always loomed so large in his mind seemed to have shrunk in the months of his absence.

Rooms that had once sprawled endlessly now appeared cluttered and cramped. Even the kettle pond at the back looked narrow and intimate, genuinely a pond rather than the spreading lake he had unconsciously pictured. Only the ocean, crashing behind new and subtle configurations of the dunes, was big enough to outpace his memory.

The feelings he had expected rose to the surface slowly and in unexpected ways. He began to see the peeling paint on the clapboard exterior, a shutter torn loose in the winter nor'easters, displaced cedar shingles in the garage roof. But now his reaction was less contemptuous than pitying – *he* had moved on so far and yet this place only appeared to have become more like itself.

Paul was so involved by these impressions that over a week had passed before he became aware that there had been real changes. And the biggest, of course, in Cora-Beth.

Having arrived home for the summer vacation a good month before he was due, his chest still swathed in elastic bandages, he had found it easy to avoid her. His aunt had a loathing of sickness or injury, and Louisa – a plumper, more serious Louisa than he remembered – brought him his meals in his room.

Paul welcomed the isolation. His abrupt departure from Curwen – explained, with indecent haste, as 'a year's independent study (with an option for further extension)' – had been more traumatic than he had first realized, much more than the beating which had put him in the college infirmary for four days.

There had been something awkward about the academic solicitude which accompanied his recovery – 'Don't worry about your spring term exams, Paul,' his tutor had told him on an unexpected infirmary visit. 'Just concentrate on getting yourself well.' And then, later, as he had begun to move awkwardly about Jackson once more, 'Have you ever considered taking a sabbatical, Paul? I really think you've got the self-motivation to make good use of it. Why don't you give it some thought?'

He had, but he still had projects to finish – work more immediately pressing than vague prospects of travel, even more than any desire for revenge on his attackers, whose actions he judged to be as inexplicable as they were extreme.

And yet when he had first returned to the Fine Arts building his tutor had shown more embarrassment than enthusiasm. Suddenly the darkrooms were booked up until too close to the exams to be of any use. Studio space was in short supply, equipment already allocated. As the excuses multiplied Paul had seen the unease growing in the face of his tutor – a stocky and acerbic Pole who had never before gone to such lengths to explain his actions and clearly resented doing so now. 'I think you should give more consideration to continuing your studies elsewhere,' the man had finished, so coolly he could have been making a threat, or giving a warning. 'I mean that very seriously.'

His manner had impressed Paul, but not enough to quell his confusion and growing annoyance. He had made his own threat – or warning – to see the Dean of Freshmen.

'That would not be wise.' The tutor's tone was dangerously flat. Then he had startled Paul by darting forward suddenly and prodding his chest with a hard finger. 'This is *personal* advice. Take it.' And the conversation was over.

But Paul had ignored the advice, seeing no alternative, and Dean Howell had eventually agreed to an appointment – late on a dry, dusty afternoon that seemed more like high summer than late spring.

The Dean of Freshmen had listened in silence, almost slumped behind his desk as fierce sunlight shone directly into Paul's eyes from the window facing him. Its brightness made him squint, turned the Dean into a dim, sprawling silhouette which took shape only when a slight movement would draw a flashing reflection from his horn-rimmed spectacles. The man seemed withdrawn, brooding, his few direct glances at Paul sharp and vulnerable, as though he were sulking.

When at last Paul finished, the Dean had been silent for a moment, then slowly breathed out in a low sigh that to Paul's surprise became a dry chuckle. 'You astound me, Mr Hanna.'

The Dean straightened, blocking the sunlight. His expression, Paul now saw, was a mask of strained hilarity. 'You stretch my credulity, you really do.'

'I'm sorry. I don't think – '

'No,' the Dean interrupted him. 'I don't think you do. I think you lack some fine but vital connection between your apprehension of a deed and any awareness of its effects.' He paused. Paul blinked, now more confused than ever, alarmed even more by the disparity between the Dean's looks and his words.

'You seem unable to take a hint, Mr Hanna. Several hints, in fact.'

'I just want to finish my projects and take my exams.'

'You won't.' The Dean's smile was glacial. 'Not while I continue to be a member of this administration. And if Curwen were not so well disposed toward legacies – particularly those whose families contribute sums in excess of five figures to college funds – you would not be here now.'

Paul felt blood draining from his face. Then Cora-Beth *had* bought him his place. Outrage rose in him.

'But my work is OK – you said it yourself – you asked me to do Barbara's portrait.'

'Oh yes!' There was no more humour in the Dean's voice, even of the most bitterly ironic kind. His eyes sharpened behind his lenses, quivering with a surge of uncharacteristically fierce emotion.

'I did ask you to take my daughter's portrait. I didn't ask you to bang her in my own home – I didn't ask you to knock her up, either, you little shit!'

The outburst left Paul's mind a yawning blank. He found himself grasping for words. 'But she – I didn't –'

'Yes you did. Oh, you most certainly did.' The Dean's fingers fluttered birdlike on the desk top. He glanced down at them sharply, as if disciplining an unruly student, and the tremor stopped.

'Fortunately the clinic where she is staying can take care of the physiological side. Psychologically, things aren't so simple. She was due to start college in the fall – I doubt if that will be possible now.'

'Dean Howell –' Paul began.

'No, *Mr* Hanna!' the Dean's voice sparked. 'I don't want

214

to hear what you have to say. I don't want to hear from you ever again. I just want you to know that under normal circumstances I'd have you up before the Administration Board and I'd make damn sure you got expelled. Since that would involve even further hurt to Barbara, I'm not going to do that.'

He took his first breath in moments; his cheeks shook with the effort of self-control. 'Instead I'm going to forward a petition on your behalf for a withdrawal from studies. Or you can call it a leave of absence or a sabbatical or whatever you damn well please. All it means, however, is that you leave this college – voluntarily and permanently. And preferably as soon as possible.'

Dean Howell leaned back in his chair, releasing the sunlight again so that it shone full into Paul's face, causing him to shut his eyes.

'I don't want to see you again, Mr Hanna,' Paul heard from darkness. 'Neither does my wife. And neither does my daughter. Shut the door on your way out.'

He did not understand. None of it made any sense.

He couldn't see why Barbara Howell had not taken precautions. They were an elementary fact of life. If he'd even suspected something might happen he would have taken rubbers. But it had been *her* father's house – *her* initiative. If she didn't even know the state of her own body . . .

The injustice of it all gnawed beneath his incomprehension, breaking out in fits of anger. What did rules mean if the rule-makers changed them at will?

Back at the Cape he kept his anger and his outrage in reserve, a first defence against the possibility of his aunt's wrath – a second defence, too, because nebulously but certainly he blamed her for his blunders in the outside world.

But there was no wrath – in fact, hardly any interest at all. Cora-Beth greeted him vaguely, enquired after his injuries and left him alone. At first Paul thought this might be circumspection; later he began to wonder who was avoiding whom, and his outrage, rather more irrationally, surged again. Didn't it matter to her what he did?

Only then did he realize how quiet the house had become – almost as it used to be. There had not been one party, not even a single visitor during the nine days he had been back.

Finally, his curiosity piqued, he sought out Cora-Beth. It was mid-morning, but nowadays she appeared to be rising much later than usual and she was still in her room.

Something made Paul hesitate at the door, brushing the wood quickly with his knuckle before he walked straight in.

Cora-Beth was dressing, bending next to the bedside table with her back to the doorway as she stepped into a pair of dark silk drawers. They were all she wore. To Paul her body looked thicker than when he had last seen her naked – perhaps six months before. The curve of a breast, visible beneath her left arm, seemed less rounded, less full.

'Cora-Beth – '

Her head jerked round as if stung, her face twisting in shock and annoyance. 'For God's sake, Paul, can't you knock?'

Immediately she yanked up the drawers and snatched a slip from the bed, wriggling it swiftly over head. Paul stared in surprise – never before had he seen his aunt show the slightest degree of bodily embarrassment.

'I did.' Paul gestured vaguely. 'I just wanted a word.'

'Good God.' Cora-Beth drew the slip straight and turned away, still flustered. She picked up a brush and began whipping it through her hair. 'I'm going to be down in five minutes. Surely you can wait that long?'

When she said no more, Paul shrugged and breathed out. 'Well, sure – I just didn't know when you'd be finished.'

'Well, now you do.' Her back was to him, straight and taut. He grunted and left.

On the landing he realized what he had seen in her eyes – even more surprising than the sudden onset of modesty. Fear. But what did Cora-Beth have to be afraid of?

Louisa was at the bottom of the stairs, working her way up with a vacuum attachment. 'Is my aunt worried about something?' Paul asked her.

The short, dark woman looked up from her kneeling position, smoothing aside a loose strand of hair with her forearm and squinting at him above the noise. When she turned off the vacuum he repeated the question.

Louisa shrugged, curling her full lower lip dismissively. '*Los anos*,' she said, and re-started the machine, leaving Paul none the wiser.

That afternoon he tested his newly healed ribs by taking a first swim in the vaulted pool. He had forgotten how extraordinary the structure was – or perhaps never noticed before: a kind of water-filled Gothic conservatory. It was like swimming in church.

Bushes and scrub oak shielded the extension on two sides, but the sun's rays still burned through the glass. Even with the cooling vents open, high against the ribbed roof, the atmosphere was exceptionally warm, steamy yet vapourless.

As Paul ploughed through it he had the powerful sensation that the water had mixed with the air to form some curious syrupy fluid which completely filled the room and in which he was suspended. It was a pleasant sensation, and for the first time since his return he felt himself relaxing.

Halfway through his third length a sharp sound, like the blast of an unusually shrill car horn, sounded very faintly from the front of the house. He ignored it until a shadow suddenly intruded itself into the silvery kaleidoscope of water and glass-reflected sunlight that surrounded him. Standing, Paul turned.

A figure stood pressed to the outside of one of the window panels, arms outstretched between two wooden ribs. Sunlight came from directly behind it, but the silhouette was clearly female. Then Paul saw where the brightness made a blonde halo around the head.

'Diana!'

The shadow of the face formed into a broad, white-toothed grin as he splashed across the pool. Diana jumped up and down and waved. She was dressed in jeans and a white cheesecloth shirt – bra-less, he saw, when she suddenly flattened herself against the curving glass, squirming in a mock dance so that each breast mounded and rotated.

As Paul's mouth fell open she gave a muffled laugh.

'Come round!' he shouted, pointing to the back of the house.

Her sudden appearance seemed a miracle. It threw into abrupt relief the gloom of the preceding weeks. It was as if he had suddenly woken up, switched into a state of heightened awareness as sparkling and brilliant as the sunlight sprinkled in the water about him. It made him breathless.

He had only just crossed the pool again when Diana, still laughing, came through the doorway into the house.

'I thought I'd do something disgusting just so you'd know who it was,' she grimaced mockingly. She leaned over him at the pool's edge, her face bright and hot. Perspiration gleamed along the lines of her collar bones where they

218

showed through her shirt's open neck. Her hair looked shorter and stragglier than when Paul had last seen her.

He took in the details wonderingly, ricocheting between the delirium inside himself and the extraordinary fact of her presence. Struggling to reconcile them, he could only grin.

'Hi,' he said at last.

'Hi yourself – that's what I love in a man, eloquence! What are you doing here, anyway? I thought you were still at college. Is Cora-Beth around?' She straightened, turning her head away and frowning. 'This place is like a morgue.'

'She should be here. She's probably upstairs – she seems pretty quiet these days.' It was an effort for him to marshal his thoughts. He didn't want to talk about Cora-Beth.

Diana was still frowning. 'She sounded kind of low on the phone. I better go find her.' She spun round, making Paul start in the water.

'Hey! Are you just passing or what? I mean, don't we say hello?'

He reddened as she stared at him, her features lightening in the brilliant smile he knew of old.

'Why, *Paul*, I'm deeply flattered – of course we'll say hello. Properly, I promise. But I've been driving all night. I really need a shower.'

'Take a swim instead!' Paul rose onto his toes, splashing the water around him with his hand in a sudden, almost desperate anxiety to keep her there. Her face dropped and his heart shrank in fear that he had betrayed too much of his excitement and made himself look silly. 'Come on, it's great!' he persisted, hearing himself bleat. 'Are you really staying long?'

The girl's eyebrows lifted. '*Uuugh* – that depends.' She groaned. 'I'm hiding from this guy from Hartford. Did I ever tell you about him?'

219

Paul frowned. Then he remembered. 'Not the one with the big . . . ?'

'Right! Never move in with someone just because you have a great time in bed, Paul. What a disaster! Why do guys think they can run your life for you just because you like screwing them!' Her tone sharpened with a touch of bitterness that seemed alien to her. Paul nodded, feeling an odd twist of emotion as he imagined her writhing on cool sheets with somebody else. Somehow the thought had never reached him before.

'So you're expecting this guy to follow you?'

'I doubt it. I've got his car outside!' Diana gave a broad grin, making Paul laugh. 'Damn it,' she said, 'that water looks great.' Paul grinned as she kicked off her sandals and began pulling at the buttons of her shirt. 'I didn't tell Cora-Beth *when* I'd arrive.'

Paul paddled backward across the pool, watching as she threw her shirt aside, unzipped her jeans and smoothed them down swiftly and matter-of-factly, rolling light, patterned briefs with them. Then she dived, slicing past him underwater in a flurry of pale limbs, and all Paul's memories of her body, its softness and hardness, its warmth and its excitement sparked again inside him, like shrugging on a favourite but long-forgotten coat.

As she surfaced, shaking her head and gasping, he lunged toward her. Seeing him, she squealed and struck out toward the deep end, clutching breathlessly at the edge just as Paul caught up, his arms smacking against the marble on either side of her head, trapping her. Both were laughing.

'Oh, *God*!' she gasped at last. 'I'm too tired for all this leaping about!'

'We don't have to leap,' Paul grinned. Holding the edge, he let his body sink against hers. His groin bumped the

220

roundness of her bottom; his stiffening cock nudged her cheek. He dropped an arm, pressing himself closer, bringing his hand up under her breast. 'I wonder if you can do it treading water.'

'Paul.' Diana twisted toward him, pushing her hip into his crotch; her grin wavered. 'Let me get my breath back, eh?'

Paul hesitated, then was forced to let go her breast and clutch at the pool side to keep his balance. As the girl turned her back again, he grinned, reached down and slid his hand up the inside of her thigh.

'*Jesus, Paul!*' She jerked round with a violent splash, her face drawn with sudden anger. 'For Chrissake, I'm not some Barbie doll you can screw about because *you* feel horny! Give it a rest – just for once, OK?'

Paul blinked at her, deeply shocked. As a blush rose up his neck, the girl glanced away, her tone softening only slightly. 'Jesus, Paul – I know this place is Liberty Hall but a girl needs a break sometimes.' Then she paused, staring suddenly across the pool. Paul turned.

Cora-Beth, her bright red kimono pulled only loosely about her, stood motionless by the door into the house. She looked distracted and pale, hardly aware that she was not alone. There was a slip of paper in her hand.

'Cora-Beth?' Diana called, frowning.

'It's Bernard,' Cora-Beth said quietly. 'I've just heard. It's his heart. He's dead.'

'I suppose if I'd loved him I'd have more right to feel like this,' said Cora-Beth.

She sat, blank-eyed, at the kitchen table, gazing at the range where Diana was preparing tea. Her face was almost gaunt, deep lines bracketing her mouth; her hair looked straight and dull, combed free of its usual lustre.

Paul, sitting diagonally opposite her, noticed these things only peripherally. Diana absorbed him. Why had she rejected him? He could accept that she was tired, even irritable as a result. But she had been tired at Curwen and they'd been making love in moments. Was she still thinking of her Hartford man? *Give it a rest – just for once.* Hadn't she wanted to make love at other times?

It wasn't simply the lack of sex between them that racked him – it was the denial of that intimacy he had glimpsed at the end of her college visit. Losing that seemed suddenly unendurable.

'How *do* you feel?' Diana asked, turning as she poured the tea. Her shirt, tucked loosely in her jeans, clung in damp patches to her body, outlining a stretch of stomach, the undercurve of a breast.

'A little bit numb,' said Cora-Beth. Her mouth lifted in a fragile smile, which included Paul. Caught unawares, he responded automatically, then dropped his eyes awkwardly.

He was embarrassed by the situation, by Cora-Beth's uncharacteristic display of vulnerability. He had seen his aunt's ex-husband perhaps a dozen times – and not at all in recent years. He remembered a grave, self-possessed man, large and balding, interested only in speaking to Cora-Beth. That was all.

'But there are no problems, are there?' Diana said, setting down a cup in front of Cora-Beth and slipping onto a chair next to Paul. 'I mean, he's taken care of you financially, hasn't he?'

'Oh, that was all settled a long time ago – this won't make any difference.' Cora-Beth picked up the cup, balancing it between her palms. She paused, her gaze unfocusing again.

'I just wish – I could have been fairer – '

'Oh come on, Cora.' Diana twisted on her chair; she drew her legs up under herself in a way that was half childish, half provocative to Paul, whose heart squeezed at the line of her thigh, the pout of her rump. 'You didn't hide anything when you married him. He took his chances, and when he couldn't take any more he pushed off. Don't blame yourself for that.'

'I don't. Not for that.' Cora-Beth sipped quickly at her tea and set it down. Her eyes, sharper suddenly, flickered at her nephew. 'There's something I have to say to Paul. Do you mind, Diana? Why don't you take your things upstairs? It's your usual room.'

Diana registered surprise, then said quietly, 'Yes, sure. Of course.' She uncurled herself from her chair and left.

Disconcerted, Paul watched her go.

Cora-Beth's voice surprised him. 'I don't think I've been very fair to you either, Paul.'

He looked at her quickly, dreading another quiet smile drawing him into a conspiracy of feeling he didn't want. He wanted to be outside, with Diana, or simply outside. Then, as his aunt took a breath, still looking into her tea cup as though ashamed to go on, or finding the words too painful, he felt a grudging guilt at his selfishness.

'Oh, I don't –' he began, falteringly.

'No, there are things you don't know,' Cora-Beth interrupted him. 'Things I couldn't really tell you until now.' He waited for her head to rise, but she did not look up.

'I've never seen very much point in marriage. If I had, I would never have married Bernard. I did it because he wanted me, he was rich – and I wanted to spite your father.'

Paul's swift glance mirrored his aunt's.

'My father?'

223

'I was very fond of your father, Paul.' She paused momentarily, her gaze wavering in a kind of embarrassment which only disconcerted Paul the more. As though realizing that, she seemed to chide herself.

'No, "fond" is a meaningless word. I was closer to him than to anyone else I have ever known – anyone I will know, I think. We were the same. It was as simple as that. He told me once' – the embarrassed look returned – 'if he were to cut his skin he would find my skin beneath.'

This time Paul did not look away. She had his attention now, more fully than in years. The idea that his mother and his aunt had ever been rivals for his father's affections was utterly new to him.

'But he married my mother instead?' he asked, tentatively.

Cora-Beth breathed in. 'If I could have accepted marriage I would have married him, but the question never arose – because he was already married.'

'Alre – ?' Paul blinked as the implication of the remark sank in.

His aunt's smile was gently cynical. 'I never had much respect for an institution that could be shattered so easily.'

'Did my mother know?'

'Oh yes.' Cora-Beth nodded briskly. 'I loathe dishonesty. Unfortunately your mother didn't see things in quite the same way. Keeping your father was more important to her than feelings – '

'But if she and my father got married in the first place – didn't they have feelings too?'

'Relationships change, Paul. If people are wise they allow each other the freedom to deal with that. Otherwise the changes come anyway.' Cora-Beth sighed. 'Your father realized that, of course. But your mother never would – she wouldn't let herself.'

Catching Paul's look, she hurried on, 'I'm not blaming her, Paul. Things weren't the same then, and Victoria and I never thought alike anyway. But I did blame your father – he knew differently. But the moment Victoria became pregnant with you he gave in to her completely. He surprised me a lot. I expected more from him, and that made me bitter for a while. Bernard just happened to be there at the right moment.'

She paused and Paul took a deep breath, feeling the atmosphere thick with an intimacy he hadn't known with his aunt for over two years. But this intimacy was emotional, intellectual rather than simply physical; for the first time he felt she was treating him as an adult. He was still wary, but surprised and intrigued by the change as much as by any revelation of a past he barely remembered.

'It's all over now, surely,' he prompted her.

'No.' Cora-Beth shook her head decisively. 'It isn't. When your mother and father were killed I realized I'd been given a second chance. A chance to know someone like your father again – through you, Paul.'

Her eyes fixed him, brimming suddenly with an intensity he'd seen only once before, in the throes of sex. But he was not in her bed now. Her voice grew soft. 'You are *so* like him, Paul. I've watched the resemblance grow year by year – it's been uncanny. It's not just the way you look, it's the way you speak, the way you walk – the way you are!'

Paul recoiled, the intimacy suddenly soured. Her tone, her longing repelled him instinctively even before he could rationalize his distaste.

'Did my father get thrown out of college too?' he snapped angrily.

Cora-Beth shook her head dismissively. 'That's not

important, Paul. Your home is here, anyway.'

'I don't *want* a home!' he cried, kicking back his chair and leaping up. His face blazed. 'I want to finish my work! I want to get my degree! I don't care what happened twenty years ago!' He paused, breathless, glimpsing uncertainty and confusion flicker across his aunt's face. And the sight – almost unique in his experience of her – abruptly curtailed his anger.

He saw her not as a figure of obligation or personal frustration but as a photographic subject – coldly and clearly. There were lines on either side of her full, balanced lips too deep to be the result of a momentary expression. There was a rawness in each cheek, a bruised puffiness beneath each eye – marks of a fatigue no sleep could remedy. It was as if overnight the fine edges of an exquisite sculpture had softened subtly, leaving its excellence still visible but blurred.

And Paul understood what Louisa had meant on the stairs. *Los anos.* The years. Years whose effects Cora-Beth had, until now, always seemed to avoid. He sighed, realizing his fists were clenched in anger, and relaxed them.

'Paul.' Cora-Beth started out of her chair. 'Paul, we've got to talk – it's not how you think it is – I don't want you to be unhappy – this is where you belong. We can be together here – like we always have been – it'll be wonderful, I promise you – *Paul!* Come back!'

But he had turned and moved quickly out into the hallway, skipping up the rear staircase. And it was not until he had slammed his bedroom door and thudded onto the bed that he remembered that, along with so much else, he had also inherited his father's first name and every word Cora-Beth had just spoken could have been addressed directly to that long-dead stranger.

226

He did not know the girl.

He knew the warmth of her body, the soft weight even the most petite form could offer as it moved beside him in the closest proximity. He knew the hard edges of her thighs beneath her clothes, the cushioned peaks of her breasts. But her face was hidden to him — masked by swathes of musky-scented hair too near to his cheek.

Such closeness smacked of the most intimate familiarity — but of lover or mother, he could not tell.

They were beside a lake — the kettle pond as he remembered it, broad and deep, wind-ruffled and sparkling in the sun. A head bobbed among the ripples. It was grinning, the teeth hard and white, then an arm waved. And as Paul recognized Kyle Stevenson he realized that the water was not the kettle pond at all but a stretch of the Connecticut River just below Curwen.

'Paul,' Kyle said, and his voice seemed next to his ear, though he continued to wave and splash some distance away. 'You've just got to learn to do the right thing. That's all. After that, the rest is easy.'

He said it again, but less distinctly, as a second head appeared in the water beside him. It belonged to a girl, her face cupped by thick, damp hair. Like Kyle she was grinning and waving. To Paul's surprise he saw it was Barbara Howell. What was she doing swimming with Kyle? To Paul's knowledge they hardly knew each other.

But then the couple laughed and threw their arms around each other and, with a stab of fear, Paul realized he had been mistaken. The girl was Diana. He was instantly confused and agonized: Diana and Kyle had never met, had they? She had only been on campus for one night. A terrible suspicion assailed him that the man in Hartford was really Kyle — could they have conspired together?

He was so concerned he did not notice for a moment that they were no longer in the water, but a room. Somewhere high with bright sunlight streaming in the window — Diana's bedroom at the Cape? Mrs Howell's attic retreat?

227

Paul could not be sure, only that Diana and Kyle, still laughing and smiling, lay entwined together in front of him, not making love, but nude. And, despite an upsurge of anger and pain, the thought that any moment they might make love brought him suddenly and thickly erect. The reaction was an embarrassment. Doubly so because of the physical discomfort and the nearness of the faceless, long-haired girl who still clung to him. Her body seemed to sense his excitement, pressing even closer; her hands, strong and supple, caressed him, sliding downward to grip his cock. He felt her weight, hard yet enveloping. And saw Diana's face, turned toward him, smiling broadly and brilliantly. 'Take my picture, Paul,' she said. 'It's all right. I don't need clothes. Take my picture. Take it.'

He shuddered awake in unfamiliar darkness and in his confusion felt the swirl of panic. Twisting his head, he looked for the pale rectangle that should have been above and to the right – the window onto Little Yard. But there was only more darkness, and a dimmer, squarer outline on the wrong side of the room.

His panic peaked and then he knew where he was. He took a breath, slowly rationalizing the tangled emotions of his dream. Diana and *Kyle* . . . ? The thought tempted him to grin, just as he remembered the stiff ache at his groin, and realized he was not alone.

The warm body of his dream still butted his hip. There was a soft pressure, reaching from his neck to his knees, cupping him, spoonlike, from behind.

He stopped breathing and moved his hand back. He touched a warm flank, soft and fleshy. Sliding his hand down he found the bony edge of a knee; reaching back, the smooth curve of an inner thigh, the prickle of curled hair.

He grinned, his heart accelerating. Diana – she'd recovered from her tiredness, stolen into his bed. He turned over on the mattress, feeling the body beside him stir too. Warm breast-flesh pillowed his chest. Warmer breath rasped against the curve of his throat where lips fastened and sucked and his nostrils filled with a thicker, muskier odour than he had ever known before in Diana; the familiar citrus tang had changed into something richer, riper, almost over-ripe. It surprised and excited him.

He gave a low chuckle as he continued to roll, mounting the soft limbs as they parted welcomingly below him. He had known Diana would come to him. The rejection had only been a passing mood – she was as eager as ever: this restored everything –

Their urgency redoubled with his renewed confidence. Her sex was loose and liquid under his fingers. Her fingers found and levered his swollen cock forward and down.

He sucked in breath as his tip swam in the moist folds of her flesh. Her knees rose on either side of him. He heard her gasp as he eased between outer and inner lips, her hands reaching back to his buttocks, urging him forward.

Something was wrong. In the gasp, in the touch of her flesh. In her smell.

He stopped, his heart booming in his chest. Vivid lights flickered behind his eyes. Joy had blinded him as effectively as darkness. The body below him, just discernible now, was not Diana's.

He felt it tense around him, sensing his unease, as a knot of disappointment and disgust tightened in his stomach.

'Paul?'

He gasped, grimacing, pushing himself back off the mattress.

'*No!* Paul, don't stop!'

The hands on his buttocks suddenly gripped, pulling him forward. 'Paul, it's all right. I gave my word to Bernard I never would – but it's all right now he's gone. We can – we *can!*'

He groaned, twisting to beat at her arms, and slipped, his cock bumping through her opening, sinking deep, making her jerk and cry out.

'*Yes – yes!*'

And he was deep in her, his cock feeding on her slickness and heat, its own force responding, contracting to spurt.

'*Get the hell away from me!*' Gathering himself, he pushed backwards, pulling audibly free as she gave a low grunt, as if stomach-punched. Then a gasp and a whining sigh as his cock erupted, spattering her body in the darkness.

She was groaning as he lurched off the bed. He stumbled across the floor, close to retching, his loins spent but frustration a dull blockage in his bowels.

'Paul – ' Cora-Beth whispered. 'Paul – Paul – '

He knocked against a chair; steadying himself, he felt jeans across the back and grasped them.

'No,' he breathed. The door handle was against his hand. His blood tilted like mercury in his veins, threatening to unbalance him. 'No.'

He fumbled the door open and was gone.

The Atlantic invaded him, its icy inrush so impossibly fierce he felt his own heat shrivel to a tight, desperate knot in the pit of his stomach. As he surfaced his mouth stretched in a soundless shriek. His legs thrashed in the dark, slow-moving swell. Then the knot uncurled – a tingling glow spread from his centre until it coated him from head to toe like a fresh, fiery skin.

His plunging dive had taken him only a few yards from the shore, but the dunes were now barely visible under the starless sky. The ocean moved like oil, its limit marked by

the dim phosphorescence of low surf. Far to the east, past
Hyannis and Chatham, a dull pink showed along the line of
the horizon

He had tramped to the beach in darkness, not thinking of
his destination until he arrived. Then he had wanted to
plunge past the surf and swim endlessly until the Cape
house was just a memory. The chill of the water robbed him
of that impulse. Instead, its iciness became a punishment, a
purging. He felt tainted by Cora-Beth and all she represented, a taint that went deeper than thought, infecting
every part of him – to be expunged ruthlessly. Everything
she was, everything she'd ever told him was a sick joke – a
joke at his expense. All his blunders outside this place
started with her – her longing for that 'free, loving,
orgasmic experience' – with a man who had died eighteen
years ago. A man who had simply fucked her better than
anyone else.

He felt betrayed and abused, mentally, spiritually, physically. Her slickness was on him like the slickness of her
sex – not just tonight but through a host of nights and days
when she had pulled him to her bed or drawn the sweetness
from his loins or watched as he had pleasured others, taking
her ultimate pleasure by proxy – until another death had
cancelled that final constraint.

The rush of memories brought him close to nausea. He
swam faster, churning the water, pushing against the
current.

His tutor at Curwen had been right after all – he *could*
make use of a sabbatical, somewhere where Cora-Beth's
sickness did not extend, beyond East Coast and West.
Canada? Mexico? Or even Europe . . .

A ship's light winked far out in the Sound and brought
him back to the present. The fire on his skin was cooling;

the ocean's cold touched his limbs again.

Calmer now, Paul turned toward the shore, kicking with the swell. One bright spot still remained in the chaos of the night. In Diana he had glimpsed an intimacy beyond sex, something more mysterious, more complete. Now was the time to tell her, to pursue that path wherever it led.

He was shivering when he eased open the french windows and slipped through into the rear parlour. The house was silent, filled with the grey gloom of dawn.

The painted floorboards of the landing creaked underfoot and Paul hovered at the far end, listening. Still there was no sound. Only his door seemed open; no light showed anywhere.

A muffled grunt made him start. His heart thudded wildly. He did not want to encounter Cora-Beth again – not tonight, not ever, if he could manage it. But the sound was not repeated. After a moment he moved quietly to his door, peering carefully through the open gap. His mattress was a paler grey in the general dimness. It was unoccupied.

He went inside, holding his breath as he pressed the door shut. Then he switched on his bedside lamp, dried himself fully and dressed.

Packing took shorter time than he had anticipated. But he had hardly unpacked since arriving from Curwen. It was almost as if he had never expected to stay.

There was a pale light spreading from the window when he finished. He paused, his thoughts churning. Diana was only a room away and his Atlantic confidence wilted. He could think of nothing to say to her.

Then his eyes fell on the bed and he felt Cora-Beth's touch again, the spurting treachery of his loins. Nauseated afresh, he realized he had no choice.

232

Diana's door was closed but off the latch. It opened noiselessly. With the dawn entering by two windows, the room was almost light. Warmth blossomed in Paul's breast as he saw the rumpled outline in the bed and his certainty returned, urging a grateful smile.

He allowed it to surface as he tiptoed across the floor. The thick coverlet was drawn up around the pillow, hiding the girl's head, making the curled hump of her body look childish and vulnerable. He reached for the edge, ready to smooth the coverlet back so as not to alarm her. But as he touched it the sinous shape collapsed. Shocked, he drew the coverlet back on nothing. Diana had gone.

He stood blinking in confusion. There had been no one downstairs. He had passed her car still parked outside. Then the muffled grunt he had heard on the landing sounded again, sharper now. A cold sliver of foreboding dropped in his centre.

He sighed, squeezing his eyes shut. He should go now, at once. Every instinct, every fear, every memory prompted it.

He let go the coverlet, went back onto the landing and gripped his own door handle. A softer sound came from Cora-Beth's room. Gentle as a sigh, thin as a shared whisper.

As he turned toward his aunt's door he felt that the darkness in the air had changed to treacle. Every inch he moved through it was a slow beat of his heart, cancelling the one before, reiterating the possibility of retreat. But he didn't retreat; he simply put a hand against Cora-Beth's door and pushed it open.

The window was uncurtained and the glow of a pale rosy dawn was in the room. It touched everywhere but the bed where the two figures sprawled like unkempt statues. Paul knew that both were naked, though he could see only Diana plainly, her heart-shaped rear upraised to him as she knelt between his aunt's widespread thighs.

For a moment it seemed to him a deliberate tableau – an attempt to shock or tantalize like so many others in this bizarre household. Then he heard the grunt again, a whimper and a soft, insistent lapping and he knew that both were quite unaware of him.

Turning away, he believed his mind as smooth and hard as marble, impervious to reaction. The moisture that spilled from his eyes seemed to come from somewhere else.

He was at his own door when he heard Diana's call and the hurried slap of bare feet.

'Paul? Is that you – where are you going?' She hung round his doorway, her face glistening and overheated in the orange light of the lamp; strands of damp hair plastered her forehead and cheeks. She blinked at the parachute bag over Paul's shoulder, the portfolio below.

'I'm just – taking a trip. Don't let me – break you two up.' He snatched up the portfolio, not looking at her, not wanting to speak.

'Hey.' Diana frowned and came into the room, closing the door quietly behind her. 'You can't just slope off like this. Cora's pretty shaky at the moment.'

'Sorry,' Paul interrupted, staring past her. 'I'm sure you can console her exactly the way she wants. I have to go.'

Diana peered at him, then her face broke into a wondering grin. 'Paul, you sound *jealous*.' She shook her head in disbelief. 'Don't you *know* Cora and I have been going together for ages – long before I knew you.'

'Look.' He felt his small control slipping; he gestured with his hand to stop it trembling. 'It's none of my business.'

Diana's frown returned. 'Paul, I *love* her. I always have –

234

'that's why she chose me to go with you.'

'What about – ' Paul snapped and swallowed, losing himself in anger – at her, at himself for the tears that welled again. 'What about other people loving you?'

'I love you too, Paul.' She touched his arm. 'I love you both. There's no law about loving more than one person at a time, is there?'

Paul grunted. 'Did you ask your friend in Hartford?'

Diana sniffed, letting her hand drop. 'He was a dork. His attitude was totally unrealistic.'

'Oh, I see.' Paul was nodding again; clutching his baggage he moved round her. 'I understand – looking for something better with a person than a good fuck is unrealistic. Right, I see that now.'

Diana stared at him, silent a moment. To Paul her blandness was a torture, doubly cruel because he could see it was entirely appropriate to everything he knew of her, everything he wanted to be close to.

'I'm sorry I turned you down in the pool earlier,' she said at last, softly. 'I had to see Cora first. It wasn't that I didn't want to fuck you – '

'No, you just wanted to fuck her first!' Paul snapped, unable to stop himself. But the girl simply blinked at him slowly, her gaze steady.

'You can fuck me now, Paul. We can do it on the bed. We can do it standing here if you like.'

She moved only slightly, but the lamplight touched the slope of her breast, the tip of a stiffened nipple, arcs of gold in the dark, bushy mass between her thighs. In that instant Paul felt his loins contract, his anger distorted and blunted. She looked so totally, so unstoppably desirable. Seeing the spark in his eyes, Diana smiled.

'Or why don't we go back to Cora's room? She'd love

235

us all to be together.'

'*No!*'

His bark made her start, and she blinked as if slapped.

His face worked in fear and rage. 'I don't want to fuck you! I don't want to fuck her! *This* is what's unreal – it's like a mad wet dream. It's not true. None of it is true. It's all stupid – deluded – lies! Lies that crazy woman feeds on!'

He choked on his own vehemence, reduced to waving his free arm impotently. His eyes streamed again, beyond his control. Then he saw Diana's expression.

It was cold. The fire had sunk from her eyes, from her flesh. She seemed to shrink back into shadow, as if covering her nudity. 'You've ruined it haven't you?' she said. 'You've ruined everything Cora tried to do for you. That makes me so angry, Paul.'

'*You! You're* angry!' He shook his head, too incredulous to laugh. His thoughts boiled, so jumbled he could no longer order them. He swallowed, abandoning the effort. 'I have to go.'

'If you do,' said Diana, 'you won't see me again.'

Her quiet stare was like a needle skewering his heart. If he pulled away it would rend him inside.

A footfall sounded across the landing. Panic flared in Paul's eyes and he snatched at the door handle. 'I just want – ' he said, looking back at the naked girl, and stopped, not knowing what he did want any more, only what he did not. Then Cora-Beth's door rattled and he rushed down the landing, not looking her way.

His trailbike took him as far as Providence, where he sold it to a dealer less than a block from the bus station. The next bus to leave was a Greyhound to New York. He was in the city by early afternoon, en route to Kennedy within minutes.

His despair was a kind of liberation. He felt light-headed, distanced from everything around him, as if the pain of the last few weeks had temporarily absolved him of any further responsibility toward anything.

Aimless travel only compounded the effect. He had chosen directions and destinations at random, uncaring at first and then exhilarating in the freedom of a split-second commitment. Only at the airport's first international desk did he pause – the earliest available flights were all European and the fares astronomic.

He had a wallet stuffed with traveller's cheques unused from Curwen, but the cheapest seat would swallow more than half of them. He agonized a moment and found it impossible to stir his numbed mind enough to care. He chose Paris.

Then, as the desk clerk wrote the ticket, news came of a cancellation in a flight currently boarding. There was room in first class. If he was in a hurry and willing to pay?

The cost would drain him of all but a few dollars. As he handed over the traveller's cheques he told himself, with the tiniest twist of fear, that he was being insane. And it was only as he turned away from the counter that he noticed the flight was to London.

In the plane he sat next to a man in a crumpled safari suit who was snoring gently. After take-off Paul closed his own eyes and when he opened them again over an hour later the man was still asleep.

Paul was glad. He didn't want the slightest obligation to talk. The aircraft's droning artificiality matched his mood, soothing his senses as it dulled them. A cramped, hermetically sealed world where even the air smelled unreal.

But in his emotional deadness his mind still sought to

237

work. Paul found himself opening his portfolio, sorting idly through prints he hadn't looked at since leaving college. Odd points began to occur to him – ideas for cropping old prints in new ways. He was pencilling notes against the back of one when he became aware of being overlooked. He turned his head and saw that his fellow passenger was awake, gazing down at the photographs with evident interest.

'Nice pictures,' the passenger said, his accent English and faintly mannered. 'Are they yours?'

He was in his forties, with a heavy, leonine head, the look of an aristocratic boxer – battered yet refined.

Warily, Paul answered him.

'Do you mind telling me what camera you used?' his neighbour asked.

Paul's terse answer was intended to deter interest. But to his surprise and diminishing annoyance, the man laughed out loud.

'Good God! It's years since I used one of those. Marvellous machines!'

Paul immediately became aware that the Leica was resting in his parachute bag just above his head. He fought his conscience a moment, then accepted what appeared to be inevitable. He rose and retrieved it. The man took the camera with a kind of glee, turning it over appreciatively in his hands.

Paul asked if he was particularly interested in photography.

'It's how I earn my crust,' the man grunted. 'At least I do when the buggers pay me.'

He reached into the seat pocket in front of him and pulled out a glossy magazine folded at a spread of fashion pictures. Taking it, Paul turned the cover over and saw it was

'You did these?' He glanced back at the picture credit, his interest suddenly quickening. 'You're James Kingsley?'

'Uh-huh. That was only a one-off, sadly, but I live in hope.' The man handed back the camera. 'Beautiful little thing, isn't it? I'd use one today if it was practical.'

Paul nodded as he put it away. 'I'm Paul Hanna,' he said, sitting again.

The man pointed at the topmost print on Paul's lap. It was his view of an abandoned fishing shack on Cape Cod Bay, taken in the last moments of sunset. 'What kind of exposure did you use on that?'

Excitedly, Paul began to tell him.

8
RACHEL
1975

Swathed in an ankle-length dressing gown, her head turbaned in a towel, Josey skittered into the tiny, steam-filled kitchen, fingers splayed in front of her.

'Oh, do us a favour, Rachel. Pop a fag in my mouth and light me – my nails are taking an age and I'm dying for a puff. They're in my pocket.'

Rachel unplugged the electric kettle and turned as Josey twisted to one side, juggling her hip in Rachel's direction.

'Oh, do you like that?' Josey bobbed her hip again, her small, high mouth breaking into a bright smile. 'Do you think I should work it into my patter? Get them all leaping into my shower cubicle – '

'Idiot,' Rachel murmured. She took a packet of cigarettes from Josey's pocket, extracted one and popped it between the other girl's lips. Replacing the packet, she picked up a box of matches from the breakfast debris on the table.

'You'd do better to demonstrate your shower person-ally,' she said, carefully striking a match.

Josey grimaced. 'No thank you. I spend enough time out of my knickers as it is. I *don't* really want to do it in the middle of Woolies.'

She brought her cigarette closer to the match flame by bending from the waist and pursing her lips. It was an odd, coquettish gesture – the gesture of a small child eager to please. It made Rachel grin, feel self-consciously but genuinely proprietorial, despite Josey being a good three years her senior and half a head taller.

The feeling was a good one and the best reason Rachel knew for accepting the blonde girl's offer to share this cramped, ill-decorated attic at the back end of Camden. *'I'm sure this Derek is a decent fellow,'* Josey had said. *'But he's still a fellow, isn't he? What if he has one too many one night and decides to get frisky?'* The word 'frisky' had made Rachel smile; it described Derek too well.

Then the reality of her situation had come back to her – aided by the wintry, rubbish-strewn view of Kilburn High Road, beyond the window of the café where they sipped scalding coffee. She'd had enough 'friskiness' from Barry Drew to last a long time.

'Give it a month, if you like,' Josey had gone on. 'Then we'll see. You'll be doing me the favour. Since my boyfriend pushed off I can't stand being there on my own, and I can't afford to move.'

'I can't afford to move in,' Rachel had said, pointedly.

With a swift shake of her head, Josey had dismissed the thought. *'You'll* get work. Your figure's all right, isn't it? It looks it.'

Rachel had shrugged.

'Max is as good a start as any.' The older girl had paused as Rachel's eyebrows lifted. 'I know he's a wanker, but he had his little chums in today. He goes on these sex jags – anyone else, it'd be booze or drugs. But he knows the business backwards. Just don't sign any model releases until you've got cash in hand. He can be a bastard paying, if you let him. And he can't sell your pictures without a signature – '

And as Josey went on, Rachel had listened, fascinated as much by the girl as the unfamiliar and bizarre world she

241

described – she seemed so normal, so untainted, the very opposite of the seedy glamour of May. The more Rachel saw the possibility of dignity in this situation, the more she warmed to Josey.

'And, anyway,' Josey had finished, her voice dropping in the half empty café, 'if I'm going to open my legs in front of any photographer, I'd rather it was a dirty old bugger like Max I couldn't give a toss about. Hell'd have to freeze over before I let *him* lay a finger on me – and I think he's almost realized it!'

And as they laughed together Rachel had made her decision. She had moved to Camden at the end of that week . . .

'Andrew was asking after you.' Josey spoke through twin streams of smoke. Something tweaked at Rachel's heart.

'Andrew?'

'You know – Griswold, Grisly, whatever – the fellow at Norman's party.'

Rachel remembered a crowded lounge in a large white-painted terrace overlooking a common, french windows and expensive carpets, pretty girls and men in business suits chatting smartly through cigarette smoke and the clink of glasses; the familiar, hateful clenching of her stomach as she saw herself treading here as a gauche fraud; Josey's firmly encouraging arm at her back, the blonde girl's astonishing familiarity – her normality – with the most intimidating of the crowd.

And then, at the very moment Rachel realized they were ordinary, or at least approachable, human beings under the glitter – though she felt unable to do more than watch for the moment – someone had handed her a glass. . .

'Andrew *Gridley*. How were you talking to him?'

Josey took another puff and deposited her cigarette on

the edge of a dirty saucer. She began towelling her damp hair. 'His company's auditing the agency. He's always in the office. That's why Norman asked him to the party. Didn't he say? Norman's very impressed. Not the only one, by the look of it.' Tilting her head, she gave a sideways smirk.

Colouring, Rachel turned away to the coffee she had been making.

'Of course, he's not a bad-looking fellow.'

Rachel glanced back, breaking into an annoyed grin as she saw Josey's look of elaborate innocence. 'Well, what did he say then?' she snapped.

'He wanted my telephone number – for a party he's thinking of having,' Josey added as Rachel's expression tightened. 'But somehow I don't think I'm going to be invited.'

'Why?' Rachel began, and stopped at Josey's widening grin.

'Oh come on, Rache. He was all over you at the party. He's not going to want to take *me* out, is he?'

Inside, Rachel's hopes flared, but she quickly stifled them; it was her newest resolution to keep her expectations low and so avoid disappointment.

'And pretending you don't care,' Josey murmured with frightening telepathy, 'isn't going to make the slightest bit of difference either way.'

Rachel sat defensively with her coffee; she felt criticized, her privacy invaded. Sensing it, Josey changed her tack. 'Are you going to be in lunchtime?'

'I don't know. I've got to see Max about the *Prince* pictures. I think he wants to do another set.'

'Can you manage not be back before about three? Norman's taking me out to lunch and I've a feeling we'll end up here – I know!' Josey sighed at Rachel's disapproving look. 'He's a boring old fart, but he also owns a model agency, and if I'm not going to spend the rest of my life doing nudie pics or handing out shower leaflets in Woolies I've got to be nice to him. There's some chat going around about catalogue work.' She draped her towel over her shoulder and picked up her cigarette again. 'Anyway, I quite like him.'

She made for the door, her expression growing impish. 'Not that he's as dishy as Mr Grisly, of course.'

Rachel's face dropped suddenly in shock. 'He doesn't know – does he? About my pictures?'

'Andrew?' Josey paused in the doorway. 'As far as he's concerned you're my flatmate – and you help out at the agency occasionally.' Then she shrugged. 'I wouldn't worry about it. As soon as he sees you in all your glory he's going to be battering the door down – and he won't be using his fist!'

Frowning, Rachel sipped at her cup. She did worry, more than she liked to admit, even to herself.

'Would you like a drink?'

The glass had been extended to her almost carelessly, as if it were an afterthought and she really were as out of place at this party as she suspected. But as she took it, rather gracelessly to show that she could be equally indifferent, she had seen the face above and realized it was diffidence not carelessness that had prompted the awkward manner.

The face was pleasant: smooth and open with wide, clear eyes, straight, dark hair and even features just a little too sharp at nose and chin to be blandly handsome; it belonged to a young man in his early twenties, dressed as smartly as every other man in the room, but not at all as comfortable about it as they appeared to be.

The contrast intrigued Rachel as much as his looks appealed to her.

'Do you know anyone here?' he said quickly. 'Norman invited me but I only met him last week.'

Rachel told him, pleased to accept the role of co-conspirator in a room full of unnerving strangers. He had said he worked for an accounting firm, only as a trainee at the moment, a general dogsbody, but he was studying and when he qualified everything would change.

The studying and the job impressed Rachel, and when he asked what she did she said without thinking, 'I'm temping, actually, just as a secretary.'

In fact she had done numberless high-street leafleting jobs during some of the winter's bitterest months, and once spent a day with Josey sprawling in bikinis across some obscure piece of marine equipment at a trade promotion. That, and her single session with Max, had been the extent of her modelling career.

She covered her lie by fumbling for a cigarette and, to her delight, the young man instantly produced a lighter.

The smoking habit had come from Josey, and she still barely inhaled, but the confidence it gave, the cool, appraising looks possible through veils of curling smoke – carefully practised in the mirror – seemed invaluable in social situations.

The young man accepted a cigarette himself, lit it but then only pecked at it in gaps in the conversation, using it, Rachel saw, in much the way she did. Obscurely that pleased her.

But why was he still so nervous? It wasn't an unpleasant nervousness – more a kind of self-conscious, self-mocking verbal fumbling that exploded into mutual giggles. He was easy to talk to, funny in unexpected ways and he was good-looking – he must have chatted up dozens of girls. How did she come to have such an effect on him? If she was *that* unsettling why did he stay – out of politeness?

Then a burst of laughter from Josey across the room distracted her, and when she turned back it was to catch his eyes rising from her figure with a look of extraordinary intensity – a look that contained an all too familiar hunger but softened by self-restraint, by a kind of regret.

It lasted only a fraction of a second, dissolving instantly in a grinning blush – he even said, 'Sorry, just dreaming . . . . ' But in the same instant she had understood the reason for his awkwardness and been astonished and immensely pleased by it. Not even Donny had looked at her like that.

She found herself sharing the warmth of his blush as his hand reached for her glass. 'Can I get you some more? White, isn't it?' he said. She saw the glass was empty as she gave it up. Then, with a smile, he disappeared in the crowd.

Rachel's awareness of the party returned almost with a jolt – the conversation had absorbed her so completely her surroundings had ceased to matter. Now she knew she was standing on her own with nothing in her hands and no one to talk to.

As she reached for another cigarette a face caught her attention in a small group a few feet away. A young woman in a severe but flattering black dress, her dark hair lifted high, her features narrow and sculpted, exquisitely made-up, was watching her. She was very striking, almost certainly one of Norman's 'legitimate' models, her gaze cool, appraising, subtly contemptuous. It seemed to say, 'I see what you are and it's not *that* much.'

It was a look that Rachel envied, one that she had seen

246

wither unwelcome men at even greater distances, but this was the first time she had received it herself and its force shook her.

She dropped her eyes quickly, ostensibly to light her cigarette. When she raised them again the girl was still gazing at her. The disdain was now so open it sparked a sudden anger. *Would you look as cool stripping off in front of a camera? I doubt it!*

The thought came so powerfully the girl's eyes darted away abruptly, giving Rachel a quiet buzz of satisfaction. And suddenly Josey was there, flushed and beaming.

They had a lift home – one of Norman's friends in a Jaguar en route to Hampstead. It was late; there'd be no taxis this far south of the river. It was too good an opportunity to miss. But the car was going now.

For a moment departure seemed unthinkable. But as she went to protest, the reality of the situation intruded. Reluctantly, Rachel let herself be drawn away, scanning the crowd in vain for the one familiar face.

In the entrance lobby Josey pushed Rachel's coat into her arms as a horn sounded through the open front door. At the opposite end of the hall a group of laughing men and women were clustered around the door to the kitchen where the drinks were kept. But the young man who had introduced himself as Andrew Gridley was not among them.

Why had she said she was a secretary?

The question left a sick feeling in her stomach as she stepped off the bus at Lord's. It was a bright, summery day and there was a small queue outside the cricket ground. Passing it, she turned down Lisson Grove.

She knew the answer to her question, of course: she was trying to impress. Andrew was 'nice', not by simply being

247

more pleasant than any other man she knew – with the exception of Derek – but respectable, acceptable too. Like one of the boys at the local grammar school at home – in fact a minor public school; boys whose smart accents and expensive uniforms had earned them mild derision at Rachel's school, and secret envy. None of the boys she had known had been likely to become accountants.

That would be something to fling in her father's face – sweeping up to the door of his council house in a Jaguar with Andrew at the wheel, watching May's expression as she stepped out.

She quashed the fantasy with annoyance. Only one thing impressed her father, and she wouldn't be going anywhere with Andrew while she claimed to do one thing and Josey contradicted her. That is, if he ever bothered to phone her at all.

She paused outside a tall, modern apartment block and consulted a slip of paper in her handbag. Reassured, she walked down the short, curving driveway, past a parked Volvo and a BMW, and entered a glass-doored, carpeted porch.

Two further glass doors were locked. To one side was an entry-phone grille, a row of buttons adjoining a list of flat numbers and names. Rachel pressed the button with 'M.A. Wallace' against it. A woman's voice answered.

Max Wallace's flat was on the fifth floor, one of a dozen anonymous doors in a long, spartan corridor which had an insinuating but strong chemical smell, as of new artificial carpeting. Rachel had never been here before; on the telephone Max had mentioned his studio was being hired out today.

A blonde woman opened the door, smiling as Rachel introduced herself in the intimate, restrained manner of nurses or medical receptionists. She was severely attractive, in her thirties, Rachel judged, dressed in sweater, slacks and high heels. She invited Rachel inside.

'Max is just seeing someone. You can go in, if you like. I'm sure you won't disturb them.'

The woman indicated a closed door off the small, windowless entrance hall and, before Rachel could answer, moved busily toward the open door of a kitchen to one side. 'Oh – ' She turned in the doorway. 'Would you like some coffee?'

When Rachel declined, the woman smiled again. 'You *can* go in – He *is* expecting you.' She nodded encouragingly as Rachel turned to the closed door.

Voices murmured on the further side. Rachel took the door handle hesitantly – her first experience of interrupting the photographer was still etched in her memory – but the woman continued to watch her. With a deprecatory smile, Rachel tapped gently on the door and put her head round the edge. Inside was a small dining area, largely filled by a broad and very modern mahogany dinner table. A waist-high room divider separated it from the remainder of a long, sandy-coloured lounge, one wall of which seemed entirely glazed, curtained with a creamy net.

Max stood against it, fumbling with a bulky-looking camera. Another man was at his side. But all Rachel noticed was the figure resting on hands and knees, neat rear upraised to her, in the middle of the dinner table.

It was a girl, quite nude, her body slim and shapely, very lightly tanned. As Rachel blinked at her she turned her head, saw Rachel and grunted, expressionlessly, 'Hi.'

'Hello.' Rachel spoke as vaguely, not at all certain she should be here – just as Max looked up from his camera.

'Rachel! Hi!' he rasped. 'Come over here, out the way.

I'm nearly done. Rachel's one of my best models,' he told his male companion, giving her a crooked and, she assumed, ironic grin. He seemed to her unusually sprightly.

The second man nodded at Rachel as she skirted the room divider, his eyes skipping down her figure and up again as she passed him. It was the kind of curt, automatic male response she did not appreciate – particularly from a man like him.

He was lean and thirtyish, with hard eyes and a fleshy, lightly pockmarked face bisected by a dark, neatly trimmed moustache. His clothes had a neat appearance too – an expensive leather jacket, newly pressed jeans, polished shoes – but the neatness seemed unfamiliar, an ineradicable roughness, a seediness showing through.

Rachel merely glanced his way and found a chair at a small writing desk in a corner of the room. As she sat, no more certain of her role than when she had entered, Max was lifting his camera.

'Turn your head to the right a bit, love. That's it. Look at me.' The camera flashed. 'Now I want you to get down off the table and just walk about.'

Rachel watched as the girl hesitated, then climbed down with dainty rather awkward movements, her breasts swaying gently. They were small breasts, pale under bikini marks, less firm than they might have been, Rachel considered, but not badly shaped.

The girl stood up, brushing from her cheeks stray wisps of untidy russet hair, most of which was gathered in a loose bun at the back of her head. 'Like this?' she said in a soft, barely audible voice.

'In front of the divider,' Max prompted. 'Don't bother to pose. Just move about. Be yourself.'

The girl stepped around the end of the room divider,

turning to look over her shoulder at Max as he took another picture.

'Lovely,' he said.

She began to pick at objects resting on the divider top, a china figurine, a paperback, glancing up at intervals toward the camera. The flash unit flared again and again.

Unconsciously Rachel's eyes narrowed in scrutiny. The girl had a nice figure – even if her tummy seemed a little too rounded – and her small, heart-shaped face with its large eyes and petite mouth was attractive. Its blankness of expression had first suggested dullness, even stupidity, but now Rachel saw there was a quietly self-regarding quality about her – a teasing awareness in the way her gaze lingered, for only fractions of a second, on the two men watching her.

The paperback slipped from her fingers and she bent quickly from the waist, her bottom high to the camera, her eyes flickering at Max as she rose. It was a momentary look, but filled with a secret exultation that struck Rachel as irremediably tarty. She wondered if Max found her attractive.

'She moves very well,' the photographer murmured.

The man at his side nodded authoritatively.

'Oh yes, Christine's very experienced. I mean, she knows all the poses.' His accent was a dull London monotone; he shut off abruptly as Max gave him a sharp look.

'I thought you said she hadn't tried any of the men's books before?'

'She hasn't. I mean, experienced as an amateur.'

Max grunted and returned to his camera. 'What d'you mean – clubs, stuff like that?'

The girl had reached the window wall and was leaning against a chair.

'Some, but mainly modelling for me at home, perhaps getting a few friends round – all serious photographers, mind. We study all the mags very carefully.'

'Uh-huh . . . . Sit on the chair, love, will you,' Max called. 'Good – cross your knees.' He squinted through the viewfinder. 'Ever tried any mixed modelling?'

'You mean with other girls?'

'And fellows.' Max took another picture. 'Now stretch both your legs out, love – that's it – straight in front of you. Not so close together. Just do what feels natural.' He wound on the film and glanced questioningly at the other man.

'We've done the odd few poses at the end of sessions. Sort of semi-serious. A couple of the lads are fairly keen. Christine quite enjoys it, don't you, darling?'

'It's all very tasteful,' the girl cut in suddenly. 'It's not disgusting or anything.'

'No, 'course not,' Max said quickly and lined up another shot. 'It's just there's a big demand these days for stuff that's a bit more graphic than the usual books. The difference is piddling – they have these bloody silly rules. But it's worth more money. It's mainly for abroad, anyway, so you're not going to see it in your newsagent's. Then there're films, of course.'

'Films?' The man looked startled. 'You mean blue movies?'

Max grunted and took the picture; both the man and the girl watched him closely. 'That's just words, isn't it?' he said, looking up. 'The average blue movie is what you see in the West End, with the censored bits left in. They fake it all up, anyway. It's a good opening if you've got a flair for it. ' He shrugged. 'Give it a bit of thought. I can set something up if you're interested.'

The man glanced quickly at the girl. 'Film star, eh,

Christine? How about that?'

The girl seemed uncertain. 'I don't know. Aren't I going to be in the magazine?'

'Oh, that's something else,' Max said. He put down his camera. 'Let me take a look at these test shots first and I'll get straight back to you. You can get dressed now, love.'

He glanced at the man as the girl rose and went back into the dining area; she turned her back, lifted a bra from somewhere below the room divider and, with the same deliberation she had shown throughout, began to put it on.

'Get her to lose about half a pound to flatten that tummy.' Max spoke quietly. 'And try some sun-ray treatment on the boobs – not much, just enough to even out the tan. Oh and next time' – he raised his voice, including the girl – 'leave your underclothes off the day of the shoot, love. Saves waiting for the marks to fade. Your hubby'll stop you getting touched up on the Tube.'

He gave his low, throaty chuckle as the girl smiled wanly; she was straightening a sweater over clinging, dark cord jeans.

Her companion ducked his head toward Max. 'About these films you mentioned.' His eyes flickered back toward Rachel and his voice dropped. 'When you say "more graphic" I take it you're referring to a certain amount of – genital contact?'

Max frowned, then he nodded. 'Well, whatever it takes,' he muttered. 'That's not a problem, is it?'

'Oh no, no, shouldn't be at all.' The other man rubbed his moustache briskly. 'As I say, Christine's very experienced.'

Max was still frowning. 'Tell you what – if you want to know more about it, I can arrange for you to sit in on a movie shoot. Let you get the feel of things.'

'Really?' The man's eyes were bright. 'That would be great. I'd really appreciate that.'

The hall door opened and the blonde woman put her head round. 'Oh, darling, could you show Mr and Mrs – er – Sewell out, please,' Max called.

With handshakes and hesitant smiles, the couple made their exit. As the front door clicked shut, Max turned to Rachel, shaking his head in amusement.

'*Quel wankeur*, eh? *Quel wankeur*.' He grinned in the lop-sided conspiratorial way he judged to be charming.

Rachel sat stonily as he drew very close, his grin broadening. She had just seen her father and May again, in all but actuality, and the experience had both sobered her and left her uneasy.

'Will you use her?' she asked.

'Oh yeah.' Max nodded, still grinning, looming over her. 'She's got a good body, knows how to move it. She likes it, too.'

'What about her husband?'

'No problem. I'll let him watch. That's what gets him going. I'll give him a bloody heart attack!' He laughed and leaned forward, making Rachel shrink back, but he was reaching for a light-box on the desk behind her. He switched it on and opened one of several boxes of transparencies.

He began to lay out the transparencies across the bright mica surface. Rachel glanced down at them and then looked closer. She saw herself, sitting on the edge of a bed, dressed in a black silk chemise.

'Thought you'd like a look before I finished sorting them. It's not a bad set.' Max sniffed and found an eyeglass, bending over for a closer examination.

Suddenly absorbed, forgetting his proximity, Rachel

bent over too, twisting on her chair. One by one, bright and extraordinarily colourful, images of herself, each differentiated by the smallest movement of head or arm, sometimes only of eyes or mouth, paraded across the light-box.

Rachel was astonished. Physically, it was her – *very* physically when the shoulders of the chemise began to drop and first one then another rounded breast rose into view – but it was a self she hardly recognized. It was like looking at a stranger who had somehow borrowed her face and figure, a stranger who was sleek-skinned and lush and very, very glamorous. Was this how other people saw her? No wonder men stared at her on the Tube.

Then Max put down another transparency, picturing her in mid-blink so that only the whites of her eyes showed and she looked demented. She burst out laughing.

'That's what you ought to do more of,' Max murmured, grinning at her sideways.

Her brow creased. 'You mean, look as cracked as that?'

'*Laugh* a little, *cry*, if you like – get more animation into it. You got a great little body and it photographs well, but the poker-faced bit only works up to a point. Believe me – I'm only trying to help.'

'*Relax, Rachel. Forget about the camera. Just take your time, love.*'

She had sat in her underwear in a studio so cold her nipples had felt like bullets inside her bra. Tracey, who had made her up with surprising skill, busied herself behind Max. *Don't go*, Rachel had willed with all the force of the tension inside her. *Don't leave me alone with him.*

She took the eyeglass as Max passed it over and looked at the picture he had indicated. It was a three-quarter-length view of her standing against a light-coloured surface, which gave her flesh a warm, almost olive hue. She was nude, posed as if surprised, one leg slightly in front of the other, arms back, breath held in, she remembered, to give her body poise, her bust its maximum extension. She looked at her face. The lips were slightly apart, as if about to voice a protest; the eyes, dark and almond-shaped, glistened with a withering contempt, a fierce dare to the viewer both to stare and to suffer the consequences.

'Now that's a look to blister paint,' Max chuckled.

Rachel breathed in, feeling herself colour. Its venom embarrassed her, even directed, as it was, against a man like Max.

'I just look so annoyed.'

'No.' Max shook his head. 'It's great. They'll lap it up at *Prince*. That'll be a full page, I bet you. It says passion, that does. It says, "Come on and get it and I'll rip your balls off!" They'll love it. They'll *love* it.'

Grinning, he moved away across the room. 'A bit more of that and I can get you a centre in any mag on this island.' He began to rummage in a drawer. 'Your friend Josey's got the same look, but she's got no force behind it, no emotion. She just wants to pick up her money and piss off.'

Rachel turned back to the transparencies, unwilling to comment on her flatmate, but even more puzzled by Max. During their photo session he had not made any kind of advance – had even shown a kind of gruff sympathy – but it had been an hour before her heart-beat had resumed anything like its normal rate. Inwardly her nervousness had persisted almost to the end, only forgotten when she had concentrated on a series of precise poses. Had Max done that deliberately?

She had come away from the studio both gasping with relief, and convinced that she had ruined everything by being wooden and awkward, hopelessly tense. Yet in these

256

pictures Max had made her look exotic, dramatic, even beautiful. The contrast between the man who could do that and the one she had seen abusing himself in front of Josey seemed extraordinary.

'Here.' She looked up. Max was at her side, holding out two ten-pound notes.

'What's that for?'

'On account. I'd like to do another set with you.' He frowned. 'Come on, take it! It doesn't happen that often.'

Rachel obeyed him, hesitantly. 'I don't understand.'

Max began replacing the transparencies in their boxes. 'I showed some of these to an American mag. Looks like they want to do something. It'll be more money than last time. That's just to keep you in touch.'

Rachel's face grew rigid. 'This isn't this "more graphic" thing, is it?'

'No!' Max screwed up his face at the thought. 'That was just to keep the wanker on the boil. No – they're just getting more crotchy in the States at the moment. But it's all stylized – heads and legs chopped off, big close-ups. Personally I think it looks fucking dreadful, but it's making a fortune. ' He looked at her suddenly. 'I meant it about never seeing the stuff over here, though. Those mags never cross the ditch.' He sniffed, hunching over the light-box. 'Look, I'll give you a bell about it in a couple of days, OK?'

It was Rachel's cue to leave. She rose. 'Thanks for letting me see the pictures.'

'Oh, by the way.' Max turned quickly. 'I wasn't bull-shitting about movies, either – I got a lot of contacts. It's where you make the real bread. There's travel too. You could do a lot better than that po-faced cow earlier.'

Rachel stiffened. She shook her head abruptly. 'No. Never.'

Max shrugged. 'Suit yourself.' He went to turn, then halted again. 'I've got to put a name on these trannies. I can never think of anything. You got any ideas?'

Rachel paused. Then a thought crossed her mind, so frighteningly delicious its daring almost made her catch her breath. She voiced it instantly, before her courage failed.

'What about "May"?' she said.

She was a fool. She saw it so clearly now.

Listening to Derek, to Josey, to Max – she hadn't needed to take her clothes off if she could look as good as Max had made her, as good as that snooty girl at Norman's party. She could be a proper model – in fashion, in TV ads, anywhere.

But now Andrew would see her pictures and think she was another May because she had lied about it from the beginning. May! There was a bitter irony in choosing that name. Just to spite her father – just to have him wander into a newsagent and see how much better his daughter was than the ridiculous woman he had married . . .

Angry and confused, she clattered up the staricase to the flat, head down, heedless of her surroundings until, rounding the dim second landing, she collided with a pillar of dark, clean-smelling worsted.

She sprang back with a gasp as a hand clutched at her elbow, steadying her.

'Rachel! Are you all right?'

She caught her breath, blinking at the stocky, prosperous-looking man above her, his handsome middle-aged face frowning and solicitous.

'Oh, Norman – I mean, Mr Bealby – yes, I'm fine.' She smiled, still confused, as he let go her arm. 'I'm sorry, I was miles away.'

'Actually I'm glad I saw you, Rachel,' he said. 'We might have something coming up. Can you talk to Deirdre in the office in the next couple of days?'

He went to step past her. Rachel's eyes brightened. 'It's not anything to do with catalogues — mail-order catalogues — is it?'

Norman halted, looking surprised. 'I don't think so, dear. What made you think that?'

'Oh — just something I heard.'

The man became thoughtful. 'We've only used you for leafleting, haven't we?'

'There was a marine trade promotion.'

'Oh, yes. When Angela couldn't make it — that was kind of you to help out.' Norman smiled, as if remembering something. 'Well, we're always happy to look at zed cards or portfolios.'

He started to move again and Rachel back-stepped to forestall him. 'I've just finished some work. If I showed you some pictures, would it be worth trying for any catalogue jobs — in future, I mean?'

This time Norman's smile was strained. 'It's a very specialized field, dear. They all want the girl-next-door look — everything to reassure the mums. And they tend to be — pernickety — about other work . . . . ' He trailed off, snatching a glance at an expensive wristwatch, and immediately broke into a brisk trot. 'Bye for now! Don't forget to call Deirdre, will you?' he called over his shoulder.

And Rachel was alone on the landing. Josey had told him about the *Prince* shots. The realization came to her as the street door thumped distantly. *They tend to be pernickety* — he'd screwed Josey and she'd told him. Rachel couldn't believe it. Josey was already sleeping with him just to get better work, and she still had to sabotage Rachel's chances.

Incredulity turned to cold fury, which grew and grew. She thundered up the stairs, wrenched her key in the lock and threw open the door on the small living room.

Josey was leaning over the glass-topped dining table in the corner, peering at a sheet of paper. She was dressed in a white slip, stockingless, her blonde hair ruffled; her face was exultant.

'Oh, *fantastic!*' She bounced up, catching sight of Rachel and breaking into an ecstatic smile. 'Fantastic!'

Such unexpected enthusiasm blunted Rachel's anger. Scowling, she pushed the door shut behind her.

'It's from Dave! You know Dave, the boyfriend who was living here before you moved in?' Breathless, Josey shook her head in happy wonder; she returned to scanning the letter hungrily. 'I never expected to hear a word. He went off to France or somewhere – but he's settled now, he's got a flat, he wants me to go and see him. He's even sent me the cash for a ticket. Isn't that *incredible!*'

Shrugging off her coat, Rachel slumped into a sagging armchair. 'Great.'

Josey glanced up, hearing her glum tone. 'Oh, I know I haven't made much of him beforehand but he really *was* lovely. And you know how you don't dare get your hopes up because the chances are he won't even remember your *name* after a couple of days.' She laughed, pressing her lips to the now crumpled paper. 'I mean, somebody *must* care if they're willing to pay your fare halfway across the Continent!'

'Good,' said Rachel, 'then you won't need that catalogue work you just screwed Norman to get.'

Josey's face was suddenly blank. 'What are you talking about?'

Rachel sniffed. 'You're not telling me you've both been

260

discussing the weather dressed like that? I *saw* him on the stairs.'

Josey frowned. 'So what? I told you he'd be here.' Her face changed. 'I never let Norman lay a finger on me until Dave was long gone, if that's what you're fussed about.'

Rachel's eyes blazed. 'I'm "fussed" about *work* – about queering other people's pitches by telling Norman *everything* – and telling boyfriends too!'

Josey said nothing, then she took a deep breath and sat down. 'You really pick your moments, don't you, Rachel?'

Something in her look pricked Rachel's wrath. 'What do you mean?' She was suddenly uncertain.

'I didn't get any work from Norman,' said Josey quietly. 'There is no catalogue coming up. What there is, is a brochure for sex aids. It's something Norman's agency won't touch because he doesn't do glamour work, but he thought the contact might be useful to me because he knows I do. Only he found out today they don't want a blonde – they want someone dark. So I suggested you – though I really don't know why I bothered.'

As she finished, Rachel's face was pale. She chewed her lip, her eyes dropping. 'Oh, shit.'

Josey gave a sigh and straightened in her chair. 'But today,' she said briskly, 'absolutely nothing is going to upset me because I really don't give a toss any – '

'Josey, I'm sorry.' Rachel looked up. 'I really am. I just got so het up – '

The telephone on the dining table trilled, interrupting her. Josey picked it up.

'Hello – oh, hello. Yes, I'm fine and . . . ? Oh, so you're finished at the agency, are you? Well, good luck.' She glanced across the room at Rachel. 'Yes, she's fine too . . . . Mmm. Well, actually she's between temping jobs at the moment – Yes, well, secretarial work is a bit hard to find these days.' Josey's gaze narrowed as she spoke. 'No, *here* . . . . Would you like to talk to her?'

Josey extended the receiver across the table, her hand over the mouthpiece. 'Don't you *dare* ever say again I don't look after you!' she hissed, eyes bright.

Swallowing, Rachel jumped up; she grasped the phone, 'Hello?'

The voice at the other end was hesitant. 'Oh, hello – Rachel? I don't know if you'll remember me. We met at a party the other week. My name's Andrew – Andrew Gridley – '

The realization that she loved him came in a single instant – without debate, or doubt; it was, simply, a conclusion, a summation of every bubbling feeling that accompanied her sight of him, his touch, his continuing and curious hesitancy.

How, after three, four, half a dozen dates, could he still be nervous of her? Why did each phone call begin on that note of uncertainty – as if he expected her to have forgotten him?

'Simple,' said Josey. 'He's crazy about you.'

'But he doesn't *do* anything. I mean, we've only just started holding hands – he hasn't even kissed me properly.'

'Perhaps he's queer.'

'No . . . *no!* He's just shy – sometimes I think he's afraid of me.'

'Great! That's exactly where you want him.'

'Josey!'

'He just can't believe his luck, that's all.'

'Neither can I!'

'Well, give him a nudge. You fancy him, don't you?'

'I think he's gorgeous. But *I* can't do anything – I can't

make him grab me. He might just want to be friends.'

Josey's look was old-fashioned. 'I should be going to see Dave this weekend. I won't be back before Tuesday, longer if I can manage it. Invite loverboy round. You'll soon find out how friendly he wants to be.'

Rachel sighed long and deep. 'I just wish I didn't *care* so much.'

Josey wrinkled her nose in a swift smile. 'Mmm. Great, isn't it?'

They both laughed.

She slipped the empty dinner-plates into the sink, glimpsing her dark reflection in the windowpane above it. The hair she had spent the afternoon pinning up in an elaborate bun still looked intact. The fact did not ease the rippling tension inside her. Then she noticed a reflected movement in the glass and half turned.

'Oh, thanks.'

She moved to let him deposit the dessert dishes in the bowl. He was wearing a pale blue shirt she liked – she approved of his taste – and dark hopsack trousers that fitted beautifully. They brushed her dress and she felt the urge to touch them. Instead she reached out, twisted on the tap and squeezed washing-up liquid into the bowl.

'Washing-up time,' he said, loosening his cuffs. He began rolling his sleeves.

'No, don't be silly.' She frowned, turning off the tap. 'You're the guest. These are just soaking – anyway, it's late.'

He glanced down at his wristwatch. His forearms were well-shaped, smooth, pleasing to look at. *Why did I mention the time?*

He looked up awkwardly.

263

'What's the matter?' she asked quickly. She knew it must be nearly midnight. He shared a house in Wimbledon. The Underground stopped running soon. On any previous date he would have left her by now.

He smiled thinly. 'It's just that I've got a stack of work tomorrow.'

Rachel didn't reply. She felt cold. 'It was a really fantastic meal,' he said.

Annoyance stirred under her rigid calm, and she built on it to smother the sourness of her disappointment. But he was still gazing at her, as if waiting for her to react.

She dropped her eyes. 'I'll get your coat.' And went to brush past him, but to her surprise he didn't yield. She was still as his arms came round her, his head angling down.

The kiss was hurried and lopsided, his lips bumping the side of her mouth. Then they found each other and she was rising on tiptoe, opening her mouth on his, pressing herself to him with all the unfettered urgency of weeks of uncertainty and fear and longing.

They undressed in the bedroom, silently, on the carpet between Josey's small double bed and Rachel's narrow single. The gas fire, the room's only illumination, popped gently, its warmth prickling the flesh of Rachel's back. And it was only as she rose, naked but for her briefs, reaching down to smooth them off, that she looked directly at Andrew, and immediately stopped filled with a sudden dread.

He was kneeling, the warm orange light full on broad shoulders, a smooth, hairless chest, the white of underpants distorted by a blunt ridge angled across his thigh. There was a kind of wondering pain in his face.

She had done something terribly wrong. By undressing

264

so quickly, by moving instantly from kitchen to bedroom as if there were no alternative, no persuasion necessary, by cheapening herself in his eyes . . .

As she went to open her mouth he spoke first. 'You're so – so – *beautiful*.' The words were a dry whisper. 'I just can't – tell you. So –'

Then his breath caught in a grunt and a fierce shudder. Gasping, he dropped his head. Rachel looked down, frowning at his moan. And saw the stain of damp cotton spreading at his groin.

'Oh, God, I feel such a – Jesus, I'm sorry, I really –' He was gabbling, scarlet-faced. Rachel turned to Josey's bed and pushed back the cover. Swiftly, she peeled off her briefs and slipped between the sheets. She lay on her back, drawing the coverlet up to her neck.

'It's all right,' she said. 'Just take them off.'

She watched him, a steady blink betraying her nervousness, as he shrugged off his pants, turning slightly away from her in the dim glow. Then he eased onto the mattress at her side.

His flesh was warm against hers, his breathing deep. He sighed. 'I feel so –'

'It's all right.' She moved against him in the warm darkness. His chest was soft; she tucked her head beneath his chin, moving her loosened hair against his shoulder.

'It's all right. Don't worry. Everything's all right.'

'Lift your bum higher, Rachel,' said Max. 'Higher than that! Now reach back – no, between your legs. That's good. That's lovely. Now touch the sides of your fanny – just fingertips.'

'I can't do that.' She was on knees and elbows, on cushions of silvery satin, brow resting on forearm. She turned her head. The photographer was behind her, crouching under a golden umbrella,

265

Tracey impassive at his side.

'Rachel — come on! I've got a brief to follow. It's one lousy shot.'

She sighed. She moved her hand.

Click!

His hands moved on her, slowly, wonderingly as if the flesh she knew so well, its tautness, its roundness, its unremarked folds were some kind of miracle, impossible to believe. His eyes shone and she basked in their disbelieving joy, sinking into his warmth, borne up by the swelling tide of his excitement.

This was not the hurried, guilty conjunction she had known with Barry Drew; this was unstinted and total, a mutual giving and receiving that mingled tenderness and touch, flesh and feeling in ways she had never dreamed possible.

She felt herself beautiful. He made her beautiful. Until now she had never really believed it.

Click!

'That's better, Rachel! That's a million per cent improvement. Now keep that look — bring your hands down — legs just a little bit wider. That's great! No, don't move — don't lose it — just keep that feeling.'

Her head was back; the pale blue of the background rose above her. She heard murmurs.

'We got the Vaseline?' Max's softened rasp.

'What do you need that for?' Tracey querying, making a point.

A pause. 'Oh yeah, what d'you know?' And louder. 'Now Rachel — just stay as you are — don't move an inch — and we'll go again.'

Click!

He was always with her. His words echoed in her head, his

body left its imprint on hers – in hers.

On the Tube, heading for Kilburn – '*Just one more shoot for the Yanks, Rachel. Come on, if they like a girl they're all mad for her, but they go off the boil if you piss them about. It's better money*' – her thoughts wandered to Josey, three weeks gone, and immediately Andrew's seed, fresh from that bleary-eyed morning, dropped within her.

A flush started from the dampness in her briefs; it turned her face scarlet; her flesh burned for him with an immediacy that frightened her, and drew curious glances from the commuters opposite. *If only you knew – if only.* In her mind she was naked to him.

Click!

'*And again – that's fabulous – now on your side – bend your knee – bit more – bring your arm up–* '

He was with her in the limbo of the studio. There was no camera, no spark and whine of the flash, no grating murmur from Max. She lived in him. He lived in her. And he touched her – so clearly her body twitched, her heat drummed. She dared not open her eyes to be disappointed.

There was a spring in her centre, a coiled, breath-devouring spring that gathered and tightened. She felt her breath on him; his fingers brushed her, bristling the fine down of her abdomen, the straggling curls below.

Lightning struck with dizzying force, cleaving her from crotch to head. It was so sudden, so totally unexpected her whole body jerked spastically; she rolled sideways, gasping in shock. Then, just as quickly, sat up, pressing a hand to her brow, shuddering violently.

'*Are you all right?*' *Tracey watched her from the shadows beyond the lights.*

'*I don't know.*' *Rachel shuddered again and sucked in breath.* '*It's stupid – I just came over so strange.*'

267

Then she saw Max's face, surfacing from behind the camera, dark and questioning, watching so intently that she laughed, suddenly and inexplicably embarrassed to her core.

'And who's been screwing in my bed?'

'*Josey!*'

The blonde girl leaned in the doorway to the bedroom, hand on hip. There was a flight bag over one shoulder, brightly coloured carrier-bags about her feet. She looked tired and bedraggled and radiant.

Beaming, Rachel slammed the front door, stepped over a suitcase and skipped to her friend. They hugged.

'Why didn't you phone or write?'

Josey cocked an inquisitive eyebrow. 'I see – afraid I might surprise you and young Grisly in the act?' She glanced back through the bedroom door. 'Does look like the springs have had a good bashing. I suppose it *is* thingymajig . . . ?'

Rachel nodded, her smile glowing.

'Didn't I tell you?' Josey prodded her arm, letting down the flight bag. 'An intimate little dinner, inquisitive flat-mate out of the way – Bob's your uncle, or Andrew, or Dave! Is he staying here now?'

Rachel's face changed. 'Oh, no – I mean, he's stayed overnight quite a lot, but he's got his own place. I'd have tidied up your bed if I'd known you were coming.'

Josey shook her head. 'That bed's seen enough wild humping – a bit more isn't going to make any difference. Not to me, at any rate. Not any more.'

She paused as Rachel's eyes widened. 'You don't mean . . . ?'

'I'm only here to collect my things.' Josey shrieked with laughter. 'He wants me to move in – now, this minute. Isn't

268

it incredible – incredi*bule! Incredibule!*'

She began leaping about the room, flinging her arms wide, throwing Rachel into fits of laughter.

'So you turned him down flat,' she managed at last.

Josey's face went instantly straight. 'Oh, of course. I mean a girl's got to look after her reputation.'

'Naturally.'

Their expressions cracked. They laughed maniacally.

'I still can't *believe* it,' Josey collapsed at last into an armchair. 'His flat is *vast* – three big bedrooms – the bathroom is bigger than this living room! Central heating, not that we'll need much of that.' She grinned and sighed. 'God, he is *so* nice. He's got this engineering job to do with NATO. He's not in the army or anything, but they give him a kind of honorary rank. It means he can shop in this NAAFI supermarket place where the prices are so cheap. He might be able to get me some work too. *Not* modelling. Something in an office – '

Rachel settled on the sofa opposite her. 'Do you want to live in France, though?'

'It's not France, I got it all wrong.' Josey lifted her eyes in mock exasperation. 'It's Belgium. Near Liège. Right out in the country. They don't even speak French. It's Flem something – '

'Phlegm?' Rachel made a face.

Josey hooted with laughter. 'They sound as if they're having a good hawk.' She mimicked the action, making Rachel grimace still further.

As the laughter subsided, Rachel grew serious. 'Isn't it a bit risky, going so far so quickly?'

Josey smiled, pausing before she answered. 'No. I can see how it could look like that. And I *know* I'm not the most cautious lady in the world! But it doesn't feel that way at all.

It just feels right – it feels natural. For Dave as well as me. Even if it all went completely wrong in a couple of months – and I hope to God it doesn't! – it would still be right. Do you know what I mean?'

Rachel nodded slowly. The room had grown quiet. 'I don't think I would have done before Andrew. But I do now.' She smiled.

Josey's returning smile widened, then abruptly she sprang up. 'Well, where is loverboy? This is celebration time! Champagne and roses and After Eight mints!'

Rachel laughed. '*After Eight mints?*'

'Well, I couldn't afford champagne and the florists were shut.' Josey dived for a carrier-bag and began rummaging.

'Andrew's working tonight,' said Rachel. 'He's got exams in a couple of weeks.'

'Then we'll get fat alone!' Josey lifted a small dark green carton aloft with a cry of triumph. 'And you can tell me all the things about Grisly you wouldn't dare to if he was here.'

It was a kind of intimacy Rachel had temporarily forgotten, a sharing of secret hopes and fears and desires with affection but without the tensions, the unspoken obligations of a sexual relationship.

At first such an opening out made her feel guilty – surely only Andrew deserved this? But as she and Josey talked – drinking cheap Algerian red over the remains of a Chinese take-away, a single celebratory candle, planted in a saucer, lighting the room – her feelings changed.

What took place between Andrew and herself was something rarefied and exalting, something she could not imagine living without, but it was also different, a joint creation; and apart from it, rather to her surprise, she

270

discovered she was still the uncertain, ordinary, hopelessly insecure person as before.

'I just live in dread,' she said quietly, 'of those *Prince* pictures coming out. I don't even dare ask Max when they're due.' She sat on the carpet, back against the sofa, knees outstretched; the candleflame at her side painted her face with wavering strokes of shadow.

Opposite her, propped against the armchair, Josey frowned. 'You mean, thingy still thinks you're temping?'

'I say I do the odd job between looking for modelling work, which is true.' Rachel spoke defensively. 'I go to every agency I can. I've heard every excuse there is a hundred times. "Our books are full – get a proper zed card – get a proper portfolio." Except I can't afford a good photographer to do either. And the agencies who arrange it themselves say, "Oh, you're too short to do fashion, your figure's too full, we only take trained girls – have you ever considered nude work? Experience isn't so important there." '

She mimicked the open vowels of the last agency representative she had seen, making Josey hiccup with laughter. The blonde girl reached a packet of cigarettes off the carpet, handing one to Rachel.

'I thought you said you were still working with Max?'

Rachel leaned forward to light her cigarette from the candle. 'Only to pay the rent for this place!' She breathed in, lifting her head to blow smoke through her nostrils. 'It's all for abroad anyway. I'm not going to do any more in this country. I've made up my mind.'

Josey looked sceptical. 'I really wouldn't worry that much, Rachel. When I first started I was in half a dozen mags within a couple of months and *nobody* I knew recognized me. I was quite peeved!' She drew on her cigarette.

'You'd be surprised what a difference makeup and lighting make, honestly. And just being stripped off. Most men don't look beyond that.'

'What about Dave? What did he think about it?'

Josey grinned at the memory. 'He said he did recognize me – this was when I first met him – so I admitted it. It turned out he'd mistaken me for a completely different girl!'

'You mean, you wouldn't have told him otherwise?'

Josey shook her head, breathing out smoke. 'I would have, eventually, once I'd known it was reasonably serious. Dave wasn't stupid. He knew I was modelling – he'd have worked it out for himself soon enough. Anyway, he doesn't care about the past. Neither of us do. It's only what happens now that's important.' She drank from her glass, snorting with sudden laughter just as she swallowed. 'Just as well!'

Grinning, Rachel asked why.

Josey blotted her lip with the back of her hand. She shrugged. 'Oh, he met Norman a couple of times. I don't think he'd be too impressed if he knew Mr B and I had got it together. And he *loathed* Max.'

Rachel stiffened, the cosy, semi-inebriated atmosphere suddenly undermined. She stared at her friend. 'You told me hell would freeze over before you'd let him lay a finger on you!'

Josey looked up in surprise. Then she grinned. 'You've got a good memory! *I* hardly remember saying that.' The grin faded as Rachel continued to stare at her. She glanced down into her glass. 'Well, actually it was a bit of a white lie.'

'Oh *Josey*! How could you – with him?'

'I *didn't* – with him!' Josey's brow creased in annoyance. She tossed an exasperated look at the ceiling. 'Honestly,

Rachel, you can be a pain sometimes. *You're* the one who's working with the man!'

'But I wouldn't have – if you hadn't said what you did.'

Rachel blinked as the older girl was silent, gazing across the shadowed room. At last Josey sighed.

'I don't want to quarrel tonight. I really don't.'

Rachel breathed in. She knew she was being silly and felt guilty and contrite for souring the evening. But the sense of betrayal lingered and nagged. 'It was just – it just seemed a bit unlikely, you and Max,' she said flatly.

Josey drew deeply on her cigarette. 'This is all such a fuss about nothing,' she murmured. Then, more positively: 'You know Max and his missus shoot porno films at his studio.'

Rachel's mouth opened in surprise. 'I didn't know *he* did it – I thought he just knew people.'

Josey sniffed. 'They do a lot of it there – Max and others – it's how he pays for the place. I'm surprised he hasn't asked you about it.'

'He has – three or four times.'

'Well, he asked me too.' Josey paused and smiled.

Rachel stared at her. 'You mean, you said you would?'

'A couple of times, five or six altogether, I suppose. Oh, Rachel!'

Josey's eyes widened over a wry grin. 'Don't give me that oh-how-could-she look! You're making a big deal out of nothing. It didn't mean a thing to me. I wasn't going out with anybody. They all took about as long as a normal shoot – and they paid a lot more. And, anyway, I was curious.'

'Curious!' Rachel felt ridiculous for reacting as she did, but her heart still bumped, her face still burned.

'Yes!' Josey was laughing, unable to stop herself, through

a look of pained sympathy. 'Oh, come on, Rachel – you must have fantasized about situations where some gorgeous stranger comes up and just *does* you, beautifully. I just wanted to see what it was like.'

'What was it like?'

'Sexy.' Josey grinned. 'Very sexy, sometimes. Not wildly, orgasmically *fantastic* – but better than some screws I've had. Better than dear old Norman! Actually we seemed to spend most of our time giggling – it's very hard to be madly passionate when you have to stop every two minutes so they can move the camera.' She halted then sighed. 'Oh, dear. Now you think I'm some depraved trollop –'

'No, I don't,' Rachel snapped, colouring at her lie and ashamed of it; she sipped quickly at her glass. 'Do you think you'll ever tell Dave?'

'I would if he asked – I hope he doesn't because he'd probably insist on having a copy!'

Rachel smiled thinly. She wanted to be friends again. 'I always wondered why Max didn't try anything while we were working. I mean, like when we first met –'

'Poor old Rachel!' Josey's sympathetic smile was back. 'You must have been lying there with your pussy in one hand and a blunderbuss in the other!'

As Rachel's smile broadened, the blonde girl sat up. 'Not that Max wouldn't try his luck if he thought he stood half a chance.' She suddenly laughed out loud, startling Rachel. 'Isn't it a *crazy* business! Can you imagine anyone paying Dave – or Andy – to drop their pants for a few photos? "Come on, Davey, you don't look *interested* enough. Let's put a bit of *life* into it." '

She imitated Max's slurring rasp with an accuracy that brought astonished laughter to Rachel's lips.' "Oh you got to be longer than *that*!" ' Josey dissolved into hysterical giggles and slumped back, bosom heaving, eyes closed. 'Oh, God,' she said, recovering slowly. 'Oh, God, I shall miss it all.'

Rachel looked up, her laughter subsiding. *'Will* you?'

'Oh, yes.' Josey sniffed. 'I've enjoyed myself. I shall miss my little thrill.'

'Thrill?' Rachel was eyeing her over her glass.

'Yes! Don't give me that look again, Rachel! I happen to like stripping off – it gives me a nice feeling, most of the time. And I've never known anyone any good at this lark who doesn't feel the same. Why not? It's a natural female thing – at least I think it is.'

She lowered her head, defensively, and drank. 'And don't go all holier-than-thou,' she added, glancing up with a hint of pettishness. 'You wouldn't be getting all this work from Max if you weren't giving him what he wanted. He's not exactly David Bailey, but he's not a fool either.'

Rachel put down her drink and was silent, gazing at the candleflame. 'Have you ever – ' She paused, not lifting her head. 'Got carried away, in a session?'

Josey's eyes narrowed, an impish grin taking hold. 'Rachel, have you been a naughty girl?'

Rachel turned to her. 'Seriously. Have you?'

'There was one guy who tried to jump on *me* – one or two nice things developed after shoots . . . . ' Josey frowned. 'Has Max had a go at you?'

'No.' Rachel shook her head dismissively and got up, lurching suddenly as the effects of the wine hit her. Josey continued to watch as she balanced herself against the sofa arm. 'Oh, God I feel quite squiffy – ' With a gasp she plumped down onto the sofa cushions, a magazine crackling beneath her.

Josey climbed to her feet, more carefully than her flatmate, and picked her way past the failing candle. 'Time we had a nice hot coffee,' she mouthed.

Rachel screwed up her eyes in the abrupt flood of light from the kitchen. She suddenly felt small and chill and tired and she wished Andrew's arms were around her, snug and warm in Josey's big bed.

'I really wouldn't lose any sleep about *Prince*,' Josey called above the rumble of the kettle. 'There are worse magazines about, believe me.'

Rachel stirred, hearing again the crackle of glossy paper. 'I just want to earn a living as an ordinary model.' Frowning she pulled the magazine from beneath her. It was thick and brightly coloured, folded back on its spine to show a fashion page of a grinning girl performing a cartwheel in a park. The model looked to Rachel much plainer than herself. She turned the page toward the light and read, 'Photographs by James Kingsley.'

'Have you ever gone straight to a photographer, Josey?' Rachel asked.

'Once – when I first started,' Josey called. 'I phoned up this magazine about some guy whose name I'd seen in it. They were really snotty, so I said I was his sister just back from Australia and we'd lost touch and I was only here for a couple of days.'

'And?'

'I went round and saw him. He was gorgeous, really nice too. We had a lovely time.' Josey appeared in the kitchen doorway with two mugs.

'And he gave you some work?'

'Oh no.' She handed a mug to Rachel. 'But we had a lovely time! Drink up.'

The telephone woke her just after nine, its ringing dinning

276

through her frail head with the force and rhythm of its pounding. Through slitted eyes she saw Josey's bed was empty.

She stumbled into the living room, too pained to do more than murmur for her flatmate. A shower hissed behind the bathroom door. Sighing, she rested her elbows on the table to prise up the receiver.

'Hello, duchess?' The voice's cheerfulness seemed a needless cruelty.

'Derek?'

'You sound terrible – been celebrating have you?'

She blinked in surprise. 'Yes, I have but – '

'I've just seen it in Smith's. Thought I had to ring and congratulate you. It's fantastic! Made my week.'

'What are you talking about?' Her annoyed confusion changed abruptly.

'*Prince*, Rachel.' Derek laughed. 'Didn't they even send you a copy? The mean buggers. Here – you don't get a commission, do you? I'll go back and buy half a dozen if you like.' He paused as Rachel's silence lengthened. 'Aren't you pleased, love?'

'What ?'

'Aren't you chuffed? The pictures look fabulous, really beautiful. Didn't I tell you you could knock the others for six? You're a natural, Rachel. A natural.'

Her fear was a void inside her, a numbing silence that spread, engulfing the day.

She moved through the hours mechanically, helping Josey pack, paying a brief visit to Norman's agency to pick up a long-awaited cheque, only remembering to pay it into her account moments before the bank closed.

At three o'clock Andrew rang. Josey answered the phone

and held the receiver out toward Rachel. 'Just ask what he wants,' she mouthed. '*Rachel!*' Josey glared. 'Talk to the man!' Rachel took the phone.

He had to study that night, but they could share a meal at his place before he started. Could she meet him there? She said yes. He had to ring off at once. Work was murder that day.

She put the receiver down, chewing her lip. There had been no rancour in his tone, no sign of anger, but no particular affection, either – only the urgency he professed. Was that an excuse to hide his real feelings?

Rachel was suddenly aware of Josey staring at her. 'Rachel,' the flatmate snapped. 'Stop it!'

But she did not, churning over numberless scenarios in her head as she rattled down the District Line. *'What are my friends going to say, Rachel? And the people at work! How can I introduce you as my girlfriend when everybody's sniggering behind our backs? I'll be a laughing-stock. I'm sorry, darling, we're going to have to say . . . . '* Or worse. *'Did you do it deliberately? Do you hate me that much? Or do you just enjoy acting like a tart?'*

His room was at the top of a Tudor-style semi on the edge of a railway line. The large hall was littered with bikes. *Top of the Pops* roared from the living room as she made her way up the stairs.

Andrew's door was ajar. He used a kitchen table as a desk, jammed into a dormer at right angles to the bed. Books and folders spilled across a faded, tawdrily patterned carpet. He sat with his back to the doorway, hunched over papers, reading by a swivel lamp clamped to the edge of the table. The air was thick and warm, though Rachel knew he could not have been home for more than half an hour.

'Darling?'

278

'Hi.' He did not look up, his tone was neutral. Rachel paused. He had been as distracted several times before when he studied, increasingly so in recent weeks. Perhaps he had simply begun concentrating earlier.

'I picked up some chicken pies on the way over, darling,' she said brightly, coming in. 'I thought we'd save time. They'll only need heating. Do you think we can use the cooker?'

She had dropped her carrier-bag on the bed and was undoing her coat before she noticed the stiffness in his turned back.

'How could you do it?'

There was ice in her veins, the void inside her welled up suddenly, filling the room. In a dozen mental run-throughs she had found no answer, beyond secrecy, beyond not being found out.

'What do you . . . ?'

'How?'

Why wouldn't he let her see his face? If they just looked at each other . . .

'Andrew, I'm just trying to earn a living as a model. It's not easy getting started. Lots of girls – '

'No.' He shook his head emphatically. 'No, I don't believe that.'

Under her fear a sense of injustice stirred anger. She curbed it, drawing in breath. 'It's not *that* bad a magazine. It's well known. I've got friends who read it – '

'Like the messenger boy I took it off today, the one I found wanking over it – over you!'

His words were almost a shriek, but Rachel only noticed his face, jerked towards her, contorted in a rictus of agony that made her catch her breath, the moisture filling and spilling from his eyes.

He snatched bright pages from the tabletop, flinging the magazine across the bed at her in a rustling mass. 'Look at it! *Look* at it!'

'Darling, please!' The tears broke from her. The magazine didn't matter any more, excuses didn't matter – all that did was that his pain should cease, the terrible rending of everything she held precious.

'How does a photographer get you like that? What does he do – screw you a few times? Or just let you play with yourself!'

'*Andrew!*'

He jumped back from his chair in absurd over-reaction as she reached a hand toward him, stumbling against the bed. And her eyes caught the crumpled pages on the counterpane.

A naked girl crouched before a man naked from the waist, her tongue extended toward the tip of his semi-erect penis.

Blinking, Rachel clutched at the magazine, pulling page from page. Pages of girls with legs and rears splayed, of huge gynaecological close-ups, of men and women together.

It was not *Prince*. It was something cruder, harder, even the colours were garish and raw.

'But I don't know what this is – I've never seen it before.'

'Jesus, Rachel! What kind of bloody idiot do you think I am!' Then she saw it. The pale background, the scattering of cushions, herself sprawling, splay-legged, open mouthed, eyes closed in fierce concentration, her exposed crotch a ring of dark, spreading hair, a finger buried in the pink, swollen flesh.

'But I didn't.' She was shaking her head, the tears starting again. 'I swear – I couldn't have.'

She turned a page. '*WHEN A PORNO MODEL LOSES HER COOL*', she read. ' "Normally I like it hot and hard, but sometimes a camera's all I need to get my juices oozing," says model May.'

May.

'I thought you just *looked* like that – I didn't think you *were*!' His words came like blows – she saw him flinch from their force. She understood every hurt, every twist of self-lacerating pain, every agony of a trust despised, defiled, discarded. And she could say nothing.

'Jesus, Rachel – Jesus, *Jesus!*' He shook his head, tears flying from his cheeks. 'I loved you – I *loved* you!'

It was too much. She darted toward the door, out onto the landing, down the stairs, running. And all she saw, as she went, was her face beneath the magazine headline. A face exulting in the knowledge of its own excitement, its own daring, the sharing of a secret and illicit joy.

It was the face of the girl she had seen auditioning at Max Wallace's flat. The face of her stepmother.

9
PAUL
1975

The wardrobe's surface had the appearance of a rich, pink brocade, until Paul touched it, and realized it was an illusion: oil-based paint had been applied with a clever, stippling effect on a cheap wood veneer.

Shaking his head, he twisted the small, rusted key in the wardrobe door. Nothing happened. He tried again, rattling the whole unit this time. Both doors cracked open just as a shelf collapsed inside. Cables, wires, switches, all tangled inextricably with the remains of several tripods and camera fittings, avalanched over Paul's feet.

'Oh, for Chrissakes!'

'Paul! You found that tripod yet?'

The finely pitched voice boomed down the corridor outside. Paul glanced round in annoyance. In the three years he had worked for him, his employer's talents had always far outweighed his patience.

Paul stepped back from the mess on the floor, treading awkwardly on the claw of a long-dead armadillo and almost slipping. The tiny, windowless room, not a great deal deeper than the wardrobe itself, was piled ceiling-high with a bizarre assortment of elderly photographic equipment and discarded props: stuffed animals and plastic palm trees, racks of period clothes, traffic signs, piles of ancient gramophone records, a huge Victorian hip bath, upended and dusty, its enamel base flaking. He knelt to retrieve sections of tripod as footsteps sounded outside and a figure appeared in the open doorway.

'My God, I haven't looked in here for years.'

James Kingsley was wearing his working clothes, dark green British army sweater over imaginatively patched corduroys, a dark red bandanna and well-worn moccasin slippers. Early attempts at a beard completed the vagabond effect.

'What is all this stuff, anyway?' Paul asked, tugging at the wire.

'Good heavens!' The photographer's weathered face broke into a smile of genuine delight, growing unexpectedly boyish. He stepped into the room.

'Where did you find it?' Paul indicated the wardrobe.

'I painted that thing at art college – I thought I'd chucked it out years ago!' He was grinning as he squatted at Paul's side, picking at the twisted cables. 'This was something I was playing about with, must be ten years ago now. My little contribution to the swinging sixties!'

Paul glanced at him, amused by the man's unfailing capacity for self-distraction. It was impossible wholly to dislike a man who could forget to be tetchy.

James was nodding. 'I got the idea from some theatre work I was involved in. A friend was doing theatre in the round – street theatre, really. A lot of improvisation. Fascinating stuff. The idea was to set up three or four cameras roughly in a circle – all on auto-wind and controlled from one point. Then the model would be in the middle, where I'd direct her on a sort of one-to-one basis. Firing off cameras as we went – '

Paul frowned. 'What was the point?'

James shrugged. 'I just got fed up with hiding behind a viewfinder all the time. I thought I'd get a more positive

283

response if I could get the model reacting to me rather than a blank lens. A bit of cinema verité, I suppose – or camera verité.'

'Did it work?'

'Not really.' I kept getting the bloody wires mixed up. Professional models got a bit twitchy, too. They're trained to relate to a camera, not some silly burke trying to be Eisenstein.'

Revived memories of the experiment seemed to dull the photographer's enthusiasm. He grunted, rising. 'I got some good results with amateurs, though. Made a couple of art editors happy.'

A doorbell rang far below. 'Damn! That'll be those prints from Metzer's. Can you deal with them, Paul? If I don't get this set straight today I'm going to get crucified. Tell them to tell Hugh there's a cheque in the post.'

'What about the tripod?'

'Forget it. It'll take too long. We'll hire one.'

James vanished with a haste that left Paul exasperated. Working for the man was as frustrating as it was educative. He pushed the wires and tripod pieces back into the wardrobe, propping it shut with a plastic palm. Then he switched off the light.

The corridor outside led past two work-rooms and a small kitchen to a stairwell. When Paul had first come here they were bedrooms and a lounge, with the original living room below converted into a studio.

Now, as Paul descended the stairs, he moved into an open studio area that occupied almost the entire ground floor of the Victorian terraced house. Toward the rear a curtain of high screens concealed James's set-building activities.

Paul went straight to the front door, which opened

directly into the studio space, and looked out. The narrow front garden was empty. He faced the cluttered façade of the identical two-storey terrace opposite, the double ranks of parked cars. Then a horn sounded and he saw the Jaguar slotted into the kerb a few yards to the right.

A short, dark-haired man in a camel-hair coat stood up from the driver's side and waved. 'Paul! Can you give us a hand?'

As Paul approached, a slim, serious-looking girl with dark, reddish hair backed from an open rear door. Seeing her, Paul broke into an embarrassed smile. She returned it quietly.

'Hello, Paul.'

'Andrea – I was expecting a van. This is a surprise.'

The girl's pale eyes softened. 'I hope it's a pleasant one.'

'All part of the service,' the dark man cut in, taking a large framed print from inside the car and handing it to Paul. His voice was rich and throaty, his eyes dark beads that gleamed at the young man.

'Take very good care of it, dear boy. That's worth four hundred on the gallery walls and I want a cheque to cover it and the other three.'

'Jimmy told me to tell you – '

'It's in the post – I know,' the other interrupted, reaching into the car again. 'That's partly why I'm here. I may also be able to do him a small service.' Carefully he positioned a second print in Paul's hands.

'You're not thinking of another photograhic exhibition?' There was excitement in Paul's face.

The dark man's thick eyebrows arched warningly. 'Dear boy, I've explained to you a dozen times photographs do not make a gallery money. Original paintings, yes – etchings, yes – lithographs, yes – even limited-edition prints. Photographs merely create publicity – *if* they're suitably outrageous. And the Metzer just doesn't happen to need publicity at the moment, thank you very much.' He turned with two more frames. 'Andrea, take one of these, will you?'

'Hugh, you old bastard! What are you doing here? Don't you trust the GPO?' James had appeared at the front door of the house, beaming effusively.

'It's not the GPO I distrust – it's you,' Hugh Metzer declared, locking the doors of the Jaguar. 'And don't call me an old bastard in public. I try to retain some dignity, even in the depths of Fulham.'

Paul and the girl fell in step as they followed him through the garden gate.

'I thought you might call at the weekend,' she said, glancing at the young man with a swift, shy grace. She had fine, regular features, not a pretty face, but one that could be beautiful.

Paul shrugged. 'I had to get my Covent Garden pictures finished. Jimmy was panicking all last week, as usual – I didn't have any spare time.' He looked at her. 'Are you rushing back to the gallery? We could have lunch at the pub.'

'Why do you think I came?' She sidled against him, smiling conspiratorially. She kept close, adding covertly, 'I was afraid you didn't want to call. After last Thursday –'

Paul glanced at Metzer's back. 'Don't be silly. Why should you think that?'

But as he paused to let her enter the house before him, her reluctance to sever even this momentary bodily contact seemed far greater than his.

He felt alien in this cramped city of clipped accents and

obscure class differences. More alien, he sometimes thought, than he would have done in his first, admittedly random choice of Paris. There, at least, he could have worn his foreignness on his sleeve – his separateness obvious and clear-cut from the moment he opened his mouth.

Here, where his soft, New England accent often passed without comment, the familiar and the non-familiar merged disconcertingly, creating pitfalls even now.

He had begun by feeling obscurely reassured seeing landmarks like Piccadilly or St Paul's, only to be flummoxed by the Byzantine intricacies of the Ungerground system, puzzled by licensing laws plainly designed by tee-totallers, confused by the unprovoked politeness of complete strangers who would wait to hold a shop door open for him, while others would trample him underfoot to cram onto a rush-hour bus.

He had never thought of himself as particularly 'American': he had no interest in baseball or football, Cora-Beth had made execrable apple pie, and *Twilight's Last Gleaming* struck him as ungrammatical nonsense. But his awareness of that aspect of himself – an aspect, he now realized, that permeated his character – had grown rather than diminished.

Now, the slightest news item from the States, or a corner grocer's blank look as he thoughtlessly asked for 'Jello', would bring a surge of emptiness, of displaced longing. It was, though, something he could live with, unlike the cold terror which had surfaced within moments of his arrival here.

Suddenly his problems had seemed trivial, his wild flight ill-considered and foolish. He had no friends in this country. He had squandered his money recklessly, and now a crippling exchange rate – not to mention a cost of living

287

that seemed extraordinarily high – was decimating the residue.

The horrifying thought that he had made the most appalling decision of his life had been subsumed, partly to his relief, in an urgent, practical need to raise money. To find some kind of a job.

He had expected his call to James Kingsley to yield, at best, a polite refusal – at worst, a denial that they had ever met. But the extremity of his recklessness had proved to be its reward. Kingsley's studio assistant had walked out the day before Paul's call. To the young American, eking out the last of his depleted dollars in a student hostel, the offer of such work appeared heaven-sent.

The reality was less inspiring. Kingsley was not an ideal employer; periods of profound lethargy alternated with frenzied activity, when Paul was expected to remedy situations that missed disaster by a hair's breadth. And sometimes not even that.

But the work was varied and the man a gifted photographer with a wide reputation – as much, unfortunately, for his indiscipline, as his pictures. More importantly to Paul, he enjoyed giving advice and encouragement. Paul had learned a lot he would never have been taught at Curwen.

His social life had come a poor second to that process. It developed fitfully through flatmates and chance acquaintances. He found English men friendly and frequently enigmatic, the women even more so.

He had been out with several, though rarely more than two or three times with the same girl. He had slept with four – a ludicrously small number by Cape standards. But those standards no longer applied.

The first two had reminded him of Diana, the third was

deliberately her complete opposite, the last simply the impulsive gratification of an appetite. None had given him more than momentary physical satisfaction – the last not even that.

By fleeing the Cape it seemed that he had only succeeded in hiding deeper within himself. The legacy of his life there was a curious form of impotency.

He told himself he was over Diana, but he longed more than ever for the kind of intimacy he had glimpsed with her. The knowledge of its possibility mocked anything less – certainly the thoughtless liaisons that had led so easily to disaster at Curwen.

He told himself he wanted closeness, trust, genuine warmth before anything else. And the contradictions he sensed in that, without really appreciating them, had led him to Andrea.

James and Hugh were arguing with the companionable bluster of old friends as Paul stacked the prints against a completed wall of the set. It depicted a corner of a highly stylized country drawing room, intended for a fashion spread. The models who would occupy it were due the following day.

'Paul,' said James, breaking off momentarily, 'can you organize some coffee?'

'I'll help you,' Andrea offered. She followed Paul upstairs. 'I did mean it – about not calling,' she said as they went into the kitchen.

'So did I.' Paul frowned at the all but empty coffee-maker. He began to refill it. 'I really did have to finish those pictures – I've got a magazine waiting to see them. And I needed to be up very early Friday morning, too.'

He glanced at the girl quickly and her face crumpled into

289

a guilty grin. 'What is it?'

She shook her head, half turning away. He smiled at her. 'Come on.'

'Oooh!' She raised exasperated eyes to the ceiling. 'I'm doing exactly what I promised not to. I *know* we agreed to be sensible.'

'Hey, talk to me – we're supposed to be fond of each other.'

Andrea's grin faded. 'Well, that's the point, really, isn't it?' She dropped her eyes, pressing the tips of her fingers together. 'I know we've both taken a bashing emotionally, me with my ex-fiancé, you back home – and we decided we'd take things very easily – '

Paul leaned back against the kitchen worktop. 'Now you've had enough?'

'No!' The girl looked up, alarmed. 'Not at all. It's just – we've been seeing each other for nearly two months now – and it's been marvellous. But I wonder if we shouldn't have moved on.' She groaned theatrically. 'This is *really* difficult!'

'This is all because I didn't stay Thursday night, isn't it?'

'That's part of it.' Andrea paused, then sighed, deeply embarrassed. 'I know from what you've told me you've been involved with quite a few girls. I can't help wondering – if you're thinking of them all the time.'

Paul sighed and took hold of her, clutching her to him as the distress showed in her face.

'I feel so stupid,' she murmured into his shoulder. 'I got so fed up with people leaping on me. You've been so nice – I've no reason to complain.'

Paul squeezed her and pecked her on the cheek. 'It's OK – really – it's my fault.'

She pulled back to see his face; her own was solemn. 'It

does matter that we fancy each other.'

'You're right.' Paul nodded decisively.

'Experience isn't everything.'

'Doesn't mean a damn thing.'

Her mouth was curious, the top lip longer and thinner, curving over the lower to give her a serious, sulky appearance even in repose. But when she smiled, as now, her whole face changed.

Voices rose from below.

'Let's get this coffee,' Paul said. She nodded as he gave her a final squeeze.

They were each carrying two mugs down the corridor when they heard the front door crash. Frowning, Paul went to the head of the stairs, just as the door opened again.

'Sorry, Paul!' James's voice echoed through the house. 'I'm lunching with Hugh. Hold the fort, will you?'

The door slammed again before Paul could answer. He turned to Andrea with a look of blank incomprehension that made her laugh. His gaze took in the mugs in his hands. 'I didn't even *want* coffee.'

'Never mind the coffee. What on earth is this in here?' Andrea had turned to the storeroom; its door still hung open. She poked her head into the dark interior. 'Good heavens! Aladdin's cave!'

'No, Kingsley's,' Paul said. 'The man never throws anything away. Careful, you'll get filthy in there.'

But she was already inside, giggling then shuddering as she touched the armadillo shell with her foot. 'This is like something out of Monty Python!'

Paul squeezed in behind her. 'You can't see anything.' He reached back for the light-switch.

'Don't do that.' As he turned to her she moved close to him, bumping the mugs he still carried against her open coat. 'Give me those.'

She took them from him, placing them carefully next to hers on the end of a cluttered shelf. Then she turned to him again, even closer now, so that their faces were almost touching in the semi-darkness.

'Well?' she murmured softly.

The kiss was slow and leisurely, the gradual parting of lips, the sly darting and intertwining of tongues initiated almost entirely by Andrea.

Paul's first sighing breath brought a swift response. She squirmed against him, inhaling fiercely herself as her stomach nudged the stiffening pressure in his jeans.

Paul believed himself detached, his mind stilled while his body lived its own reactions; memories of too many lovers flitted below the quiet surface. He had hoped in a vague way that when this moment came it would occupy him wholly, completely, but it did not.

He was surprised when the kiss ended abruptly as the girl's passion seemed to reach a peak. Then she was fumbling below him, kicking a clear space among the debris on the scuffed carpet. 'Pull the door to,' she said. He twisted toward the gap, uncertainly. There was hardly room in here for two people to stand.

She hissed, 'I can't do this in the light!'

The daylight shrank to a thin bar along the bottom of the door. The darkness was close and musty. Paul started as fingers plucked at his belt. His zip crept down, stuck, crept again.

'Andrea –'

'Don't! Or I won't be able to.' Her voice was almost a whine.

He breathed in as her hair brushed the exposed skin of his abdomen. She pulled him free slowly and inexpertly, as though hampered as much by general unfamiliarity as the gloom.

Her hands moved on his swelling flesh with a mixture of delicacy and uncertainty, rousing long-buried memories of pleasure that were not all entirely pleasant. The touch of her tongue – soft and trembling – caught him unawares.

She lapped the rim of his tip – once, twice, in quick succession – wary of its strangeness, and snatched a breath as he reacted with a fierce contraction.

Immediately she was pulling him between her lips – a hurried, awkward movement that provoked a further spasm, jerking him momentarily away from her mouth. Paul could sense her reluctance, her determination to go on regardless.

'You don't have to.' He touched her shoulder in the darkness, felt the dismissive shake of her head.

'Do it in my mouth – I don't mind.' This time she held him more firmly, sinking her lips right over him so that he butted the roof of her mouth, her tongue sliding round.

He could feel her shivering, her whole frame tensed with a terrible apprehension. But suddenly the urge to push, to pump, to pursue that swift, sweet explosion of joy was intense. He heard her moan at his first surge. And in the instant that he knew his disappointment – the knowledge that he had merely gratified a momentary and selfish impulse, and even that too soon for the greatest pleasure – she suddenly spluttered, pulling away from him and choking violently.

'Are you all right? Are you OK?'

'Yes, yes.' She gasped, a pale, indistinguishable shadow in the light from beneath the door, and was still. 'I just wanted – to show you I wasn't so – inexperienced – ' She ended in a small, self-derisive grunt.

'It was lovely,' said Paul. 'It was a lovely thought. Thank you.' And he flinched in the darkness for the grossness of his hypocrisy.

Outside the pub he watched Andrea's taxi bear her away toward Metzer's Chelsea gallery and then walked back to the studio early. To his surprise James was already there, carefully positioning Hugh's loaned prints on the walls of the set.

'Boucanier,' he said as he saw his assistant. He seemed unusually cheerful.

Paul frowned. 'Don't they make tyres?'

'That's *Pirelli*. Same industry, different product. But they do bring out a very classy calendar.'

James smiled meaningfully. Paul settled on a high-backed dining chair that was part of the set. 'You're trying to tell me something about your lunch?'

James's smile broadened. 'My good friend Hugh, it transpires, knows the art director of the agency which handles the Boucanier calendar. They've done some very good stuff in the past – mainly abstract – spent a lot of money. Now they've decided they want something livelier, sexier, to please the plebs as well as the art directors of this world. In other words, girls. But not pin-ups. They're looking for a kind of upmarket spontaneity. And – guess whose name has been mentioned?'

Paul prodded a finger dramatically in James's direction. The photographer inclined his head.

'But that's great!'

'It's fan-fucking-tastic!' James stepped back from the print, smacking his hands together. 'I've been waiting for something like this for so long. The budget's going to be extraordinary – no more farting around with home-made carpentry jobs.' He aimed a mocassin at the set wall, re-membering to miss it at the last moment. 'It'll do you a lot of good, too. You're going to pick up a hell of a lot more on a big international shoot than you ever will doing teenage fashion spreads in this place!'

His face dropped suddenly. 'But for God's sake don't spread this around. If they got even a hint I was jumping the gun, the whole thing could just – '

'Who am I going to tell, Jimmy?'

James picked up another print. 'I'd prefer it if you didn't even mention it to Andrea – not unless she says something first. It's that tight.'

The photographer caught Paul's expression as he spoke the girl's name. 'Didn't you have a good time at lunch?'

'What?' Paul stared at him blankly. 'Oh – yes. Yes, it was lovely.'

It was well after ten o'clock before he reached home that evening, treading heavily up the liftless stone staircase to the fifth-floor flat he shared. He heard the telephone ringing as he fumbled for his key, and scowled when no one seemed to be answering it. When the door eventually opened he found the flat in darkness.

Putting on the hall light, he traced the telephone wire to the room of a new arrival, a young Australian who seemed to make an alarming number of long-distance calls. The instrument lay beside the bed.

The caller was Andrea, her voice small and distant. 'I've ruined everything, haven't I?'

'No, you haven't.' Why did he feel so empty, so hollow?

'I shouldn't have done it like that.'

'You didn't do anything wrong.'

'But it wasn't right, was it? I mean, for us.'

Paul hesitated, not knowing what to say, except the truth. 'No,' he breathed at last. 'But it's not your fault.'

'Oh, God, who cares whose fault it is?' She sounded almost bright. He waited, not knowing what it meant. Then she was quiet again. 'I do like you, Paul. I think you're very talented, too. I would like us to be friends.'

'We always have been. My feelings haven't changed.'

There was a soft grunt at the other end of the phone. 'No.' He could barely hear her. 'I better go, Paul. Take care.'

He said goodnight and put down the receiver.

The slow rumble of traffic across Putney Bridge came through the bedroom window. Sitting on the end of the bed, Paul glanced across at the silver and ochre glow of the night. His Australian flatmate had left the lower sash open.

He couldn't hide his relief over Andrea, but an overwhelming guilt suffocated any lightness of spirit. She was a warm, attractive, loving girl, whose warmth and love he had deliberately cultivated, whose attraction he had kept at bay – for the simple, and safe, reason that he did not respond to it. Now he knew his own stupidity. There was no earthly point in looking for intimacy by ignoring its most powerful aspect.

He fell back on the Australian's crumpled duvet, feeling something hard in the middle of his his back, but too weary to do anything about it. How straightforward life had been when he believed there were rules – subtle guidelines everyone else had mysteriously learned and somehow forgotten to pass on to him. He felt the urge to grin at the thought, but its corollary checked him.

There were no rules, only muddle. All you could do was put your head down, struggle on as best you knew how – and hope in the process to take some genuinely sensational photographs.

Immediately, the lump in his back became intensely painful. He twisted onto his side, yanking the obstruction from under him. It was a rolled magazine, dog-eared and disintegrating. The cover seemed to be missing.

Paul glanced round for a reading-lamp. Finding none, he saw a plastic camping-lantern next to a rucksack on the floor. It took him a moment to locate a switch. A feeble glow illuminated the bright pages of a men's magazine.

He flicked through it idly, grunting at the bland lighting, the flash-lit exposure that concentrated solely upon the warmth and vitality of naked flesh. The memory of Lawrence Hoffman and his legendary *Playboy* collection brought a smile.

It was easy to dismiss it all as technically sterile, but the erotic impact was undeniable. Vaguely he became aware that a face had lodged in his mind. He turned back through the pages, momentarily distracted as other faces and poses caught his attention. And then it was before him.

The girl was a brunette, with rich, chestnut hair circling her shoulders. Her figure was both petite and shapely, her skin faintly olive, her breasts high and full – perhaps a little too full for her frame – her pubic hair a dark, thick wedge rather than a triangle.

Her poses were entirely conventional, even a little stilted. But, as Paul looked at them more closely, it was her face that drew him. It had her body's mixture of delicacy and slight over-lushness: high cheekbones, large eyes, full expressive lips. A kind of wary knowingness that was not in the least bit teasing but profoundly sexual. And, in a way, Paul could not analyse, almost familiar.

The realization brought a sinking twist to his stomach – a sign of the most powerful attraction, preceding even the thump of his heart or the throb of his loins.

Astonished, Paul gave a grunting laugh, pushing the magazine away. It had been months since he'd had such a reaction; abstinence was plainly giving him delusions.

A key rattled in the front door. He sprang up, darting toward the hall, then stopped and went back to roll up the magazine again, stuffing it beneath the duvet.

He went straight to bed, dreaming hotly and wetly of Cora-Beth and waking, troubled and uncomfortable, an hour before dawn.

10

RACHEL
1976

She was in a kind of darkness, a slow, sensual dream where self-consciousness, conscience, even at times consciousness itself dwindled almost to nothing. All she knew were sensations – pleasures to be cultivated, pains to be avoided: none entirely pleasant, none wholly unpleasant. But all better than memory, better than thought.

'Cut! OK, ladies, relax for a moment. Don't move.'

Rachel breathed in and opened her eyes, blinking in the harsh camera-light. Immediately it clicked off, leaving bright after-images, the relief of cooler air on her exposed flesh.

She sighed and leaned back in her heavy, well-padded chair, resting her head on the high, carved back. Voices rose, people moved in the hot, crowded room.

It was the living room of what, by its isolated position, Rachel had taken to be a farmhouse. Beyond the long window at her back, netted to half-height in the Dutch fashion and now thickly curtained, neat fields stretched to a neat line of trees. Beyond the trees a broad, steel-grey river someone had called the Meuse moved with glistening speed. Rachel knew the place only as the conclusion of a twenty-minute taxi ride from the nearest staion.

'Are you all right?' The girl curled between Rachel's knees was looking up at her, concern in her dark, shadowed eyes. She moved to see Rachel better, kneeling, resting a thin arm on Rachel's bare thigh.

'I'm fine, thank you.' Rachel smiled gratefully, then, glancing down at the girl, frowned. 'You're a bit damp. On your cheek.'

'Oh.' The girl's accent was French, her voice tired. She reached up, brushing lank brown hair from her face. She wiped the dampness away with the side of her hand.

'You're very – copious – down there.' She nodded at the thick, straggling beard between Rachel's thighs, smiling faintly as Rachel coloured. 'No, it's good. I'm so dry sometimes – it's impossible – and I hate Vaseline . . . . You're English, aren't you?' Rachel agreed. 'I thought so. I don't see many English girls in these films.'

'It's the first time I've been to Europe – '

'I must have a cigarette,' the girl interrupted her, climbing awkwardly to her feet, her long, pale body oddly graceless in its nudity, her small, pointed breasts hardly moving. Immediately she cursed, falling back into a crouch. 'Mustn't move,' she muttered to herself. 'This Dutchman is as bad as the Germans. Excuse me!'

A young man in checked shirt and jeans paused as she called. When she put two fingers to her lips, he nodded, lowered the transformer box he was carrying, and produced a cigarette packet and disposable lighter from his back pocket. The French girl received cigarette and light with visible relief.

'Thank you. I'm sorry,' she said to Rachel. 'I was up very late last night and I couldn't find this place this morning – I don't know Holland very well – only Amsterdam.' She drew deeply on her cigarette, exhaling with a long sigh of satisfaction.

'It seems an odd place to pick,' Rachel said.

The French girl shook her head, evidently enlivened by the cigarette. 'Not really. Maastricht is very close to Belgium and Germany. Any problem, they can be out of Holland in a short time. There won't be – I'm sure,' she added hurriedly as Rachel's face fell. 'I've worked for the man who produces this before – he's very careful. Oh no!'

Rachel turned where the girl's gaze had rested. Across the room, beyond the barrier of lights and camera equipment, and the bustle of half a dozen technicians, two young men stood talking just inside the door.

The taller – ascetic-looking, and almost unhealthily thin in a loose, cotton jacket – was the director. His companion was smaller and darker, with the open, mobile features of a clown; he was wearing a short, blue silk dressing gown.

'What is it?' Rachel asked.

The French girl looked away, frowning. 'I know this man – I was with him in Sweden in the summer. I didn't know he was going to be here.' She sucked moodily at her cigarette, the darkness of fatigue gathering again in her eyes.

'Is he a friend?' Rachel said warily. Both men were approaching.

'We were working together. He's too big for me – it hurts me.'

'*Françoise! Commment vas-tu?*' The clown-faced man was above them. Grinning broadly, he bent to kiss the French girl on each cheek.

'Armand,' she said, turning her head for him.

They spoke rapidly in French, the man enthusiastic, the girl indifferently polite, until Armand, whose eyes had been flickering continually at Rachel, finally nodded to her. '*Et ton amie?*'

'*Elle est anglaise.*' Françoise touched Rachel's leg. 'I'm

301

sorry, I don't know your name.'

'Marie,' said Rachel. The French girl introduced herself and the newcomer.

'Marie.' Smiling, Armand rolled the name round his tongue, his accent thick. 'I like it. You are very attractive, Marie.' His eyes barely moved down her body. In a quiet corner of her mind it amused Rachel that nudity made that male reflexive action quite redundant.

'Armand is a Belgian,' Françoise said. 'That means he only has to be half as charming as a real Frenchman.'

Armand gave a move in her direction. The director, who had been talking to a cameraman behind the Belgian, turned suddenly to the group.

'OK! Everybody together now? That's good. I want to go through the next shot.' He spoke briskly as if with a permanently uncleared throat. The man looked not much older than Rachel, the long, sallow cheeks, under rimless spectacles, still bearing traces of acne. She wished he were less fraught and humourless. He looked at the French girl.

'Now we start with Françoise and Marie together as before. Françoise gets up and moves to right of the camera.' He indicated the direction. 'Now, Marie, you are left unsatisfied. You touch yourself – you understand?' Rachel nodded. 'Make it nice and sexy, OK? Not too fast because the camera is looking straight at you. In fact, sink down a little in the seat so we can see better.

'Now.' He stabbed a finger at Françoise. 'You come back into shot with Armand, leading him as if to say, "Here is a wondeful gift for you – " '

'Do you want me to say that?' the French girl asked as Armand grinned.

The director looked momentarily non-plussed. 'Yes – yes, that might help,' he decided. 'It'll all be dubbed later,

anyway.' He paused, resuming his train of thought. 'OK –
you bring Armand to here.' He pointed to the right of the
chair. 'Armand in profile to the camera.' He grasped the
Belgian and manoeuvred him into position. 'Françoise
kneels *here* – in front of him – *not* hiding Marie – and she
sucks him. OK?'. He turned quickly to Rachel. 'Marie sees
this happening and is very excited – she wants some, too.'

Armand chuckled softly.

'Then Françoise gets up again, she takes hold of Armand
by the cock.' This time the Belgian laughed out loud,
prompting a faint smile from Françoise. 'She leads him to
Marie.' The director's vague mime even made Rachel
smile. 'And she guides him into Marie's pussy. Like a
nozzle into a car – at a gasoline station.' Behind him
Françoise's cigarette donor sniggered. The director ignored
him. 'I think it'll look very good. I'll want a big close-up
later.'

Armand frowned. 'Do we stop for that?'

The director shook his head. 'No, keep straight on. I
want you to fuck Marie on the seat. OK, Marie?' He gave
her only a fleeting glance. 'And Françoise kneels to the left
and kisses and strokes her – you make love to them both
while they make love.

'Then, when I tell you, swap over so Françoise is kneeling on the edge of the seat to keep it steady, Armand behind
her, Marie kneeling to one side of Armand, stroking, kissing
him – '

Armand's frown had deepened. 'So I fuck Françoise from
behind as she bends over the chair?'

Françoise watched the director carefully as he nodded.

'This is just a pussy fuck, isn't it? You know I don't do *en
arriére?*'

The director nodded again, more briskly. 'It's under-

303

stood.' He took a breath. 'Now, finally, Armand, when you feel you're going to come, kiss Françoise' back or shoulder – doesn't matter where. OK? Then pull out and I want you to come off in Marie's face. So watch for this, Marie. Be ready to turn to him so you show a profile to the camera.' He paused. 'I think that's it.'

Armand and Françoise exchanged wondering glances and grinned.

'And all this is going to be one take?' the Belgian said.

The director blinked, expressionless behind his spectacles. 'If you think you're going to come earlier, just make the same signal.'

Armand's grin broadened. 'Oh, I can fuck all day and all night – if you want me to. In fact, why don't you just turn the camera on these ladies and me and we'll improvise the whole film. OK?'

Rachel caught a sly look of caution in the French girl's eye. The director's face registered nothing. 'Oh, I think it's a good piece of action. Shall we walk it through – just to get it clear in your minds?'

He moved away without waiting for an answer, and immediately began talking to the technicians, missing Armand's sour grimace. The Belgian reached for the cord of his dressing gown. He spoke to Françoise in a swift babble of French, then looked at Rachel and smiled. Rachel glanced at the French girl queryingly.

Françoise shrugged. 'Oh, he's just talking nonsense.'

'Don't be such a liar!' Armand chided her, throwing off his dressing gown.

Underneath he was naked, his body lean and well-muscled, marked by a curious rectangle of thick black hair between his nipples. His eyes locked with Rachel's, half amused, half judging her reaction.

'I was saying to our good French friend here,' he told her, beaming, 'that if you enjoy fucking as much as you look like you do then we're all going to have a marvellous time today.'

As Rachel blinked at him his hand dropped between his legs, sliding his fingers round the broad, dark pink cylinder of flesh that hung there. It was already almost as long as her own hand and growing as she looked.

The apartment block was low and modern, two sand-coloured boxes arranged at right angles to each other in a quiet, lamp-lit street just behind the older part of the small Belgian market town.

The taxi dropped Rachel beside a grassy forecourt. She struggled with a fare that was now francs instead of guilders. Then she was alone.

The twenty-mile journey, from low flat fields to gently rolling hills, whose outline could only just be discerned under the moonless sky, had taken less than half an hour. The sudden silence and emptiness of the street seemed an anomaly.

For the past three days, all had been bustle and rush: a flight to Schiphol, a hurried meeting in an office over a picturesque canal where girls lolled in red-lit windows, a train ride to Maastricht – change at Utrecht, change at Eindhoven – a taxi along the Heugam road, a turn-off leading, apparently, across empty fields. Names, numbers, directions on a scrap of paper. *'They'll look after you,'* Max had said. *'I know these people. They're good. We do a lot of business.'*

And now tired and sore and alone, she was on another strange street with another strange name she could barely pronounce.

The flat number, at least, was clear enough. The front door was one of a pair in the corner of a concrete stairwell, beside a clean lift. She heard Josey's voice before the door opened.

'Rachel!'

Josey was dressed in ill-matching slacks and sweater, her hair tied back with an elastic band. She was securing it as she saw her visitor.

'Hello, mum.'

Rachel grinned as pleasure replaced the astonishment on Josey's face.

'But how . . . ? Why didn't you phone? Or write? Or – never mind!' They embraced, both laughing.

'I would have called,' said Rachel as she was drawn inside, 'but I'm only here for a few days. I haven't worked out the taxis and the trains yet, let alone the telephones. I'm not being awkward, am I?'

The narrow entrance hall opened out into a wide living room-cum-dining area as large and airy as Josey had once described it. A burly, dark-haired man was slumped in front of a television set. He sat up abruptly as he saw Rachel.

'Course you're not being awkward,' Josey said, ushering her forward. 'You don't know my favourite man, do you? Get up, David! He's got so lazy since he became a father. Rachel, this is Superdad.'

Rachel shook hands, astonished by the man's size. She had pictured someone lean and cuddly, a jollier version of Andrew; this man was a good six foot and barrel-chested, but there was a warmth in his strong, even features.

'Nice to meet you, Rachel. We wondered when you were coming to see us.' He grinned as she congratulated him.

'Well?' Rachel turned to Josey. 'Where is he?'

'In with us at the moment.' Josey nodded to a far door. Beaming, she led the way.

The bedroom was large, dwarfing the sprawling double bed, and even more the carrycot in its shadow. They leaned over it. In the semi-darkness Rachel saw a small, bundled form, a pale, bald head and closed, wrinkled eyes.

'He's so tiny,' Rachel murmured wonderingly.

'He didn't feel like that on the way out,' said Josey, grinning at Rachel's wary glance. 'Pick him up.'

'Won't I wake him?'

Josey shook her head. 'He's due for a feed about now, anyway.' Rachel received the warm, shawl-wrapped bundle nervously. 'Just keep your arm under his head,' Josey told her. 'The rest is easy.'

Rachel looked at the small head, soft and malleable, against the sleeve of her coat. The baby seemed impossibly vulnerable. She wondered if she should feel *more*.

When she was sure she held it securely, she smiled at Josey. 'I still can't believe it – you're actually a mum!'

'I couldn't believe it either. You know I was nearly two months gone when I left the flat – it must have happened the first night I spent here.' Josey's voice softened as she glanced toward the door. 'I tell you, I doubt if his nibs would have been so keen on wedding bells without it! Not that it wasn't a complete accident.'

'But he's pleased – you both are?'

Josey laughed with a gentle irony. 'Yes – now, if you forget the nights without sleep, never going out, the birth, the pain, no sex.' She paused at Rachel's appalled expression. 'Yes, it's gorgeous – he's gorgeous. I never realized. You just can't.'

She pressed the shawl away from the baby's face. It breathed in suddenly, its tiny mouth puckering. Both girls

307

smiled. Then the face crumpled up and a high, thin, complaining wail began.

'Now, that's a suppertime call,' Josey said, gripping the bottom of her sweater and pulling it up. She sat on the edge of the bed, stretching out to take the baby from a relieved Rachel. The child nestled in her arm, its head fastening instantly on the nipple of a swollen breast.

'Look at those – I've gone from thirty-four to thirty-seven: it's driving Dave berserk, and he can't do a thing about it!'

Fascinated, Rachel watched as the baby sucked powerfully, feeling her stomach contract at the thought of a bizarre discomfort.

'Makes me wonder how floppy I'm going to be when this part's over.' Josey grinned up at Rachel, who was astonished yet again by her friend's capacity to appear normal in almost any situation. 'Can't imagine Max being very interested in me then, can you?'

'Do you still miss working?' Rachel asked abruptly. 'Modelling, I mean.'

Josey grunted softly, smiling. 'I'm sure I sound like every other woman who's ever had a baby, but this is what it's all about.' She cupped the baby's head and, now that her eyes had adjusted to the dimness, Rachel saw that its apparent baldness was in fact a covering of fine blond hair. 'This is what it all leads up to, isn't it? Really?'

Her gaze fixed on mother and contentedly feeding baby, Rachel was both unwilling and unable to reply.

She ate a late supper with them, sharing the strong Belgian beer Dave favoured, talking in the vaguest way of her work just across the border, joining in, as best she could, in a close domesticity that seemed as suffocating as it was enriching.

But she had come seeking just such an intimacy – with Josey initially, with her husband and child by extension. And, within the limitations of nappy changes and feeds and bouts of colic, it was offered to her. The fact that she could not respond wholeheartedly was her fault, she realized, not theirs.

Too much had changed – in her former flatmate most obviously; even Josey's extraordinary flexibility hadn't totally encompassed the sea-change of motherhood. She was someone new, as new to herself, Rachel suspected, as anyone else. But Rachel had changed too.

In the months since Andrew, she had often wondered if she was becoming hard. Her grief had been sharp but very short: pain had turned suddenly to indifference, not just to Andrew but to everything else.

Even Max's betrayal – shrugged off as 'a cock-up with the agent; they're all sharks, love' – hadn't seemed to bother her so much any more. Nor had his repeated offers to appear in his films. In the end agreement had been a matter simply of whim, the balance tipped by overdue rent.

Those first attempts, with Max himself behind the camera, had been ludicrously easy, almost enjoyably so: little more than extended strip-teases from a variety of stock uniforms – a maid, a nurse, an air stewardess. She had writhed in mock frenzies in showers, in beds, on office desktops – sometimes alone, sometimes with other girls. The men had arrived gradually. Young men, for the most part, would-be actors, would-be models, chance acquaintances of Max or Tracey, or friends of friends, recruited with promises of free sex, of realized fantasies of one kind or another.

Their habitual modesty after the final disrobing always reassured her. In the dark surrounds of Max's studio, under scalding lights, her own nudity represented an exalted kind of normality; it was a badge of acceptance, a source of perverse pride – the only pride of which she was entirely sure.

But to the men who came there, ready to feast on her vulnerability, the situation was reversed; even the most confident, the most smoothly handsome revealed the limp – or not so limp – flesh between their legs with a hint of trepidation, aware that the judgement Rachel could make, consciously or unconsciously, would be final and irrevocable.

Their plight grew as filming began. Not so much in the milder of the two versions they enacted of every scenario: fondling and caressing, stroking and kissing, they would slide between Rachel's thighs to simulate penetration and passion by front or rear, as each shot contrived to conceal all but the faintest suggestion of censorable erection.

But in the 'harder' version there was no such concealment. While Rachel could demonstrate deep arousal by a smear of judiciously placed Vaseline and an ice cube applied to each nipple, her partner's excitement was not so easily counterfeited, or controlled. Climaxes came too swiftly or, more commonly, not at all. Glycerine and milk could substitute for the products of passion, but not for the absence of visible interest.

It was a bizarre activity, as absurd as it was sordid. A confluence of bodies – a problem of sexual practicality.

So had she regarded her first genuine act of filmed sex – with a man whose name she could not remember; but his body had been flabby and his penis small – so small it had entered her without her realizing as he rocked between her widespread legs and only his stuttering grunt as he spent himself told her the event had taken place.

310

She had gone home, chastened, shocked that she was not shocked, that no outrage or shame or more than the mildest disgust had disturbed her indifference. Hadn't she done as much with Barry Drew – a man she hadn't loved, often hadn't even fancied?

What she did now was no different from Josey sleeping with Norman Bealby for work, only perhaps less hypocritical. It bore as much relation to making love – to what she and Andrew had done – as a lingering kiss with a casual date she might never expect to see again, though in fact her dates and her interest in sex outside the studio had dwindled almost to zero.

She *was* hard – hard, she concluded, with the learned resilience of maturity, of bitter experience, and grateful for it. But it was only at this moment, sharing an evening with people whose openness and unself-conscious affection for each other made them strangers to her, that she realized how thin and brittle a shell that hardness was.

It was late by the time they had finished eating and Josey's invitation to use the spare bedroom was gratefully accepted; accommodation had been provided at the farmhouse, but it was unclear to Rachel whether or not the activities of the day were expected to continue behind as well as in front of the camera, and she had been wary of staying. She had, in any case, only taken the work in order to make this visit.

She was already in bed when Josey popped her head round the door for a final goodnight. The blonde girl was in her dressing gown and only awake at this hour, she explained, because the baby had for the first time slept through a whole six-hour period the previous night.

'You know the most sensual pleasure in the world?' Josey asked. 'Sleep,' she answered herself. 'Pure, blessed sleep. A baby really makes you appreciate the simple things.'

And then they talked – easily, openly, as they'd done so often in the Camden flat – resurrecting older versions of themselves, giving them new and temporary life.

The relief that flooded through Rachel was intense; she had forgotten the simplicity, the sheer joy of uninhibited confession. But when she finished there was a puzzled frown on Josey's face.

'You're taking all this so *seriously*, Rachel. I only did those films with Max for a laugh. Are you really enjoying it?'

'Enjoying it?' The question seemed monumentally irrelevant.

'I mean, this Dutch lot sound pretty heavy. Do you really want to be involved in that scene? I thought you wanted to get into straight modelling.'

'I did – I do.' She could feel uncertainty, confusion, swirling below the surface of her mind, threatening to break through.

'Well it took me nearly four years to find out I wasn't going to get anywhere,' said Josey. 'How long were you trying before all these films? It can't have been a year. That's no time.'

Instinctively Rachel balked at the note of criticism – the thought, *It's easy for you to say now*, rising to her lips. But she knew her anger reached beyond that, far beyond.

'Don't say that,' she murmured. The intimacy was fading. She wanted sympathy not judgement.

'I think you're selling yourself a bit short, Rachel –'
'Josey!'

The baby's cry started high and rose higher, penetrating the bedroom wall easily. 'Jo–sey . . . !' came Dave's weary, sing-song call. Josey made for the door.

312

'That'll teach me to get my hopes up,' she sighed. 'Sleep tight. Dave'll give you a lift in the morning. We're used to early starts.'

Rachel shared her friend's wan smile of irony. Then she was in darkness, nestling down under the fat continental duvet, listening as the sounds of crying died away.

She was sweating. She could feel pores prickling all over her body — from the heat of the lights, from the effort of balancing on the edge of the chair, the bare flesh of her rear grooved by fretwork, her bent knees and open thighs bearing Armand's weight with each downthrust.

The Belgian's face loomed above her, dark with strain, shiny with sweat of his own. A bead splashed between her breasts.

'I can't,' she whispered. 'I can't.'

'Yes, you can. Just relax.' The director was to the left, higher, above the glare of the lights, the blank stare of the whirring camera.

'It's too big — he's too big.'

'Don't be silly now, Marie. Françoise had no problem. Slowly, Armand.'

She gasped as the pressure increased at the neck of her womb. In a spurt of panic she jerked her head up, staring down where the Belgian supported himself between her thighs, the engorged mass of his cock stretching her lips, buried deep but for one, two dark purple inches.

'Oh, God.'

'She's smaller than me, I think.' The French girl's voice was somewhere behind.

'I want this shot! She has to take him — all of him. Now try, Marie. Slow, easy strokes, Armand. That's right.' And to the cameraman, sotto voce: 'Pull back to get her face.'

'No!' She bucked under the Belgian's sliding thrust, jerking herself back in a vain effort to avoid the force that plugged and filled and strained her.

'No— no — Jesus!'

313

In the silence of the flat, tears that had remained unwept for months seeped quietly into her pillow.

11
PAUL
1976

'I honestly don't believe this,' said James Kingsley. 'We've had location-hunters tramping around the Bahamas and leaping up and down Austrian Alps for three months. We have roughs of every conceivable shot. We have models booked – we have airline tickets booked. And the silly French sods can't make up their minds where they want this sodding calendar to be set!'

Discreetly, Paul set down a mug of coffee next to the deck-chair in which Pat Dealy, the Boucanier calendar art director, was slumped. He was James's age, a gaunt, lugubrious man, with a heavy, hawk-nosed face and hair that flowed thickly almost to his shoulders, despite a totally bald crown. He was dressed in a Hawaiian beach shirt and jeans.

He sighed gently. This speech of James's had recently become a daily occurrence.

'I mean, it's nearly March, for God's sake!' the photographer snapped. 'How long do they expect the snow to last?'

'We've probably got till Easter,' the art director added without conviction.

James gave an incredulous gasp. He was leaning against his desk in what was now his office, but had once been a front bedroom of the Fulham house. Behind venetian blinds rain poured down.

315

'Do you know what the Austrian Alps are *like* at Easter? It's a beargarden, Pat! The chances of finding any of our locations clear is minuscule – we're going to have gawping tourists in every other shot!'

'Jimmy.' The art director spoke quietly, bending forward in the deck-chair. 'It could just as easily be the Caribbean. I warned you at the start Boucanier are not the easiest people in the world to deal with.' He raised a hand as James gasped again. 'They take their time because they like to be right. And this is a new venture for them. Don't worry about plane tickets or models. That's just a question of money, which is no problem –'

'But that's my point!' James cut in. 'Even if we have to fly off to the Andes to find some snow, it's taken us nearly six months to get the right girls together. Not just in looks but in abilities – girls who can ski, girls who can scuba, girls who can do both. For pity's sake! We're already going to have to ditch half of them when Boucanier finally pull their finger out. I can't guarantee getting them all together again instantly.'

The art director nodded and sipped at his coffee. 'I've been in two minds about this all-action look. I really think we're going to have to fake most of it, anyway.'

'Oh, Jesus!' James smacked his forehead. Then he shook his head as if the blow had been overdone, and laughed. 'Don't throw all that back into the melting-pot! You'll have young Paul here badgering me about his Grand Obsession again.'

Paul, who had been sorting negatives at a corner table, looked up with a frown. 'I don't have any grand obsession –'

Both men were grinning at him; the tension of the

moment had eased, he realized with some resentment, at his expense.

'What about your porno lady?' James said.

'She was in *Prince*, not *Wankers' Weakly*.' Paul went back to the negatives. 'We were supposed to be looking for new faces – "sexy without being obvious", I think were your words. *You* told me to find out about her.'

'Which is this one?' asked Pat.

'Some girl – called Morrison, I think – Paul was very keen on,' said James. 'Paul, have we still got the pictures? What did happen about her, anyway?'

Paul went to a bank of filing cabinets next to the door and began rifling through drawers. 'The mag put me on to some photographer called Wallace. He really didn't want to know. I think there was something dodgy about the model release. She probably never signed it, or she was under age. He claimed he'd lost it – didn't even have a phone number. Here it is.'

He pulled out three magazine pages stapled together and handed them to Pat.

The art director raised his eyebrows appreciatively. ' "May Morrison",' he read. ' "Our plucked petal from the flower shop!" ' He laughed. 'Nice bod.'

'Jimmy thought she was a bit obvious,' said Paul. 'I tended to think that was just inexperience.'

As Pat shrugged, James said, 'We've gone for this sweet, Bardot look with the others – slightly nymphet. She just struck me as a little too femme fatale. There's nothing mock-innocent about that face. But I offered to look at her –'

Simultaneously the telephone and the front doorbell rang. As James picked up the receiver from the desk, he

317

nodded at Paul. Paul went downstairs and found Hugh
Metzer on the doorstep under a dripping umbrella. He led
the gallery owner back upstairs.

As they reached the landing a whoop of joy, fading into
an extremely poor attempt at a Tyrolean yodel from James,
burst from the office – closely followed by James himself.

'Paul – we're on. Hugh! This is perfect! You can help us
celebrate. Come on in – I know there's some wine around
here somewhere.'

Grinning broadly, the photographer dived into the
kitchen. In the office Paul introduced Hugh to the art
director, who was now standing beside the desk, his expression quietly beatific.

'That was Toulouse,' he said. 'They've taken the snow
option.'

'I've been praying, *praying* for this day!' James gasped
breathlessly, reappearing with an open wine bottle in one
hand and four glasses tucked against his other elbow. 'Not
bad for an old atheist, eh?'

He deposited bottle and glasses on the top of the filing
cabinet and began pouring furiously. 'Hugh,' he said,
handing over a glass, 'what happy chance brings you this
way?'

'You did, actually, old boy.' The gallery owner spoke
drily. 'You invited me to lunch three weeks ago. Andrea
confirmed it with you yesterday. I only accepted because I
assumed you were paying.'

'You're right!' James chuckled in happy surprise. 'This
Boucanier business has been driving me spare. But no
more!'

At James's prompting, they raised glasses and toasted
the good news, Hugh somewhat self-consciously. As James

318

lowered his glass, the full implications of the moment finally sank in and a look of vacant panic Paul knew only too well settled on his face.

'*Christ*, there's so bloody much to do! We've got to get out there straight away, Pat. I need a good week scouting round before we fly out the girls – longer if we can manage it. *Shit!* The girls – ' Hurriedly he rounded his desk, flopping into his chair and scrabbling at the debris that covered the desktop.

'We've got to cancel the options on the scuba models. Paul – ' He paused, as if suddenly aware of the impression this outburst of mild hysteria was creating. Instantly, and just as disturbingly, he became visibly calm. Then he thumped the desktop with both fists as thought to underline a momentous decision.

'No, this is silly. Pat and I have got to get to Austria as soon as possible. Paul – I'm leaving everything here in your hands. Sorting the girls, keeping tabs on the make-up man and the stylist – you can fly out with them when Pat and I are happy with the locations. All right?'

Paul nodded, having expected no less, and was rather pleased at the prospect of a James-less studio. James immediately turned to Pat, and began talking quickly, pausing only to cast a swift smile at Hugh. 'Five minutes, old son – OK? Help yourself to the booze.'

With an audible sigh, the gallery owner recharged his glass and sought round for a chair. The deck-chair was all that was in sight. Frowning, he leaned over it, and picked up the sheets from *Prince* that Pat had left.

'What's this, Jimmy? Taking up soft porn in your old age?'

James looked up. Paul, who had been listening in to the

discussions, turned too.

'Oh, some girl we were trying to trace,' James said hurriedly.

'Should have asked me,' Metzer grunted. 'She's with Norman Bealby's agency.'

'You know her?' Paul asked, astonished.

'I gave her a lift after one of Norman's parties last summer. He's a very old friend. I *assume* she's one of his girls – she was at the party.'

James laughed. 'Isn't that incredible? Paul's been chasing all over the place for her.'

'I'll give Norman a call, if you like,' said Hugh.

James shook his head. 'Thanks, but we've no time to look at anyone new now.' He wavered as he caught a slight movement from Paul. 'You can do it for my assistant's sake, if you like. I think he's smitten with the lady.'

'Not so sure about "lady",' Hugh said, glancing back at the pictures and frowning. 'I don't think Norman would be too happy about these. His girls are all very *haute couture*.'

But when the gallery owner looked up again, James had retreated once more to his discussions and only Paul was still turned his way, his young face curiously intent, bearing the fading trace of a blush.

Something was happening. He felt strange currents stirring, in himself, in everything around him. Sparks of excitement he had inexplicably forgotten – joys that had been dulled in overlong concentration on something that had seemed worth every effort, but which was no longer quite enough.

He felt a fullness in him, a burgeoning of old confidence, old certainty, as disturbing as it was exhilarating because there appeared no good reason for it. The go-ahead on the

Boucanier project felt less a cause than a symptom.

He had always regarded his sojourn with Kingsley – his whole time away from America – as an extension of that original flight from the Cape. Something fleeting, temporary, until the anger and the pain that had brought him so far had burned itself out. Staying so long had been, in part, a kind of mental laziness.

Now that thought had occurred to him, alternatives were suddenly possible. He was a better, more experienced photographer – James and even Hugh Metzer admitted it; he had sold pictures to magazines – and he had enough material for a show.

More importantly, he knew James's methods intimately; he could predict the photographer's approach on almost any subject and, as had occasionally been necessary, counterfeit it. He had, simply, learned all from his employer he ever would. He could see no reason, once the calendar shoot was over, why he should not strike out on his own.

The decision emboldened him as he came into the studio the following day. He expected a wild flurry of activity before James made his departure, then with luck a peaceful day or two to pursue his own work before following his employer. None of that happened.

It was as if the weeks of inactivity and frustration, waiting for the Boucanier decision, had secretly conceived a brood of horrific problems, which now seized their opportunity to burst forth.

James's intention to take the first available flight proved impossible. The chalet that had been provisionally booked for the Boucanier entourage turned out to be occupied until the end of the week and then, after enquiries, too small to accommodate photographer, assistant, stylist, make-up person, art director and four models. A second, adjacent chalet was immediately booked. That was later found to be occupied until the end of the following week.

By lunchtime, in a hair-tearing mood, James had ordered Paul to make alternative arrangements in a neighbouring location. And right in the middle of it came a phone call from Andrea.

'Hugh said to speak to you rather than Jimmy because he knew things were likely to be a bit chaotic.'

Paul's first inclination was to laugh; he could hear James and Pat bawling at each other in the studio below. But he felt unable to; since breaking up, he had talked to Andrea infrequently — as a result of circumstance rather than choice. He still felt a residual guilt, though he knew from James that she was seeing someone else regularly.

'What is it, Andrea?'

'This'll probably make more sense to you, Paul. The girl in the naughty pictures doesn't work for the Bealby agency. She did do some promotion work for them a couple of years ago, but only on a casual basis. There's no contact now. There's also — ' She paused. 'I'm trying to read Hugh's appalling handwriting. . . . There's apparently something a bit unsavoury about her. No details. Sounds fascinating.'

There was an odd note to the girl's voice, hinting at something more than idle curiosity; it puzzled Paul.

'No name?' he asked.

'Not written down here. I could ask Hugh when he gets back.'

'No, it's OK. It's not important. Thanks, Andrea.'

She made a slight sound of hesitation, giving Paul the impression that she wanted to speak further, perhaps more privately.

He was surprised when she said, rather warily, 'This was

322

a professional rather than a personal enquiry, wasn't it, Paul?'

Now Paul could laugh. 'Do you think Jimmy's lusting after some naughty model?'

'I was thinking more of you, actually.'

Paul's laughter was louder than before. 'No, sorry. It was strictly professional. A calendar candidate we were tracing.'

'Oh.'

'You sound disappointed.'

There was a silence at the other end and Paul wondered if his levity had upset her in some way, though he could not see how. Then she said, very softly, 'It'd just be nice to see you settled, that's all.'

It was the affectionate, quietly apologetic tone of a fond aunt enquiring after a favourite nephew, touching and sensible and wholly old-fashioned. Paul grinned, moved almost to pity by it but pleased. He knew precisely why he had let things go so far with her – and just as precisely why they had stopped short.

'Take care of yourself, Andrea. I've got to go now. Jimmy's screaming.' He put down the phone, chastened and a little awed by the girl's lingering regard.

But why was everyone pushing him into relationships – or so it seemed? First James, now Andrea. Was the confidence he felt, the change in himself, simply undifferentiated lust? A lust obvious to everyone but himself?

The ringing telephone cut off the thought. The travel company hiring the original chalet had managed to re-organize their bookings. The chalet and its neighbour would be free at the end of the week. Paul was on his way to tell James the good news when the make-up man called to announce that he had just broken his wrist and expected to be in plaster for a month.

It was two more days before James and Pat finally caught a late-night flight to Munich, leaving Paul with enough work to justify bedding down at the studio. By that stage he didn't mind at all. A house free of James's hysteria and Pat's lugubrious mumbling was reward enough. He would have agreed to almost anything.

His first free day, however, did not provide the relief he had anticipated. James's plan had been to assemble all the remaining members of the team and fly them out together under Paul's tutelage. But organizing so many busy individuals at such short notice proved a nightmare. The best that could be managed was an extended exodus, lasting two, possibly three days.

The evening had arrived before Paul could begin the work he had planned for that afternoon – checking and servicing the two reserve cameras James wanted, assembling and clip-testing samples of film.

It was well past midnight before he finished. Drained, he collapsed on an unstable camp-bed James kept for emergencies in the corner of his office, unable to relax because the enormity of his task was only now becoming clear to him. He slept fitfully, woken twice by sudden reminders of jobs undone, calls unanswered.

The third time, he found the room in deep gloom, rain pounding behind the blinds. He felt awful, mentally but not physically tired, despite an aching neck, a pain where a strut of the bed had grooved his hip. The night's insomniac panic had been insane; he was becoming as bad as James.

Then a faint and familiar trilling reminded him why he had woken. He sprang up, throwing off the old blanket he had found to cover himself and pulling on his sweat-shirt.

In doing so he caught sight of his wristwatch. Ten-thirty. He had planned to be on the telephone by nine.

Cursing, he dragged on jeans and sneakers and hurtled downstairs, his footsteps slapping and booming on the stripped boards of the studio. The doorbell rang again as he fumbled open the front door – annoyed that the caller should be so persistent, angrier at himself for letting the day slip away from him.

A stranger – small and feminine, not much larger than a child – stood defensively within the shadow of the porch. She wore a beige trenchcoat, dark from the waist down with rain; a green patterned scarf clung damply about her face.

'Oh, I'm sorry to bother you, but does James Kingsley work here?' Paul nodded, frowning. 'Uh-huh, but he's in Austria at the moment.'

'Oh.' The girl's brow creased; her full lower lip twisted as she chewed it. Her cheeks were flushed, shiny with damp. She seemed to reach a decision.

'It's just that I heard he was auditioning models for a calendar and I think he was looking for me. My name's Rachel Turner.'

12

RACHEL

1976

'Are you sure you haven't had a letter?' said Max. 'It'll be from Germany. *Bundes* something or other. You couldn't miss it.' Even over the telephone his disbelief was clear. 'Why don't you nip downstairs and have another look? I know what these flats are like.'

'Max, I haven't had it,' Rachel told him. 'And I'm not even sure I want to get it. I'm really not interested in that kind of work any more.'

Why couldn't she be more emphatic? Why couldn't she simply tell him: it's over, the stripping, the sex pictures, the random fucking . . . Or simply put down the phone. But a fear held her back. A fear that the face she glimpsed in faint reflection behind the grey nets of the sitting-room window might only be capable of expressing anonymous passion, counterfeit desire.

'I know what it is, Rachel.' She heard the slow grin in Max's drawl. 'It's seeing that old flatmate of yours again with her kiddie. Every woman gets broody once in a while. You'll get over it, love. You're on a winner here. I got very good reports from Holland – '

'Max, there's someone at the door – I've got to go.'

'If you don't hear by the weekend, let me know.' Max spoke rapidly. 'I'll get in touch with them. Everybody's very impressed.'

She put down the receiver and sat quietly a moment at

the dining room table. Then she reached out and picked up
the rumpled sheet of paper in front of her.

> Dear Marie, [she read] We would be most grateful to do
> business with you. We are auditioning for a new pro-
> duction of our company. There will be substantial
> rewards for performers who are selected.
>
> If you like to attend, please be at the address below at
> the time requested. We would be pleased to see you in
> Munich and would make you a warm welcome.

The address appeared to be a hotel, the time was an
afternoon a week hence.

A warm welcome. She made a grunting sound, which faded
into a long sigh. She watched her fingers crumple the letter
as if they moved of their own volition, the paper folding and
bending and collapsing on itself along creases made the
dozen previous times she had crushed it to a tight ball.

She needed a friend. Someone to say, '*Snap out of it, Rachel.
You're OK. You'll find work. Two, three months without an offer is
nothing. You'll be all right.*' Even if she wasn't.

But Josey was hundreds of miles away with worries of her
own, and Derek had helped convince her that *Prince* was the
right path in the first place . . .

She was so tired of being alone. It became harder and
harder to rise every morning in the silence of the flat, to
dress, eat, make up and walk out to new agencies, new
photographers, old refusals – quite apart from bills that
devoured her Dutch earnings at an ever-increasing rate.

How easy it would be to say yes to Max, to take up this
German offer, to rejoin Françoise and Armand and all their
kind in that bizarre camaraderie of heedlessness and self-
contempt.

327

But now, at least, she had a timetable of sorts. A week to find something – anything – to show there were possibilities beyond Munich.

She let go of the ball of paper and stood up. It was still before nine in the morning. Beyond the window a dull sky darkened. Far below, in a canyon of back extensions, commuter trains rumbled toward King's Cross.

She was on her way to an agency in New Bond Street, cutting through Hanover Square from Oxford Circus when she found herself in the narrow walk-through where Norman Bealby's agency was housed. She paused by the brass plaque beside the red-painted door.

She had called only once since Josey's departure, having got nowhere with a series of phone calls. A receptionist with fine blonde hair, a cut-glass accent and an air of bored tolerance made it plain there was little point in her returning.

Rachel had half expected as much. Her connection was via Josey; she had often wondered how much her flatmate's influence with Norman had pushed work her way. With Josey gone, Norman would have no more interest.

But that was only an assumption. Circumstances changed, and she had promised herself to pursue every opportunity, however unlikely or personally hurtful.

She was early for her New Bond Street appointment. She opened the red door and went up the steep, carpeted stairs.

She had developed a mental trick, more a superstition, that if she imagined something she expected to be unpleasant or painful as turning out in the worst possible way, then the reality would always fall short. Fate would be deceived.

In reality, it rarely worked. She imagined a blazing row with the receptionist, telling the girl exactly what she thought of her, storming out, while secretly praying that someone new and more sympathetic would be sitting at the reception desk.

But the girl was still there, icily polite over a coffee she seemed reluctant to abandon. They were only interested in girls with zed cards – if she cared to leave hers? They did see new girls in person occasionally, but only by telephone appointment. Neither Mr Bealby nor his assistant were in yet, so nothing could be arranged. Would she ring back? – though their books *were* full at the moment . . .

Rachel clattered back down the entrance steps, stifling frustration and a lashing anger. Her name meant nothing here, and her only consolation was that the receptionist's bland rejection seemed designed for all unwelcome new-comers rather than her in particular.

She was so involved in these thoughts that she hardly noticed the woman passing her on the stairs until a voice said, 'It's Rachel, isn't it? Josey Burman's friend?'

Rachel turned in surprise. The woman above her was in her late thirties, tall and thin and very smartly dressed. She spoke with a cultured, rather fey accent. Rachel recognized Norman's assistant.

'Oh, hello, Deirdre.' She smiled; the woman's smartness and apparent efficiency had always been at odds with a vaguely distracted air, which Rachel found reassuring.

'How odd to see you here – Norman was only talking about you yesterday.'

'Me?' Rachel's heart stilled.

'Yes, it was something about calendar work. Boucanier? It was James Kingsley, anyway.'

329

Boucanier. Weren't they something to do with cars? But she knew Kingsley's name. She'd seen it in a dozen magazines.

'Have you been trying to get in touch?' Rachel's voice rose excitedly. Why hadn't the receptionist said anything?

'Well, it's not our cup of tea, really. I think Norman had the idea we'd lost touch with you after Josey left. She went abroad, didn't she?'

It didn't matter what Norman thought or intended or cared. Work was on offer with a prestigious name. 'I could see Mr Kingsley any time —'

'Well, I wouldn't get my hopes up,' the woman cut in, her brow furrowing, as though she had revealed more than she should and was beginning to regret it. 'It was a very vague enquiry. I wasn't aware of any urgency.'

'Have you got Mr Kingsley's number or address?'

Deirdre's frown deepened. 'I think I ought to phone first. Most photographers aren't very keen on models turning up unannounced. Let me talk to Norman. Why don't you telephone in a day or two?' She was already turning away.

'Deirdre, you might as well let me know. I can find out his number easily enough, anyway.' Rachel spoke so harshly she felt herself blushing immediately, her heart thudding. She opened her mouth to mitigate her tone, but Deirdre had paused, sighing faintly.

'Well, all right,' she said suddenly. 'I'll give you the address now, but I'd really be very annoyed if this got back to Norman.'

The lowering skies opened as she left the Tube at Parson's Green. Waiting with a cluster of ex-passengers at the booking hall entrance, she watched heavy rain hiss off the roofs and tyres of passing cars. She had no umbrella, only a thin scarf in her shoulder-bag.

Everything inside her told her to move, to go *now*. Time mattered more than a bedraggled appearance. Hurrying contained a fierce hope; its disappointment might crush her. She waited two minutes then pulled on the scarf and ran.

The street could have been where Max Wallace had his studio – the same Victorian façades but marginally tidier, smarter cars, the odd exotic colour. The house she stopped at looked no different from any other, except for plain roller blinds on the lower windows.

The rain had not eased; the day was almost night-dark, but she could see no lights inside. With growing misgivings, she pressed the doorbell. She felt embarrassment rising as she rang for the third then the fourth time. If the photographer *was* in, busy in a darkroom perhaps, he wouldn't thank an over-persistent caller. Each time she forced herself to count longer, and on the fifth heard footsteps crashing on bare boards.

The door opened with such force she almost flinched. A young man stood there, pale and flustered and sleep-fugged, his thick fair hair spiked as though he had just tumbled from bed.

Rachel paused, uncertain. Even with a bloom of morning beard he looked ridiculously young to be Kingsley. Then, as he answered her question and the disappointment welled in her, she no longer saw him. Simple bravado made her talk on.

Something changed in the young man's face. A look of distraction, of ill-concealed annoyance sharpened suddenly into surprise, and interest. 'Look, you've come this

331

far, you might as well come in. I'm Paul Hanna.' He moved back for her, pushing a hand through his hair. 'I'm James Kingsley's assistant.'

She stepped into a surprisingly large area of bare, sanded floorboards and white-painted walls and ceiling, the lightness creating an almost luminous gloom. It came into harsh focus as a light-switch clicked. Rachel blinked at a small forest of stands, a step-ladder, the half-dismantled flats of a set. Loosening her headscarf, she turned to the young man.

'So Mr Kingsley's chosen all the models for his calendar?'

'I'm afraid so. He's scouting locations around Mayrhofen at the moment. He'll be shooting within a week. He wouldn't have time to change his mind, even if he wanted to.'

Rachel, nodded. 'Do you think I would have stood a chance – no, that's silly.' She shook her head, the damp ends of hair flapping on her shoulders. 'I'd better go.'

'Well, have a coffee or something. Dry off, at least.'

She looked at him again, puzzled by the look of interest, of a kind of ardency. Was he holding something back, or was it simply the usual reason?

She found herself examining him in the quick, almost animal way she had refined over the past year. He had a pleasant face, as open as Andrew's but more rounded, stronger, though the eyes seemed as diffident – even more so, or perhaps more subtle. A gentle face – capable of determination? She couldn't decide. He really looked very young, almost innocent in an urgent, troubled fashion that was quite appealing.

These thoughts flickered through her mind as her gaze darted down his body, appreciating its leanness, its muscular neatness, the unemphatic, compactness at his crotch. All boiled down to one question: *could I do it with him?* The answer was yes, but it meant nothing. Being able to and *wanting* to were worlds apart. And anyway, she had no more interest in sex.

She frowned. 'Are you American?'

'Yeah – I'm a foreigner.' His smile transformed his face, involving every part of it. Its warmth communicated itself, causing an involuntary tug at the corners of Rachel's mouth, which she resisted. She was not here to be sociable. And he looked too innocent to desire her, even in Andrew's inhibited way.

'Perhaps I could see Mr Kingsley when he gets back. Do you know when that'll be?'

'Probably not before the middle of next month. Why don't you leave some details? Have you got a zed card?'

Rachel's face dropped. 'It's being reprinted.' She glanced down quickly at her bag. 'I'll leave you my number.' She rummaged for a scrap of envelope; the young man found a Biro on a nearby window-ledge. 'Where did you see my work?' Rachel asked, as she wrote.

She saw him hesitate and the thought went through her that it must have been one of Max's sex magazine sales – something graphic and crude – and her heart shrank. But the young man answered easily, 'Might have been a trade mag – I don't know. Jimmy was looking for new faces all over.'

The trade magazine was just possible; there had been ads for three or four in the Josey days.

'Sure you won't want a substitute for your calendar if someone doesn't turn up?'

He grinned at her brittle smile. 'The way this project is turning out I wouldn't be in the least surprised – it has been

333

a nightmare!' He paused. 'I'm sorry we didn't get in touch sooner.'

'You know where to find me next time.' Rachel pushed the scrap of envelope into his hand. He asked if it was an agency.

'No, I prefer to represent myself.' She smoothed her scarf, folded it and put it on. 'I've really got to go. I've already missed one appointment.' She moved swiftly to the door, drawing him after her.

'No coffee?' The request was clumsily done and too late. Mentally she was already outside.

'No, thanks. Oh –' She turned in the open doorway, her eyes narrowing. 'Where did you say Mr Kingsley was shooting?'

He looked uncertain. 'A place called Mayrhofen. It's near Innsbruck, I think.'

'Thank you. Sorry about the coffee!' And with a swift smile she had gone.

The heavy rain had stopped, replaced by a thin, fading drizzle. She walked quickly .

13
PAUL
1976

Her presence lingered with a peculiar intensity, as if she'd worn a most potent perfume, though he had noticed none. But he was aware of a rich, almost an over-rich muskiness, much more unsettling to the senses than Diana's orangy piquancy – his previous yardstick of desirability.

It had flowed from her almost carelessly – the olfactory equivalent of her sudden, unusually direct glances that seemed to assess him so frankly he didn't know whether to be flattered or annoyed. There was a darkness about her, the opposite of Diana's breezy openness.

He had only recognized her when she had said who she was – the magazine photographs had been crude, formula approximations, catching no more than an outline of her vitality. He could take marvellous pictures of her!

He paused, still standing near the door, grinning at the force of his reaction. Did he want to photograph or fuck her? He was sure he would enjoy both, but there was something more complex, more elusive in her that attracted him. He wondered what Hugh Metzer's friend had meant by 'unsavoury'. Not simply the *Prince* pictures, surely?

No, he had seen her tense, as though steeling herself, when she'd asked him where he'd seen her and he'd responded accordingly. He could imagine that appraising stare, the lush edges to those mobile features, the figure beneath slotting credibly into the most erotic contexts. It was a part of her darkness – as was her evident unease at the thought of discovery.

He felt again that odd sense of familiarity, of recognition he had known on first seeing her pictures. But it was not her he recognized. It was something in her – a sexual direct-ness, a sense of experience, a confusion.

He glanced at the name and telephone number in his hand, momentarily surprised that it was not May Mor-rison. But he would hardly expect a real name in a maga-zine like *Prince*. Rachel Turner. A neat, squarish hand, both feminine and assured.

He had been really quite inept about that offer of coffee. Had he forgotten how to talk to girls who attracted him? It suddenly occurred to him that he had not been attracted to any girls for what seemed like an eternity. Sparks of for-gotten excitements . . .

Then the telephone rang, jolting him from his reverie. It announced a frantic Jimmy, and the day began.

Three of the models could get away on Saturday – the fourth was on holiday and wouldn't be back till Monday. A new make-up person – a girl – would also be free the same day. The stylist was skiing at Verbier in Switzerland until the weekend and would drive on to Austria. 'If he breaks a leg beforehand,' warned James, 'I'll go and break the other one personally!'

Speaking from his Mayrhofen chalet that evening, he seemed marginally brighter. The process was all too familiar to Paul: alternating panic and euphoria, moving closer and closer together until the moment the photo-grapher stepped behind the lens and a quiet, businesslike calm would take over – for most of the time. The fact that

Paul understood those feelings exactly did little to mitigate their effect.

'The sceneery is bloody fantastic here – I'd completely forgotten,' said James. 'We're going to have to tighten up the shots or we'll just lose the girls. Pat's getting worried about balance. I've been doing some rethinking about action shots. I'd like you to bring over some of the remote-control units tomorrow – '

'Tomorrow!' Paul interrupted. He'd existed on coffee and snacks all day; there hadn't even been time to wash, and packing hadn't started yet. 'What about the girls?'

'Oh, they can manage a flight on their own. You can pick them up at Munich on Saturday. We've got a good hire-car. Just make damn sure they've got their tickets. Now, have you got a pen?'

Grimacing, Paul reached across the jumble of James's desktop.

He tumbled into his own bed, still unwashed, just before one in the morning. There were the remains of an intimate dinner for two in the living room. By the giggling protests coming through the wall from his Australian flatmate's room the occasion was moving quickly to its natural conclusion.

Lying half undressed in the darkness, Paul realized the day's events had squeezed any further thought of Rachel Turner from his mind. He was surprised how much of a loss that seemed.

Another giggle penetrated from next door.

Undifferentiated lust – was that all she offered? After all his protests, all his grand gestures, was he just grasping for another of Cora-Beth's 'free, loving, orgasmic experiences'? How exquisite an irony – sabotaged by his own gonads!

But the joke felt too glib. If he was so strongly attracted, it was in a way that he didn't recognize – no swift, direct impulse, no sentimental, Diana-like glow – only a kind of tremulous unease, a kind of inner quaking so deep-rooted and so ambiguous he might only be imagining it anyway.

He had her number. He would find out soon enough once the calendar was done.

He fell asleep to the creaking of bedsprings and slept dreamlessly.

His aircraft dropped out of low cloud above a grey, chequerboard landscape early the following afternoon. Touch-down followed swiftly.

It was his first landfall on non-English-speaking Europe – three years overdue – and he wondered if he should feel more excited. Perhaps an over-exposure to British phlegm was affecting him at last.

The airport seemed small and unhurried, the national differences visible only in matters of detail. The air was chill as he filed from the plane and squeezed with his fellow passengers – all of whom appeared to be tourists – into the widest bus he had ever seen.

At the terminal building he made straight for the first free luggage trolley and gazed beyond Customs for any sign of James. There was none, which was ominous; Paul had taken care to telephone his arrival time before picking up the equipment from Fulham that morning. He sat down to wait for the luggage to appear, while another bus pulled up and the arrival hall quickly became crowded. Suitcases began to thump on the nearest carousel.

As Paul glanced towards it, a pair of legs caught his eye among the passengers clustering around the carousel's rim.

Rather fine legs, clad in dark nylon, balanced on black high heels.

The crowd moved and he glimpsed a tight-waisted winter coat, dark hair overflowing the collar. Then, in a swift, darting movement, at once delicate and decisive, the head turned and he saw the profile – sharp-eyed and brooding, the lip chewed in a moment of worry.

His heart dropped in his chest with the force of a piston. The coincidence was too great. He was looking at Rachel Turner.

14
RACHEL
1976

The touch at her elbow made her start.

'Rachel Turner?'

Her eyes widened from fearful suspicion when she saw who it was. She smiled a wide, brilliant, spontaneous smile. She saw its effect in the young man's face, flattered that it seemed so startling.

But sheer relief had provoked her reaction. This meeting was a chance so remote she had hardly dared dream of it – and a complete vindication of every desperate hope.

'This is – a surprise.' Paul laughed at a word that appeared to him completely inadequate.

There was a breathlessness about him, a kind of excitement which seemed rooted in her – not, disconcertingly, on the physical level she knew so well, but more totally, almost as Andrew had been with her, which was absurd because this young American hardly knew her at all.

'Hello – it's Paul, isn't it?' she said. 'You must have been on the same flight.'

'Or the one after.' He grinned, enjoying the unlikelihood of it. Then, as if becoming aware that his grin was becoming vacuous, said more seriously, 'Are you on holiday here?'

'No, I've got a few days' work in Munich.'

He nodded companionably, digging his hands into the thick quilted coat he wore. 'I'd no idea you worked in Europe. It's probably why we didn't track you down so quickly. Is it anything exciting?'

The question caught her unawares. She kept her face straight as she shrugged. 'Oh, the usual – trade things. Nothing spectacular.' She gathered her breath. 'I don't actually start till after the weekend. It's really odd running into you like this. I was just thinking I might wander over and see your boss, if I found time . . . '

Her heart bumped as she let the sentence hang, too frightened suddenly to finish it. But the young man simply smiled.

'Jimmy? Well, you won't have to go far. He's picking me up any minute. Or I hope he is.'

She felt a surge in her breast, the thunder of blood in her ears. The recklessness, the connivance of this venture which had seemed so extreme, so impossible, except in her deepest hopes, *was* right, her feelings had shown her exactly the right way.

She became voluble. 'It'd only be for a few minutes. It just seemed silly, being so near, *not* seeing him, since he'd asked for me. I didn't realize, when I saw you, how close I was going to be – there's no distance at all on the map. I know, of course, everything's settled for the calendar – ' She checked herself, seeing the uncertainty flicker across Paul's face. His eyes slid away from her and she was gripped by a terrible fear that she had bored him – he would simply nod politely and walk away and her single contact with Kingsley would vanish.

'You're going to miss your luggage,' he said, nodding at the carousel.

Rachel turned. The belt was full; passengers were jostling at the edge. They moved forward into a gap. As Rachel saw her suitcase and reached for it, Paul leaned forward and lifted it first.

'Do you mind if I claim my trolley with this?' he said. 'I've got a pile of stuff coming through and I don't want to lose it.'

She waited while he collected his own luggage from a different carousel, lending a hand with his two aluminium gadget-cases, a bulky aluminium trunk and a suitcase. Her help was tentative, but gave her all the excuse she needed to stay close, establishing links of familiarity which improved her confidence.

As they went through Customs, the official said, 'Together?'

She found herself watching Paul as he shook his head. 'Just good friends,' he said, making her smile.

In the terminal hall there seemed to be no one waiting for Paul. Frowning, he went to the glass doors at the end and looked outside at the taxi rank while Rachel guarded the trolley. His frown had deepened when he returned.

'I smell a cock-up. Look, I'm going to find a phone. I can't really keep you hanging about.'

'Oh, don't worry about me. I'd only be sight-seeing anyway.' Even to her, her brightness sounded brittle.

Paul looked dubious. 'What about settling in somewhere?'

'Oh, that's all taken care of. I can just get a taxi to my hotel whenever I like. It's no problem.' She paused. 'I really don't want to miss the opportunity of meeting – Jimmy.'

Paul raised his eyebrows. 'It doesn't look like there's going to be much opportunity – '

A hiccuping Tannoy interrupted him. Through an echoing gabble of German his own name was discernible. Rachel exchanged glances with him as the Tannoy barked again in English, 'Will Mr Paul Hanna of flight H901 from

London please come to the information desk.'

They found it at the end of the concourse. A crisp blonde woman read from a scribbled note. 'A Mr Kinley – Kinsley? – rang to say he has been delayed. Will you find a taxi to Mayrhofen?'

'*Shit.*' Paul shook his head in disbelief.

'Weren't you going to get a taxi, anyway?' Rachel asked.

'There was supposed to be a hire-car.' Paul looked at the laden trolley. 'I was counting on some manual help.'

'I'll help.'

He glanced at her and grinned. 'That wasn't a hint.'

'I know.'

Paul's grin broadened as he searched her face. 'OK,' he said at last. 'But I've no idea how far it is.'

'It's about a hundred and twenty kilometres,' said the blonde woman, looking up. 'About two hours on the auto-bahn.' She smiled. 'It depends on your taxi-driver.'

'You'll never get back here today!' Paul cried.

Rachel shrugged. 'Then I'll stay in Mayrhofen. One night away isn't a problem. I told you I don't start till next week.'

Paul's shoulders drooped in a mocking gesture of accep-tance.

He likes me, Rachel thought. *He's happy if he can find a reason for me to stay with him.* She would do her best to keep him thinking that way.

It had been dark for an hour when the small Audi pulled to a halt in a narrow, brightly lit main street. Rachel yawned and looked out at the shuttered windows of a hotel. Hard-packed snow lined the pavements. Moon-booted pedes-trians tramped by.

As conversation lapsed, the darkness and the wavering

343

pattern of lights on the winding valley road – some from clusters of low-roofed houses, others winking distantly from improbable heights on either side – had made her drowsy. She sat up now, guiltily aware that she had slumped against Paul's shoulder, as the taxi-driver left the car.

'Just getting directions,' Paul said easily, and stretched his arms. 'I'm sorry this has taken so long.'

'Don't be silly.' He seemed untroubled that she had moved away from him on the rear seat. She wondered if there would be a chance to use a mirror before they arrived.

The driver was back almost immediately. They drove on at speed as the main street dipped and curved. Abruptly they turned off into a shadowy side-road of solid balconied houses. Wide wooden eaves, piled with snow, loomed out of the darkness. Just as abruptly they stopped beneath one.

The driver got out and went straight to the boot. He seemed anxious to be unloaded and away. Paul joined him. Then, more reluctantly, Rachel too, frowning and slipping in the soft snow which covered her shoes.

All three brought the luggage to a carved dark wooden door. Curtained windows glowed on either side. Paul nodded towards them. 'At least that's encouraging.' He pulled notes from a wallet and handed them all to the driver.

As the taxi disappeared, he knocked on the door. It jerked open at once. A tall, shaggy-haired man in a loose sweater hung in the doorway. 'Paul! Thank God for that! At least something's working out on this bloody awful day – come on in!'

'What on earth happened?' said Paul.

'Ask the demon driver inside! Drove into a bloody glacier this morning!' The man snatched away the two gadget-bags Paul was carrying and deposited them inside. 'Totally

344

buggered the hire-car. We've spent the day getting the damn thing back – no end of hassle with the hire company.' Paul handed him his suitcase. 'I mean – a glacier! They're not exactly hard to miss. Did you bring the remote units?'

He ducked past Paul, reaching for the large aluminium trunk and stopped short as he saw Rachel standing behind it.

Paul introduced them, briefly explaining her presence. 'Rachel's been a great help,' he finished. 'I kind of promised her you'd run a couple of test shots while she was in the neighbourhood.'

Rachel heard the hesitancy in his voice and felt her stomach tighten.

'Did you now?' James shook hands with her over the trunk. 'Hello, Rachel.' He smiled quizzically, his rugged, bearded face not unfriendly, but not entirely delighted either.

'I really don't want to impose,' she said quickly. 'But I heard you were looking for me in London – '

'Yes.' James interrupted her with a quick smile, and Rachel threw an awkward glance at Paul, whose face registered nothing. 'Let's get this stuff into the lobby,' James continued, bending to grasp the trunk. 'I want to move it all next door later on, Paul. We didn't get the second chalet, by the way.'

'*Didn't* get it!' Paul exploded.

'It's not the disaster it sounds,' James said evenly, pulling the trunk over the threshold. 'We've a two-room apartment in the house next door. I want to use one room to store all the equipment and I'd like you to stay in the other one. The rest of us can squeeze in here. Don't look so miserable! You'll be the only one who's not sharing.' He took the last two cases from Rachel. 'You're just in time for

345

supper. Pat's doing some spaghetti speciality he knows. It's his penance for this morning.'

Rachel ate desultorily and drank less, not because she lacked the appetite – she felt ravenous – but out of a nervous need to remain inconspicuous. Clearly neither James nor the sad-eyed, balding man called Pat, who greeted her with undisguised surprise, were quite sure what she was really doing there – beyond her connection with Paul – which equally clearly intrigued James.

She didn't care. Nothing mattered until the moment James Kingsley picked up his camera and carried out Paul's promise. After that, everything would be different.

That single thought had prompted this mad enterprise, and prompted her promise to Max to accept the Munich offer, on condition that she went days earlier. And on her own, unspoken condition that there would never be any need for her to take it up. Now or ever again.

15
PAUL
1976

'Christ, I'm getting too old for this,' Pat Dealy sighed, rising from the heavy trunk which now filled the narrow gap between the twin beds in Paul's apartment.

Paul grunted and climbed over the clear bed – its companion was heaped with cases and photographic equipment. As the two men moved from the tiny bedroom Pat turned and said darkly, 'This girl you've brought isn't anything Jimmy's dreamed up, is it? You know we're only budgeted for four models.'

'No!' Paul made a face. 'I really did just run into her at the airport.'

'She knows there's no work here?'

Paul reached down to his suitcase and slid it behind a large maroon divan. 'Jimmy might be able to use her later – a couple of Polaroids now won't hurt.'

Pat sniffed. 'Well, I've no objection to you getting your leg over, son, but we're going to be busy after the weekend. Neither you nor Jimmy's going to need any more complications than we've already got.'

Paul coloured. 'Like cars hitting glaciers?'

Pat looked at him sharply. 'That was a fence-post under a pile of snow – you don't want to believe everything Jimmy tells you. And don't be cheeky.'

Paul sighed. 'I'm sorry. I just thought I was returning a favour.'

347

'Well, get your motives straight before you commit your-self next time, OK?' The art director glanced away, looking around the room. The furnishings were modest but not unpleasant. There was a kitchenette in one corner, the door to a shower room in the other, a mirror-fronted storage unit in between. Twin doors opened onto a terrace. 'At least you've got yourself a nice little love-nest. Come on.' Pat's voice rose as he saw annoyance flare in Paul's eyes. 'I could murder a drink after shifting this lot. I'll introduce you to the local poison.'

But when they tramped back the few yards to the neighbouring chalet James met them in the lobby, his brow furrowed. He pulled Paul aside and spoke in an undertone. 'I think it'd be a good idea if you took your girlfriend for a quiet drink. There's a bar just down the road. I think she could do with it.'

'Why?' Paul stared at him. 'What's the matter? Didn't you take the Polaroids?'

'I went through the motions – she's got possibilities but not for this job. You haven't been making any rash promises, have you?'

With a pained look, Pat squeezed past toward the kitchen.

'Only that you'd see her.'

James grunted. 'She's obviously got a very different idea. Look, just cheer her up, will you? She's got to be back in Munich soon, anyway, hasn't she?'

Paul nodded, suddenly not at all sure what was happening. They went into the living room. Rachel was putting on her coat. She looked pale and shaken.

'Are you all right?' Paul asked.

She glanced at him very quickly, the thinnest smile

348

forming and fading. She seemed embarrassed. 'Yes, of course. I'm very glad you could see me,' she told James. 'I really must go now.' She reached for her suitcase.

'Let me.' Paul got to it first, and a flicker of annoyance crossed the girl's face. She moved toward the lobby door as Pat appeared from the kitchen clutching a bottle of cherry brandy.

James snatched it from him as Paul followed the girl into the lobby. 'Nice to meet you, Rachel,' the photographer called after her. 'I'm sure we'll see you again soon.'

Paul lowered the case as they shrugged on their coats and James pushed the brandy bottle into his hands, nodding at it meaningfully behind Rachel's back.

Suddenly Paul found himself outside, the door closed behind him, the girl picking her way ahead of him along the pavement. Snow fell lightly out of the darkness. Too much was happening too quickly.

'Hey,' he cried. 'Rachel! This is crazy. You can't travel tonight.'

The girl slipped with a gasp. Paul dropped the case and sprang after her, grasping her elbow and steadying her as she swayed. The brandy bottle plopped into the snow. Rachel was trembling. She dropped her head, keeping very still. 'I'm sorry,' she whispered. 'I think I'll be sick if I don't sit down.'

'Don't be sorry.'

Paul sighed. They were midway between James's chalet and his own apartment house. He had blotted enough copy-books as far as his job was concerned for one night.

'Come on,' he said.

Her head resting in her hands, the girl sat at a small dining

349

table in front of the terrace doors, while Paul struggled to convert the divan into a bed. Eventually the furniture's logic became obvious.

He patted the broad mattress. 'Stretch out. I'll be two minutes.'

He went out to fetch her suitcase and the brandy bottle, feeling worried. When he got back Rachel was lying on her side on the mattress. She had taken off her coat and shoes and her eyes were closed. Her face looked grey.

He switched a small table-lamp on and put the main light off. In the semi-darkness of the kitchenette he opened the brandy bottle and found two small glasses.

'Oh, this is absolutely stupid.'

He turned and saw Rachel sitting up, her face drawn. He filled a glass and took it over.

'Drink,' he said, sitting on the edge of the divan-bed. The girl's gaze darted past him, blinking at the dim surroundings.

'I've got to find somewhere – '

'Later.' He pushed the glass into her hand. She looked at it reluctantly. He lifted her hand towards her mouth. She raised the glass, sipped and choked.

'Good for shock. Makes you forget what you were worried about.'

She sipped again, sighing as she lowered the glass. 'I feel so tired.'

'Then rest. There's no panic.'

She sighed again, more deeply, letting him take the glass as she settled back on the mattress. Her eyes appeared to be open but when he looked again, after returning the glass to the kitchenette, she was asleep, breathing shallowly.

He sat at the dining table, watching her as he swallowed

brandy, wondering how and why he had got into this situation. So much was wrong — his own ill-considered decision to bring her here (for what? To please her? To get off with her? Any other reason was self-delusion) — her bizarre reaction to a refusal that *must* have seemed inevitable.

Was there really any job in Munich? Surely she wouldn't have come this distance on a single remark in a single conversation? No one could be *that* desperate. Unless that 'unsavoury' element supposedly in her background was unimaginably dire.

He felt himself floating in a sea of contradictions, aware that he had deliberately set himself adrift, but for no obvious reason beyond the girl and the elusive qualities he had seen in her — qualities that changed the longer he was with her, growing more complicated, more involving and no clearer.

All that *was* clear was that she disturbed him. Watching that softly sculpted face, childishly untroubled in sleep, he felt twists of an unease that gnawed not unpleasantly but increasingly, compelling him to follow it whatever the conclusion. Somehow he could not abandon that quest — not quite, not yet.

His watch had stopped and it felt very late when he moved at last to the bedroom, his head muzzy with accumulated fatigue and the effects of the sickly sweet brandy. He found blankets in a low dresser, paused to drape one over the girl, then returned to the bedroom, undressed and climbed onto the clear bed, wrapping himself in another blanket and immediately falling asleep.

A sobbing woke him after what seemed only minutes. He lay quietly, straining his ears, half convinced he had dreamed it. Then it came again, very softly, a squeezed, snuffling sound, almost animal-like.

He opened his eyes onto the darkness. There was a different texture to the night and to himself, not quite a banishment of tiredness but a gloss of refreshment, persuading him that hours in fact had passed. Then he realized that a strip of light should have been visible beneath the closed door. He had not switched off the lamp in the main room.

He got up, draping his blanket over his shoulders and crawled to the end of the bed, stubbing a bare toe on something sharp-edged as he put his feet down. Wincing he listened at the door, hearing nothing, debated with himself, then opened it.

The faintest, snow-reflected glow penetrated the curtained windows. His eyes adjusting, he made out the outline of the divan-bed, a curled shape towards its centre.

He remembered another darkened room and another waiting girl three thousand miles and another life away. Curiosity and an aching cock had drawn him through that door. Straightforward, uncluttered impulses that seemed almost pure now. He felt an age older and a lot less wise.

'Rachel?' he murmured. 'Are you OK?'

There was a quiet intake of breath, no more. He rested a knee on the edge of the mattress, feeling the hardness of the wooden frame beneath the foam, then crumpled wool. Reaching down, his fingers touched the pleats of a skirt, bundled tights, the catch of a bra.

The girl stirred, moaning softly; he felt her turn towards him.

'Rachel?' he whispered.

Something pale moved below him in the darkness. He leaned forward, stretching down, and touched the warm flesh of an arm arcing towards him, glancing his shoulder –

a flaccid, unforced movement that could have been the flexing of a limb in sleep.

He let the contact unbalance him, and dropped on to the mattress. He was suddenly rolling against her – drowning in the soft contours of her body, sheathed in a thin slip, the close warmth of her breath, the sharp muskiness, softened by sleep, he knew from before.

'Hold me . . . ' The words came on a single breath – faint enough to be the mouthings of a dream. But he obeyed, pulling her to him, drawing his own blanket around them both.

They lay still in the darkness as he listened to her breathing, mapping in his mind the warm outline that abutted him, the firm edge of a hip against his stomach, the cushioned swell of her breasts, the knotted thickness of a nipple through the fabric of her slip.

A welter of emotions assailed him – pity, compassion, tenderness, desire – each vying with the other. And as the minutes lengthened, the tension in him grew. Why did he hesitate? Dreaming or waking, the girl was aroused – aroused enough to accept his advances. Why should he be so frightened that this girl should spurn him?

Then she sighed again, moving against him so that the stub of a second nipple touched his chest. Her hand closed on the flesh of his thigh.

His arousal struck him with the force he'd known when he first saw her photograph – something stomach-churning and deep, so sudden it set his heart drumming before his quickening blood could reach his loins. The feeling swamped all others, lifted him on a slow, accelerating tide, driving stiffness and boiling warmth into every limb so that they seemed extensions of his thickening cock.

Dazzled, he pressed his lips to her neck, turning and

smoothing his hands up from her narrow waist onto her rib cage, hearing her sharp intake of breath, feeling her body soften and mould to him. Nothing had ever seemed so natural, so right, so good.

She moaned as his hands came onto her breasts, her nipples thick between his closing fingers, the muffling nylon of her slip. Then he was reaching down, sliding the material up, scooping the rounded warmth of her buttocks as her thighs opened under him.

Her hand moved, deliberately it seemed for the first time – pushing down between their bodies, so that he breathed in to give her room. Cool fingers enclosed his penis. They drew him backward and down so delicately, so neatly his engorged bulb was swimming in folds of moist flesh before he realized her intention.

He entered her cleanly, on a dying sigh that joined their breath. Then her slim legs rose behind him, locking over his back, urging him deeper.

He felt himself expand as he thrust, as if his cock did not merely probe but merged with her, tissue with tissue, and his climax, when it came, sparked not solely from his tip but from every thickened inch of his shaft, his essence flowing outward in powerful, shuddering pulses.

Yet, when it was over and she relaxed beneath him, he felt that his organ had swollen so absolutely it had passed some limit of detumescence. He had expended himself but he was not spent. His rigidity and the dull echo of his heartbeat persisted, and the urge to thrust and thrust again, pursuing sparks of pure joy that still lingered just beyond his grasp.

It was a sensation of immense power – one he could not remember feeling before, down a long gallery of faces and bodies from Diana to Anna Hornsiger, Bernice and Cheryl,

Barbara Howell and Andrea, numberless others whose names were lost to him. But it was tempered, almost instantly, by a feeling of intense gratitude to the girl – a distillation of the disturbance she had brought to him. He felt a kind of fierce sweetness, a clenching warmth in his chest.

The old suspicion that this was due to overlong frustration died for ever in a fresh welling of desire – a desire not to spend himself once more but to give Rachel pleasures as intense, to stir that sweetness in her too.

He moved again in her, feeling her surprise – even, momentarily, resistance. Then his hands touched the point where their bodies joined, stroking, caressing, both above and below. . .

16
RACHEL
1976

Her arousal had started in a dream — a cold, clear dream of faceless bodies and stabbing organs, organs that took her and filled her anonymously under hot lights, while disembodied faces circled and stared, shiny with excitement: Donny and Andrew, Barry and Derek, Armand and Max. And always — brooding and chill, perpetually dissatisfied — her father.

It was an old dream, increasingly frequent since her Dutch excursion, and even as she dreamt it she knew she would wake sweating and damp, curled foetally in her solitary bed, hands locked between her thighs. Then would come the longing for enfolding arms, for soft words, for the simplest animal comfort of maleness — any maleness — within her.

It was that longing which surfaced as she sensed a movement beside her — a longing made achingly intense by the shocks of the day.

As the arms enclosed her, her awareness of their identity was dim — images of fair hair, boyish features, a strong, lean body, no more than that — and the certainty of a rigid column of flesh against her thigh.

She accepted it as she accepted it under the glare of studio lights, as a gesture both of surrender and triumph, as a practised skill in which she took genuine pride, as a bitter parody of every act of love she had ever committed — or perhaps those love acts themselves were parodies and these harsh conjugations were reality.

But in the darkness this partner touched her with a confidence and urgency which soothed as it excited her. She was pleased when his rasping breath, his shorter, sharper thrusts marked his climax. She

356

was surprised when he began to thrust again, at an easier, more measured pace, so that she wondered if he had climaxed at all.

For a moment that annoyed her — that he might pretend satisfaction criticized her own performance. Had she done something wrong? But she did not care. She had taken what she needed and expected nothing more — why prolong matters?

It was then that her own body began a new response. Her partner seemed not simply to be moving in her but caressing her inner surfaces while his fingers teased her clitoris and the crevice between her cheeks. Simultaneously his lips came down on her breasts, plucking and rolling the swollen tips of her nipples.

She breathed in suddenly, not understanding how he could touch her in so many places and so well, as if not one but two or even three were making love to her with equal expertise.

She sensed his own pride in his abilities, yet it was a curious, almost self-denying variety; if a caress provoked a sigh of pleasure it would be repeated, embellished, elaborated until the sigh came again, deeper and more appreciative than before.

Very soon she found herself wallowing in a kind of waking and utterly sensual dream — not the heedless swoon of the studio, where she sought her own feelings with a deliberate concentration. Here every nerve end seemed tingling and alive of its own accord, elevating her from mere pleasure to a form of super-awareness in which she began to feel extraordinarily, breathlessly beautiful, both deep in herself and utterly beyond. A glow burned in her womb, spread suddenly like a fire from the throb of her nipples to the sweetness between her legs. And lightning struck. A cold, clear bolt, splitting heart and head, snatching breath away — even the ability to breathe — in one fierce, racking spasm. Repeated, it made her convulse and cry out, as she felt her partner groan and burst inside her.

She lay stunned, disbelieving as waves of utter intensity ebbed and dispersed.

Then, gasping for forgotten air, the reaction set in and she was weeping uncontrollably, clutching at the stranger who had touched her so deeply, who had become in a single instant and at a time when least expected not merely a partner nor a friend but something new and quite terrifying.

She lay curled in the darkness, wrapped in an afterglow as warm as his encircling arms.

She felt at peace, a superb bodily peace she did not want to give up or disturb with thought because she knew thought would bring questions and doubt. Simultaneously she was embarrassed by her tears, grateful that he had done no more to acknowledge them than hold her. Grateful too for much, much more.

She listened to the slow beat of his heart through his cushioning chest, the murmur of his breath. Did he say nothing because there was nothing to say? Perhaps he did this half a dozen times with half a dozen girls every week. She did not know him at all. And he certainly did not know her, and might never want to. Then he took a deeper breath, expelling it slowly in a half-sigh and she heard his smile in it and took courage.

'That's never happened to me before.'

She felt him move, dipping his head to her. 'Did I just *deflower* you?'

His tone was so exaggeratedly sincere it brought an involuntary hiccup of laughter from her, which he echoed. She nudged him lightly, tucking her head closer. 'You know what I mean.'

There was silence, and for a moment she thought he did not.

'Mmm.' He paused as if considering it. 'I'm glad. It was good.'

She would have preferred something more effusive. She

stirred, turning toward him, wanting suddenly to see his face.

His body was a long, pale outline stretched out beside her in the gloom, his face a moon shape, tilted up to her. Then it moved and his eyes caught a fragment of light from the window and she realized he was staring at her, watching as if the darkness were no impediment at all.

The mystery of what had happened struck her afresh. She had been with men who were better looking, stronger, sexier – but none of them had affected her as he had. Not even Andrew. Why should this man be so different?

'I've made a lot of trouble for you with your boss, haven't I? I didn't mean to. I think I've been a bit mad over the last few days.'

He shrugged. 'I'm not complaining.'

His apparent casualness troubled her. Nothing was ever this simple, this easy. It was foolish to pretend it was. 'You shouldn't be so trusting. You don't know anything about me.'

'I know you. I think I know you very well.' His quiet confidence stilled her. It held no arrogance, no bravado, merely a certainty that was suddenly chilling.

'How can you say that?' She spoke in no more than a whisper.

'I don't know.' He seemed amused by the thought, almost apologetic. 'It's crazy. I just do.'

And then she knew real fear. Because this man had breached the final barrier that had been her proudest and most cunning defence, had in a moment rendered her so vulnerable that his capacity for hurt could be beyond anything she had ever experienced before.

17
PAUL

He had never worked so hard, never loved so hard.

Rachel would stay or he would go. He was not conscious of giving an ultimatum, merely of stating a self-evident fact. To his surprise James appeared amused by his protégé's instant and seemingly oblivious commitment. 'I was beginning to wonder about you, Paul. No one can be *that* dedicated to taking pictures, not even me.' Or perhaps the photographer's amusement was at the expense of Pat Dealy, whose resentment at the girl's reappearance was immediate and unrelenting; after almost a week in each other's company the two men had refined their mutual antagonism to new, though allegedly creative, heights.

And yet, to Paul's secret relief, Rachel fitted in smoothly. She knew photographers, she knew shooting schedules, she was good with the models when James's demands became excessive, which was frequent. She was both bright and unobtrusive, complementing Paul's role by allowing him to concentrate on film and equipment, cameras and lenses, technical aspects of his job where his skills were best employed. After a week of accelerating success even Pat's gruffness mellowed and Paul smiled at an overheard remark from the art director to James that two assistants instead of one might have been a better plan from the beginning.

But such matters seemed no more to Paul than icing on a

very private cake. Watching Rachel tramp about snow-fields, clipboard in hand, dwarfed as much by borrowed anorak, salopettes and moonboots as by the gleaming and inhuman peaks on every side, he found it increasingly hard to comprehend her separateness. Only hours, sometimes minutes, before, he had linked his body with hers, mingled with her juices, taken her most intimate odours and inter-stices upon himself in bouts of emotion that exposed him as utterly as they seemed to expose her. In his mind they were still in that small, cramped apartment where they spent every evening and every night. Yet now she could exist apart from him, laugh, smile, chat, function perfectly well, as if that miraculous door into their deepest feelings could close again as suddenly as it had opened and all would be as before.

Then, as emptiness and uncertainty invaded him, he would catch her gaze, see her dark eyes soften and glow and know the night's mysteries were not lost, but hoarded away, cherished and safe in some joint and precious memory. It was in those moments that Cora-Beth's words – forgotten for so long – echoed through his mind. *If he were to cut his skin he would find my skin beneath – We were the same – It was as simple as that.* Yes. He could see it now; he could even understand how such a feeling could reverberate down twenty years. It was only his aunt's attempts to revive it that he could never forgive.

And then, after a fortnight, with the calendar well ahead of schedule, and James and Pat talking amicably, high freezing winds swept southward from Germany, raking the Zillertal Alps and most of the Tyrol with two days of freakish blizzards. In their chalet James and Pat fumed while the models grew bored and the stylist and make-up girl played patience. In their apartment, hardly able to believe their luck, Paul and Rachel made love.

Paul was padding from the bathroom when a sudden burst of light made him throw up his arm. 'What are you *doing*?'

Rachel laughed infectiously. Crouching by the bed, she was naked like him. She clutched a camera and flash unit to her bosom and rose, backing away as Paul stumbled across the room.

'No, you're not having the film,' she warned. 'I want to keep this one.'

Paul paused, frowning. 'That's Jimmy's favourite camera — he'll go berserk if anything happens to it.' Then, as Rachel's grin persisted, he dropped his eyes and sighed as he saw his all but vertical erection. 'Oh, *Jesus* — '

'I want a picture of it. I think it's beautiful — especially just now. *No!*'

She leapt back, holding the camera high with a breathless giggle as Paul lunged for her. He halted again, pressing a knee against the side of the bed and raising a hand in surrender.

'Promise you won't hurt the film?'

Paul nodded.

'Cross your heart?'

Paul obeyed. 'Trust me,' he said. 'I'm a photographer.'

Rachel made a sour face, pondered a moment, then gave the camera to him. Immediately he thumbed a catch and flipped open the back panel.

'You *swine!*' Rachel gaped at him in outraged disbelief. 'You *promised!*'

'Sure.' Paul grinned, turning over the camera to show her. 'No film.'

'You *sod!*' Her plunging fist caught him full in the stomach, pitching him off balance and back on to the bed.

As he bawled in mingled pain and laughter, she leapt after him and continued to pummel him unmercifully, striking all but the bloated shaft at his crotch. At last he grasped her to him, pulling her lips down on to his. As they kissed her struggling slackened, their breathing deepened; both relaxed. They had curled together on the mattress when they came up for air.

Paul smiled. 'Can you imagine Jimmy getting *that* on the end of the Boucanier pictures?'

Rachel pouted. 'I don't know what you're so shy about. You don't seem to have been too fussed about it back home.' She gave a sudden high, chuckling laugh, throwing back her head.

Paul grunted questioningly.

'I just remembered something Josey and I talked about once. We were going to do Polaroids of all of the men we knew really well – you know, *things* in all their glory – and paste them round the bedroom walls against ruler marks. Just to encourage the newcomers – '

'Oh, my *God*!' Paul groaned, raising his eyes ceilingward.

Chuckling again, Rachel pressed her head close to his. She grew quiet. 'Thank you,' she said quietly.

'Thank you for what?'

He frowned, moving his head back to look at her, but she kept her eyes down.

'For making me laugh about sex – I could never do that before, not with anyone I was involved with. It was never fun before it was beautiful.' She looked up then, her gaze deep and clear, drinking him in. 'Before you made it beautiful.'

He sucked in breath, wrinkling his nose semi-comically, grateful, embarrassed.

'I mean it.'

He swallowed, believing her. 'I'd like to take your picture,' he said. 'Properly. I've wanted to right from that day in Fulham.'

She blinked and lowered her head against his chest, breathing in the scent of his skin. 'No, not me,' she said. 'Us. I want you to take pictures of us as we are now – the way we feel. Everything. So that we can never forget.'

'*Everything*?'

He tried to smile, pressing his chin down to see her. But she did not move, merely nodded, the perfume of her hair thick in his nostrils.

'I know you can make it beautiful because it is. I want you to make up for all the times when it wasn't. I know you can do it.'

Her seriousness, her certainty, humbled him. He did not know what to say. And then, as her head continued to nuzzle his chest, moulding comfortably against the curve of his throat, his mind wandered, only for an instant, to the technical problems of such a shoot.

She was easy to make love to, easier than any other woman he had known. She seemed made for it, not merely in the shapeliness of her figure, the fullness of her breasts, the mobility of a face whose dark, brilliant eyes could shade from bright openness to fierce sexual interest to heavy-lidded desire in the space of seconds. It was in a manner, too, that matched independence, boldness, even sharpness, with the most delicate femininity, the most unexpected reticence.

'What are you looking at?' She sounded uncertain. She was below him as they sprawled, head to crotch, weary from the late hour and their own exertions, his arm arching over her upper thigh, his forearm flat on the mattress. With fingertips he traced the corrugations of her sex, wondering at the loose, dark pink folds that seemed permanently exposed.

'Don't *peer* – ' She shuddered lightly as his finger brushed the soft tip of her clitoris.

'You're always moist. Did you know that?' He glanced up at her, and smiled. She lay quietly, blinking, watching him. 'I'm not peering,' he said. 'I'm admiring. I think you're lovely – all of you.' He bent and kissed her, breathing in her sharp musk. He felt the air ease from her lungs. 'How can you be so shy about that?' he asked, lifting his head.

Her eyelids flickered and he sensed the tension in her that always accompanied any reference to her past. He wished she were not so vulnerable about it.

'It just seemed – clinical – that's all.'

'But you can't have minded before – in your work?'

She twisted suddenly, rolling on to her stomach, dislodging his arm. But not swiftly enough to hide the flush rising about her neck.

'That was different.'

'How different?'

She sighed, and he was penitent for having forced her. Before he could say anything she replied: 'That wasn't *me*.' She paused, her voice softening. 'I'm only me with you.'

Such words curdled his heart, compressing a sweetness there that was like a pain. They expressed a trust so total, so all-inclusive, his mind almost rebelled in disbelief, in protest at the burden it imposed.

But it was simultaneously a burden that swelled his self-esteen beyond all measure. He felt deeply male, deeply in control, and the responsibility tempered any egotism – for the most part.

It emerged when they argued – brief, sudden squalls, as spontaneous as they were lacerating – eruptions of selfhood (he realized much much later) into an over-pressurized intimacy. Then she would become irritating and obtuse, absurdly, almost contemptibly fussy, something smaller and dowdier than the fabulous creature of his obsession.

Lovemaking, too, brought such moments. Once, early one morning, he watched her emerge, pink and damp, from the shower room, her towelled hair still dripping odd droplets on to hard-nippled breasts, others glistening in the casually brushed thicket of her pubis. She was oblivious of him, thinking him asleep, and the sight of her – and perhaps her obliviousness – brought him instantly and thickly erect.

As she turned to the full-length mirror in the storage unit, bending slightly from the waist to towel her hair afresh, he slipped from the bed, making her start as his hand suddenly palmed a breast from beneath, the other smoothing the spare fleshiness of a buttock. Her surprise turned to grins and feigned annoyance and then a swallowed sigh as his fingers gently stroked each nipple.

Deliberately he said nothing, smiling but forcing her to bend still further forward, arms and legs outspread, hands pressed against the front of the unit. Then, releasing her, he sat quickly between her legs, his back to the mirror, raising himself on his hands to plunge his face into the forked junction of her body.

He licked and kissed, her, massaging her *mons* with his brow, teasing her clitoral hood with his nose, parting her swelling lips with his tongue and trailing its tip from clitoris to anus, devouring her soft and moistening surfaces in an accelerating frenzy of lust. She moaned and gasped and writhed, pushing herself down on to him until her knees gave and she began to shudder and sob, held up only by his hands propping her thighs. He had pictured himself rising between her arms, rising into her and lifting her on the hard spike of his excitement. But her panting collapse, even if his strength had allowed it, made that impossible.

Instead he half pulled, half carried her to the divan-bed, deflected the arms that reached for him, positioned her carefully over the end, legs parted, buttocks upraised. Then, kneeling, he entered her, pushing deep as her breath was expelled in a rasping gasp.

And as he pumped, fast and slow, chasing her climax as he avoided his own, he realized he was seeing her not as an object of affection, not as a source of solemn or tender joy, but simply as a body – no more than female flesh, to be pawed and moulded and *fucked*.

Images flashed through his mind, then – of a past she had described only in general terms. Images of strangers who took her not in this bodily heat but coldly – clinically – holding back their own desire and hers for the snap of a camera shutter. Or perhaps they had merely used the excuse of that sound to slake a lust as powerful as his, to cleave her and fill her with their arrogance, the contempt of *cock* for *cunt*, denying all but the sweet power of the prick, the hard spurt of the seed, because the sexual obviousness James had referred to – the tartiness, he meant – deserved no more. And so he came, lashed by storms of jealousy and vicarious excitement, heedless of her pleasure, making a cruelty of his last, stabbing thrusts.

Lying beside her in his exhaustion, seeing her once more as Rachel, he was shamed and chastened by his own contempt. Yet as he touched her shoulder by way of sup-plication she turned her head, showing her face as warm and sweat-streaked as his own, and murmured in a kind of quiet wonder, 'It's better when we don't think of each other, isn't it? Isn't that strange?'

Click!

She straddled him, rising and falling slowly, watching his face for the slow ecstasy of his movement in her slick passages, anticipating, mirroring the effect of every squeeze, every hesitation, every unexpected jerk she gave him. Then she realized she had heard something and her face lost its joyous absorption.

'What was that?' She turned her head, pulling him where he was deep inside her.

'Nothing. Don't worry.'

Her eyes caught the camera propped on the small bed-side table, directed not at them but at the mirror she faced. She looked back at Paul, confused. 'Did you put it on a time release?'

Her lips curved, echoing his amusement as he shook his head. He pulled back the rumpled sheet at his side. There was a small, black, rectangular block five or six inches long with a button and two tiny red lights in the face. He thumbed the button and the camera clicked and whirred.

'It's a remote unit with a motor drive. Remember that trunk Jimmy had me drag out here? It was all this stuff. He hasn't even looked at it yet.'

'So that's why you wanted me this way round –'

He grinned as she looked up into the mirror.

'You're a pervert, you know that?'

'*I'm* a pervert!' He laughed. 'This was all your idea, remember?'

But there was no rancour in her face. 'You should have told me. I wasn't ready.'

'You weren't supposed to be ready! That was the whole

point. What's the use of you posing as if it were just another shoot? It's got to be the way we are now. That's what you said.'

She considered this, her expression growing quiet and ruminative in the open way of a child; it made him smile and love her, though he did not show it.

'It feels odd, somehow –'

'So you don't want to do it? I only set it up because it seemed so important to you.'

'It is. I do want it.' She bent and kissed him drily on the lips and sat up, thoughtful again. 'Couldn't you just let it go off on its own? Like one of those booths?'

'There's an intervalometer somewhere in the trunk – I could work out something with that. But – ' He glanced down at his crotch. 'I'm kind of otherwise engaged at the moment – '

Her hiccuping laughter squeezed him and made him wince. She looked back in the mirror, eyes widening. 'My God – that'll be so rude.' She lifted herself, watching their pubic hair unmesh, starting to slide herself off the fleshy, glistening column that impaled her. Her expression became mischievous, scheming and then embarrassed, as if at her own thoughts. She chuckled, shaking her head.

'Tell me – ' He was grinning.

'Let me press the button – at the end. You won't know, will you? I mean, when I'm ready.'

He looked at her. 'OK.' He pushed the control unit down the mattress towards her. 'Now we can both reach – *shit* – '

'What is it!'

He sighed. 'I think I'm losing my edge – '

Her look of alarm changed to one of dark and knowing calculation. Her eyes fixed on his, trapping them. Out of sight, her fingers reached down, curling and encircling the root of his shaft. 'I don't think *that*'ll be a problem,' she smiled.

Holding him rigid, she began gently to rise and fall about his re-embedded length, swaying faintly from side to side, forward and back, not shifting her gaze. As he breathed in sharply, Paul's finger closed about the black control unit, squeezing the button on an involuntary spasm. The camera shutter winked open and shut with the smoothest *click!*

The pictures changed things.

As they continued, Paul and Rachel grew at once more intimate and more wary with each other. It was as if a further door had been opened in their relationship, but neither seemed willing to rush beyond the threshold – from fear of what might be revealed either to the other or, perhaps, to themselves. Their jokiness and self-conscious-ness before the camera faded – in Rachel, to a quiet watch-fulness, a simultaneous awareness and non-awareness that what were once acts of love had now become performances too.

Paul's feelings were more openly confused. Having sex while being watched was all too familiar to him from the Cape, and gave him no qualms in itself, but he was making love now. His emotions were engaged in quite different ways, and the fact of observation – however impersonal – was both an intrusion and a kind of tainting.

He found himself growing more critical of Rachel, watching her for signs that her actions were no more than camera poses, indistinguishable from a thousand others she had performed with different partners, marks of an exhi-bitionism that mocked their present intimacy. If he saw such signs – or thought he did – he would despise her utterly, his contempt matching the degree of his arousal. She was fulfilling the erotic promise in her features, in her body, deriving her excitement from showing herself off, from arousing his excitement as she had aroused so many others', randomly, undifferentiatingly.

How, suddenly, he hated those others! And how, too, he hated her for making him feel so exposed, so irrational, so vulnerable — for so exalting the act of love that lust by itself could seem tawdry. But the moment he responded to those feelings he was invariably surprised.

There was a time when she knelt between his knees as he sat on the end of the bed. Three cameras watched them, one on either side positioned on bedside table and chair, the third locked by a clamp to the shower room door, surveying the entire room on wide angle. An intervalometer on the dining table operated each in turn — one at five second intervals, one at ten, one at fifteen.

As she stroked him and licked him with a touch like moist velvet, coaxing his tired flesh into fresh rigidity, the room filled with the crisp clicking and whirring of the mechanisms, a timeless clockwork which trapped his mind, divorcing it from the tingling pleasure at his crotch. When a touch of particular delight recalled his attention he was astonished by his size.

Rachel's eyes widened with appreciation of his pleasure. They were upraised to him as the tip of her tongue teased the sensitive gland below his bloated crown, her long fingers pressed as if in prayer against either side of his shaft. Her eyelids half closed in a look of such warmth, such self-absorbed desire, his organ twitched in involuntary response. With the faintest of smiles, keeping her eyes on his, she rose, drawing his erection down into the soft valley between her breasts.

371

He swallowed, his heart booming, as she closed the warm, curving flesh over his shaft, her smile widening as she began a slow, rhythmic stroking. He wanted to cry out, to grasp her, to fling her to the bed and spend himself within her, but the swelling joy stopped him. A moment, a second more – until he knew he pivoted on the point of no return.

As his muscles tensed to lift him, Rachel's head moved in a half gesture of dismissal, her fingers increasing their pressure on his captured organ. He saw in her face the possibility that he should finish there – now – saw her pleasure at anticipating his. And for that instant the memory of Cora-Beth reared in his mind – the way she had stroked him to erection and beyond – what obscene pleasure had *she* taken in the thoughtless ejaculations of a boy? Suddenly Rachel seemed to share that obscenity – worse, to touch a knot of that same sickness in himself. It made him surrender to the surge of sperm. He groaned, gushing self-indulgently and copiously between her breasts, watching her gasp with each fresh spurting as his seed splashed high up her neck and chin.

Afterwards the feeling of that instant left a sour taste, robbing the act of all meaning but simple physcial release, pointless in itself. And then Rachel looked at him, smiling a quiet smile of satisfaction, as though the climax had been as much hers as his. She put her fingers to the space above her breasts, moving them wonderingly where his seed still glistened on her skin.

'All your babies,' she murmured. 'Hundreds and thousands of babies . . . '

And her smile wiped clean all hint of sourness, of taint, of selfishness and fear, leaving him with a sense of awe. The simplicity, the mystery of her was unfathomable to him – he understood then that only by loving her would he ever encompass it.

Later he would wish he had used the moment to say so. For the next day, quite unexpectedly after six extraordinary weeks, James announced that the calendar was done.

'What are these?'

Paul grunted at the photographer's query, not really listening as he completed an awkward trim on a print. He glanced round to see James bending over a drawer in a corner of the darkroom. Then he looked again more urgently. It was the cabinet he used to store his own work.

'Hello, hello – picturing your own fantasies, Paul?'

Paul darted from his stool as he realized what his employer had found. James held a large monochrome photograph of a naked girl falling away from the camera towards a bed, laughing, arms extended, her hair and breasts appearing to float. Below it were sheets of stiff card patterned with contact prints.

'Isn't this Austria? No wonder we never saw you two. And I thought you were just having naughties – '

'Jimmy!' Paul clutched at the photograph but James simply turned away, continuing his scrutiny.

'It's got a nice feel to it. You obviously know how to get the best out of your lady friend – '

Paul sighed uneasily. 'We were just messing around. They're holiday snaps, for Chrissakes, Jimmy – '

'Don't be so prickly,' James murmured, peering at the contact prints. 'I can't imagine you shot this on your own equipment. Good God – you must have spent hours getting this many angles. Wait a minute – ' He gave a barking laugh and looked at Paul, grinning. 'You devious sod! You

373

used my remote units on this, didn't you?'

Abashed, Paul felt his face redden. Before he could speak, James laughed again, looking closer at the rows of small pictures.

'This is *my* camera verité trick! You cheeky devil!'

'Jimmy — ' Paul began. But the photographer was still grinning, shaking his head in excited disbelief as he turned the sheets of card. He stabbed a finger at a a row of pictures.

'How the hell did you manage a sequence like that? You must have had the control panel up your bum — '

'Intervalometer — and three motorized cameras, two, five and ten second intervals.'

'Nice.' James nodded, turning over another sheet. 'Well, I can see where I went wrong — '

Paul looked at him, forgetting momentarily his urge to snatch the photographs away. 'What do you mean?'

'Not enough contact with the model. I should have been on the same side of the camera. God, you can't have more control than actually screwing the woman — '

'Look — ' Paul's anxiety returned. He reached for the sheets.

James suddenly frowned. 'This layout,' he said. 'You've chopped these contacts about deliberately — '

Paul hesitated, his hand falling. 'It's — something I tried back home once. It's a kind of mixture of collage and strip cartoon — you see a sequence of views rather than individual pictures. It was pretty crude the first time I did it, because I only had one point of view. But with three or four different angles, different distances, it seems to work better — '

He halted, deeply unsure not of what he had done but that he should talk about it at all.

James grunted and straightened. 'It's interesting. I'd like

374

to show Hugh Metzer – if only to prove my ideas weren't so crazy – '

'*No*.'

James looked at him in surprise. The young man's face was dark, his eyes fierce.

'You're not that identifiable, Paul. Neither is Rachel, for that matter. It's all shot in natural light, isn't it?'

Paul grasped the pictures and pushed them back into the drawer, shutting it. 'They're just private experiments – that's all,' he muttered, moving back to his stool.

'OK.' James shrugged behind him. 'But you can't afford to forget about good work when you're trying to make a name for yourself, Paul – especially with smack-in-the-eye stuff like this. Life is too short.' Whistling, the photographer went out.

Good work.

He knew the photographs were good. As he printed and arranged the best, working steadily in spare moments, never quite acknowledging the priority he gave them, they continued to inspire in him that twitch, that pleasurable unease – so close to the sensation of love – that he was breaking new and startling ground, new at least to him.

He had felt it during the first weeks of shooting, finding, as so often before, that the sideline rather than the main path of a project proved the more rewarding. After all the effort he had squandered on other photographs, it was those he had begun as an indulgence, a pastime, almost a joke, in which his abilities had flowered.

But the irony was doubled, because, if he had not started by regarding the pictures as serious artistically, in personal terms he had never seen them as anything else. They were

375

woven into the fabric of his relationship with Rachel, touching every part of it. He could not, should not judge them apart.

Yet oddly Rachel's interest in them seemed slight. She had asked to keep only one – a simple head and shoulders portrait of them both smiling at the camera, a shot which bore almost no relation to the situation portrayed so graphically in every other picture. It was as if the act of taking the photographs had expiated something – the end product was unimportant.

Or perhaps she was simply too intent on her new life. Paul had given up his shared flat and moved in to Camden within days of returning from Austria. The privacy, the self-sufficiency of Rachel's flat, which she could not support alone, made the logic of the move seem inescapable. There seemed movement too at last in Rachel's own career. A photographer friend of James's had organized a zed card. She was registered with new agencies. Small trade jobs were coming her way. She had a new confidence, a new certainty. Visibly she glowed.

Paul had been afraid that the return home might have changed the relationship, lessening the intensity of Austria. But if anything it deepened, spreading into an equally close domestic intimacy. He saw a new Rachel, a Rachel who functioned improbably, delightfully, in the most mundane and familiar surroundings, charging them with the warmth, the excitement they had jointly created. And when James, flushed with Boucanier's favourable reception of his photographs, suggested a fortnight's break by way of celebration and thanks, even offering a friend's weekend cottage on the Norfolk coast, the couple had embraced the idea enthusiastically.

Perhaps it was gratitude, perhaps a feeling that he and

Rachel had somehow outgrown the Austrian photographs, depriving them of their rawness, that made Paul suggest James show a selection to the owner of the Metzer gallery. A very limited selection – one Paul would make himself – just enough to demonstrate the pictures' quality, to establish Paul's credentials for future work. But as he had spoken the words – in so casual a way he could not be sure James had even taken them in – he had felt that thump in his chest that signalled an irrevocable decision.

Later, travelling northward by coach with Rachel at his side, he reviewed the moment again and again, diluting its importance until – with a sense of relief whose intensity surprised him – he suddenly realized he had forgotten to make the promised selection. Even if James wanted to, he could not act on the suggestion. It had to remain in abeyance until Paul's return from holiday – and perhaps even longer, perhaps indefinitely.

Smiling a smile that Rachel returned, unaware of its cause, he relaxed in his seat as the flat acres of Norfolk swept by the window. He had nothing to worry about. Everything would be all right.

They were in the last hours of the holiday, curled in a bed as warm and as deep as their intimacy, high against the carefully exposed rafters of an attic bedroom, when a distant trilling reminded them there was a telephone in the cottage. They joked as they searched for it, tracing a cable from the hallway to the tiny living room, unearthing the squalling instrument behind the curtain of a window seat. In fourteen days they had hardly spoken to a soul, living a dream between sea and sky and bed.

It was Rachel who picked up the receiver. She giggled and squirmed as Paul caressed her from behind, pressing himself against her naked back.

'Can you hang on?' she said, putting a hand over the mouthpiece and turning to Paul. 'I think someone's taking the mickey. They say it's the *Daily Mirror*. They want a comment about some exhibition of naughty photos in Chelsea. Some MP or someone's kicking up a fuss – '

Then she saw the look on Paul's face and her disbelieving smile froze. He took the receiver from her fingers, not meeting her gaze.

'Hello,' he said. 'Can I help you? This is Paul Hanna. Yes. The photographer.'

EPILOGUE
A Letter to Paul

I thought of you last night as my husband made love to me.
Doesn't that sound a dreadful admission! As if I yearned for
some long-lost erotic past and the present were a terrible
disappointment. It isn't, of course, and I don't yearn – at
least only in those wistful, self-indulgent moments everyone
is entitled to once in a while.

But I do think of you. I think of you a lot, even after all
this time. I wouldn't like to say how often I've tried to
gather those thoughts together and make sense of them.
There must be dustbins full of unfinished letters somewhere, never mind the dozens I did finish and still keep
tucked away, in an old shoebox. Most of those written in
that awful time after Norfolk.

How I hated you then! Not in the 'instant-dislike' way I
remember you criticizing me for (I'm really very mellow
these days) – and not because I didn't believe that James
Kingsley had given your pictures to that gallery without
your permission. I hated you, in spite of everything else,
because I could see you *wanted* those photographs to be
seen, desperately – even when you were denying it to the
newspaper people, and having to retract it all later, even
when you were attacking James (he knew you *so* well), but
especially when you were talking to me. I watched you
agonizing and agonizing over the hurt you did us – and *still*

going on. *That* was what killed things between us. Not the Sunday newspaper people chasing me down Camden High Street or ringing at three in the morning. Not the big splash in *Prince* which were just old pictures of Max's dug out of the files. Not even the foul phone calls which meant changing the phone number twice.

Recognition meant more to you than *us*. Not just my feelings – or yours – but the living thing we had made between us, which seemed so extraordinary, so unique, it deserved our loyalty. I couldn't understand how you could betray that. Betraying me seemed small beside it. And, because I couldn't understand, I had to leave, because understanding, even more than the sex, was what made us so special.

What did I say in my goodbye note? I can't remember – something silly and banal the way the most important things always are. But the endless one-sided conversations I had with you afterwards, hidden away in my little room in Josey's apartment, scribbling page after page! I was so terrified you'd track me down, most terrified of all that if you did I wouldn't be able to stop myself going back, regardless of everything else. Then, as the weeks went by and I realized I'd covered my tracks only too well, all my frail resolution started to waver and I was frightened in a different way – that I would never be myself again. You were so deeply involved in me, you touched so much, I couldn't physically exist without you. That was the worst time of all. I owe Josey and David so much for holding me together then – as if one helpless individual wasn't enough in their household!

But, bad as it was, it was also the beginning of a new me. I slowly started to realize I could never be the way I was because there never *had* been much of a me before you. All there had been was a small, quaking soul hiding inside a face and a figure that said something completely different, something bold and glamorous and sexy, everything those *Prince* pictures tried to make me. So I had tried to be what those pictures showed because that was what the people I loved seemed to want – right from my father down to poor little Andrew.

And then you arrived, Paul (isn't it funny? I wanted to write 'darling', and I had to stop myself – only my husband deserves that now). And suddenly all those wonderful, beautiful things two people can do together when they make love weren't just motions to go through in front of a camera or – worse – in someone's bed. They were real, they had an importance and a beauty and a wonder I hadn't even dreamed before. But just as important they were part of me – a part I'd never really acknowledged before then. Even the posing for pictures – I'd *enjoyed* that – even when it was with Max. I was only able to admit it to myself when I was with you. And you looked so shocked when I suggested it! I think that's when I really knew that you loved me. I had actually made Mr Experience blush! But I did it because I wanted you to understand and I thought you of all people would, and I wanted you to get the benefit because you more than anyone deserved it. Of course, I didn't realize that benefit would be as much professional as personal.

And here I come to the point of all this rambling. I remember so clearly my feelings when your *Lovers* book first came out. I had no fears of being publicly exposed again – I'd given up modelling by then and gone back north and was trying very hard to be anonymous. But I did fear the personal pain of seeing those pictures again, reliving that time once more. For a long while I promised myself I'd never open the book. It was part of a past that was over. I don't even remember how I came to change my mind. I only know that when I did turn those pages for the first time I found myself looking at strangers. Strangers with oddly familiar faces and bodies, but strangers none the less. Ghosts from another life which I happened to have lived myself.

But they were beautiful strangers and their closeness and their joy shone through every picture. I could see why so many people had bought the book. I could also see how talented you were, Paul, and how agonizing it would have been for you to hide that talent. I could even understand how pictures so beautiful could weigh in the balance against the feelings they showed. If any bitterness remained then that moment cured it. I knew that you were still within me as deeply and as surely as when we first made love, and when my husband and I made love only a few hours ago.

I'm not talking about adultery-in-the-mind or hinting at anybody's inadequacies. Quite the opposite. I mean my own capacity to love – to love in every way a woman can, to her utmost and beyond – to be in the fullest sense a *lover*, Paul, which is what you gave to me. I can think of no greater gift beyond love itself.

This is what it has taken me so many years to put into words. Why they should suddenly come together now is a mystery to me – probably as mysterious as that we should ever have found each other in the first place. But the reasons don't really matter. All that matters is that the words are true and that they have been said, even if they never get beyond my dusty old shoebox of precious memories.

I wish you all the joy you once gave me, Paul, and all the joy you have enabled me to have since.

With my love

RACHEL

Southport
Lancashire
England

1 June 1986

BESTSELLING FICTION FROM ARROW

All these books are available from your bookshop or news-agent or you can order them direct. Just tick the titles you want and complete the form below.

☐	THE COMPANY OF SAINTS	Evelyn Anthony	£1.95
☐	HESTER DARK	Emma Blair	£1.95
☐	1985	Anthony Burgess	£1.75
☐	2001: A SPACE ODYSSEY	Arthur C. Clarke	£1.75
☐	NILE	Laurie Devine	£2.75
☐	THE BILLION DOLLAR KILLING	Paul Erdman	£1.75
☐	THE YEAR OF THE FRENCH	Thomas Flanagan	£2.50
☐	LISA LOGAN	Marie Joseph	£1.95
☐	SCORPION	Andrew Kaplan	£2.50
☐	SUCCESS TO THE BRAVE	Alexander Kent	£1.95
☐	STRUMPET CITY	James Plunkett	£2.95
☐	FAMILY CHORUS	Claire Rayner	£2.50
☐	BADGE OF GLORY	Douglas Reeman	£1.95
☐	THE KILLING DOLL	Ruth Rendell	£1.95
☐	SCENT OF FEAR	Margaret Yorke	£1.75

Postage _____

Total _____

ARROW BOOKS, BOOKSERVICE BY POST, PO BOX 29, DOUGLAS, ISLE OF MAN, BRITISH ISLES

Please enclose a cheque or postal order made out to Arrow Books Limited for the amount due including 15p per book for postage and packing both for orders within the UK and for overseas orders.

Please print clearly

NAME..

ADDRESS..

....

Whilst every effort is made to keep prices down and to keep popular books in print, Arrow Books cannot guarantee that prices will be the same as those advertised here or that the books will be available.